Since Antonius

by

Alexander Francis

Since Antonius

Foreward

This book was a work meant to happen. A few years ago, I wrote *Revenge of Jesus* and, at the time, ruled out any related work or sequel because of the large effort and laborious research needed to make such a book both exciting but also historically accurate as much as can be done with a fictional effort. After awhile, and as I completed additional unrelated works, the images from *Revenge of Jesus* kept coming back to me at odd times. No, I wasn't yet finished with it. There had to be more because one of the main characters had disappeared back into the maw of time leaving the fictional living, and me, to always wonder about his fate. So, I think I actually wrote this book, *Since Antonius*, to close the book, as it were, on the subject in my own mind. The characters in this one complete their mission for all time and leave the past to the past.

I need to give credit to Wikipedia for being my main research tool and for providing a clear understanding of ancient names and concepts, as well as providing many public domain images which makes this work come to life. Frequently, I donate funds to Wikipedia and if you can afford it, please do also.

I hope my readers enjoy *Since Antonius*, and if they do, it would be awfully nice to hear about it.

Alexander Francis

Other Novels by Alexander Francis

Revenge of Jesus

Are We A Band Yet

Mick Grundy…Spy Hunt

Mick Grundy…The Russian Connection

Mick Grundy…Elapid

Geminknot

Beware The Exit

The Green Scarf

Memory Gap

The Copy Candidate

Please visit afnovels.com for more information

Table of Contents

Flora(Proserpine). Fresco from Stabiae (cubiculum w26 of the Villa of Ariadne)
This work is in the public domain

Chapter 1

What Does It Mean?

Herculaneum, July 2020

Cosimo stepped into the street just in time to avoid the cluster of tourists headed toward him on the narrow sidewalk, engaged in talk typical of visitors to this ancient historical site, full of awe, their cameras close at hand or pressed against their face. Cos shook his head in amazement; they never even saw him coming. He continued walking over the rough paving stones, lost in thought, looking down at the surface but not really seeing anything, his mind actively pursuing other images, other tasks.

"Cosimo," she called softly. He turned toward the voice just behind him, and when he saw her, he stopped abruptly, smiling and turning fully to face her. Rachel was strikingly attractive. Her big soft eyes and her long, shining, dark brown hair would arrest the attention of nearly any young man. But her main appeal, to Cos anyway, was her enveloping voice which seems to flow over and around him. A voice he could listen to for eternity, without a doubt.

Rachel came alongside, smoothly folding her arm in his, and looked up at him with a bit of humor in her eyes. "Don't you eat lunch, Cosimo? Ever?" she added for emphasis.

"Funny you should ask. I was just heading toward the concession area with lunch in mind. Would you care to join me for a soggy piece of pizza and a small cup of bitter coffee?"

"Not a chance, Cosimo. I have a different plan, one you will like better," she answered, her smile becoming broader. She held up a small and tattered black toolbox for him to notice.

"I get it. We are going to dig up our lunch from some ancient source. Have you thought that, after nearly two thousand years, it might be a bit hard to chew?" He laughed at his jibe knowing she intended otherwise.

Instead of answering, she stopped and looked at the signs above the ancient openings to the interior of villas which were now mostly open to the sky, their roofs long ago incinerated along with most interior contents. A few had undergone limited preservation with new roofs and stairs, but the majority of structures remained unprotected to the elements and roped off to the constant flow of tourists. Rachel was obviously seeking a specific location and, after a bit of study, found it.

"This is the one," she announced and started toward it, providing a gentle tug on his arm in that direction. Cosimo laughed again, while being led, and noticed that he and Rachel were collecting the attention of several tourists. Both were wearing the obligatory tan jumpsuits and white hard hats required of staff. Above Cosimo's left breast was embroidered his name in contrasting blue thread. It read "Cos" on the top line; the second line stated "Milano," indicating his university affiliation, at least for the summer season. Rachel's second line read "New York."

She confidently strode to the street door of the villa which was blocked by a white chain draped from side to side barring entrance to the throngs of visitors. With a quick glance at Cosimo, she lifted the chain high enough to slip under, then turned and waited for him to follow. With a bit of a grunt, Cosimo passed under the chain, and they entered the narrow and vaulted entrance typical of most villas. The floor was tiled and in reasonable condition given the incredible age of the place.

"This unit is off-limits," Cosimo observed as he stood there taking it in, hesitant to go where prohibited without permission. Rachel didn't answer or look back but proceeded into the *atrium* area before stopping. Reluctantly, Cosimo followed her. They both looked around like tourists and, like tourists, were also in awe of the place.

"It's still under restoration, mostly it's repair to stabilize the site from further damage from the elements," Rachel answered his unasked question. "I have been here twice before, few of us undergrad students have had the opportunity."

"I sure haven't," Cosimo assured her. "There is an upstairs," he observed and pointed to the reconstructed balcony guard rail and wooden *transennae* wrapping around the room in three directions. The roof and supporting beams were also new, replaced exactly to match the original structure.

"Sure is. That latticework was what we were constructing last week. I don't think the public will ever make it up to the second level because there is too much to protect up there and never enough guards."

Cosimo twisted, looking up at the opening in the roof and down toward the marble rectangular pool below it at floor level. "So, now that there is a roof, does the *impluvium* actually work?"

"There is supposed to be a cistern below to collect the rainwater, but I don't know if it is even there anymore or ever was. All I know is that the water goes someplace," Rachel answered, her hands up with palms inverted. Cosimo smiled at her use of a typical Italian mannerism. She was learning quickly and, perhaps subconsciously, adapting to her surroundings.

"Want to go up and have a look?" she asked and, without waiting for an answer, started for the stair entry off to one side of the room.

Cosimo shrugged and followed her up. After all, he was here to learn about Herculaneum and so far all he had done was clean up after tourists. Besides, he and Rachel were part of the staff, at least they had uniforms with name tags.

They passed by several rooms opening onto the balcony. Most were rectangular and small without an opening of any kind to the outside, making them at first seem dark and forbidding, but all the walls displayed elaborate paintings on smooth plaster, and much of it remained in vivid color, making the past come alive as almost nothing else could. One room contained the wooden framework for a bed, and though carbonized, it was a shock to see it sitting there ready for its occupant's night sleep.

"Amazing!" Cosimo exclaimed. "It's nearly like going back in time up here."

"I knew you would like it," Rachel commented. "The spot I wanted you to see is just ahead." She led the way toward a large arched opening in the stone wall which was about waist height. In front of the window, a circular slab of white marble sat on an elaborately carved pedestal base. Two decorative stone stools were at opposite ends of the table, making it an elegant and private location for the fortunate people who occupied this villa originally. "The view today is, of course, the mountain of rubble put there by Vesuvius two thousand years ago, but before that event, the panorama would have been the Bay of Naples. A choice spot I would say."

"And I would also. I assume you brought lunch deceivingly disguised as tools?" he asked.

"Indeed. Hungry?"

"I could not refuse for many reasons, and one of them is your very pleasant company."

"Does that mean that you are also hungry for me?"

Of course he was, Cosimo thought, but Rachel was more than just a desirable woman he had the good luck to encounter. He was attracted to something else, something inside of her, that he couldn't quite comprehend. He was afraid to let himself be pulled in by desire alone, afraid of the consequences of rejection but most afraid of following his baser instincts and losing something much more valuable. The truth was he just didn't know her that well.

"Rachel, I need to admit something to you."

"Yes?"

"You are so confident, so…beautiful, so…in charge that it frightens me a bit. I feel like a school boy around his third grade teacher."

"So, does that mean that you are frightened of me or of yourself?"

"Good point. Myself, I think. You are very hard to resist," he admitted.

"Well, Cosimo the schoolboy, I have only invited you up here so that you can see areas of this site that you would otherwise not see. Whatever made you think that there was any other reason?" Rachel responded, accompanied by a broad smile.

"The other thing is more sensitive, Rachel," he said in a lowered voice, looking directly into her eyes. "I really am attracted to you but… ."

"Come on, Cosimo. You are a big boy now, and you can confide in your third grade teacher. After all, I'm here to look after you." Rachel followed that statement with a hardy laugh.

"Well, there are always a lot of other men hovering around you. And you give them the Rachel personality treatment just like you do me."

"And, so what if I do? Are you saying that you want to be the only one in my life or, to put it another way, you don't want to be one of many?"

"Sure. That's about it," Cosimo admitted. "I would like to feel that you could be mine. What man would want to share you?"

Rachel stopped smiling and became serious. She put her arms on the ancient table and leaned toward him, her eyes roaming his face as she spoke. "Think of me as you would a fancy, expensive, Italian sports car. Everybody wants it, but the only one who will drive it home and park it in his garage will be the one who earns it. Want to eat now?" She sat back, letting what she said sink in a bit, then smiled her engaging smile at him and picked up the lunch box.

Out of the small tool box came a demi-sized bottle of wine, two glasses, and, folded neatly in foil wrapping, two perfect panini sandwiches, the cheese still hot from the grill. "And there is dessert, Italian chocolate, of course," she explained.

"You are amazing. And finding me at the right moment when we were just feet from this secret spot!" Cosimo shook his head in appreciation. He looked at Rachel across the ancient table admiring her anew. They had only been introduced a short month ago during orientation for the new incoming students assigned to work at the historical site of Herculaneum. Once their glances were exchanged across the room, it was a sure thing that they would become companions as often as circumstances allowed, yet circumstances kept them apart so often that occasionally days passed before they met again. And there were other men pursuing the radiant Rachel, she seemingly enjoying the attention. Cosimo considered giving up the chase, however each time they locked eyes, his pulse told him that Rachel was worth the wait and the effort.

Cosimo relaxed and looked around at the ancient villa once again. It was sumptuous, compelling. The lower floors were entirely covered by marble mosaics, tens of thousands of individual pieces, selected and positioned by color, creating a majesty of patterns and images. The walls had been painted by hand to expand the room size and included fanciful Roman temples, walkways, and distant landmarks. Then, on other surfaces, there were paintings of celebration showing well-dressed women engaged in various domestic pleasures.

Cosimo ran his hand across the marble table top, and for a brief moment, he felt what the original owner himself felt in this very spot. It was an intense sensation, and it caused him to take a deep breath.

"Something wrong?" Rachel asked.

"Not at all. For a moment, I thought I was actually here."

"You are here, my dear. How do you mean that?"

"I had the sensation that I was here, though back in time… before the eruption, sitting in this very spot with you across from me."

"I could see us back in time together. We would make a handsome couple, don't you think?" Rachel smiled, catching his eye, making it impossible to determine if she was teasing again.

"It must have been a fine life, at least for the wealthy," Cosimo added.

"Until they all burned together on that last, fateful day. Have you seen the bodies down in the boat sheds?'

"I glanced at them on the way past once. Almost too gruesome to contemplate. I don't want to go down there again."

"Yes, horrific. On the other hand, there is another emotion which comes to me when I really study the bodies. There are couples together holding onto each other as well as mothers with their children. It's very touching to see people in the last moments of their lives caring for others. And the experts tell us that, at least, it was over quickly for them."

"You are a caring person, Rachel. You would have done what they did if you had been there. But to change the subject, what do they have you doing every day? I hardly ever see you," Cosimo complained.

"As you did, I came here wanting to dig things up, find things, discover the past. We all did, though there is no excavation being done any longer, and it looks like there will never be any again, at least in our lifetimes. There is no money for it, they say. They have me working odd jobs, helping where I can. And what are you doing with your time?"

"The Italian government oversees more ancient sites than the rest of the world combined. There will never be enough money to even protect what they have now. I think the right thing to do is stop the digging because even the small site of Herculaneum is rotting away before our very eyes. As for what I do, it seems that most of the time I'm sweeping up debris left by tourists or emptying garbage cans. At least they have put me out as a guide on occasion, mostly because I speak several languages. Still, I'm lucky because I am actually here taking in the romance of this unique place, wishing I could see it before the year 79 AD."

Rachel frowned for the first time. "I speak English and not much else. How did you come to be so fluent in other languages?"

"Well, of course I speak Italian since I was born here. My mother is from Israel and taught me Hebrew at a young age. My father taught me Latin, also from a young age. They both are fluent in Greek, and I also took that in college. Then there is English, a necessary language if I was ever to speak to a Rachel. Thank God I know that one."

Yes, I thank Him for that also. Isn't your father rather famous in the fashion industry?" Rachel asked, already knowing the answer.

Cosimo chuckled. "Oh, he is, and I'm sure you've seen his handsome face all over the place since you've arrived. So that lets me ask you about your parents, doesn't it?"

"I have nothing to hide, Cosimo. Both my parents work in the banking and financial areas of New York. Money is not a problem for them."

"So here we are together in this fabulous historical site digging around in the dirt of the ancient past. I don't think that money means much to either one of us except to allow us to pursue what we love."

"You could have added…to pursue someone that we might love."

Cosimo sighed. "This very spot you have selected may just be the most romantic spot in all of *Italia*. It could have been two thousand years ago or now, and the effect on me would be the same. Sitting across from you, admiring your beautiful face, and listening to your captivating voice has created a powerful feeling within me and one that I will carry with me the rest of my life. This is one of those treasured moments that you only get a few of in life. Thank you, Rachel."

"You are wrong, Cosimo. This is the first of many with us, and you and I will remember them all."

Cosimo reached across the table and covered both of her hands with his, their eyes never leaving each other's face.

"Are you free to go with me to see the sights in Naples tonight?" Cosimo asked, nearly whispering.

"A date, a real date with the debonair Cosimo, you mean? Of course…why did you take so long to ask?" Rachel replied.

"Then, before we return to our assigned tasks, how about showing me around this villa you seem to know so well?"

"There is a lot to see downstairs, just follow me," she said and stood up.

Once again in the *atrium*, Cosimo had a moment to look around and take it all in. He was very familiar with the typical *domus* from this part of Roman history, and he realized that this particular structure was from a much earlier time than the first century AD.

"Rachel, did you hear an approximate date on this villa?"

"Not exactly, although the curator said that it was constructed at least two hundred years prior to the event in 79 when Vesuvius erupted. In addition, there were areas of major damage in the earthquake of 63 which were repaired, altering the floor plan. Wonderful place, isn't it?"

"It's intimidating to think that some folks lived better during those times than anybody does today. I've never seen a modern home this elaborate. Are there any?" Cosimo asked.

"I've seen a couple but never with this much craftsmanship. It does teach us one important thing," she hesitated, then turned to face Cosimo, her face serious, "you can't really own anything in life. You may possess it temporarily while you are alive, yet this place is now owned by all of us, and really, it always was. Even the items, their personal treasures, they were buried with are dug up and put on exhibit to be enjoyed and admired by all people. My father once told me that all you have in life is yourself, and I know he was right."

All Cosimo could do is nod his head. Rachel was much more than a pretty face. Thinking about her across from him upstairs made him realize that in many ways Rachel was the embodiment of all women throughout time. She was the past and the future. In his mind floated the images of all the Roman statues of women he had seen, their nobility and timelessness crafted in stone for all eons to follow, for humanity to see and appreciate and marvel at the importance of women. Rachel could have been any one of them but was actually all of them at the same time. Suddenly it dawned on him, man's reason for existence was to protect and nurture women, to ensure that they could have and raise their young. The existence of the human race depended on it and nothing else mattered.

"Cosimo?" He felt a soft hand on his shoulder, saw her head cocked at an endearing angle as she tried to determine what made him seem so lost in thought.

He took her hand, kissed it, and held it against his chest. "Sorry, Rachel, I think it's this place doing something to me. I feel connected with the past here more than any other place I have ever been. It's like you and I have always been here in some way."

"We better finish seeing this *domus* before they come looking for one of us," Rachel said with a soft voice, her eyes shiny with emotion. She took his arm, and they walked toward the daylight of the enclosed courtyard, the *peristylum.*

Stepping up on the elevated *tablinum,* the office of the *paterfamilias,* the male head of the house, Cosimo stopped to look around. This was where the business of the father of the family was conducted, where he spent most of his waking time. He tried to envision standing here receiving guests and business associates who were loitering around the *atrium,* each waiting their turn at mounting the *tablinum.* Where did he sit, Cosimo wondered, looking for clues that were not there, long ago destroyed in the furnace of the eruption and by the passage of time. Then he saw something of interest on the floor. Bending down, he used his hand to wipe away the dust over a paving block of stone. There was lettering just at the surface, a name perhaps. He knelt down and blew away the rest of the dust. Yes, there were two words crafted in bronze and inlaid into stone. An odd place for such a thing. *"Quoniam Antonius,"* he said aloud, then stood up.

"What does that mean, Cosimo?" Rachel asked.

"The first is one of those words that means different things in different uses. English is full of those, and so is Latin. Usually, it roughly translates as 'since,' at least as far as I know. It's interesting, to say the least. What is it doing right here in the middle of the floor?" he wondered aloud.

"Somebody should know. After all, this area of Herculaneum was excavated long ago," she ventured.

"And so it was, but since then, no one has come in here for a long time. What if no one of importance ever actually saw it? What if it were covered in dirt and just escaped notice?" Cosimo's face was alive with questions. There was something important about this inscription, however his personal experience with antiquity was just not enough to deliver any meaningful explanation.

Chapter 2

It's a Matter of Opinion

Marcus Annaeus Lucanus (39 AD – 65 AD)

Cosimo leaned on the trunk of his car, his hands supporting his face as he watched her come toward him. She was dressed in white, poured into a dress unique enough to be a designer original, a formfitting one at that. When she saw that he was looking, her face broadened into a big smile, her exquisite teeth contrasting with her natural red lips, and she waved one of those lovely female hands back and forth to signal that she had noticed him. He sighed, thinking that Rachel was just too much woman for him, often making him feel inadequate in some vague way. Not that she ever tried to, it was just that Cosimo didn't feel prepared or mature enough to encounter a woman such as the one now coming toward him, a big smile on her face.

"How did you know that I like sports cars, Cosimo?" she asked while appraising his little yellow convertible.

"I would count that as just good luck," he answered while coming around to open the door for her. "Want to go anywhere special?" he asked after she was seated and the door closed.

"I trust you, Cosimo, and besides, I know nearly nothing about the hot spots in Naples."

"You wouldn't mind then if I take a small detour to see somebody before our evening starts?"

"Of course not. I'm sure if it interests you, it will me also."

"Well, it's about that inlaid stone we found today. It's driving me crazy, and I have to ask somebody about it. You don't mind?"

Rachel laughed, "I don't mind. A date is a date, and I go where you go. Honestly, I don't understand why finding that particular stone has you still interested."

"You may know that my dad is usually called 'Tony,' but I've heard my mother call him 'Antonius' on occasion all of my life. Perhaps it's just the association with his name that intrigues me. And there is that first word, *Quoniam*. It doesn't make sense to me to pair those two words together."

Cosimo concentrated on driving through the vigorous Naples traffic while Rachel concentrated on watching him. Each time he glanced over at her, he noticed a small grin. "Rachel," he called over the noise, "is it too windy for you? Should I put the top up?"

"No!" she yelled. "I like it." She patted his shoulder and then let her hand fall to his biceps. "Not bad, Cosimo," she said as she felt the muscle appreciatively. "Are you into weight lifting?" she asked.

"Not really. I have been a sparing partner for my father for a very long time. It has built me up."

"I must know more about that business. You can tell me all about it at dinner."

They pulled into a parking lot, and Cosimo shut down the motor, pulled the top up, and latched it. "This is it. We have to go find Father Cantoni on the second floor. He is expecting me."

Rachel looked around but saw no indication of where they had arrived. "What is this place?" she asked.

"San Luigi. It's a Catholic seminary. One of the faculty is rather famous for his knowledge of Latin. I want to see what he thinks our inscription is all about."

Once on the second floor, Cosimo consulted the small scrap of paper in his hand and found the appropriate door. He whispered to Rachel, "I'll bet they don't see many women up here. You'll be a nice surprise." She rolled her eyes and smiled. Cosimo knocked softly and waited for an answer.

The door opened to reveal a short elderly man dressed in black with a priest's collar brightly evident. He looked Cosimo and Rachel up and down before standing aside and inviting them in with a wave of his arm. Before speaking, he went to the other side of his desk and sat down. "*Per favore siediti,*" he requested and motioned to the chairs near his desk.

Cosimo cleared his throat, then spoke softly, "*Possiamo parlare in inglese?*" and nodded toward Rachel.

"Certainly, my son. I speak English rather well if you don't mind the British accent," Father Cantoni agreed, looking intently toward Rachel as he spoke. "I would have guessed this young lady was *Italiano* by the way she looks," he chuckled. "My ordination does not prevent me from observing, by the way, how attractive she is. Hope you don't mind, my dear?"

"It's a compliment, Father. Always nice for a woman to hear. My parents are both Italian, by the way, so you are not wrong. I was raised in New York so my Italian is rather rough."

"And you are Cosimo Solomon, the one I spoke with earlier? And you have a Latin phrase you want translated?" Father Cantoni inquired.

"Correct, Father. I did have two years of Latin in college, though what I need is a more profound knowledge of Latin than I have. You come highly recommended by the staff of Herculaneum."

"I see. So this is something from a discovery, a recent discovery?" Father Cantoni looked interested and rocked back a bit in his chair.

"You see, we found a stone, a floor paver, in the *tablinum* of one of the villas which is currently undergoing some stabilization repair. I'm not convinced that it has ever been noticed previously. It has an inlaid bronze inscription which is intriguing to say the least. I wonder if you can give me some ideas about it." Cosimo dug out his phone and then passed it to Father Cantoni, the image in question on the screen.

"*Quoniam Antonius,*" Father Cantoni read aloud, then continued to look at the image for a moment before passing it back to Cosimo. "Seems simple enough on the surface of it. It's a message about a fellow named Antonius. I think a common interpretation would be 'For Antonius,' or 'Since Antonius,' something like that. Or it could mean 'Because' or even 'Whereas.' Another thought is that *Quoniam* was, on rare occasions, used as a term of praise." He paused, looking at Cosimo for any comment.

"And just why would they put this in the middle of the floor?" Cosimo asked.

"To answer that, first ask yourself why any plaque is installed anywhere. It was placed there to remind and inform. Something placed on the floor in a working area of a *domus* would serve as a reminder to the occupant about this fellow Antonius. A common Roman name, by the way, in that time period. Or it could be there to send a message to someone who may eventually see and understand the message. To understand the message you would have to know something about the parties involved, otherwise speculation is mostly a work of fiction." He finished and glanced at Rachel who was listening intently. "Would you care to comment *signorina*?" he asked politely.

Rachel looked back and forth between Father Cantoni and Cosimo before speaking. "Seems to me that the use of the inscription and its placement is deceptive on purpose."

Father Cantoni leaned back again and appraised her comment in silence, obviously thinking it through again. "Please explain, *signorina*."

"Well, the message isn't clear. If you translate '*Quoniam'* as 'Since' then the message is nonsense. Just a crazy little statement which only arouses a shrug. If you use 'For' then it might just imply something rather dramatic. Does the message mean the entire house is 'for' Antonius or just this room? Or…what if it means that under the stone is something meant for Antonius. Something precious or even a message of some sort?"

Cosimo raised his eyebrows, waiting for Father Cantoni to speak first.

"Well, that's nearly what I said first when I suggested the word 'For.' I agree with you," Father Cantoni confirmed.

"Do you mean that there may be something under that stone?" Cosimo asked looking back and forth.

"Who knows, my son…who knows. Why don't you lift the stone and find out?"

"Because doing anything like that would have to be approved by the Superintendent himself, in person. As you know, all excavation has stopped there for good as far as we know," Cosimo answered.

"My opinion, for what it is worth, is that the message creator and Antonius are both long since dust, and it doesn't matter any longer. Besides, if you and Rachel could think this through, don't you think someone else would have also? Perhaps there was something under the stone which is no longer there," Father Cantoni suggested in a comforting voice. "Or more likely, the message meant something else entirely."

"Thanks for your time, Father. I was informed that you are one of the most informed students of history anywhere in Italy, and I can see that is correct," Cosimo said, standing up.

"Thank you, Cosimo, for the undeserved praise, yet before you both go, I get to ask a few questions. Do you mind?"

They both sat down again and glanced at each other, unsure of where the questions will probe.

"Rachel, are your parents Catholic, and are you?"

"Yes, Father, on both counts. I am a faithful Catholic."

"And Cosimo," Father Cantoni said turning toward him. "What is your faith? I would presume that your Italian heritage would also mean Catholic. Am I mistaken?"

It was an embarrassing question, and Cosimo could feel his face flushing. "Well, my mother is Jewish, and I have been extensively taught in her faith. My father was born in Rome, like I was, but he seems to have little interest in religious matters. For me, I have gone on with my life and studies and not thought about religion much at all lately."

"I suspected as much, although I can't tell you why other than some deep feelings within an old priest and Jesuit. One request I have of you both, if you will permit."

"Sure," they both said at once, then laughed at the synchrony of it.

If for some reason, fate brings you two together so that you want to be in union, please let me perform the ceremony. It would be my honor."

"Father, you should understand that we have only known each other for less than a month, and we are currently on our first date together," Cosimo responded. He glanced at Rachel and saw the smile.

Rachel got up and extended her hand toward Father Cantoni. He accepted it with both hands and stood also. "I would be honored also, Father, and if such a thing would ever happen, I would insist that you be there."

There may be more places to dine in Naples than any other place in the world of the same size. Cosimo chose with care and selected an upscale yet small and private cafe where the food is remarkably good, and the service is even better. They sat in a quiet corner out of view from every other table, a burning candle between them. Cosimo took the liberty of choosing the selection of food, making sure to pick items popular and particular to Naples.

The plates had been cleared, and the only thing remaining was to finish the excellent red wine just poured into their glasses. So far, conversation had been limited to the food and things to do in Naples and Italy in general. Cosimo couldn't take his eyes very far from hers which were glistening softly from across the small table.

"Enjoyed your company, Rachel. Lovely night, great food, and the most delightful companion. Thanks for coming with me."

"I was hoping to hear something about being with me again," she teased. "Say, do you know anything about people getting married by a devout priest like Father Cantoni?"

"Not really. Is there something special I should know?"

"They won't marry a couple unless both are Catholic or there is a pledge to become Catholic. That's why he asked about your religion."

"Interesting man, Father Cantoni. Tricky also," Cosimo laughed. "Isn't the entire subject very premature though?"

"For certain it is," she agreed. "To change the topic, do you have any more plans regarding our troublesome paver?"

"Does that mean that you are also troubled?"

"Since I virtually led you to it, I am troubled if you are. We are in this together, my handsome companion."

"Then, I will go to the top man, stir the water and see where it goes. Don't get your hopes up about seeing what is under that stone. It's an uphill battle, and if we were to succeed in looking under it and finding nothing, our reputations will be a laughing stock around the site. Young idiots, they will say." Cosimo studied her for a moment before adding, "Sure you want to be considered part of this?" He hoped she would. It would give them something in common, and he wanted any reason to see her again, and again.

Chapter 3

Up the Chain of Command

Marcus Aurelius (161–180 AD)

It was starting to feel like a fool's errand, and Cosimo was not encouraged that his request would ever be taken seriously. He stopped at the reception desk and waited for the attention of the secretary who was busily typing on her keyboard. She had glanced at him when he came in so he knew that she was aware of his presence. It had been a long morning, consisting of seeking out one permission after another in order to wind up here, waiting to see the *Supervisore degli studi*, himself only another cog in the huge ladder of those in charge of the archaeological site of Herculanum. Earlier he had sought, and eventually found, his immediate supervisor, a graduate student, making him a more senior level than Cosimo, only to be told to seek out the professor in charge of summer students. Professor Gimbolie had listened impatiently to Cosimo's theory, dismissed him with a wave of his hand, then turned away. "Take it up with the *Supervisore,*" he had said before disappearing around a corner.

Well, here he was in the office of the *Supervisore,* waiting for another dismissal of his pet theory. If only someone in charge would give it a little consideration… Cosimo thought. On the other hand, perhaps his idea of a message beneath a paver is just ridiculous, as everyone, except Rachel, has told him.

"*Signore* Cosimo Solomon," she called, looking over her glasses at him. She motioned toward the door behind her with a jerk of her head and resumed typing. Cosimo got up and, with some apprehension, opened the door to the private office of the supervisor of students. He had previously encountered people in charge at his university, and those meetings had rarely been satisfactory.

The room was cluttered with drawings along the walls of various artifacts or architectural elements, each held by clips or tacks which gave a temporary nature to the room, as if the drawings could be snatched off and put away in a hurry. Behind the metal desk was a short balding man whose chief feature was a prominent nose, of the sort which has been deemed a proper 'Roman nose.' The sign on the desk noted the occupant was *Supervisore Termineto* in bold brass letters.

"I am given to understand that you have a pet project which has caused you to solicit the opinion of nearly everyone working in Herculanum at this moment," Dr. Termineto stated dryly. "Let's hear it from you. Tell me your idea." He tapped his pencil on the desktop, waiting for a response.

It suddenly dawned on Cosimo just who this *Supervisore* was. Dr. Termineto was a senior archeologist at the University of Naples, author of several books regarding the excavations at both Pompeii and Herculaneum. In other words, an expert, perhaps *the* expert. Cosimo felt his mouth go dry.

"One of the other students and I found an inscription inlaid into a paver near the center of the *tablinum* in a *domus* just now undergoing preservation. I found it interesting to say the least. A couple of days ago I showed it to Father Cantoni who agreed that it was unique at least. I believe that it may indicate that something is buried under the paver, a treasure or message."

"And exactly what is the inlay you mentioned?"

"*Quoniam Antonius,*" sir," Cosimo stated, offering his cellphone with the picture showing.

Professor Termineto took the phone and studied the image for a moment. He shrugged without looking away from the image, then handed it back. "Frankly, I don't know what it means, if anything. Your idea, then, is to remove this stone and look under it?"

"Exactly. Don't you think this is a message to do just that?" Cosimo asked hopefully.

"Do you know why, Cosimo, these Roman floors have lasted two thousand years, even under tons and tons of rock and ash? I'll tell you. They are very well designed and constructed. Better, in fact, than any modern floor. Under the pavers, or mosaic tile, is a layered construction consisting of compact rock, sand, and Roman concrete. The final layer of mosaics were placed with precision and pushed into the still wet concrete or mortar to us. This took a great deal of skill to do, and we believe a large floor could have taken a team nearly a year to complete. Under your inlaid stone then, you will find a solid base extending down for some distance. Hardly a place to hid anything. Besides, getting that stone free will be very destructive to the floor, not to mention the stone itself. If I were living back then, I would have chosen a better place to hide something."

"I see," said Cosimo. "Then why was the inscription put there in the middle of the floor?"

"The reason is lost to history, I'm afraid. But I do congratulate you on finding something that no one else has managed to previously notice and for thinking about the subject in depth. That's what it takes to be a good archeologist, and I'm proud of you for being persistent about it." Professor Termineto stood up and looked Cosimo up and down for a moment before speaking again.

"How about you and I going to look at this stone? I would like to see it first hand." He smiled and came around to pat Cosimo on the shoulder. "Say, I met your rather famous father one time, though he won't remember the event. An impressive fellow and you remind me of him just now. You have the same look, the same nearly confrontational stance about you. A good copy I would say!" he laughed and motioned toward the door.

They talked as they walked down the stone paved streets of the uncovered Herculaneum while Professor Termineto continuously pointed out interesting features, giving Cosimo a rare mental glimpse at the city covered nearly instantly by the cataclysm of fire and ash in the year 79 AD.

"Have you taken note of the personal graffiti written on these old walls, Cosimo?" he asked, stopping by a corner of a building and pointing some out.

"Not really, Professor. Mostly I have been cleaning the litter dropped each day by our invasive species of tourists."

Professor Termineto chuckled and then started tracing the old scratched comment written at head height 2000 years ago. "I would guess this was a man about your age caught up in fascination for a girl who ignored him. He scrawled his frustration here for all to see. It translates 'He who is seen with Marcia is a dead pigeon.' I wonder if the threat worked or were they both killed separately in the eruption before Marcia came to her senses?" He chuckled again, and they moved toward the *domus* of the inlaid stone in question.

Cosimo held up the white chain to allow Professor Termineto to enter and then ducked low and came in also.

"Here is a fine mosaic entrance, Cosimo," he said, pointing down at their feet. "A typical scene of geometric repetition and done in a style which predates the Roman conquest of this city. As you surely recall, this area was taken by the Romans from the Samnites about 321 BC after several battles, and there were several more rebellions afterwards. The area around here even helped Hannibal during his invasion. I am often surprised to realize that the Romans didn't destroy this city after that treasonous act. Then, once again, Herculaneum fought on the wrong side during the civil war of 82 BC. After that, Herculaneum was assimilated totally, only to be destroyed by nature a hundred years later." Professor Termineto paused, inhaling deeply while looking blankly toward the distance. "History, not artifacts, is the most interesting subject to educated people such as you and I."

He walked toward the *tablinum,* lit by a slanting evening light, the sun nearly level with the horizon as seen through an opening to the west. "This is a lovely place, Cosimo, my favorite domus so far excavated in this little city. In its glory, there would have been curtains of highly embroidered and decorated fine wool draped over the various openings. Some would have been held back by a contrasting woven cord. We see no furniture in here now, but we are sure that impressive wooden furniture, consisting of chairs, tables, and even couches, would have been scattered tastefully about. And the walls, Cosimo! We see traces of paintings now, however try to imagine every wall brightly painted, expanding the living space with scenes of mythology, of war, of restful images of water, temples and sky. And the floor was level, bright and polished as we can only imagine now. I also see in my mind the people in here with their lavish clothing, the women with their braids and fashionable hairdos."

"And do you also see the slaves, bent to their work, keeping in the shadow of that life of splendor?" Cosimo asked.

Professor Termineto turned to face him, holding his gaze. Cosimo regretted his caustic remark because Professor Termineto looked on the verge of anger.

"You have a lot to learn, Cosimo Solomon," he remarked with some sadness, not anger. "There is that sad fact about Roman slaves, for sure, although Romans frequently freed their slaves, married their slaves, and saw to their needs. Many, perhaps a majority of people, living in Herculaneum were freed slaves, some of them became rich and influential. There is a remarkable structure near the center of the city, just off the forum. You should see it. It is a meeting house of freed slaves, all of whom became an integral part of the city and made wealthy because of their own ingenuity and efforts."

"Remember, the owner of this home was called the *paterfamilias* which translates 'father of the family.' They included the family slaves in that term. Some slaves were even buried alongside their masters just as family members were. The subject is very complex, Cosimo. You would have to consider the situation of each slave independently to weigh your concept of slavery."

"*Grazie, Professore,*" Cosimo said, tipping his head. "You are correct, I have much to learn."

"Now about that stone, *mio figlio,* before it gets too dark in here," Professor Termineto reminded him.

"Right at your feet," Cosimo answered, pointing at the stone just inches away.

Professor Termineto looked down, then squatted with some difficulty next to the stone while brushing away the dust with his hand. "I have not encountered a marker such as this one. Unique, at the least." He continued studying the stone for a time in silence, then stood erect. "There is something different about this particular stone. Have you a pocket knife with you?" he asked.

Cosimo produced a small folded knife and held it out for inspection.

"That will do, " Professor Termineto said. "Take a small blade out and probe around the edge of your stone and tell me what you find."

Hesitant at first because he didn't understand what he was supposed to discover, Cosimo pushed the small blade into the joint next to the inlaid paver. It pushed in easily. He tried around the stone on the other sides with the same result.

"Now try probing a joint several centimeters away."

This time the blade hit solid structure. Cosimo stood, folding the knife. "Does this mean that the stone is loose?" he asked.

"It means that you are not as crazy as you sounded earlier." Professor Termineto stroked his short beard, lost in thought, looking alternately between the stone and Cosimo's face.

"See here, Cosimo," he began. "Don't think that you have accomplished anything, anything at all…yet, though there is a glimmer that you are on to something of interest. I will discuss this with the *Direttore Delle Antichità*, who has responsibility for this entire site, in a day or so. Until then, you would be wise not to think of it and go on with your work and your studies."

Chapter 4

A Link to the Past

No untroubled day has ever dawned for me.

Lucius Annaeus Seneca (54 BC – 39 AD)

The decision had taken two weeks, but at last, the day had arrived. Cosimo was waiting on the down ramp, his foot against the railing, looking down in contemplation at the remnants of the ancient city and its rectangular street patterns. Because of the early hour, the site was empty of tourists, and in its silence, Cosimo could almost hear the echos of ghosts who still filled the streets. Below and close by, the arched openings of portals rose darkly, sheltering their ancient dead who still huddled there in commonality, still hiding from the furnace blast which inexorably came racing toward them down the slopes of Vesuvius. The docks, originally at sea front, now faced weeds where waves once lapped, a towering wall of stone where a vista of the Bay of *Neapolis* once was seen.

Cosimo felt the immediacy of Herculaneum, the life of the place, the objects remaining so real, so unchanged from a specific moment in time, and its people still moved through these streets pursuing their lives. He felt as though he was back with them, as if he knew them, was part of the pattern of life, breathing the same air as they still do.

"Thanks for waiting!" Rachel said, taking his arm before he realized that she was beside him. "You didn't even hear or see me coming. I must be losing my touch," she teased, smiling her familiar yet still tantalizing smile. Cosimo always felt his eyes tracing the lovely bow of her upper lip and, as always, continually astonished by its perfect shape and how utterly attractive it was. He didn't remember previously noticing any woman's upper lip and was convinced that no other lip had ever been so appealing.

"You are indeed worth waiting for," he said, still mesmerized by her lips. "They said to be there by 7:00, and we have plenty of time yet."

"Aren't you excited? Do you have any jitters of expectation?" she asked.

"I had a sleepless night trying to control my nerves because all I could see when I closed my eyes was that stone coming free in my hands."

"Did you find out who, exactly, will be there and who will get to lift the stone?"

"Professor Termineto is running the show, and, I assume, he gets to decide exactly what happens. He just didn't tell me anything but to show up at 7:00. As far as I am concerned, it doesn't matter who gets to do it."

Without further discussion, they started walking down the concrete ramp, descending from the modern city of Ercolano, lying above and astride the archeological site, downward toward the ruins of antiquity. It was in some ways like time travel, from the now into the past, just by descending a ramp. Once back on the stone paved streets, they saw the orderly rows of brick and stone lining up just as they did in 79 AD, the curbs and the doorways still hinting what it felt like to walk these streets surrounded by the sounds, the smells, and the cacophony of life.

As they walked, Cosimo reached out for Rachel's hand, and with a glance up at him, she accepted. They walked for a moment hand in hand with no conversation, both lost back in time, their mind's eye seeing Herculaneum for a brief moment exactly as it was.

"Here!" Rachel blurted, abruptly stopping. "Have you seen this place?" She let his hand go and turned to enter a small open stall. It was a *thermopolium*, still nearly intact, its counter top paved with irregular tiles, the opening of its large ceramic pots still flush with the counter. "It's a fast food joint," she laughed, while running her hand over the counter top, glancing back at Cosimo who was watching her intently.

"Sure, I've seen it. Some call it a *caupona* or a *thermopolium*, though you are right, they served hot food here. On the back wall you can still see where the wine was stored. Ready for breakfast?" he joked.

"What are you serving?" she asked.

"I recall hearing that they found chickpeas and flava beans in some of those vats. Want some?"

"Most assuredly and with a glass of wine, if you have it."

They rejoined hands and headed once more down the ancient sidewalk. Ahead at a street corner, a group of people crossed with long strides heading with purpose to something important.

"Looks like we will have a bit of company this morning," Cosimo remarked, his mouth going dry.

"You and I will be famous, at least for a day," Rachel observed.

"Better hope there is actually something of interest buried in the dirt under that stone," Cosimo said softly.

Cosimo and Rachel entered through the unchained entry way. Across the *atrium,* they could see several people standing in the *tablinum,* most of them studying the floor. There was a large movie camera on a stand, a technician standing behind it adjusting his controls. Another was positioning a long microphone boom. Professor Termineto noticed their arrival and moved toward them, arm extended in welcome.

"Well, the star of our little show has arrived," he said with a flourish and then took closer note of Rachel. "And you, my dear, you don't escape notice either. I don't believe I've been introduced, though I'm aware that you are a student here on loan to us from America."

Rachel smiled and said nothing, preferring the spotlight remain on Cosimo. She managed to slide slightly behind him and nudged him to move forward.

Before speaking, Cosimo glanced around at the assembled spectators, trying to decipher who, exactly, they were. Professor Termineto noticed his hesitation and pointed out the invited guests.

"This fellow is Amelio," he said, pointing to a thickset man dressed in a well-worn jumpsuit as if ready for hard labor. Cosimo noted that Amelio carried a small toolbox and that Amelio was not smiling. "And these distinguished *gentiluomini* are my fellow faculty members who are rather excited to see something of interest come out of the ground today."

Cosimo nodded to turn to each of them and then waited for additional instructions from Professor Termineto, who obviously was in charge.

"Well, time to start the process," Professor Termineto announced. "Amelio, please vacuum any debris and soil away from this inlaid stone." Amelio had a small handheld vacuum ready, got on his hands and knees, started the little motor, and began. Professor Termineto turned to face Cosimo, "Amelio has tools with him for you to insert, which should, we feel, enable you to remove the stone. However, if there are difficulties, then we will need additional permissions to proceed any farther. You do understand?"

"Yes, Professor," he answered. He did understand that there would be no additional permissions granted if the stone resisted extraction. There was a chance that it would work, however permission was intended only for this one morning, and failing that, the stone would remain forever in place. And this entire event would be recorded on video for the world to see, fail or succeed.

Amelio got up, finished with his part. Cosimo could tell by his threatening look that Amelio would much rather that he be the one to gloriously lift the stone and, in doing so, achieve a singular moment of fleeting fame. He was obviously jealous of a young undergrad student getting credit for something usually left to the professional and full-time staff.

"The probes, please," Professor Termineto instructed Amelio. Two slender probes with hooked ends were produced and grudgingly offered to Cosimo.

Cosimo could easily grasp the intended method of removal: one simply slid each tool between joints on either side, twist to engage the hooks, and then lift the stone unharmed. If it worked, that is.

The camera lights came on, and Cosimo could sense the mike being lowered to just above his head. He took one last look at the tools in each hand before getting on his knees, positioning himself above the stone.

The first pull was a bit delicate and failed to accomplish anything. Then Cosimo put a bit more force into the effort with the same result. Not a hint of motion from the stone. He inserted the probes in another spot and tried again with still not even a fraction of displacement. There were murmurs of misgiving coming from behind him.

"*Non funzionerà*," Amelio muttered, and Cosimo could hear the tool box lid flipping back. "Move over," Amelio growled, also getting on his knees. Two more probes were inserted, then Amelio made a motion to stand up. They both put their backs into the effort and then someone excitedly called out, "It's moving!"

The stone slid slowly and steadily upward when suddenly it came free, tumbling to one side as a gaping hole in the floor was produced. They all peered into the void trying to determine if any object was visible other than the expected Roman concrete underlayment.

"Start digging, Cosimo. You are an archeologist, remember? We dig, but carefully," Professor Termineto encouraged. A small spoon excavator was passed to Cosimo while a bucket suddenly appeared from someplace and was placed beside the opening.

It didn't take too many spoonfuls of soil and fine sand before a fist sized hole through the supporting concrete was unveiled. Cosimo carefully spooned out the sand filling the hole, emptying each load into the bucket to be analyzed later, if needed. He was starting to feel a bit desperate because the hole was rapidly getting deeper and becoming harder to excavate using the small spoon. Doubt was begging to grab him as well, as sweat ran freely down his arm into the deepening hole while his silent audience breathlessly observed every minute detail as if he were a surgeon performing life saving surgery. Yet another spoonful of gravel laden dirt was excavated with several sets of eyes following its progress from the hole to the bucket with still no hint of the much anticipated buried message.

As he looked again, there *was* something different in the hole. A hint of yellow metal beamed through the dust, and as he brushed the area, a small chain link came into view, its attachments disappearing into the depths.

"I found something!" Cosimo murmured, and the small crowd closed in to see for themselves this prize, this message, from the distant past. Behind him, he could hear Rachel clapping loudly.

"Be especially careful, Cosimo. Better to use the vacuum at this point," Professor Termineto suggested. The vacuum was grudgingly passed from Amelio while Cosimo gathered a firm hold on the metal chain. As soon as the vacuum hose was brought to bear, the dust cleared, like a fog lifting from a passing ship at sea, and there it was, a metal cylinder about the size of a short water pipe, capped at both ends, faint engraving on its side, just waiting to be plucked out of its hole. A gift from the distant past, exactly what everyone wanted to see. Someone was patting Cosimo on the back while the rest applauded.

"Well done, Cosimo," Professor Termineto said, smiling broadly at him. "We will be sure and give credit to the person who discovered what all the rest of us had missed for so many years. Congratulations, my son." He shook Cosimo's hand as did the other professors. Amelio nodded in his direction, about the most Cosimo could expect. The warmest applause and the most gratifying gesture was from Rachel who wrapped her arms about his neck and planted a very welcome kiss on his cheek, all recorded by the ever present video camera.

"Professor, we have to acknowledge Rachel as part of this because without her help and encouragement, we would have never had success this morning," Cosimo said, enveloping her shoulders with his arm and pulling her toward him.

"Of course, Cosimo. Women throughout history have been denied their just due. Nearly every discovery by a man was accomplished with female assistance. Thank you, Rachel, from all of us for this contribution to the history of Herculaneum."

Professor Termineto held up the cylinder for the camera and also for all present to see. It dangled and twisted on its small chain, tantalizingly still holding its secret message, safe from the elements and safe from prying eyes.

"What happens now?" Cosimo asked.

"Well, this part is for the experienced laboratory technicians to decide. I believe it will be cleaned and photographed and, perhaps, subjected to imaging studies to see the insides before it is opened. There is no rush, Cosimo. It has been a long time getting to us, and we need to look at all aspects of this before rushing to get it over with. Recall how damaging previous digs at sites all over the world have been and how it caused the loss of what they were there to protect. In good time, we will know the truth."

Chapter 5

A Sudden Reversal of Opinion

All things by nature are ready to get worse

Virgil (70 to 19 BC)

It felt different this morning having people, some they didn't know at all, acknowledge them with a wave and smile, occasionally adding an appreciative nod of their head while passing. Rachel and Cosimo were seen together so often recently most would think that they had been joined forever rather than just a couple of weeks. Their success with the stone and its sealed message was the current talk of the archeological minded who seemed nearly numberless in the environment of Herculaneum.

Across the small table, graced with their usual morning *cappuccino* and *mostaccuoli,* so typical of *Napoli,* they smiled their usual smiles at each other, talking mostly with their eyes and their hearts.

"I am going to miss you when you return to New York," Cosimo said. "Is there some way to make the summer last a bit longer?"

"Ah, the famous, or notorious, summer romance with a handsome Italian like you. Your curly brown hair, your tanned skin and dark eyes, and your exquisite English with its memorable accent are all the stuff of dreams. I couldn't have imagined such a summer as this one has been, and it is causing me to dread the time that I have to leave. Can't you move to New York and go to my school?"

"I am thinking; can't you move to *Italia* and go to my school?"

"I can't speak enough Italian, though I wish I could at the moment, given enough time around you…"

Their romantic breakfast was interrupted by a shadow standing beside their table. "*Scusami*," the tall young man said. When they looked at him he continued, "You are Rachel Lucchese and Cosimo Solomon?"

"Yes," Cosimo answered for both of them as he glanced up and down at the man standing beside their table. He had seen this fellow before, somewhere near the administration building.

"*Supervisore Termineto* demands your presence in his office," he said, then started to walk away.

"Wait!" Cosimo called to him. "Does that mean right now?" he asked.

"*Si*," was the answer, and they both watched as he disappeared through the open door without a glance backwards.

"I should think this is good news," Rachel mused. "It might mean that the secrets of our discovery have been analyzed and ready for us to see."

"A rather odd thing to do is to demand our presence so abruptly and by messenger. It concerns me." Cosimo felt some vague dread or apprehension creep into his thoughts. Perhaps there was nothing of value in the mysterious cylinder. He had heard that the imaging study had shown there to be a rolled object of thin metal inside, yet until it was actually opened and examined, there was only speculation to go on.

"Better finish our breakfast, Cosimo. He must be waiting on us."

On the way, Cosimo was filled with anxiety. Professor Termineto had, up to this point, exhibited the height of professionalism and courtesy. In fact, he had gone out of his way to interact and instruct, far more than any other faculty member he had ever encountered. Cosimo couldn't fathom a change of heart, especially after his theory about the stone had proven so correct.

"You know, Cosimo, you are thinking more about an old stone than the woman beside you. I feel insulted." Rachel smiled with her eyes to let him know she was kidding, just a way for her to pull him out of his trance.

Cosimo smiled at her in turn and grasped her free hand. "I know, my lovely Rachel, I am ignoring you, and I'm sorry about it. Will you let me make it up by taking you out again tonight?"

"Do I have to answer?" she laughed.

Indeed, they were expected because the private door to the *Supervisore* was standing open, its occupant seated behind his desk looking right at them. They entered and stood before the desk, not clear about the reason for the summons.

"You will sit, both of you," he said with authority, then called for the secretary to close the office door.

"Is there a problem, *Supervisore?*" Cosimo asked.

"*C'è sicuramente*, Cosimo. Or should I address you as Cosimus?"

Cosimo looked puzzled. He glanced at Rachel, who was staring at him also, waiting for a reply. "I don't understand. I've never been called Cosimus."

"I'm angry, Cosimo, very angry. This is the biggest hoax I've ever encountered. I have to ask why you would so easily toss your entire education for a bit of cheap publicity?"

"What ever you think I've done, I assure you that you are mistaken. Couldn't you just tell me in what manner I am supposed to have perpetrated a fraud?"

"I don't need to explain it to you because you already know all about it. I am here to dismiss you both because I'm sure it took two heads to figure this one out. The Herculaneum project is closed to you both, and I will be sending a negative report back to both institutions. I earnestly hope that both of you are dropped from the rolls of your universities, and as of this moment, neither of you are to be permitted to enter this archeological site again."

Cosimo stood up, angry himself, with fists clenched, his nostrils flared. "Wait just a moment. I don't accept this without some proof of what we did to bring this reprimand on. Show us some evidence."

"Very well, Cosimus," Professor Termineto sarcastically responded and reached in his desk drawer. He flipped a photograph to Cosimo without any explanation.

Cosimo and Rachel looked at the photo together. It was a close up of the side of the cylinder they had discovered. The metal was now clean of debris and corrosion, exposing the elaborate engraving which was in Latin.

APERTVM. EST

ANTONIVS. SEVERIVS. MAXIMVS

EX

PAVLO. FABIO. PERSICO. COSIMVS

"In case you have forgotten your Latin, it translates 'to be opened by Antonius from Cosimus.' I had an assistant look up this Antonius Severius Maximus. Guess what she found? It is the name your father often goes by when he wants to look like a Roman *centurion*. Everybody in *Italia* has seen or heard that name before.

We were confused at first until we opened the tube and read the message so nicely imprinted on copper."

Cosimo looked stunned. He stared at the photograph trying to make sense of it all. "Look, Professor, I don't know anything about this. The first time I ever set eyes on the cylinder was when we both saw it together as it came out of the ground. And to accuse Rachel of any wrongdoing is particularly grievous. She and I are both entirely innocent. There must be another explanation."

"There is no other explanation possible. I have kept the contents of the message out of the press, and there will be no mention of it after this day. So your attempt to gain your moment of fame has backfired. You both are dismissed, and I don't want to hear from you again."

The *supervisore's* face said it all. The conversation was over and finished and so was their education in archeology. Cosimo flipped the photograph back on the desk, stood and looked at Rachel to do the same. She had recovered from her initial shock and was tight lipped and pink tinged.

"Now, I get to say something, *Supervisore,* in our defense. I am an American, and we don't get tossed aside so easily. I can tell you for certain that the first time Cosimo was ever in that villa was when I brought him in to see it. The stone was there at the time, looking just exactly as you saw it. We didn't tamper with it or dig it up because that would be against everything we have been taught. If there was tampering with that stone, we are not the perpetrators, we are the victims. I had a lot of respect for you and the way we were treated, and I don't want to think otherwise. However, I'll tell you that I won't be kicked out of school for any charge you may toss at me, and you will have to answer for anything you may say about me."

She stood erect and took Cosimo's arm in hers, the fire in her face not dying out. Cosimo had a moment to resume thinking and cool down, and he decided to make one last offer. "Professor, you mentioned my father and his advertisements. I have seen those also, although I always thought it was just for marketing for one of his products. You may not know this, but my mother is a rather well-known archeologist herself, and for whatever reason, my father is a recognized authority on ancient Roman life, and he has given many lectures on the subject. He is well respected and would never pull a stunt to deceive anyone. I suggest that you allow him to talk with you, and perhaps together, you can figure out why and how this was done."

"I do know about your mother, Cosimo, and I respect her, which is one of the reasons you were treated so deferentially. Even though your father is more of a showman and businessman, to my recollection, and not educated in our profession, I will agree to meet with him for discussion, if he would wish to do so. Remember, the best thing to do, Cosimo, would be to admit this entire affair…own up to it before it also embarrasses your whole family."

"May I see the contents of the message?" Cosimo asked.

"I don't have time to humor you any longer this morning. Please leave."

On the way back up to the student locker area, there was little conversation between them. Finally Cosimo spoke, "I hope you don't think I had any part in any deception, Rachel. Whatever they do to me, I couldn't stand for you to be involved in any discipline. I know you are innocent."

"As I know you are, Cosimo. Don't worry about me though, because my family has a lot of connections and a very long reach. I hope it doesn't come to that." After her comment, Cosimo gave her a long questioning look. There was always more to Rachel that you could see by looking at her.

"I need to ask something of you, Rachel. Please agree."

"If I can. What is it you wish?"

"We are done here, I'm afraid. Will you drive back to Rome with me and stay with us in our home until you have to leave for New York?"

"It would be an honor, Cosimo. Could you also give me a tour of Rome while I'm there?"

"Thank you, Rachel," he answered.

Chapter 6

Home Is Where the Hearts Are

It had been a lovely car trip from *Napoli* to *Setteville*. They kept the convertible top down the entire time, even though the noise generated prevented most casual conversation. Rachel took in the sights of southern Italy, remembering that her ancestors on both sides were Italian while regretting her limited knowledge of the Italian language. She felt a stranger to this land yet also a strong, innate pull toward it.

"I hope your parents speak English, Cosimo," she yelled over the wind.

"Surely they do, among several other languages," he replied.

The car slowed and took a turn into a residential area, one of impressive luxury homes. In the distance, the low hills created a pleasant view, and it wasn't hard to imagine this area as rural prior to its present dense settlement.

Cosimo stopped at a gated entrance, flanked on both sides by towering stone columns. "Rachel, please activate the opener," he asked, pointing to the small device tucked under her sun visor.

The driveway curved toward a mansion properly situated behind and beside neat rows of olive trees, all carefully manicured. Cosimo stopped just short of the stately entrance and shut the motor down. "Welcome to our humble home," he said, waving his arm toward the house. "Let me take you in for introductions, and I'll get the bags later."

Rachel recognized the face of Cosimo's father, Anthony or 'Tony' as the press usually called him, nearly instantly. He was more handsome in person than in his many photographs…and much more muscular and masculine than she would have ever imagined. Nearly obscure by comparison was Cosimo's delicate mother, but a second glance disclosed a face of classical timeless beauty with perfect features and glossy black hair. Rachel suddenly felt outclassed by the physical beauty of these two for the first time in her life.

"Hi, I'm Rachel," she awkwardly said and moved slowly toward them with her hand extended. Her hand was warmly taken by Cosimo's mother who smiled and introduced herself.

"Hello, Rachel. Please call us by our first names while you are here. I'm Mary, and this is Tony, whom I'm sure you recognize."

"I do know his face by heart as does nearly everyone."

Tony put a hand on her shoulder and said, "I know some of the story, Rachel. Please stay with us as long as you like until we straighten this out." He turned to Cosimo and picked him up in a bear hug and spun him around. "Hey, I missed having you as a workout partner. I think I am getting soft."

Rachel had time to look around as they were seated in a large room containing many works of ancient art including several life-size bronze busts of both male and female Romans. The room was tall, and at the top was an impressive dome of stained glass depicting an epic event of some sort.

"You have an impressive collection," Rachel observed, continuing to look around the room.

"We are proud of our masterpieces. Some are excellent reproductions of items I helped excavate at one time or another, and others are indeed real and priceless. That's the reward for being an active archeologist. At times, there are antiquities that can be acquired legally and with the permission of the host country. And I understand that you are also pursuing a degree in archeology?" Mary asked.

"Well, I thought so until this morning. Now I don't know what my future is. And the worst thing is, I haven't told my parents yet. It happened so fast, right out of the blue, as they say."

"Cosimo, can you tell us what happened this morning?" Tony asked his son.

"You are involved in this, *Papà*, at least that is one accusation we heard."

"In what way?"

"A few days ago, we uncovered a cylinder of bronze buried under a slab of stone in one of the villas. The overlying stone was engraved with the words '*Quoniam Antonius.*' To make a long story short, Rachel and I found it and came up with the idea that it was some sort of message. Well, eventually, we got permission to remove the stone and look under it. This was done under the direct observation and encouragement of the *Supervisore* of students, Professor Termineto, who was there in person. After the cylinder was removed, it was sent for examination and that was the last time either of us saw it. This morning, Professor Termineto said that the inscription was somehow addressed from me to you as a publicity stunt. He refused to give me permission to see what was in the cylinder. Then he kicked both of us off the site and is going to try to blacken our name at our schools."

Tony considered this for a moment and quickly glanced at Mary to read her thoughts. "And what was the inscription, do you remember exactly what it said?"

"Sure, it was '*apertum est Antonius Severius Maximus ex Paulo Fabio Persico Cosimus.*' " Cosimo watched as his father's expression changed. His face became pained as if, suddenly, he had received a hard punch to the chest. Cosimo noticed the long look between his parents. This was something they were involved in for sure. "Does this mean something to you?" he asked looking back and forth between them.

"If you mean, did either one of us have a hand in planting that cylinder in Herculaneum for some nefarious reason, the answer is absolutely no. We had absolutely nothing to do with it." There was a long pause as Tony considered his words carefully. "However, we did know a person by that name many years ago before you were born. The coincidence is too much for mere chance. I will have to read the actual message to be positive that it was intended for me."

Cosimo recalled what the professor had said, "He already agreed in principle to meet with you, although you should know that he thinks of you as a showman and businessman, his words exactly."

"I can go, Anthony," Mary said, her smooth voice pulling everyone's attention to her. "Since I have the credentials he will respect, he may be more willing to discuss it with me."

Tony stood up, and one look at his dark face told everyone that his opinion was different. "The professor thinks the message is for me then I'm the one who will read it. He can hardly refuse." His anger was just below the surface, and it was a side of him that Cosimo rarely had seen.

"And if it helps, my family has many contacts in Italy that may give the professor incentive to reconsider his decision regarding us," Rachel offered.

"I'm sorry, Rachel," Mary said sweetly, "I didn't hear your last name, and aren't you from New York?"

"My last name is Lucchese, and I was born in New York, but I have many relatives who migrated from Italy, and I understand many more still live here."

Mary smiled, pondering the name, Lucchese, which went around in her head looking for a connection. She had heard that name previously…some place.

"I will travel to Herculaneum in the morning and read the message," Tony announced. His statement put an end to further discussions.

Rachel woke with a start, glanced at her watch, then looked around the room, unsure at first where she was. The bedroom was sumptuously appointed with dark mahogany paneling and furniture, contrasting with the white bed linens floridly embroidered with bright silk. The bed was a rich four poster one, hand carved from floor to the top finials. She twisted to a sitting position, stretched, and looked out the large window, a view which showed an olive grove stretching out to the horizon. Her parents' home just outside the city of New York was also an estate designed and furnished to indicate great wealth, and she was used to such surroundings. Still this one was special. Here, each room was more like a museum with interesting art and ancient carvings on display, really too many to take in all at once. There was a feeling of history all around her, the handwork of long dead ancient people who had once lived and flourished, now remembered only by the work they left behind.

She paused in thought, her mind seeing Cosimo more clearly than if he had been standing just in front of her. A handsome creature, his curly dark hair fitted to his scalp just as perfectly as a cap. Now she understood his nose, which was prominent, though not overly large. It was a Roman nose, adulterated by a Jewish nose, cumulating in a near perfect combination. Rachel took a deep breath. She had to find out more about his parents. Hers were very particular, and to convince them of her valid interest in this young masterpiece, she had to produce more than just physical evidence. Though she had seen Tony many times in still photographs, she now realized that the man in person was much different than his images. She sensed a raw power just below the surface of this cultivated icon groomed for public consumption. Tony was clearly capable of violence, a lot of it, and it coursed through his body, held in check by slender threads, likely attached to his lovely wife. And what about Mary? She seemed to project an image of a lovely middle-aged woman, educated and cultivated way beyond what Rachel expected to find. There was no obvious attempt made to appear to be anything but what she genuinely was. Rachel decided to focus on Mary, whom she was sure would tell her anything she asked about the family.

After a shower and dressing in modest but fashionable clothes, Rachel started descending the large curved staircase. There, at the bottom, waited Cosimo, smiling up at her as he rested his arm on the lower stair railing. His eyes caressed her body from her hair to her feet then returned to focus on her face.

"You must have slept well because you look wonderful," he said softly.

"I did. Perhaps I dreamed about you," she retorted.

As she neared the last step he offered his arm and she accepted. "Hungry for breakfast?" he wondered.

"As long as I can dine with you and your parents, I will relish any dish offered."

"Well, *Papà* left for Herculanum before we got up. I think he is anxious to resolve our problem and restore our good names."

"Yes and to read that mysterious message," Rachel proposed. "Any ideas about that, Cosimo?"

"It's a mystery to me. We'll find out tonight when he returns, I expect."

Mary was waiting by the table as they turned the corner into the dining room. She was dressed in a white gown which flowed around her slender figure like a painting from ancient times.

"Ah, both at the same time. However did you manage that?" She asked and gave a little laugh and a sideways look.

"Simple, I waited at the foot of the stairs for an hour for her and didn't mind a bit," Cosimo answered.

After they sat and the food was served, Mary broke the silence by asking, "Rachel, are you in your senior year at school?"

"Yes, same as Cosimo. At least we are as of September, I hope."

"Anthony will get this matter corrected. You shouldn't worry at all."

"Can you tell us about this man who buried a message in such a strange way?" Rachel asked while watching her face closely.

"He was a good friend to us both, and I can say that we both loved him, almost as much as he loved us." She looked toward Cosimo and held his eyes before completing her announcement. "Cosimo was named after him, though he never knew that fact until this moment."

Before the stunned Cosimo could react, Rachel pursued the subject. "What do you mean by 'almost'?" she asked.

"He gave his life for us, to save us and to insure our happiness. He even started Anthony in his current business before he left us."

When Mary finished, tears started down her face before she quickly wiped them away. They could sense that Cosimus was an important person in her life, perhaps the most important person other than her husband.

"I never recall hearing about Cosimus, *Mamma*. There obviously is a lot I don't know," Cosimo said.

"There is, dear, much you don't know. However don't press me on this subject just now. We have to wait and hear from your father first and then, perhaps, we can discuss this further. I think you are old enough now, though… " She couldn't finish. She could go no further toward a subject that had been off limits for over 20 years. A subject they never discussed any longer, even in private. There were too many emotions, too many memories, which would emerge and surround them. Better to go on pretending.

"Can I ask where you and Tony came from?" Rachel ventured, slightly changing the subject.

"Of course, my dear, and I understand fully why you would ask such a question. There is a simple forthright answer for you. I came from Israel, born in a small settlement just north of Jerusalem. My parents, both of them, were archeologists which is why I ended up in the same profession. Anthony was born in Rome, grew up there and educated there. We believe that, in his youth, he lived nearly where this house is now."

Rachel contemplated Mary's last words for a moment. The house seemed to be much older than it could be if her statement was true. She decided to move past that…for now. "How could you two have met and fallen in love, born so far apart?"

"Yes, that is a good question and rather hard to answer fully," Mary said, recovering enough to smile again. "The short answer is that we were assembled as a team because of our language skills. Would you care for more coffee?" Mary rose and took the porcelain pot from its heated cradle and waited for her reply.

Rachel could sense that the conversation about such topics was over for the moment. "No, I've had enough stimulation," she answered. Her answer was greeted by a quizzical look from Mary but no comment.

"Rachel, would you care to go to Rome today and see the sights?" Cosimo inquired. He had intensely studied the previous exchange between Mary and Rachel, trying to gauge why certain questions were asked and what answers were given and also withheld. He respected his mother enough not to intervene or push for information until the time was right. Also, he began to suspect that a full disclosure of the past will not only be painful but life-changing, and some doors, once opened, cannot be closed again. There had to be a sound reason that he was never fully informed about this touchy subject.

Rachel was looking down lost in thought but suddenly perked up, beamed a smile at him, and responded, "That would be wonderful. Might I buy lunch for us at some spot that we will remember forever?"

"That would include any of the several cafes within sight of the Roman Forum," Mary suggested. "Good plan, Rachel. If Anthony were here, we would go in with you. He knows every haunt and hollow of that place and can tell stories about it for hours."

After they left, Mary went up to her room and closed the door. The tears started in earnest this time and so did her sobbing. The flood gates of the past had opened again, unexpectedly bringing with them memories which had been put safely away in a corner of her mind. All her inner eye could see was Cosimus, his last wave at them before he disappeared forever, suddenly gone as if life itself was just a dream. If they had been able to mourn over his body or toss his ashes someplace, that would have kept his memory in perspective, they could have come to terms with his loss. As it had occurred, he was gone in an instant as if he had never lived at all. At the time, she felt as though a blanket had been tossed over her head, smothering her, with no time to correct things which had happened or reverse irreversible events. Her eyes had bulged at what she saw, she had screamed and cried, all to no avail. Anthony had held her in his strong protective arms, however he too streamed with tears.

She lay face down, her face in the pillow, her body shaking with regret and loss. Cosimus had died for her and for Anthony. She could not change what happened then nor could it be altered now.

Rachel pulled on Cosimo's sleeve, getting his attention but not his eyes. He was busy avoiding the intense and fast traffic of Rome. "You have to speak loudly, Rachel," he shouted over the noise of the bus just passing on the left.

"I have an idea," she said in his ear.

"So?"

"You know the big museum near the Forum?"

"You mean the *Musei Capitolini*?"

"That's the one. Can you take me there?"

Cosimo looked at her for as long as the road would allow. He wondered why she would want to begin her excursion with another museum. Her face was just too pretty to decipher her motives. All he saw when he looked at her was her perpetual smile on a beautiful yet distracting face. He braked and took a turn, heading up a different street. As the car slowed, the ambient noise diminished enough for conversation.

"Well, all of what you want to see is pretty much in the same area so the answer is 'sure,' but what do you have in mind?"

"I understand that the *Musei Capitolini* has an extensive collection of records also. It just occurred to me to search for the two names on the cylinder and see what pops up."

"But," Cosimo protested, "we already know that the names were *Papà* and their mutual friend. What we don't know is why."

"What is bothering me is the use of Romanized names. It makes them sound like they were copying actual historical names. And why would they do that?" Rachel asked.

"Tell you what I think," Cosimo began, "I think my father's Roman name is just to enhance his image when he dons all that Roman armor. You can't take that seriously."

"What is you mother's maiden name?" Rachel bluntly asked.

"Solomon," Cosimo answered.

"You ever wonder why your father adopted her last name?"

"I never really asked. I don't know why, and now I realize that I never questioned it." The conversation stopped for a moment as Cosimo searched his memory for answers. This will be an interesting day, he told himself.

Office of the Supervisore degli studi, Herculaneum, 9:00 AM

Tony could tell by the secretary's expression that he was expected. He closed the outer door and stood in front of her desk, staring silently at her, waiting for acknowledgement of some sort.

"Well, I recognize you from the many photos I've seen of you, in case you are wondering," she said. "For some reason, you look bigger in real life." She paused for any comment, but he remained silent, still looking at her with a hint of glower on his face. "You may go in, he's waiting." She pointed to the door on one side of her desk.

Without a word, Tony opened the door, finding Professor Termineto seated behind his desk looking at him with a sour expression

"You need no introduction *Antonius Severius Maximus*. Isn't that what you prefer to be called?" he asked sarcastically.

Tony leaned across the desk, supported by his two thickly muscled arms, bringing his face close to Professor Termineto's. "Let me make this very clear, Professor. I had absolutely no part in any deception and neither did my son nor Rachel. If you choose to be confrontational though, then I am your man." He pulled himself to his full height and put his hands on his hips, his eyes never leaving the face of Professor Termineto. His posture and his hard eyes had the desired effect, and he could see that Professor Termineto was now not so sure of himself.

"You know what really made me angry, *Antonius Severius Maximus,* is the message itself. Not only did we nearly embarrass…no, humiliate all the archeologists who have labored at this site for so many years, we nearly made *Italia* itself a laughing stock in front of the entire world."

"You need to inform me why this is the case. How could a simple message, in your view, cause so much distress?"

"You are not serious, are you?" he sputtered. "The 'message' was skillfully placed to give the impression that it was from before the eruption of Vesuvius. I mean, how else could it get there under an undisturbed paver? We archeologists were supposed to be excited about this new find and give the press a heads-up so that maximum publicity would be gained. The giveaway was that your son was the one who 'discovered' it, and what did he discover? I'll tell you…he found a bronze tube engraved with your name and a metal scroll inside with a personal message to you."

"You do know, don't you, that many Roman names were similar and reused just like some names are today. Can you be so certain that I am the one to whom it was intended?" Tony said deliberately, trying to keep his anger in check.

"Certain? Oh, I'm certain. The letter is written in English. Or can you explain how a language not developed for nearly fifteen hundred years after the eruption of Vesuvius could have been placed prior to that event?"

Tony visibly slumped, his anger gone. A nostalgia mingled with regret came over him, and there was no longer doubt in his mind. The letter was actually intended for him. A letter written by the noble Cosimus, his friend and companion, now only dust, dead for nearly twenty centuries.

"May I read the message?" Tony asked, this time his voice was softer, the edge gone.

"In fact, you can't have it, any part of it. We need this around to prove your family's involvement in a conspiracy to use our ancient history for your own commercial ends."

"Where is the cylinder now?" Tony asked.

"It's safe in my desk drawer, still pretending to be from the past."

"Since you think that the object has no worth, then you should not mind giving it to whom it was intended. To tell you the truth, I did know the person who wrote the letter. He was my best friend and the most honorable person I ever met. He died a very long time ago and obviously placed the cylinder before his death. My family had no part in this other than the admittedly incredible coincidence of my own son being the one who brought it to light."

"I'm not sure I believe you, *Antonius Severius Maximus,*" Termineto snarled. "In fact, I don't believe you. Since I have no use for this item, you may have it and good riddance to the lot of you." He opened his bottom drawer and tossed the cylinder on the desk. It landed heavily with a dull thud, rolling and stopping just at the desk edge. Tony picked it up and inspected it carefully, turning it over and over.

"The message is still inside?" he asked.

"Yes, you can have that also."

Tony turned and softly closed the office door, then returned to stand in front of the desk. He paused for a moment, considering his words carefully.

"Professor, I do owe you something for your previous kindness to Cosimo. He spoke praise of you and holds you in high regard. So does Rachel Lucchese. What I am about to disclose should go no farther than this room. I doubt that you would repeat it because I'm sure you won't believe it either. I swear to you that what I will say is the truth, however preposterous it may seem. There is much that happened to me and others which has been kept out of the public consciousness and for good reason. If you repeat this conversation to anyone, I will deny saying any of it. Instead, I will release to the press how you were fooled by an elaborate publicity stunt. Do you clearly understand?"

"On with your story, likely I won't believe anything you say so it really doesn't matter."

"I was born in the year 03 AD." Tony let this sink in for a moment before continuing. "*Paulo Fabio Persico Cosimus* was born in the year 1995 and died two thousand years ago. He sent that message to me knowing that controversy surrounding anything written in English from that time period would create so much sensation that I would hear about it no matter where I ended up. The message is authentic and is really from the ancient past."

"Are you telling me that you and this Cosimus traveled back and forth through time?" He laughed out loud and shook his head. "Pitiful. This gets worse and worse, nearly comical. Just take your message and leave. We are done here." He waved his hand toward the door, then looked down at some papers on his desk.

"I won't threaten you, Professor, because, in your shoes, I would't believe it either, however if you value your life, you should be very careful of putting a member of the Lucchese family in a bad light. Thank you for giving me the message, and you will see no more of me."

Chapter 7

Libro Del Passato

Truth is confirmed by inspection and delay;
falsehood by haste and uncertainty.

Publius Cornelius Tacitus (56 – 120 AD)

Musei Capitolini, Rome

H e said at the end of the hall," Cosimo repeated in confusion, looking around for any sign they were in the right place.

"There!" Rachel said, pointing to an obscure door somewhat short of the end of the long hallway. Indeed the door was marked with a small sign which would have been easily missed had Rachel not been so persistent. The office which contained the computer assets of the *Musei Capitolini* was obviously not intended to be frequented by the public.

Hesitantly, Cosimo opened the door and was greeted by the sight of several booths arranged around the sides of the room, each furnished with two chairs and a counter top on which sat a large computer screen and keyboard. An attendant attired in a comfortable and well-worn sweater came toward them. He was young, thin, and wore heavy glasses in thick black frames which were positioned near the end of his prominent nose. Instead of a verbal greeting, he paused, looking them over from head to foot, obviously waiting for a request of some sort.

Rachel smiled at him and asked in her warm feminine voice, "Speak English?"

"Some," the man answered.

"We are archeology students working at Herculaneum for the summer. Recently a discovery was made which was engraved with two Roman names. We were told you could be of assistance with research regarding who these men were."

The assistant looked blank for a moment, digesting her words after mental translation. "Of course. Know how to use a computer?"

"We do."

"Help yourself," he said and motioned toward one of the booths. "If you need any assistance, let me know."

After the screen lit up, Rachel looked helplessly at Cosimo, "It's all in Italian! You'll have to do it." She pushed the keyboard in front of him.

"*Certamente*, my dear Rachel. What did you expect in *Italia*?" He laughed and pulled out the small paper with the exact spelling of the names in question. "I've heard of this collection before. It's called *Libro Del Passato,* the book of the past, a compilation of names, dates, and biography of nearly every ancient Roman from the beginning until the breakup in the fifth century. A work which is still in progress. Expect to suffer a bit doing this search because there is always an awful confusion about Roman names which were passed from generation to generation. At times, it's nearly impossible to discover exactly whom you have found and when he or she lived. But here we go… ."

The first was *Antonius Severius Maximus,* the name Cosimo's father frequently used when he dressed as the *centurion* character he had made famous. Cosimo admitted to himself many times that his father certainly looked authentic enough when dressed as an ancient Roman officer. And so did his women fans, who pursued him constantly when they were out in public. It was the price he paid for fame and fortune. Mary abhorred the public in general and also the lack of privacy fame brought with it. She much preferred her life of comparative academic isolation in a field of no particular interest to the masses who preferred the glossy and glamorous.

The list of hits returned almost instantaneously filled three screen pages. Cosimo groaned, leaning forward to see the small typeface used for the biography such as it was known. Most were from the wrong century, nevertheless three stood out as possible matches. Rachel and Cosimo found what they were looking for rather quickly and looked at each other in surprise.

"Look at this one," Rachel said, her finger on the screen under the name *Antonius Severius Maximus.* "It says he was a *centurion.* Isn't that what your father is in his photos?"

"Let's see what the source is," he murmured, his eyes looking for the citation. "Suetonius," he said louder. "That's interesting."

"Well, what did the famous historian say about our boy?" Rachel persisted.

"It says that there was an *Antonius Severius Maximus* who disappeared in the desert west of *Caesarea Maritima* in the early first century, under the reign of Tiberius. That would have been in northern Judea. It actually quotes Suetonius specifying the year as the year of the consulship of Piso and Frugi."

"Anything else?" she asked.

"No, still something bothers me about this," he said continuing to stare at the screen. "Why would anyone record what happened to some *centurion* in that part of the Empire? What would make that interesting?"

"Don't look at me. How about the other one, the same name as the man you were named for."

Cosimo typed in the second name, growing more apprehensive about discovering some ancient secret which might affect the present in some way. He had to look twice at the big screen. There was only one hit, and it was a big one, full of information. Several Roman historians were quoted. This person had been a well-known and respected figure back then.

"Wow!" Rachel exclaimed. "Jackpot. What does it say?" she impatiently asked.

Cosimo was silent for a moment, reading ahead before answering. "It does not list his birth or birthplace, something odd for such an important figure. This man was unique in several ways. He was a *centurion* for a long time then became a *legatus legionis,* or general to us, in command of a *legion,* a rather famous one, the *XX Valeria Victrix.* He was in command during the invasion and occupation of Britannia under Emperor Claudius."

Rachel looked puzzled. "So what is unusual about that?"

"The rank of *legatus* was filled by the high born…you know, the senatorial class of patricians. Not only that, being promoted from the ranks, as we say, just wasn't done at that time. Another thing…there is usually a progression of elected positions before being appointed *legatus.* This *Paulo Fabio Persico Cosimus* doesn't have any other positions listed. Either the facts are incomplete or…"

"Or what?" Rachel insisted.

"Or this man was one hell of a soldier."

"When did he die?"

"Not listed."

"Well, like you thought, there were real people who held those names. I guess we didn't really learn anything. Thanks for being patient with me," Rachel said. There was no response from Cosimo who continued to read the entry.

"Want to meet *Paulo Fabio Persico Cosimus*?" Cosimo asked, smiling at something.

"Whatever do you mean?"

"He's here. Downstairs in fact. Come, we are going down and see him in person." He rose and tugged her arm.

Cosimo had a strange sensation of déjà vu as they walked down the long isles, statuary on both sides, giving the feeling that these famous men and women somehow still occupied cold stone and bronze, still projected their power to those looking them in the face. He was positive he had been here before. A vague recollection came over him, and he reflexly paused beside a dark bronze object and then looked at the face. Sure, he had seen that face before, in his youth. This time, he stepped back to take it all in. Whoever created this masterpiece had studied the actual man long enough to understand the raw power locked up in him. The bronze was full size and was of a thickly muscled man in resplendent armor. The detail was breathtaking. Every stitch was there, every muscle fiber stood out. Yet the face was what held his attention. It was both noble and fierce at the same time. A man of total confidence and power, who had made life and death decisions in an instant. A man whom you would dread meeting in actual combat.

"Wow," Rachel said. "Wow again," she repeated. "So this is the man you were named for," she observed.

"He bears the same name, though my mother was referring to an actual living person they knew before I was born."

Rachel looked back and forth between the statue of *Paulo Fabio Persico Cosimus* and the living Cosimo Solomon standing just beside her. "You are about the same size as he was, except I think he had bigger muscles. Ever try on your father's Roman outfit?"

"Are you kidding? I would look like a kid in a cowboy suit holding a plastic revolver. No, and I was never offered a chance anyway."

"Does Tony speak Latin?" Rachel wondered.

"There are two kinds of Latin, you may know. One is ecclesiastical and the other the language of Cicero and Caesar. My father speaks the latter."

"And you, Cosimo. How are your Latin skills?"

"I can and do converse in Latin with my father. When we spar together, it's strictly Latin. I learned both from an early age."

Rachel took a deep breath and gave the statue a final look. "About that lunch I was to buy for us?"

As Mary had suggested, they found a cafe in sight of the Forum situated on a second floor balcony. This elegant coffee shop was not on the radar of the international tourists, just now swarming the streets looking up in amazement at all the ancient ruins. Most of this crowd were well heeled, dressed in posh but comfortably stylish Italian clothes, instantly recognizable as authentic by those in the know.

Rachel looked around with big eyes, then back at Cosimo who was grinning, happy that he had delighted his companion. "Perfect, Cosimo. I knew you would find just the right spot." She looked out the window and pointed. "Have you any idea what those columns over there are?"

Cosimo looked down her finger. "Sure. Those look like the remnants of the Temple of Saturn. Don't worry, we'll go over there with the crowd and stare at them and all the other remaining monuments till your feet are crying." He laughed and pointed at her stiletto heels. "That's not what you want to wear for seeing the sights of *Roma*."

Rachel shot him a not so amused look. "Do you find me attractive, Cosimo?"

"The most attractive, gorgeous woman I have ever encountered. And that's no exaggeration."

"Then just let me be that girl. The right outfit makes me feel like I want to look, and it gives a woman confidence to see the admiring eyes of men when they glance her way. Just be supportive, that's all I ask."

Cosimo put down his coffee cup and patted her hand. "I will, Rachel. I will. Thanks for putting me in my place. I know how you feel though, because just being next to you makes me want to jump and shout, 'Look at Cosimo and who he is with!' "

Rachel took a more serious tone, looking at him without blinking. "Cosimo, something is being kept from you about your family history. I'm not sure about anything from the little I know, nevertheless whatever it is, you are in for a shock. It's that last thing Mary said about you being old enough now. She didn't finish, but I sense that when Tony returns you will be told some facts which will be stunning."

"I got that feeling also. Frankly, whatever it is, I'm happy not knowing. I had a good childhood, have an interesting future, and found somebody wonderful that I plan to pursue until I catch her."

"You recall when she said that Tony was born nearly at the spot of your present home?"

"I've heard that before. So what?"

"Cosimo, your home is at least two hundred years old. What year do you suppose Tony was born then?"

"Gee, I always figured that the landscape was different twenty or even forty years ago. How do we not know that a nearby smaller house, built for groundskeepers or caretakers, was there then and gone now?"

"I guess we don't," she admitted. "One other thing," Rachel added, "I was there when you pulled that cylinder out of the hiding spot. You can't convince me that it wasn't there for centuries the way it looked. It was placed there by someone who knew that it was going to be safely buried by tons of volcanic rubble away from prying eyes and destructive erosion. And that person was smart enough to disguise the legend so that only very astute people, like you and me, could guess that something was actually there to be found. The person that buried it knew what was going to happen, and no one else did. How did he know?" she asked, a bit louder.

Cosimo looked around to be sure their conversation was not bringing undue attention. "What are you saying, Rachel? Where is this going?"

"The message, Cosimo. We have to read the message. That will tell us everything."

Chapter 8

A Message From the Past

To be ignorant of what occurred before you
were born is to remain always a child.

Marcus Tullius Cicero (106 – 43 BC)

It was nearly supper time when they arrived. Cosimo could see that his father had returned because his car was parked at an odd angle as if he were in a hurry to get inside. A knot formed in his stomach, his brow furrowed, and his mouth became increasingly dry. There was apprehension written all over his face, and Rachel noticed. After she emerged from the car she stood and softly took his arm in hers, smiling comfortingly up at him. "Nothing can happen to you, Cosimo. I forbid it. The worst that can happen is that you come to New York with me to finish your education. There, I guarantee that no harm can come to you. My family would never permit it."

"I am worried. I admit it, although I don't have the slightest idea what concerns me. It's easier to take bad news when it dribbles at you one drop at a time, but when it pours over you… ." He didn't finish because the front door opened, and Mary stepped into the light. From this distance, she looked more like a young girl than a middle-aged mother, a university professor. She was beautiful. Radiant even. Why had he never noticed before?

"Exactly the right time. You both must possess telepathy," Mary remarked, moving aside to allow them to pass. She quickly kissed Cosimo on his cheek as he went by, then smiled, her eyes bright and full of love. Cosimo considered that the news he expected might not be so tragic or gripping after all. Then he turned and looked at her again, detecting the red eyes of recent tears.

"*Mamma*," Cosimo exclaimed, turning to face her, "is something wrong?"

"No, Cosimo," she said, her voice level, "nothing has changed since you left. I just have emotions when I think of things past. Long past in this case. Come on in because we are nearly ready to eat. Rachel, you have time to freshen up before supper." It was an invitation for Rachel to go upstairs and let her have a moment alone with Cosimo. Rachel understood, and after a quick glance at Cosimo, she started up the staircase toward her room.

They both silently watched as Rachel rose out of sight without looking back. Then Cosimo asked, "Did *Papà* sort things out with Professor Termineto?"

"They talked, I understand. He can tell you the details while Rachel is changing."

"Not a chance. This concerns her also. Both our futures are in jeopardy, and she has a right to hear what happened."

"There is more to this story, Cosimo. Part of it is not for her ears to hear. It's hard enough telling you the facts and the truth."

She led Cosimo through the house toward the small study that Tony used for business. It struck Cosimo how similar things were to ancient Herculaneum after all this time. There still existed the concept of the *tablinum,* the office of the *paterfamilias.* His father held the same position of respect that the ancients used for so long.

Tony was seated behind his desk, standing as they entered. "Please close the door and sit, Cosimo. We have something you have to hear. It is time you know."

The feeling of dread returned. Cosimo sat in an upholstered chair, his mother behind him with her hands resting on his chest.

"Possibly you won't believe my story, however your mother will tell you that every word I say is true. I've never lied to you, however you were never given all the facts. I am your father, and Mary is your *mamma*. We were born and raised just as you've been told all of your life. That much you already know. What you don't know…," Tony paused. The truth was brutal. No imagination could ever invent such a tale as he had to tell.

"Tell him, *caro*. Just say it," Mary spoke firmly.

"I was born a long time ago. In fact, I was born in this very spot but in the year 03. Yes, you heard me correctly. I was born over two thousand years ago."

Cosimo's jaw opened, his mind raced. His father had told him something inconceivable, something that could not have happened. There was no rational thought possible if what he heard was true.

All Cosimo could utter was *"Papà!"* He felt like running away. There was madness in him. He couldn't have heard what he thought he heard. There was a mistake someplace.

Tony came around the desk and caressed Cosimo's face. "I never told this story until I met your professor this morning. I told him the truth also, yet he still dismissed me. His mind is closed to this possibility. You will believe me and trust in what I say, Cosimo."

"Papà, I heard you just say that you are two thousand years old. I must be having a bad dream."

"No, Cosimo, I am not that old. I mean, do I look that old?" Tony laughed and glanced at a mirror hanging on the wall. "I said I was born two thousand years ago. I met your mother…well, it's confusing." Tony stopped and looked at Mary for help.

"Cosimo, we both did time travel together. It was all made possible by an accidental discovery at Fermilab in Chicago. As I understood it at the time, it was a byproduct of a high energy project. The scientists eventually learned to control where and when an aperture through time was created. The project was carefully guarded by the American government, and after we returned, the entire thing was discontinued, and we were explicitly warned to never speak of the matter. And we obeyed that directive until now. We have wanted to tell you since you were born, though neither of us had the nerve until now."

"Why and where did you go?" Cosimo asked, the excitement rising in him.

"They sent Cosimo in first. You see, he used the same name you do now. He changed it later to Cosimus to sound more authentic for that time period. We met by accident and became friends, best friends," Tony explained.

"They came back through the hole together and that was the first time I ever saw your father, my future husband. After getting ready, four of us passed back in time together and were there, in what today is called Israel, for several months. We all came back together into this time period, then Cosimo decided to go back alone. We watched on a little monitor as he returned to the Judea of the past. He never came back. He couldn't even if he wanted to because the aperture was closed for good. Just telling the story makes me cry, and I hope you can understand why." Mary became tearful and held her head low while wiping at her eyes.

"My God!" Cosimo said. "This is the most amazing thing to ever happen, and it was kept secret from the entire world. Don't you think it's time to tell your story to the public?"

"No, Cosimo," Tony said firmly. "Never mention this to anyone. Think what would happen. People would return to the past to influence the future. They would change things. We all might even suddenly cease to exist. Or worse. This is a discovery which should have never been made, and I hope that it stays a secret and that the knowledge how to do it is lost for all time. Humans are not ready to have this much power and never will be."

"Wait!" Cosimo said. "You came here and your friend Cosimo stayed there and did it change anything, anything at all?"

"It sure did," Mary said. "Cosimo saved the entire world by going back.He knew what he was doing and gave his life to do it. It was a close call for humanity. We can never take that chance again."

There was a knock on the door. They all knew that Rachel was on the other side wondering what was being said. "Just a moment, Cosimo, before she comes in. One last thing you should know. The cylinder you unearthed was placed there by my friend, Cos, just like you thought. The message inside was written to me using English. That way, Cos knew that nobody would believe that the message was anything but a fake, yet eventually I would read the message he addressed to me and me alone. It was a particularly brilliant gambit, and it worked, just like he would have wanted. Although he died a very long time ago, his letter brought his image to my mind just as if he were standing right here talking to me in person."

Mary turned and opened the door. Rachel was standing in the hall with big eyes full of innocence, her face questioning. "Come in, dear. We are having a family discussion, and you are welcome."

Rachel came straight to Cosimo and took his arm, looking around at the others from a safe position. "Are you discussing what happened today?" she asked.

"Here is what you need to know, Rachel," Tony began. "I had a nice talk with the professor and explained to him that the message was from a friend of mine and Mary's, and he was the one who hid the message long ago with no malice or deception in mind. The professor gave me the cylinder and message to take with me, and I have it in my desk. Thanks to both of you for having the intellectual curiosity to pursue this, and we both want to thank you for enabling our old friend to speak to us from the grave in this way. I think after some time to consider this, the professor will forget it ever happened, and both of you can resume your education with no black marks attached to your record. Consider this entire episode part of your education and experience in life."

Rachel looked down at Cosimo's face. She couldn't read him like she usually did. This time, he looked lost in thought as if present in body only. Nope, she had to have more information for this jumble of facts to rest easily on her mind. "What did the message say, Tony? Can't you tell me anything?" she blurted, looking back and forth between the three other people who were also looking at her.

"Much of it is personal, I'm afraid. For your information, Cosimo doesn't know any more than you about the message. The text of it describes his life, his work, his successes, and the danger he faced. I don't feel that any of it would be understood by someone who didn't know him."

Rachel could feel the blood rising in her face. She wasn't used to being treated like a child. Being from a family who never took no for an answer compelled her to stick up for herself. "I have some questions you need to answer," she said. She could see Tony's jaw clinch, and his eyes narrow. He was morphing into the image of the frightening Roman warrior he frequently pretended to be. Or was it pretending, she suddenly wondered? Was this man standing there, his muscles tightening, actually the famed *centurion* who vanished in the desert of Judea? It was impossible, however the facts swirled in her head. There was something important which had been discussed out of her presence. Looking at Cosimo, she realized that whatever was said was hard to digest or comprehend, something that no one was supposed to know. And this friend, Cosimus, who wrote the letter, was he the model for the statue she had just seen this very morning? If there was such a thing as time travel, she would believe that she had discovered people who had actually done that very thing. But time travel was fiction, fanciful fiction, that everybody at one time or another mused about and wished that it could be true. Was it true? Was it actually possible? Had Cosimo's parents traveled in time?

There was silence in the room, and you could cut it with a knife. No one spoke. Everyone was waiting for something to happen, to either disperse or… . She decided to speak what her brain was screaming at her. "I think there is a really big secret in this room, and I'll bet I know what it is." There was no response from anybody, no movement, no denial, no conversation at all. They were waiting for her to continue, hoping that she had not guessed what had happened behind the closed door.

"You two," she said, pointing at Mary and Tony, have traveled in time. I know in my heart that is what the silence is all about, and since I have guessed correctly, you should tell me what you just told Cosimo."

Mary gasped, her hands shielding her mouth, and looked away. Cosimo said nothing but couldn't hold her gaze.

Tony stood, his hands on his hips, and studied Rachel, as if seeing her for the first time. This was a very intelligent and brave woman Cosimo had brought into his home. How to deal with her was the question. "Rachel, do you understand how preposterous your statement is?" Tony asked.

"I do, it's pure science fiction, isn't it? Yet it fits the facts as I know them, and no other explanation works. You are the *centurion* who disappeared in Judea, and now I understand why that fact was recorded by Suetonius. It was likely widely discussed and debated all over the Roman Empire. No one could understand how or why you just disappeared one day. There must have been witnesses who reported this significant event. I think you came to the future that day, and here you are. I don't know how it was done, still it happened. And Cosimus stayed in the past, dying there roughly two thousand years ago, given the emotion about him. I gather that you and Mary feel somehow responsible about it. I saw the bronze casting made in his image today, and I will never forget it. I can understand why you can't forget the real man."

Tony sat back down, reclining in his chair. "Sit, Rachel. We have much to discuss.

Chapter 9

A Luxurious Life

Herculaneum, October 51 AD

*D*awn crept in by degrees, as if sneaking in without anyone noticing, the faint pink glow turning by seconds into a warmer gold. On the moisture laden air drifted the sounds of ever-present gulls, who began their day just before the sun made its appearance over the low hills to the northeast, just past the shadow of Vesuvius still standing watch over the sleeping cities to its west.

Cos stretched and studied the ceiling, lost in thought, unwilling to actually begin his morning, wanting it instead to linger, coming to him slowly as if he were still dreaming. He slept alone as he had done for his entire lifetime, although in moments like this, he imagined how wonderful it would be to hear the soft breathing of a woman next to him, watching her face when her eyes first opened, transitioning her consciousness from dreams to reality. In his imagination, he would watch her face become a smile, her eyes sparkle with love... .

A loud noise from someplace in the house brought him back to the reality of the moment. It was time to arise and start the day. He swung to a sitting position, realizing that the many traumas of his life had made their wounds to his joints and muscles ever present. His body functioned well enough, considering his age of 46 years, most of those spent in the hard service of the Roman Legions, however he was starting to feel his years, especially in the mornings.

Once again he looked around the room and marveled. Two walls were decorated with elaborate scenes which drew the mind in, nearly accepting the premise of the artist as fact instead of mere decoration. The colors chosen were mostly in the blue restful range, befitting a bed chamber. The rear wall was consumed by large windows which held a spectacular view toward the west and the vast bay, the sea sparkling beyond, blending imperceptibly at the horizon. Already the harbor was alive with commercial ships, some heading south to the busy port of Pompeii, others slowly docking at the wharfs below, oars out beating at the water.

There was no doubt, he had finally arrived at the best part of life. The labors and risks of the past over, the rewards of earning wealth and prestige now apparent. It was a different life than he had become accustomed to, and he had not yet learned to enjoy it as much as he should. Each day was his own to spend as he wanted. He was no longer responsible for the lives of his men and not subject to the whims and orders of superiors.

This home he had purchased, a gift of luck, was a treasure, no matter in what century you could define. It was beautifully crafted and executed, expertly positioned near the harbor and convenient to everything necessary for an extravagant life. He had only lived here for several months, not enough time to fully adjust to the life of a *paterfamilias,* instead of his former title of *Legatus Legionis,* in command of the famous *Legion XX Valeria Victrix.* And other than his companions who lived with him, there was no real family, no children to care for, and most unfortunately no wife.

Since they were granted occupancy in January, the months had been full of housekeeping tasks, such as repairs, finding furnishings and cooking supplies, not to speak of acquiring an adequate wardrobe for a man of leisure and wealth. He had kept his military clothing and weapons, both from his many years as a *centurion* and, later, as a general. But what he preferred wearing now was just a simple wool tunic and cape for his ordinary, everyday life. Following breakfast, he usually went out for a brisk walk around the streets of Herculaneum, stopping to chat at the various shops along the way. Finishing his walk by midmorning, the remainder of time before noon was taken up by a gratifying soak in hot water at one of the community baths.

Then it was time to pay a visit to one of his commercial ventures, either the winery or the bakery, both wholly owned by him. The two shops adjacent to the front entry of his *villa* were stocked by his own produce, each returning a fat profit. Once a week, he and Maccus ventured out on horseback to the gladiator school just north of Pompeii. There they had a fine workout with the gladiators, enough to keep fit and to hone their already considerable fighting skills.

Even with all this business and busyness, he had become increasingly aware of a vacant spot in his life. When he passed comely women on the street and noticed as they flicked curious eyes at him, he felt a strong urge to hold a woman in his arms, one that belonged to him and him only, one to grow old with and to lie with, both in life and after. He badly needed to find a woman who could please him and one who would allow him to bestow on her all life could offer: praise, respect, even worship, along with fine clothing, wealthy and educated friends and even travel. There had been many introductions to young available women along the way, still there was always something missing in them, and he had let them pass.

The problem was, as always, Mary and his recollection of her, his mental image being enhanced by the decades of time passed since he last saw her. She would have been the one, the only one he would ever have needed. But she had fallen for Antonius, and he for her, and the rest was history. At times, she still came to mind, her radiant face, her lustrous long dark hair and, most of all, her magical eyes when they looked right at his. No woman had ever matched Mary, and he had nearly given up the search for a replacement, even though Mary will not be born for another two millennia. Mary will exist someday, however he won't be there to find her again. He understood that his fate was to become dust and to be forgotten, just part of an ancient past that few will even recall as the human race goes on to different pursuits.

Cos slipped a loose fitting tunic over his head and tied the waist string taut, slipped on a pair of sandals, and walked out to the balcony, pausing a moment over the *atrium*, his arms folded on the railing, once again impressed by the incredible floor below paved with thousands of small multicolored marble fragments creating a realistic image of the sea bottom and the gods who inhabit it.

Maccus stopped below to look up at him, smiling his crooked smile, his familiar wrinkled face, his earnest, loyal face which Cos had seen for years, never really tiring of the man. "I see you are up, *Dominus*. Ready for breakfast?"

"I am. Have you eaten?" Cos inquired, returning the smile.

"Never without you, *Dominus*."

They dined on the little table in the *peristylum* under the shadow of the covered walkway which surrounded the garden already lit by sunshine. The morning was starting out as another perfect one, a day to rejoice and remember as a fine moment in one's short life.

Cos and Maccus chose seats across from one another as they had done for so many years. The table was already laden with hot bread and breakfast wine. A bowl of dates coated with sugar rested in the center.

"And *Màthair?*" Cos asked, wondering where the elderly mother of Maccus was and would she be dining with them as usual. Cos had taken to calling her mother also and was certainly treated as her son as exampled not only by her coddling but also her gift of pointing out his many faults whenever she saw them.

"I believe that she has a fish fresh from the sea to serve. The aroma of it brings my mouth to water." Maccus poured a generous cup of *mulsum* and passed it to Cos before pouring two more, one for himself and one for his mother.

Cos had finally gotten used to the Roman practice of diluting wine with water and adding a moderate amount of honey. At times, he still missed his morning coffee, though that habit had ended many years ago, in another life, in another century.

Màthair bustled in, a platter supported by one palm, the other hand holding a pie-shaped cut of cheese. She smiled broadly at them, and after placing the hot fish and cheese on the table, she stopped to kiss each of her men on the cheek before seating herself. "Cos," she started as she sat, "did you notice the fine white bread and the sweet *mulsum* before you?" Before Cos could answer she continued, "Both from our shops out front." She shook her head with the satisfaction that both items were of excellent quality, but mostly, they were convenient to acquire.

Cos smiled and nodded at her, a verbal response entirely unnecessary. *Màthair,* to an outsider, would be overlooked as simply another sparse peasant woman wearing rough loose clothing who spoke in an accented, coarse manner. But to Cos, she was the core of his new home, the authority of where things went and who did what. She ran the household as she saw fit and as she presumed that the master of the house, Cos, would want. Both

Màthair and Maccus felt at home here, felt ownership along with Cos, and in the privacy of their home, they treated each other as equals and on a first name basis. All three knew that this practice was not acceptable out in public, and anywhere but home they assumed their roles to comply with what other Romans would accept and expect, master and freed slaves. The Master ruled, slaves and freed slaves obeyed. However in the privacy they all three cherished, they were equals, all played a supporting role and always acted with consideration for the other members of their small family.

Cos had been saved by Maccus, who at the time was part of an axillary band of fighters recruited from friendly local Gaulic tribes. Maccus was a spearman, one of many wearing no identifying uniform yet fighting side by side with heavily armed and armored Roman legionaries. He had killed a warrior who had broken through the lines, determined to kill the *centurion* who was leading his men to victory in hand to hand fighting. Cos turned in time to see the event, afterwards thanking Maccus by rewarding him with the position of servant and personal assistant. They had become close friends, and when the *Legion XX* was withdrawn from Gaul to assist in the invasion of Britannia, Maccus went with them. And when Cos finished his two year appointment as *legatus* and retired, he had traveled with Maccus to Gaul to find *Màthair,* escorting her back with them on the long trip down to Herculaneum. *Màthair* was faced with the choice of remaining in Gaul without her son to protect her, facing her elderly years without support of any kind or, she was told, to expect a comfortable life in sunny *Italia* with her son and his new friend, Cosimus. She had wisely chosen the latter. However the tedious journey across and around the transalpine region was arduous and long. All of them were glad to finally reach the sea near the port of *Genua,* their embarkation point for the remainder of the trip to Herculaneum by ship.

Cos relaxed in his chair, his new family enjoying their modest breakfast together. He could say honestly that he loved both of them, their rough country ways, their willingness to work when needed and, above all, their complete utter honesty. Old *Màthair*, though aging, still went joyfully about her tasks each day, uncomplaining and wanting nothing in return. The few times Cos had presented her with things he thought she might want, she had laughed and refused. She wanted nothing but a safe home and honest labor and, of course, the happiness of her son.

"Cos," she began, still chewing on a nice thick slice of bread. Cos had already learned that her technique of getting him to agree to something required her perception of the correct moment, one in which his guard was down. He raised his eyebrows, quickly glancing at Maccus to discover if he was part of the coming request. "You know that I am not getting any younger," she stated and then put down her bread. "It would be nice for me to help rear young children before I no longer have the patience for it." Cos nodded, keeping his eyes on Maccus, who pretended ignorance of where she was going with this line.

"And, *Màthair*, do you see any women of child bearing age in our home?" Cos answered, egging her on a bit.

"No, Cos, and that is the problem, isn't it?" She was staring at him with her pale blue eyes, her face serious.

"And, *Màthair*, what is your solution to this vexing problem?"

"Ah, it's simple for you, my son. You are handsome beyond description, rich and famous as well. Just walk down the street and pick a woman, even a married woman. Any of them would rush home with you if given a chance. For poor Maccus, it's a different problem. He is not exactly an attractive man and has no prestige or wealth. You should just buy him a bride and be done with it."

"It all sounds so simple, *Màthair.* Where would I go to buy a bride, and should he go with me or can you trust me to choose for him?"

"No, Cos, you can't do this without me!" Maccus spoke up. He looked between his mother and Cos, unsure if the conversation was even serious. "I have a suggestion, *Dominus,*" Maccus said somewhat tentatively, using his title of master instead of his first name.

"Speak it then," Cos responded.

"If you are willing to even go look, there are some women available for purchase not too far from here."

Cos rolled his eyes. A slave woman brought in for reproductive services would not be in keeping with his idea of a happy home. "You want me to buy you a slave for sex?" He demanded an answer in such a tone that it would be difficult for Maccus to agree.

"Well, as *Màthair* truthfully spoke, I am not exactly prize material for any woman. I guess we could travel back to Gaul, and I could perhaps find a willing woman there." Maccus suspected that it would take more than the search for a bride to get Cos to leave and travel north again. He and his mother had concocted a winning strategy.

"I don't want to own a slave, you both know that. Any woman brought in here has to come of her own free will. If one is purchased, she is to be legally freed immediately and then can choose to stay or go. I suspect that most will want to find their own destiny. I don't think your plan will work," Cos said to both of them.

"But, *Dominus,*" Maccus argued, "I heard that women slaves cannot be freed before the age of thirty. Is that not true?"

"I understand that is the law, yes."

"And who would buy a woman slave older than thirty?" Maccus persisted.

Cos gritted his teeth. Their arguments had been well constructed and timed, he had to concede that to them. Still it would also be nice to see children under foot, and for sure, they had enough room for them. It was little enough to do for these two people whom he cherished more than any others. "All right, we'll go this morning. How much is this going to cost us?" he asked. They both shrugged.

Carole Raddato from FRANKFURT, Germany (https://commons.wikimedia.org/wiki/
File:Roman_Empire-_Power_&_People,_Leeds_City_Museum,_UK_(15967256472).jpg), color by
AF, https://creativecommons.org/licenses/by-sa/2.0/legalcode

Chapter 10

Barely Alive

Aristotle (384 BC to 322 BC)

A camp near Vesuvius

Cos pulled the reins, slowing his horse to a walk, looking over the encampment carefully before entering. This was not a camp supervised by Roman soldiers or bearing any official status but more likely by a band of thugs selling anything they could for any price. Before they left the stables at Herculaneum, Cos had a strong feeling that there might be some danger buying slaves away from the traditional market in Pompeii. He had his *gladius*, his sword, hanging from his right side and was wearing a chain mail tunic over his cloth one. His battlefield experiences had taught him to be bold yet prepared. Maccus had never worn or owned armor, though he was wearing a short sword and knew how to use it.

Roughly a hundred *passus* away, they stopped and watched for activity. The camp seemed normal enough with men moving about, none of whom were armed. Cos signaled, and they began to walk their horses slowly into the camp, keeping alert as to their surroundings. Ahead were several large carriages which were enclosed except for small openings near the top needed to exchange air. These would likely be transport mechanism for hauling captured humans long distances.

They stopped near the carts and waited to be noticed, still astride their horses. "Are you sure that this is where you want to pull out a bag of coins?" Cos asked.

"With you by me, I fear nothing," Maccus answered. Cos glanced at his face and could see no misgivings.

"I predict that there will be no women of quality here, we should leave," Cos suggested.

"But, *Dominus*, I had a tip regarding a certain captive that I thought might suit my needs. Please."

Cos squinted, his body on high alert, and his horse, sensing his discomfort, snorted and pawed the ground, anxious to leave also. "All right. You stay with the horses, and I'll have a look," he said while dismounting. He walked around the carriages looking for an opening and discovered a cloth cover on the far side. He pulled the cloth off with a jerk and was greeted by the sight of several women huddled in one corner. Walking down the line, he did the same for three other wagons, each with the same result. A quick guess was nearly twenty women being held for sale. Most were dressed in rags and weathered furs, and all were dirty and had fearful eyes looking back at this new threat.

"Can I be of service to you?" the man said as he approached. Cos spun to the sound of his voice, his hand on his sword. "No threat from me. You need not your sword," the man assured him, moving closer.

Cos quickly scanned the man who was somewhat heavy with fat though still large. Penetrating eyes were above a scruffy beard, and he was dressed in rough woolen cloth. "Don't approach any closer," Cos warned. "Are you selling these women?" he asked.

"Of course. Why else would I have them?" he laughed. "I can see that you are very fit and ready to fight. You must be a legionnaire. Is that not true?"

Cos ignored his question. "Where did they come from?"

"I am a slave trader. My stock comes from many sources. Do you have a preference?"

"You will answer my question," Cos warned.

"Surely. I buy these women from the men who captured them. We travel long distances with them so that you may have a fine choice today."

Cos started looking more closely at the women, moving sideways from wagon to wagon. All were white, most were fair with light colored hair, and the majority were of child bearing age. As he looked them over, Maccus appeared around the corner, also with his hand resting on the handle of his sword.

"Have them stand and come forward," Maccus ordered.

The slave trader complied with hand gestures signaling the women to come forward, and they reluctantly lined up against the bars of the rolling cage. In their faces was the resignation and hopelessness of their situation, reduced to nearly worthless human flesh offered to a new owner for a few coins.

Cos silently watched as Maccus methodically went past the women, slowly looking over each one in turn, obviously looking for something in particular. Finally he stopped and pointed to a healthy blond. "Do you speak Latin?" he asked her. There was no response as she looked listlessly at him. "*An dtuigeann tú dom an uair seo?*" he asked her in Celtic. This time she nodded, holding up her thumb and first finger spread slightly to indicate a minimal knowledge of that language.

Maccus turned to Cos and said, "This one is from *Germania*, just across the Rhine. She speaks a bit of my native language. They pick up some words from the traders crossing back and forth." He turned to the trader asking "How much?"

The man stammered a bit, obviously wanting to haggle over the price. "This is a very fine and heathy one. May I inquire as to what you want of her?"

Cos spoke up, "Just the price my friend, and remember that we are not in *Roma* at the slave market standing in the sunlight. We are in shadow where there are no rules regarding slaves, and there are no papers, I presume, to claim rightful ownership. You will not get full price here."

The trader wiped his lip with the back of his arm. "For that one, for she is my best, I demand 6,000 *denarii*."

"You make me laugh," Cos said. "Take her from her cage so that we might inspect her more carefully." As he spoke he detected noise from behind him. Something was approaching and attempting to be stealthy. "You, trader," he called with menace, not looking around. "I can kill you and everybody in your party by myself and faster than you can imagine. If anyone approaches from our rear, you will soon be headless." The warning was followed by receding sounds from behind. Whoever it was got the message. The trader was sweating, only now realizing what kind of men were standing in front of him. He traded in women for a living; these men slaughtered as a profession.

Without further comment, he unlocked the cage door and opened it enough to allow the selected woman to come out. She did so reluctantly and with obvious fear, looking at Cos and Maccus with wide, wondering eyes.

"Take your robe off," Maccus ordered in Celtic. She nodded and dropped her filthy cloak to the ground, clad now in only her scant tunic. Even in this loose garment, her fine female figure was obvious. A lovely woman indeed.

"Take the rest off," Maccus told her.

"No," Cos said with authority. "We will not rob her of her dignity. You have seen enough of her. Give her back her cloak."

Maccus pick her cloak up with two fingers and held it out for her. He nodded to Cos that she was his choice and had his approval.

"I have questions, trader," Cos announced. The trader and Maccus looked at him in surprise, waiting for the questions.

"Have you or your men enjoyed the company of this woman during her captivity? Be warned that I will ask her that question, and your life will hang on her answer."

The trader's eyes wandered from the woman to Cos to Maccus and back again as he considered his fateful answer. "Not this one, you can ask her. Not once. Others, yes, but not this one."

"Why not this one?" Cos asked.

"She would fight back. Others were easier to control." There was a prolonged silence after he spoke as Cos watched him squirm waiting on the question to be posed to the woman.

"I believe you. It seems that 6,000 *denarii* might be possible in Rome, however not here. 500 *denarii* is more than enough, I think," Cos said, watching the man closely.

"That is not enough, *Dominus*. We transported and fed this bunch all the way across Gaul and the mountains. You can kill me, but I can't accept this amount for my best woman."

As Cos considered his next offer, he looked the line of women over again. One was still on the floor near the corner of the cage. "What about that one?" he pointed to the still figure.

"We expect that one to die shortly, if she is still alive. She refused to eat for the last two weeks. She is not worthy of your attention."

"Bring her out, I want to see for myself," Cos ordered. It began to dawn on the trader that the armored and muscular legionnaire giving the orders was more than just an experienced soldier. He had the power of higher office radiating from him like an aura. This man was, or had been, in command of many other fighting men. Whatever his rank, he was used to giving orders and having them obeyed without question. There were consequences to resisting such a man, he understood.

The slave was picked up and carried out, seemingly without any consciousness or resistance. Cos came forward to inspect her more closely. She was alive although not by much. She had given up and wanted to die, an end to her misery and her captivity. One eye opened as he touched her, and it looked at him for a brief moment. He had seen and administered many deaths on the battlefield, but this woman evoked a deep pity in him. After all the deaths, he owed a debt to the people of *Germania* who had mostly fought the Romans in defense as their country was invaded. He wanted to save just one. One life could not make up for the many lost, still there was an obligation to be fulfilled. He had seen enough death and loss in his lifetime. Her death was unacceptable.

"How much do you claim this one is worth?" he asked mockingly.

"She had value once. No more. She is yours if you buy the other," was the answer.

"To be fair with you, trader, we will give you 2000 *denarii*. I am giving you more than they are worth, and you know it. Accept it or we leave and look elsewhere."

It didn't take but a split second, and the trader readily agreed. He had not counted on nearly this much. Besides, it saved him the time needed to bury the sick one. It was a good deal.

"I agree. You drive a hard bargain. May I ask you something in return?" he asked.

"Ask," came the low voice of Maccus standing behind him. The sound made the trader jump. He had not realized that Maccus had positioned himself so close. It was now evident who would have taken his head off had things gone wrong.

"I wonder what rank you are, soldier?" directing his question to Cos.

"You shouldn't have to ask that about the most respected *legatus* in the entire Roman Army," Maccus replied. The trader felt like he was going to faint. This was a close call indeed, because he realized just who this man was. And he had been speaking with truth, he could have slain all of them by himself.

Cos tossed a leather bag of coins on the ground and scooped up the small woman into his arms, watching as her one eye appraised her new captor. There was no longer any resistance possible. She had given up any will to live.

They rode slowly, the horses ambling their way back to the stable. No direction or urging was necessary because the horses knew the way and also knew that food and grooming awaited their return. Cos had his arms full, carrying the small woman delicately and tenderly while thinking how to best restore her to health. So far, neither had said a word to each other, and he had made no attempt to pull back the cloth covering her head and most of her face. It was a package of unknowns. From the little he could see, she was ripe with an army of lice which busily moved along the cloth cover. He occasionally glanced at Maccus who transported his new woman behind him, her arms circling around his waist. When Cos looked at her, she looked back, some sort of satisfaction evident in her smile to him as if she fully understood that she was in no danger and, just the opposite, that she was heading toward a better life, one horse step at a time.

"A reminder, Maccus," Cos announced. He waited until Maccus looked directly at him so he could be sure his message was delivered. "Remember my order that your woman is no slave and will not be expected to service you in any way. You are directed to explain to her that from this moment forward she is no one's slave and is free to decide for herself. You need to tell her that she is free to live with us as long as she wants with the only expectation being that she do her share of the work demanded of all of us."

"I understand, *Dominus*," Maccus replied. The woman and Maccus were watching Cos, probably only one of them understanding any of his words.

"And another thing you should know," Cos continued. "If you really desire her for your own, you must win her affection, not take it. Give her the courtesy that she would deserve as a wife, your attention and perhaps gifts of things she may need or want. That's the only way she will become truly yours and you, hers."

"I will try, *Dominus*. I swear it."

"One task is yet remaining before this day is over," Cos continued. "This woman in my arms is infected with lice, as, I suspect, is yours, and she is coated with grime and filth. We need to stop by the baths and have them cleaned before we return home."

"I agree. Her odor is killing me," Maccus answered, wrinkling his nose.

"When we arrive, I will arrange for a female attendant to take them in while you go and find some suitable clothing. Also, purchase several fine combs to help rid their hair of nits."

"May I, *Dominus*, spend money freely in this pursuit?" Maccus asked with a hint of mirth about his task.

"Wisely, Maccus. Spend freely though wisely."

There were two public baths in Herculanum, one was free to the public with entrances allocated for men and separately for women, who usually bathed in the afternoon. And the other, the *Balbus Thermae*, usually reserved for affluent men, and the one most often used by Cos and Maccus. Cos directed his horse to the *Centralis Thermae* because of its women's section, and shortly, they stopped at the entrance for women. He dismounted carefully, still holding his living package and, with one arm free, tossed a bag of coins to Maccus.

"What is your woman's name?" he asked Maccus as they also dismounted.

"She is called Linza but will answer to any name we choose." The woman smiled when her name was mentioned and then started to look around, puzzled by the sound and smell of water just beyond the door.

"Then, Linza, you will wait here with me." Cos motioned for her to stand beside him. "Explain to her, Maccus, what is going to happen."

Cos wasn't sure that Linza understood anything of what Maccus said to her, still she looked willing and happy. He pounded on the closed door, and they waited as Maccus walked away, looking back once or twice at his new prize.

An attendant opened the door and appraised the three people on the threshold. She appeared as though she might refuse any request until Cos spoke to her with authority. "I need some assistance with these two women. You will call another attendant to help. Both of you will be well rewarded for extraordinary service and for any kindness toward them."

The attendant rolled her eyes, nodding though still not moving to help in any way. "I am *Paulo Fabio Persico Cosimus,* and if you refuse to assist me, I will find someone who will." That statement made the difference, and she called to someone inside. The second attendant, who quickly appeared, was a large, older woman who had seen much of the world and was not shocked by seeing two former slaves or their appearance.

"I think you will have to carry this one," Cos suggested, offering his living package to the second attendant. She accepted but frowned as she looked more closely at the swarming lice.

"We will have to burn their clothing, you know. And we will have to use soap and oil to cleanse their hair." She looked at Cos with some anger. "This one is light. Does she have any disease?"

"I was told that she was refusing food for two weeks. Other than that, I don't know."

"We will need to summon the Greek physician. Who will pay his fee?"

"I will and anything else that these women may require. Will you take charge of these two and see to their needs?"

"Yes. You should return in three hours to pick them up and settle any charges," she replied, then turned away to enter the baths. She motioned for Linza to follow, causing Linza to give Cos a questioning look, hesitating before going inside the strange building. Cos smiled at her, reassuringly pointed inside, and in a moment, the door closed, and he found himself alone with the horses.

Chapter 11

A Gift of Life

Marcus Aurelius (121 AD to 180 AD)

The streets of Herculaneum, 8:00 PM

The wait turned out to be much longer than three hours, but at last, the two women, still wrapped in large towels, were brought outside to the waiting Cos and Maccus. Linza was walking confidently, her clean blond hair glowing in the near darkness, and she was smiling broadly, glad that her new captors were waiting for her. The other woman was too weak to walk and was carried out and placed in Cos' waiting arms.

"We fed her as much as she would take," the matron said, frowning and showing concern. "The physician thought that she would have only lasted until the morrow without our care. As it is, she may still die. He couldn't find anything wrong other than starvation, though she is almost too weak to eat."

Cos carefully pulled the towel back, this time with no hint of parasites, and looked at her face. Her eyes looked back at him, clear and open this time, her face thin and drawn. "You have done a great service to me, Matron, and to this woman. I want to give you some money for your own use, and if you ever need anything from me, all you have to do is to ask."

"We all know of you, *Legatus*. You are the most important citizen of Herculaneum and the most respected. It was our honor to serve you, and there were no fees incurred in caring for your women."

"Thank you," Cos said, patting her shoulder. "Do you have any suggestions for her in the next few days?"

"Try feeding her with goat's milk tonight and, if she makes it through, then small amounts of fruit and bread tomorrow. And her lice…" the matron frowned again. "Someone needs to wash her hair every day, comb it out and reapply oil. If you do this for two weeks, she will be rid of the creatures at last."

"I will personally do it," Cos said. "It's important to me that she lives."

"Why this one, *Legatus*?" she asked.

"I never took or accepted slaves. It is wrong and evil, especially for innocent women or children to be captured and enslaved. If I can restore just one to her proper place in the world, it will ease my mind."

"Are not these two women your slaves?" she asked.

"They were sold to us as slaves though bought as free women. They will never be slaves again."

"I can see why you are so respected, *Legatus*," she said, her eyes reflecting in the fading light. "May the gods look after you and your women," she added.

The two attendants continued to watch as Cos and his family slowly walked away into gathering darkness, finally disappearing around a corner.

"Maccus," Cos began, "did you find the items I asked for?"

"All in the parcel that I carry on my back, *Dominus*. Is there anything else I should get before we retire?"

"Do we have fresh goat's milk and bread at home?"

"I heard the conversation. Our women will have plenty, I assure you."

There was no moon to be seen, and the scant evening light had disappeared leaving them to walk in nearly absolute blackness. Herculaneum shared one truth with other Roman cities of the same era: there were no lights of any kind at night unless you carried a torch or lamp with you. However, their journey was short, only a few blocks, and at last, the threshold of their home welcomed them. Once in the *atrium*, the scattered oil lamps gave a soft glow of shimmering light.

Màthair appeared as soon as she heard footsteps from inside. "What have you boys brought me?" she wondered, walking in a circle around the four.

"*Màthair*, meet Linza," Maccus said, smiling broadly as if he had brought home a prized catch from the sea. As far as Maccus was concerned, he had accomplished what he hoped to this day, and the woman he chose was even more attractive that he had hoped she would be. Clean and fresh from the baths, scented with aromatic oil, this Linza would be a prize for any man, Maccus thought. *Màthair* inspected her closely without comment, avoiding returning Linza's smile until she was herself satisfied that this was the woman who would someday bear her grandchildren. She had to be sure.

"She looks fit enough," *Màthair* finally announced. "You have my permission to start having children."

Maccus looked nervously at Cos who was silently watching this exchange. "A clarification first, *Màthair*," Maccus said, again looking at Cos instead of his mother. "Our *dominus* has instructed me to inform Linza that she is free from slavery and able to choose her own mate as of tonight." He swallowed hard, anticipating some contradiction from someplace.

Màthair nodded her approval to Cos. "Yes, our *dominus* is correct, as always. This is the proper way, and I agree with him. The rest, then, is up to you, my son." She turned to Cos and the woman whom he still carried, inspecting her also. "This one is not well, Cos. You have made a poor choice, I'm afraid."

"Prepare a room and bed for each of them, *Màthair.* They are to live with us, at least for the time being. I think this one needs a lot of rest and special care. I was instructed to give her some fresh goat's milk tonight before it's too late."

Màthair paused for a moment, considering a solution. "May I place two goats in our garden for a short time?" she asked.

"Whatever you need to do, my dear *Màthair.*"

"Put her in the gold room, Cos, and I will be up shortly with the milk."

Cos carried his package up the stairs, looking down at the face of a helpless young woman he so much wanted to save. She followed his eyes in silence, in acceptance of whatever was to happen to her, with no strength to resist or even complain. He took a lit lamp from the hall as they entered the room. It was a fine room, decorated with lavish wall paintings and furnished with a large carved bed and feather mattress. He put her softly down and pulled a cover over her, sitting down beside her in an available chair.

"Do you have a name?" he asked her. She blinked but didn't answer. He pointed to his chest and said "Cos" then pointed to her and smiled, raising his eyebrows.

"Alia," she weakly answered.

"Alia," Cos repeated. He found her hand and patted it reassuringly. There were no more words to be exchanged for the moment, and Cos just sat there looking at her, wondering just what he had rescued from the wagon this morning.

He heard *Màthair* trudging up the stairs, coming toward them. Along the way she loudly directed Linza to an adjacent room and, even louder, directed Maccus to stay out of it without permission from his mother. Cos chuckled to himself. Old *Màthair* could always be counted on to do the right thing.

"The goat's milk," she said and put a flask into Cos's hand. She correctly sensed that Cos wanted to feed the girl himself, not trusting even her to do that, at least for tonight. If the girl died before morning, he could blame no one, because her fate was already sealed before he found her.

"And where will Cos sleep?" she wondered aloud.

He rested his head against the back of the chair and winked at her. The answer was clear, he would stay beside the girl all night seeing to her needs, being there for her even if she didn't make it all the way to dawn.

Màthair shook her head and patted his arm before leaving to retire herself. And to think that this man didn't have a woman in his life. Amazing, she thought.

The goddess Diana. Ancient Roman fresco in the Third Style from cubiculum W 26 of the Villa Arianna at Stabiae. Mentnafunangann (https://commons.wikimedia.org/wiki/, color by AF, https://creativecommons.org/licenses/by-sa/3.0/legalcode

Chapter 12

The Dawn of Alia

Cease to ask what the morrow will bring forth, and set down as gain each day that fortune grants.

Horace (65 BC to 8 BC)

The pink glow of dawn crept into the gold room from the oculus over the *atrium*. At first barely noticeable then more radiant as a few direct fingers of the sun found their way to the threshold, reflecting a magical light on the wall fresco just behind Cosimo's sleeping head. His arm was resting on the bed, the other hanging near the floor still grasping what was left of the flask of goat's milk. On the bed lay Alia, her eyes open, studying Cos as he, at last, slept. Her eyes followed his masculine form from the top of his bushy head and along the muscular contours of his body. Then her wandering eyes saw the room she was in for the first time, the wall paintings, the lavish furnishings, and the floor covered in shiny mosaic tiles forming an intricate pattern of geometric shapes. Never had she seen such a place, even in her imagination, not even heard it spoken in tales or fables. She had no idea of where she was or who her captor was or his intentions. For three months, she had been held as captive along with many other women taken in raids across the Rhine, dragged or beaten unconscious by brutal Roman soldiers, and laughingly sold to slavers, then the wagon, the endless days inside, fed scraps and taunted by their captors. She had endured till she reached the point that hope was gone, that life as she had known it was over, and there would never be a return to the familiar. She became convinced that the only way of escape was self-starvation. The other captives didn't mind eating her food ration ravenously as they watched her slow retreat from life, unable or unwilling to help her. She didn't actually remember how many days she spent folded and unnoticed in the corner of the cage.

This morning she had been born again, the dawn bringing a new day, new circumstances. Although she understood none of the words hovering about her the previous day, she did comprehend that the calm soothing voices meant her no harm. It restored her will to live and the natural inquisitiveness of a person who wanted to return to life, finding whatever a new day brought.

She looked again at the large man sleeping beside her. Never had she seen a man, especially a warrior like this one, stoop to bring food and comfort to the ailing. She didn't understand how this could be so, yet there he was. He was just beside her and had tended to her all through the night. She was increasingly aware that her need to relieve herself was becoming acute. There was no chamber pot visible, and she wasn't sure she could stand by herself. She was unwilling to soil the wonderful bedding that had kept her comfortable for the first time in months.

Some sound nearby caused Cos to awaken. He blinked at first and rubbed his face, finding the flask of milk still in his hand, then remembered where he was. He looked toward his ward, finding her looking alertly back at him, the covering still held close to her neck, exposing her face alone. It was the first time he had seen her face really alive, and it was a jolt. Her hair was still wrapped in cloth meant to keep the pestilence coated in oil and also hiding any hint of its color. Her pale thin face was like ivory or at least comparative to a fine white marble work of art. Except the eyes.

They were profoundly blue and penetrated his consciousness. She was asking something of him though had no words to express her needs.

"Greetings," Cos said, smiling at her and realizing that she was not going to die after all. "Is there something you want?" he asked, knowing that she wouldn't understand but also wanting to communicate with her even if it was one-sided. She didn't answer and cast her eyes around the room near the bed. It dawned on Cos that she had to void and had no way of telling him. He got up and looked around, thinking of the best solution, then went to the door and summoned *Màthair* by calling her name. She would know what to do.

Màthair appeared momentarily and immediately looked at the bed and smiled. "Well, Cos, good work. I can see that she will live after all. Never underestimate the strength of a young woman. They are tougher than you think. Now, what is the problem?"

"I believe that she has to do her necessary functions. What do you think about me carrying her downstairs to the toilet so that you can help her?"

"Do that, and I will show her what she needs to know. And there are clothes downstairs for her to wear. They will do for now, just never again send Maccus to buy a woman's clothes."

"Can you speak to her?" Cos asked.

Màthair turned and looked directly at him. "Of course I can. I grew up on the west bank of the Rhine, and I was courted for a time by a fine young man from the other side. Most of them speak a Norse language or close enough that they can talk to each other. We spoke Celtic on our side. A very different language indeed. Nevertheless we traded with them, and both sides learned enough to get by." She turned to Alia, speaking softly and slowly, "Hvat eru þú köllumk?"

"Alia," she answered.

"Cos is going to carry you downstairs to the toilet, and we'll get you in some clothing. Are you hungry?"

Alia looked back and forth between them before answering, then only nodded her acceptance. After a glance at *Màthair*, Cos came forward and scooped her up. This time she put a thin arm around his neck while still clutching her bed cover tightly to her chin.

Cos walked onto the hall balcony giving Alia her first look at the villa in the light. She gasped, looking around with wild eyes. Other than *Valhalla*, no place could possibly look so grand. There was just so much space, so airy, so magnificent. Alia just could not believe her eyes. Cos was watching her face as they progressed to the stairs and understood quickly that Alia was stunned by her surroundings. "Don't worry, Alia, you will get used to it just as I have. Even to me, it is a marvelous palace fit for a king, and trust me, I've seen a lot of the world, even some which hasn't been created yet." Alia looked at his lips and face as he talked, still not convinced that some harm might yet come her way.

In some Roman estates and villas of the time, there was often fresh water carried in by handmade lead pipes running underground. Even a valve mechanism to regulate the flow of water was available to the wealthy. And Herculaneum was even more fortunate than Pompeii in that it also had an underground sewer system for carrying away human waste and sometimes leftover food. Access to this system was simply a direct hole placed in public places as communal *latrinea* or in private homes as a single toilet. Most often this facility was situated near or in the kitchen area. It had been the first item on Cos' list of improvements after he occupied his new *domus*. The toilet had been moved to its own room, complete with a functioning door.

He placed her carefully on her feet and stood ready to catch her if she proved too weak to stand, yet even though she swayed uncertainly, she stood, looking resolutely at him, telling him with her stern expression that she could do this on her own. Cos backed away and looked her over. She was not as short has he had imagined, and under her wrappings, he got the hint of once broad, sturdy shoulders.

"Go and eat with Maccus, Cos. I will see to getting her back upstairs when she is finished here," *Màthair* said from behind him.

"If she is able, bring her out to the table, and we will see what she can eat."

Màthair sighed. Too soon, she thought, but… .

As was their custom, Cos and Maccus sat opposite each other in the small alcove of the walkway just off of the open air garden. Along the far wall bordering the ocean was another table meant for just two people and directly above that, on the second floor, was a matching set, consisting of an oval marble top on a floridly carved base with two matching stone stools. A panoramic view of the harbor and the famed distant island of Capri, the legendary second home of Emperor Tiberius, was framed by a large opening in the wall on both floors. Cos had never dined in either location as yet, reserving those two romantic spots for another time in his life, if that moment ever came to pass.

He ate slowly, wondering if Alia would be able to join them or if she needed to be carried up the stairs back to her room.

"Are you troubled, Cos, or are you tired from the night's vigil?" Maccus asked, a hint of humor in his voice.

"No, Maccus. Where is your Linza just now? Is she permitted to dine with us?" There was a bit of tit for tat mixed with humor in his reply.

"I fear Linza is still sleeping. Should I wake her?" Maccus asked, hoping that his *dominus* would permit his entry into her room.

"Linza appears to have a strong will and a mind of her own," Cos observed. "I think you will have to work really hard to gain her affection. Do you see it that way?"

"Of course, she will fall for me. After all, I picked her above all the others, and it was my idea to fetch her from the clutches of the slavers. I am most interested in her and will buy her gifts and clothing. Is that not enough?"

"For some women, yes. For others, unfortunately, no. Time will tell. She didn't choose who rescued her, and anyway, she is a free woman as far as we are concerned."

"Yes, Dominus, but can she actually choose to leave us?"

"She can, though she should be told that she would last not even a day without protection and would shortly find herself back in slavery." Cos turned in the direction of a noise coming their way and smiled. "And it looks as though we will be joined by Alia this morning." He stood and walked toward the slowly progressing Alia supported by the strong arms of *Màthair* who was talking close to her ear. Alia had her arm over *Màthair,* and her head carried low. She was wearing a new tunic, the one purchased by Maccus, and Cos could tell that it was rough and coarsely made and much too large for her frame.

"Thank you, *Màthair,* for helping Alia join us. Do you think she can eat anything?"

"You two are much alike. Both stubborn. She wanted to try, however I think she is not yet strong enough. But here she is." Cos pulled out a chair and helped *Màthair* guide her into it. Alia looked up at him, catching his eyes for a moment. There was no smile from her, and he wondered what she was thinking.

"Let me serve you some bread and honey, Alia, and there is goat's milk, fresh from the garden," Cos told her. He rolled his eyes so that *Màthair* could see that he knew about the goats eating all the decorative plants they had worked so hard to nurture.

Alia looked around at her new companions, then at the garden lined with stone columns supporting the covered walkways. In the corners were pure white marble statues mounted on dark stone bases, all imported from *Graeci*, and all were lifelike representations of nude females in artistic poses. Then she realized that the others around the table were looking at her. She made a short, startled sound, then looked down toward her plate and its small slice of honeyed bread.

Cos had been watching her since she had come into view, his eyes never leaving her for long. Her long slender neck was visible for the first time, her hair still wrapped tightly and hidden from view, and it struck him how fragile she looked, how much like a delicate, living statue she was. He leaned back and studied her face, which occasionally and shyly looked his way for a brief moment. He realized for the first time that Alia was beautiful. The soft light played on her face as she moved, and when her blue eyes flicked at his way, it gave him a start. What a reward to realize that he had helped bring this one back to life, he thought with satisfaction, certain that Alia would quickly become an important and welcome addition to his small family.

They started chatting between themselves in a language completely unknown to Alia. She didn't understand why she was here with these people and what they expected of her. There was no denying their obvious courtesy and affection toward her, though the experience of being here was so different from anything she had ever seen or done. If only she had not been captured and dragged away from her family, friends, and the way of life she had felt part of.

"Alia," Cos said softly, "you need to eat something." He poured some fresh goat's milk into her glass and offered it to her while smiling. She turned to look at his eyes, unblinking, wishing that she had some way of speaking to him, some way of asking him what he expected of her. After a moment of hesitation, she took the glass, wondering at holding an object that was transparent yet strong. She took a sip as was expected of her but continued to look at Cos over the rim, her blue eyes speaking more than words could have, saying that he was someone she could trust.

Cos noticed her look and received her message, resolving that he would never let her fall prey to the monsters of the world again. It was a singular moment, exchanged by eyes alone and private from the rest of humanity.

Some motion in the hall attracted the attention of Maccus, who had been on alert expecting that, sooner or later, his new woman would awaken and come looking for him and him alone. They all turned and watched as she came into the light from a darkened hallway, her long blond hair now clean for the first time in months and catching the morning light in a spectacular way. She paused when she saw the group around the breakfast table, smiled broadly at them, hesitant to move closer without invitation. She was wearing the same poorly fitting tunic as Alia, neither woman looking either comfortable or attractive in Maccus' hasty selections. And she, like Alia, was barefoot, another oversight by Maccus.

Màthair motioned for Linza to come to her, and when she complied, *Màthair* bent close and spoke into her ear. Linza nodded enthusiastically, causing *Màthair* to rise and accompany her back down the hall again. She glanced back at Cos, sure that he would understand that Linza also needed instructions on the use of the toilet. Maccus looked puzzled and frustrated, craning his neck to see where the object of his desires was going with his mother.

"Not to worry, Maccus. She will return in a moment. By the way, you were certainly frugal when you bought clothing for them. I told you to spend wisely, and you certainly did," Cos said with a straight face. "I think that, next time, I will try my hand at it and see if I can do as well." His statement provoked a satisfied smile from Maccus who was always proud of pleasing his *dominus*.

Cos watched both women when Linza returned, smiling and happy. He noticed that they did not exchange greetings or even glances. There was so much for them to share, the circumstances of their lives changing so abruptly and arriving in a situation of warmth and safety. Still, there was a deep friction between them, causing Cos to contemplate why. The most obvious difference was mere fitness and body size. Linza looked normal, especially now that she was cleaned of filth. Alia had nearly starved to death and was thin and pale. Even now she could barely eat or sit up for long. They seemed to avoid each other's eyes.

"Maccus," Cos began, causing Maccus to shift his attention from appraising Linza for a moment. "Can you communicate with Linza?"

"Some. She understands a bit of Celtic, however no Latin. I understand a few words of her language," he answered.

"Ask her why and how she managed to thrive while Alia starved."

Maccus looked at both women anew, having previously never considered the topic. He glanced at Cos before speaking, now understanding his question very clearly. "Linza," he began, "did you eat the food of Alia while you were captive?" It was put to her slowly, using Celtic instead of Latin.

Linza looked shocked, her eyes wide. She clearly understood the question yet hesitated with her answer fearing some retribution. She shook her head, "no," and started tearing.

Màthair had arrived and heard the question and watched the response from Linza. "A moment please," she said while sitting down. "It's an unfair question, Cos. If you consider the situation they were in, it comes down to survival. Each person has the right to try to survive. No one ever taught these girls any morals. They came from tribes who teach tradition, not right and wrong. I think

Alia had given up the fight and wanted to die. You can't blame Linza for eating another's portion to survive."

Cos nodded at her. *Màthair* was right, of course, and he had seen the same behavior in his troops. He let the subject drop, sure that these two women would never become friends. It was something to keep his eye on.

Linza slowly realized that there were to be no more questions on the subject. She had indeed eaten every scrap she could find, and there were other things…she had flirted with her male captors, encouraging them to do more for her than the other women because in her smiles she held the promise of rewards if they helped her. Linza was worth a lot of *denarii* as a slave, a very attractive and healthy one at that but only if she remained intact and especially if she were not pregnant when she was offered for sale to the highest bidder. She was the prize of the entire crop and word got around that these slavers held a pretty package suitable for some lucky, wealthy buyer.

Alia was sagging. She had attempted to eat her portion of bread, though there was no strength left to continue. Cos was alert to her situation and had determined that there was no need to persist with breakfast any longer. Alia was clearly not recovered enough to even feed her starving body. He stood and placed his hand on *Màthair's* shoulder, "I'll take her back to her bed. Could you make some stew for her for later?"

"I will. There is a nice lamb for sale nearby that I've had my eye on. It will be ready by the noon of this day."

He knelt down beside Alia and waited until she turned her gaze toward him. He offered her his arms, and she understood what he meant. She nodded acceptance and cast her eyes down and reached for his shoulder. She was light, too light, and one of his hands pressed against her bony spine. No, she had not reached the point of positive recovery, not until she started to gain weight, restoring her body as well as her confidence. It was not only about food; he had to give her a reason to live.

Alia watched his face as they returned up the stairs, thinking of this man they called Cos and his commanding presence with the others. He was in charge of her destiny and made all the decisions regarding her and everyone else. So far, he had treated her with tenderness and respect, and she could see in his eyes that he would permit no harm to come to her. The tension faded from her body and mind. She was where she was meant to be, and she had to forget the past, both pleasant and unpleasant. Alia recalled an oft repeated expression from her childhood *"Gæð a wyrd swa hio scel."* ("We have no control over fate.") Things had happened to her that could not be undone, and there was no reward in longing for her past. This new life was what she could make of it.

Cos placed her gently on the bed, pulled her covers over her, and stood for a moment above her. He was puzzled by the new wave of anxiety passing over her features. Was it fear or some body ailment she had, he wondered. He smiled at her and turned to leave when he heard her cry out his name.

"Cos," she called weakly, causing him to turn toward her again. Her hand and arm were outstretched toward him, her eyes pleading with him. He understood now what concerned her. She didn't want him to leave her alone. He nodded to her and sat down in the bedside chair that he had used as a most unpleasant bed the previous night. He was still sore in unusual places, still unrested and unwashed as well.

"Of course, I won't leave you just yet," he said and patted her hand. She grasped his hand in hers and squeezed tightly, her eyes and her hand not wanting to let him go. Cos sighed and settled in for as long as it took for her to fall asleep. He looked at her, her big eyes unblinkingly focused on him. What a prize to be pulled from the grave, he thought.

Cos dozed, a dream floating in his head, repeating itself over and over, now and then with small differences, always with the same theme. He was running in darkness, afraid but not alone. Some person was there. He could never see him clearly, however it was someone he knew and trusted. He forced himself to wake, ridding his mind of an impending nightmare. Alia's hand was still in his, though she was, at last, asleep. He studied her for a moment, tracing the lines of her face, wondering what color her hair was, how long it was, and would it shimmer in the sun when clean. Carefully letting her hand go, he pulled the cover over it. There were things he had to do, and he had to leave her for a few hours. Nevertheless he had to leave some message for her when she awakened, something that didn't require words to express. It came to him in a flash, and he took out his small dagger, the one presented to him by a Druid in thanks for his kindness long ago on the western front of Britannia. It was a prize for sure, fabled for its origins, small enough for a woman, and decorated lavishly indicating incalculable value. He carefully placed it beside her, near the hand that had held his, and quietly left the room.

Chapter 13

A Bringer of Gifts

Many individuals have, like uncut diamonds, shining qualities beneath a rough exterior.

Those things please more, which are more expensive.

Decimus Iunius Iuvenalis (Juvenal) (late first century)

Alia woke with a start and instantly looked at the empty chair beside the bed. He was gone. She felt a sense of panic, or dread, a feeling that she was once more vulnerable and helpless to some unnamed evil which could materialize at her room's door. She sat up, looked around, and listened, the urge to call out curtailed by the possibility that it would attract attention, the wrong kind. Her hand accidentally found the sheathed knife left there by Cos, and she picked it up, turning it over in her hand watching the imbedded jewels catch the light. He had left it for her she understood, a precious gift which not only gave her a feeling of security but also fed her instinct that Cos cared very much about her. She clutched it to her breast and then the tears started. For the first time in months, she let herself cry. Each trauma she had experienced was reborn as salty tears, and there were many of them. She lay back down and curled up into a ball, still shaking, still crying though without making any noise.

Màthair paused at the doorway and slowly pulled the heavy curtain back, letting the evening light spill into the room. She could see that Alia was still there and seemed to be asleep. "Alia," she whispered and waited for a response. "Alia," she said a bit louder. This time Alia stirred, and when her eyes opened, she jerked awake with a start and shudder, looking toward the doorway with fearful eyes.

"No, no, Alia. Don't be frightened. We have brought you some fresh stew, that's all," *Màthair* said, her voice very soft. They came in, *Màthair* and Maccus, who carried the small clay pot of steaming stew by its handle. Seeing Maccus in her room made Alia look away from them. She had seen him before but never without Cos being there also. She knew enough Celtic to understand that his name meant "hammer." And he was, in body, much like the rough tool his name implied. Maccus was round of face and round of body with arms a bit too long for his shape, as if his head had been pushed back into his thick torso. He smiled at her, though it was more of a grimace, displaying flattened teeth underneath thick lips.

Màthair always noticed the repellant effect her son had on women, still she was used to it, readily accepting her share of the blame for mating with his unattractive father. "Now sit up, and we'll see how much of this you can eat. And don't refuse because Cos ordered it before he left, and he will expect us to do what we are told."

"Where did Cos go," Alia asked.

"She can talk!" Maccus exclaimed.

Màthair ignored her son's comment and sat down on the bedside chair while considering how to respond. "He said he would be back before dark, and the evening approaches, so it won't be much longer."

"What will happen to me?" Alia asked.

"Same thing that happened to us. You are to live your life, do whatever you want to do, and you are welcome to stay with us as long as you desire. While in this home, you are safe from harm and among friends."

"Am I not a slave?" Alia asked.

"No, dear. We are all free, including you and Linza. Though I must warn you that if you leave this place by yourself, you won't last the day before harm comes to you. You may even be returned to the cage again. Now eat and stop talking. You will learn everything you need to know in due time, but first you have to get your strength back."

A dark cloud lifted from Alia, her mind soaring with the new possibilities of life spread before her as if she were looking from a mountain peak at the land below. For the first time since her captivity, she smiled, grateful to be here among people who seemed to only want her happiness and not her servitude or her body.

"She's smiling!" Maccus loudly noted. His mother shot him a disapproving look, wanting him to be more restrained.

"Yes, she is," *Màthair* agreed, satisfied herself that some corner had been turned, and the girl would slowly be restored to health. Although what that would bring with it was still unknown. They still had no knowledge of her personality, her honesty, truthfulness or even her intelligence. There was much work yet to do to make this one part of a family. The other one, the very attractive blonde that Maccus thirsted over, was a different person entirely. No doubt about her beauty and sexual appeal, however it was becoming apparent that Linza would use any asset she had for gain, even a temporary one. It was troubling that Maccus could only see her curves and shining hair and not what was behind those green tinted eyes.

For the first time, Alia ate what was offered and with relish. As they watched, the bowl of stew disappeared into her, and the effect was immediate. It was mostly in her eyes, which were more alert, less fearful, but roving, taking in her surroundings in a way she previously could not.

"This is a wonderful place," she announced.

"And you haven't seen all of it yet," Maccus responded, delighted with the possibility to show her all the craftsmanship and artistry to be found in this *villa*. He still marveled when he walked through the rooms, proud to live here and very proud of being friends with its master, Cos. During their long-standing friendship, they had fought many battles side by side. When Cos was a *centurion*, he fought at the front of his men, entered into combat first, taking more risks than anyone. Maccus was there solely to protect his *dominus*, not to win any battle, yet in doing what was required, he had killed many men. When Cos was appointed *Primus Pilus*, Maccus went with him, sharing a tent along with their evening meals. His appointment as *Legatus Legionis* of the famous *Legion XX,* at last, removed them from direct combat and entitled Cos to decidedly more luxury as well as more responsibility. Maccus sighed with the memory…a glorious last two years, he recalled.

Alia looked back and forth between Maccus and his mother, appearing hesitant to ask about whatever was of concern. "I'll bet you have to go to the toilet," *Màthair* guessed. Alia nodded at her, unsure of what came next. "I think you may not be strong enough to use the stairs by yourself. A couple more days and then you might try it but… ." She glanced at Maccus, deciding if she should let him handle Cos' new found prize and, if she did, would Alia allow it.

"Alia," *Màthair* began, "Maccus will carry you down the stairs, and I will go with you. When you are done, he will carry you back up or if you feel up to it, you may sit with me in the *culina* while I prepare supper for Cos."

Alia seemed to be deciding when suddenly Maccus scooped her up and started for the stairwell. "Don't be frightened, little one, I can't harm you or our *dominus* would have my head," Maccus assured her, chuckling at his own humor. He put her down just in front of the toilet and waited for *Màthair* to catch them. Each time Alia glanced his way, he smiled broadly at her.

It had been a long day, longer than he expected. The trip to Pompeii was easy enough by horseback, but the shopping… ! Something Cos was not used to, especially buying clothing and shoes for women. He had decided that the way the two new women were dressed was not an asset for his home or to their self confidence and something had to be done. Pompeii was famous for its woolen clothing and fabrics, and being a large trading town with many foreign ships docked at its wharfs, it was an ideal place to purchase refined gifts. He carried three packages tied to his back as he walked home from the stables, deciding, after a couple of blocks, that he would be much relieved to part with them.

The evening sun was very low when he made that last, grateful turn into his home. He stopped and listened for a moment and heard voices though was unable to discern the conversation or who was speaking. Cos headed across the *atrium* toward the voices. He crossed the *tablinum* and entered the *peristylum* and realized that all the sound was coming from the small *culina* where the cooking was done. They were all in there together and all smiling. Alia was seated at a small table, and *Màthair* was tending a kettle on the fire. Maccus and Linza were standing in the middle of the floor engaged in a separate conversation.

"Well, I see that I'm in time for supper," he remarked, watching all their heads turn toward him. Alia turned and looked at him without a smile, watching his face with unblinking eyes. "And I see that you are up, Alia!" Cos commented, smiling at her while he slipped the packages from his shoulder.

"What have you brought, *Dominus*?" Maccus asked.

Cos winked at him, tossing him a bundle, "Just what you asked for, Maccus. You recall that you needed some fine things for Linza, and there they are." It took a second for Maccus to realize what Cos meant but grinned as he understood. These were things for him to give to Linza in an attempt to win her affection. Maccus winked back.

Linza understood only her name when they spoke to each other using Latin, still it was enough to suspect that the package held by Maccus was meant for her. She looked back and forth between the two men, not knowing whom to thank or what to say.

"Linza understands. Open the package and see if I got everything you wanted," Cos told him.

There, on the stone floor, the strings were untied and the overlying cloth unfolded while they all watched. Linza gasped when she saw the contents, certain now that they were meant for her and her alone. On the top was a finely made ivory linen tunic, decorated along the plunging neckline with little flowers crafted from brightly colored silk. Maccus held it up for their appraisal using his finger tips. He looked at the feminine garment and back to Linza trying to imagine how it would look on her shapely body. He offered it to her, and she took it gingerly, her eyes glistening with tears.

Next was a folded soft wool *palla*, a long, wide scarf, dyed in pale orange, complete with long knotted fringes. That it was a gift suitable for a woman of means however destined to caress the body of a recent slave was nearly unimaginable. Maccus stood and handed it to Linza without a word, watching her face as tears started down her cheeks in earnest. And there was even more. At the bottom of the parcel was a pair of soft leather shoes, and inside one shoe was a small leather bag which spilled onto the floor, spreading its gold contents for all to see. A *fibulae* of bright and highly decorative repoussage for pinning the *palla* at the shoulder and a matching set of bracelets for her arm reflected the light from the fire, causing Linza to take a deep breath. Was it possible that these gifts were meant for her? She held her hands over her mouth, while her eyes flicked back and forth between Cos and Maccus, not sure which was the one to thank.

"And one last thing," Cos said, pulling a small sack from under his cloak. He handed it to Linza and smiled, "You will need this also." Then to answer the question which would quickly come from Maccus, he explained, "It is underwear, she will know what to do with it."

Linza hesitated at first then rushed toward Cos and encircled his neck with her arms, pulling his face toward hers. "No, my dear Linza, that is not necessary. You owe me no debt for your clothing." He gently pulled her away and softly stroked her ear. "You should be thanking this man." He patted the chest of Maccus who stood there somewhat appalled by the affection his woman had displayed toward Cos. Getting the idea, Linza turned to Maccus and delicately kissed the side of his cheek, then swiveled her head to Cos and smiled, her golden hair falling seductively over one eye.

Alia was watching this little play, her eyes going from one party to the other, her ears straining to understand what was being said. She gathered that Cos was the one who had selected and bought the new clothing and jewelry, and she assumed that the second package was meant for her, yet the excitement and the newness of everything settled on her and pushed her heavily into the chair. She was very tired, too tired to take part or receive gifts at the moment. Her bed was calling her and she tried to stand, intending to head for the stairs before she collapsed and ruined the evening for the others.

"Cos," *Màthair* called out. "You need to catch Alia before she falls." Cos saw that Alia was standing, though barely. She had her head proudly up and her chin defiantly out, however her legs were giving her away because they were trembling, causing her to waver from side to side.

Snatching up the second bundle, he let Alia lie back in his arms as he picked her up. He could tell by her eyes that was what she wanted to happen. She placed her arm over his shoulder and fixed her eyes on his as they moved toward the stairs. "Pity you can't understand me, Alia. We have much to discuss when you are better." Up the stairs they went, toward the comfort of her bed and in the company of each other.

He put her down carefully and looked around in vain for a burning lamp. The room was in semidarkness, lit only by the last fading rays of the setting sun coming in a distant opening, permitting fading softness and expanding shadows to slowly envelope them. From below, they could hear Linza, her higher pitched voice full of excitement and delight. Once in Alia's room, there was a comforting silence.

Cos put the bundle he carried at the foot of her bed and added the small bag of underwear. He patted it and smiled toward her. "These are both yours, and I expect that you will want your hair washed and another bath before putting any of it on. We'll take care of that tomorrow when you are rested." He glanced at the door, wondering if he should leave or if she would still need him by her bedside at least one more night.

Alia wanted very much for Cos to stay with her. This time it was not from a fear of the unknown because she was comfortable with her new surroundings and her new friends. It was just that she wanted to be near Cos, to hear him breath, to feel the safety of his presence. She understood the hardship he endured sitting beside her all night; selfishly, she wanted him to stay.

He stood there silently thinking, trying to see her face clearly enough in the dimming light to decide what to do. She didn't reach for him as she had done previously, so he wasn't sure she needed him any longer. There may come a point at which she would feel threatened, feel that her privacy and independence was dominated by too much attention from her master. He sat down, as before, in the same uncomfortable chair, and took a big breath. As in most things, there is no one around to tell you what to do when you need advice or consolation. It comes down to an intuition of what is the proper course of action. He noticed when she placed her open hand down on the side nearest him. He put his on top of hers, and they held each other in silence.

Domus: Wall Painting in the Roman House. Los Angeles: J. Paul Getty Museum
(Public Domain) Venus and Cupid from the House of Marcus Fabius Rufus at Pompeii, most likely a
depiction of Cleopatra VII

Chapter 14

Mark These Too Few Days As Devine

Godlike the man who sits at her side, who watches and catches that laughter which (softly) tears me to tatters: nothing is left of me, each time I see her.

Catullus (? to 54 BC)

Cos realized that he was no longer dreaming but looking at the ceiling in his room, the luminescence of dawn reflecting a soft pleasant light making scenery painted on the walls come alive as though the scenes were real and not just pigment on plaster. He swung his legs around and sat upright. This was another day to look forward to with no dreads, no fear, and no responsibility. Life was as good as it could possibly be no matter what century it was. His entire life had always been a struggle until now. Being born in Rome of a fractured family and poor to boot was an asset in some ways because it taught him how to survive, even thrive, in harsh circumstances. He had paid his own way through college, taking an interest in ancient languages including Latin and Greek, and along the way reading extensively about that classic time period. Then suddenly everything changed, putting his little world upside down. He had readily agreed to travel back in time when the offer was made, as preposterous as that sounded at the time and even now. A mission they said, just a quick trip there and back, the purpose innocent, historical only. Unfortunately it wasn't that way. It was a trip designed to change the future by changing the past. A huge, ignorant, and irresponsible plot which was never going to work. There was a debt to be paid for opening that door, and the world nearly paid it. A monster from the past had come through the opening and was intent on creating chaos and widespread death.

Turning the corner at the foot of the stairs, he looked admiringly once again at the size of his palatial villa. Far down at the end of the *peristylum,* containing the garden bathed in the morning sunlight, stands a large opening with a small table and two empty end seats before it from which to enjoy the lovely and timeless view of the *Sinus Neapolitan.* He had never dined there alone or with anyone. And there was another just like it above on the second floor. There were valid reasons, of course, although it would be hard to convince anyone why, with the loveliest companion possible available to him, he had not yet taken the opportunity to share a romantic meal with just her. It was simply the way his small family treated each other. They dined together as a whole, rather than apart as separates. Only two meals were eaten together, but it was important to them to have everybody dine as equals in life, share their stories and their happiness around one table. Dining apart with Alia would hurt the others' feelings and put cracks in their unified feeling of togetherness.

There was a large dining room nearby termed the *triclinium,* lavishly decorated and furnished, suitable to entertain the most wealthy and powerful guests. It was constructed for one purpose… to impress. And it was impressive. A fantastic body of labor had been used to decorate the walls and floor, and the three long upholstered benches, meant for diners to recline while eating, were crafted from elaborately carved exotic wood. It was too much for

Cos, and he had never eaten in there. Besides, he absolutely hated eating while reclining.

Instead, they nearly always used the table and chairs sitting in a corner of the *peristylum,* the proximity to the garden and the open air most inviting. And the walk from the *culina,* where the food was prepared, was short and convenient.

Cos noticed that the table was already laden with food, and as he approached, Alia came out of the *culina* carrying another platter. She saw him, he was sure, though she didn't break stride or even glance his way. It was a game they played, her not paying him any mind until he called her name. Then she would turn her eyes on him, the shock of seeing her face again like an electric bolt out of the sky. He marveled each time at the effect she had and, like always, wondered if Alia knew her power. Only six months had passed since Alia had come into his life, and each moment of that time she had become more a part of him. She had learned Latin quickly, more quickly than he could remember learning the same language in his youth. She spoke with nearly no remaining accent to remind him or herself of her origins in the dark north woods of *Germania.*

"Alia," he whispered, and she looked directly at him. Those wonderful blue eyes fixed his, searing into his soul. Her eyes smiled as she turned toward him, looking up, her face of perfect features, her even white teeth just visible under a slight smile. Alia was a goddess visiting earth, not just a lovely girl with an inquiring mind. She was wearing a simple tunic he had purchased for her as appropriate for an unmarried woman, one expertly crafted from blue wool with long sleeves, ornamented with delicate geometric designs and tied just below her breasts with a contrasting yellow cloth. Alia had certainly learned how to wear Roman clothing, how to move gracefully under the loose layers and yet show her marvelous female shape hidden underneath, creating a visual sensuality that few women could match. She stood there, a slight amusement on her face, waiting for him to ask whatever he wanted while knowing he just wanted to see her and hear her voice. He never asked anything of her, demanded no duty or affection. Yet he frequently brought her gifts of clothing and jewelry, even exotic perfumes, expecting nothing in return, only her happiness. And she was happy, deliriously so. Happy, though not fulfilled. She wanted one thing she didn't have. That was Cos. She wanted him, loved him, nearly worshiped him. He was all she thought of from dawn to dusk, even dreaming of him most nights. Yet, so far, Cos made no move to have physical contact of any kind with her other than a brief touch on her shoulder or to hold hands when they crossed a street. His eyes told her that he loved her and desired her, and each time he spoke to her, it was with softness and tenderness. Why? It was driving her mad. When would it come?

Alia paused, lingering in front of him for a long moment, then turned away, her reddish hair catching the light as she returned to the small *culina*. Cos followed her with his eyes until she turned the corner.

Màthair sensed that Alia was different, changed from her usual buoyancy to someone moving more slowly, just in a brief moment. "Alia," she asked, pulling on her shoulder to turn her so that she could see her face. "Did something happen?" Alia shook her head 'no,' but her tears said otherwise. "Did Cos say something that offended you?" Again the shake, 'no.' *Màthair* paused in thought. She could tell the affection between those two was growing by leaps and bounds. The looks they exchanged told her that a romance had started between them. What could possibly be wrong?

"Alia," *Màthair* said, "I've known Cos longer than you, and I think I know him pretty well. He's in love with you, in case you don't know that. And you are so obviously in love with him. It's a wonderful thing, love, however when emotions are that strong, you can be easily hurt with an ill chosen word. Is that what happened?"

"No, *Màthair,* no matter what I do, he just doesn't want to touch me. I'm not good enough for him. He must be ashamed that an ignorant country girl is lovesick over him." The tears followed quickly, and Alia turned away from her, hiding her face.

"Cos doesn't think that way," *Màthair* said. "There must be another reason, and you can count on me to discover what it is."

"And how would you find out what is in his mind?"

"Simple. I'll ask him. You'll see."

"No, *Màthair*, please no. I am happy here, and I don't want to cause him to avoid me."

"Not a chance of that, Alia. Cos would do anything for you. He'll never turn you away or let anyone take you from him."

Breakfast had just started when Linza appeared in the doorway. She had let her long hair down and was wearing the seductive linen tunic she loved so much. Her waist was cinched in the perfect spot to lead a viewer's eyes toward her full breasts, and she instinctively knew what effect those lovely curves had on men. She swayed to the table looking only at Cos, and when she caught his glance, she beamed a smile at him.

"Linza," Cos said calmly. "You look very beautiful this morning, nevertheless you would look even better if you got up early enough to help cook the breakfast."

Linza blushed and pulled her hair over her ear. She had been reprimanded for the first time by Cos, and it stung her badly. She glanced at *Màthair* and Maccus who were giving her a rather hard look.

"I'm sorry, Cos. It seems that I need more sleep than others. I'll try harder to please you."

"Not to please me, Linza. It's just that we are a family, we live here together, we are all we have in the world and each of us has to help pull the cart. You understand, don't you?" Cos asked.

"Yes, Cos," she answered, tears just starting down her face.

"On this fine morning, I have a lot to be thankful for," Cos said, looking around the table at each of them in turn. "To be with my family and to have a marvelous breakfast in this sunlit corner would be enough, but I also have the pleasure of looking at the two most beautiful women ever created while I eat." His well-chosen words ended Linza's tearful moment, and she beamed with pride. Cos glanced at Alia and saw the humor on her face. She held his eyes with hers until it became awkward, and they both reluctantly looked away.

Màthair decided to take this opportunity to speak up. "Cos, speaking of family… ," she started. Cos looked up at her, sensing that he was about to get a lecture of some sort. "I am not getting any younger waiting for children to be produced by you or Maccus. How long do I have to wait?"

Cos could hear giggles coming from the two younger women, and the question made him smile as well.

"Really, I don't know what I would do without you, my dear *Màthair.* You run our home, manage our affairs, do most of the cooking, and tend to all our needs. You are my *Màthair* in every way, and I respect everything you say. This is a delicate subject, one which I have thought about more and more lately."

"Does that mean you want to have children or not?" *Màthair* persisted.

"Children should be a product of both love and marriage, would you agree?" Cos asked. He waited until *Màthair* gave her approval, then added, "We should work on the marriage part first."

Both Alia and Linza put their hands over their mouths in a reflex designed to hide a surprised open mouth. Marriage! The wonder of it, the marvel of acceptance in society. Women were nothing in Roman civilization without marriage. The fortunate women who could proudly wear a *stola* over their *tunic*, flaunted their success in life over the single women. A certain dignity was bestowed on married women for there was little else left for them in life but work and marriage.

"Want to get married, Linza?" Maccus asked, smiling his best smile at her. It wasn't the ideal time to ask her, because at the moment, she was scheming how to convince Cos how utterly desirable she was and how devoted she would be as a wife and lover. She looked at Maccus, breaking her trance for a moment to consider his offer.

"I should know you better first, don't you think?" she answered and lowered her head, her eyes remaining on Cos' face.

"You must know me by now, Linza," he protested. "After all, I buy you things all the time. What else can I do?" he sputtered in frustration.

"Now, Maccus, don't pressure her. I think things are going to change and then we will see," *Màthair* recommended, knowing that the union between Cos and Alia would be soon and eliminate Cos as competition, solving the problem she hoped.

The rest of breakfast was spent in idle conversation ranging from the price of wine, their wine, to the current office seekers in Herculaneum, who constantly scrawled their names and slogans on various walls all over town trying desperately to gain recognition and votes. It was a fine morning for a stroll and possibly a bath at one of the public facilities. Or, Cos considered, he and Maccus could go to the gladiator training facility near Pompeii and get a workout. After some thought, he realized that he would have to give up contact with Alia for most of the day. It just wasn't worth it. He turned his full attention to Alia, who was trying to avoid looking directly at him, stealing quick glances now and then, reassuring herself that he was still focused on her. She was lovely beyond words. Each turn of her head was enchanting, and her long slender neck took its share of his wonder. Her hair was perhaps the most mesmerizing, and after several months, he still couldn't decide on a name for her particular color. The Latin name should be *gingiber,* though it was more than just red. Parts of it morphed into different shades as it passed under a beam of light, some nearly blonde, others close to dark red. Whatever it was, he considered it perfect. He loved it best when she let it down, without braids or restraints of any kind, letting it flow behind her like a river of color. Most of the time, Alia keep her hair braided, pinned in a bun behind her head as did most other women who were not wealthy enough to afford a personal hair dresser. He had a sudden urge to show her off to somebody important, some wealthy or powerful man who would nearly drool with desire as she passed close by. No, that would just create problems for both of them, and he let that idea evaporate.

"Alia," he said softly, getting her to look directly at him. The others also were interested. "Care to go for a walk around town this morning with me?"

"Of course," she replied. "Do we have a destination?"

"Oh, we need to stop by our bakery to see if there are any problems," he answered.

"How should I be dressed?" she asked, a subtle smile becoming evident. Alia knew full well what Cos had in mind was to show her off a bit, his proud possession, his pet, the woman he had raised from the dead. Well, that was fine by her because she enjoyed the public display of consideration by him when they went anywhere together, especially since Cos was the most desirable and respected man in the entire area. It became especially evident who Cos actually was when they encountered a legionnaire of any rank. They all knew *Paulo Fabio Persico Cosimus, Legatus* or heard of him in some way, and all of them deeply respected him.

"Not too fancy, Alia. I thought we would stop by the forum and eat at one of the food shops."

Alia nodded, now certain that Cos most wanted just to be seen strolling with the beautiful woman he called Alia.

She chose a sheer, ivory *palla*, one large enough to wrap most of her upper body, the right arm arm remaining free. Underneath, she wore a simple tunic, one which had been dyed a dark somber red, outlined at the edges with gold thread. Before they left home, she pulled a layer of the *palla* over her head, exposing only her shining face.

Cos looked at her a couple of times in appreciation but didn't comment. They left, arm in arm, to stroll the several blocks to the forum. Since Alia was unmarried and a dependent, if not a servant, she would be expected to trail behind *Paulo Fabio Persico Cosimus* in respect for his title of master of the house. However, Cos, the man, wouldn't permit such a thing and insisted that she walk with him as if she were his equal.

"You seem to enjoy my company, *Dominus*," she said quietly. Cos looked at her with a questioning look because of her use of that title, and realized she would have noticed that the other members of their family never addressed him by his personal name around any strangers or in public.

"I do enjoy being with you," he answered.

"Am I really free to do what I want, even leave?"

"You are no slave, you know that."

"Am I a servant, then?"

"You and I are equals, you know this also."

"Exactly what am I supposed to do the rest of my life?" she asked.

Cos was silent for a moment, considering where she was going with this conversation. "You are not required to do anything but be happy. Don't I treat you well?"

"You are very good to me. Would the reason be that you feel sorry for me and are trying to make it up to me in some way?"

Again Cos hesitated. This line of questioning seemed to be leading into a trap of some sort. "Of course, I felt sorry for you. Though no longer. I can't feel sorry for the most beautiful of women who is also very smart and proud."

"So if I were ugly or deformed, in your eyes, you would treat me differently?"

"I don't think I would… ." He thought for a moment wondering if she had discovered some truth that he was unaware of. "No, Alia, it's just how I feel about you as a person. You make me feel happy just being near you."

"Then, you would miss me if I were gone?"

Cos stopped walking and turned toward her, letting others using the sidewalk pass by. "Would you leave me?" he asked.

"I don't want to, but you can't expect me to stay an unmarried servant to you forever. I was born to have and raise children. There isn't much a woman can do in life other than that."

Instead of answering, Cos resumed walking while turning over in his mind what Alia had said. No doubt that she was exercising a bit of pressure on him to act, and how could he blame her? She was, for good reason, unsure of his intentions toward her in the future. Out of respect, not lack of desire, he had compelled himself not to become physical with Alia. He didn't want her to feel obligated to submit to him since he was acting as the *paterfamilias* and had moral and legal control of anyone in his family. He did love her, without a doubt he loved her, and the concept of losing her was something he pushed away into the recesses of his thoughts. He needed to discuss this with good old *Màthair* who would know what to do.

As they walked down the sidewalk, Cos pointed out interesting features of the city, its stone paved streets, the continuous row of wealthy villas with shops on either side of the entrances. It suddenly brought strong memories of when he visited the ruins of this same city nearly 2000 years into the future. After the volcanic eruption in 79 AD, this city and Pompeii had slept under volcanic rock and ash for centuries, leaving a wealth of information and artifacts for archeologists and reigniting interest in all things ancient Roman. Being able to see it now, in its original condition, alive with people going about their everyday lives, nearly brought a tear of joy to his eyes. He always knew when he returned to the past that one fateful night, there never would be another opportunity to return home. The future was now just a dim memory of things that once was, as if the future had become his past. After years of hardship and danger, Cos had managed to make a name for himself and acquire enough money to live well, really better in some ways than he could have done in the twenty-first century. His was a good life at last, and since Alia came into his world, it was getting better and better. He could look forward to the remaining years of ease and companionship, while living in a modest but beautiful city. One fact pressed against him when he thought about it. Vesuvius was still looming over the city, and in the year 79, it was going to erase Herculaneum and most of its people from the memory of man for centuries. That would occur more than twenty-five years into the future. There was still plenty of time.

The vendors harked their products loudly to all who passed. One, a bit too forward, approached Alia from the side and touched her arm, then looked at her companion, quickly withdrawing. Alia leaned her head back and laughed, her free hand passing her face as if to shoo away a pesky fly. She looked up at Cos, squeezing his arm in the delight of the moment.

No, he could not part with this one, the one thing in his life which really mattered. It was true that she was dependent on him, but he was evermore dependent on her.

Carole Raddato from FRANKFURT, Germany (https://commons.wikimedia.org/wiki/File:Mummy_portrait_on_wooden_tablet_of_a_woman,_from_Fayum,_c._AD_150,_National_Museum_of_Denmark,_Copenhagen_(12993278095).jpg), color by AF, https://creativecommons.org/licenses/by-sa/2.0/legalcode

Chapter 15

A Trip to the Arena

The Love-god inflames more fiercely those he sees are reluctant to surrender.

Tibullus (51 BC 19 BC)

Cos had chosen for himself a bedroom, not more lavish nor larger than assigned to the others in his small family. It was entirely adequate, and besides, all the bedrooms, the *cubicula*, were decorated with exquisite wall art and fine furniture as well as breathtaking floors of naturally colored marble mosaic tiles. This one did have one advantage over most of the others in that it had window openings on two walls, one of them overlooking the harbor. The shortcoming was that, in the cool months of winter, it was drafty if not frigid. Still, nearly anything was better than the tents pitched in far away lands he had slept in for so many years of his young manhood.

It had been another nearly sleepless night. Tossing and turning, his mind burned with thoughts and desires fixated on one tenacious subject. Alia. She had become his partner, at least during his dreams, and when he awakened without her warm body next to him, his sleep world seemed preferable to the real one.

There was a sound in his room. Cos came suddenly fully awake and sat up in bed, looking around for a source of the noise.

"I didn't want to wake you, Cos, however it is time you got up," *Màthair* said. She was seated in the only chair in the room, close to his bed and smiling in his direction.

"*Màthair?*" Cos croaked. "Something wrong?" He rubbed his eyes and remembered that he wore no clothing under the bed cover.

"No, Cos. We need to talk, and this is the only time I can speak to you apart from Alia."

"Can you return after I put on my clothes?"

"I will sit right here and wait while you dress."

"*Màthair,*" he said firmly, "I don't want to walk around naked in front of you."

"You should know, Cos, that I have seen many men and boys in the nude in my time, and it doesn't bother me in the least. In fact, I like it."

Cos sighed. Arguing with *Màthair* was most often pointless. "Then I'll stay right here, which is probably what you want anyway, and we can have your little discussion. What do you want to talk about?"

"It's about Alia, of course. She wonders, I wonder, why you resist touching her in any meaningful way? And I question why you don't take her as a mate? She certainly would like it."

"It's very complicated, *Màthair,*" he said and settled back in bed. "She is my dependent and has no family, no contacts with her people, and is therefore not in a position to resist any advances from me. Of course, she would feel obligated to do what I wish since she has no other choice. And…because I saved her and care for her, she has naturally become attracted to me. Need I go on?"

"All that may be true, Cos, but the fact is, she is desperately in love with you."

"Sure, I can see that. However there is one thing you don't know about Roman law. Given my position, I am not allowed to marry a slave or former slave."

"No, I did not know that." She paused for a moment thinking through this new gordian knot. "Does the law matter within this house?" she finally asked.

"It does. Any children born between us would be considered illegitimate and would not become Roman citizens and all that entails. And, just as bad if not worse, Alia would not have the right to any of my property in the event of my death."

"Things can't go on like they are, Cos. Both of you are suffering needlessly, pining away for each other while you are only separated by thin layers of cloth. What are you going to do about it?"

"There must be a solution, *Màthair,* but so far, I haven't found it. There is another, even bigger problem we have not discussed." He stopped and looked at the ceiling, unsure of how to say what troubled him.

"Don't tell me that you are unwilling to accept this young beautiful woman as a mate. In what way is she not suitable?"

"Alia is in every way suitable and desirable. Nevertheless, *Màthair,* she is nearly half my age. I am old enough to be her father, and at times, I look at her and realize that she is just a child, and I am in my middle years. I can't do that to her. I love her more than that."

"For goodness sake, Cos," *Màthair* blurted. "You don't know that your maturity is partially what is appealing to her? And you should know that many women die in childbirth…more often than animals do. Therefore, choosing a young healthy woman to bear your children is a very wise thing. On this subject, you should just ask her what she thinks."

Màthair stood and pushed the chair aside. "Now get out of bed, and I'll help you get dressed. I want a good look at you, and this is as good a time as any."

Màthair turned the corner and entered the cramped *culina,* finding Alia already at work preparing the morning meal. Alia looked up and studied her face for a moment and returned to her task. *Màthair* paused in the middle of the floor waiting for the right moment to speak. Unusual for her, she was temporarily at a loss for words.

"I talked with Cos this morning, and we discussed you and how he feels toward you," *Màthair* finally said. Alia put down what she was doing and stood upright, looking at her face intently, waiting for the rest. "He told me he loves you but is concerned about being too old for you. That is one of the reasons he has hesitated toward you."

"And the other reasons?" Alia asked.

"He feels that you may feel obligated to accept his advances and wants you only if it is by your own free will."

Alia thought it over. This information was no surprise to her because she had guessed as much. Perhaps she could have pushed a bit harder, certainly Linza had done that and more. In fact, the only thing Linza had not tried was to completely disrobe in front of Cos or jump on him in his bed. Her tactics bore no fruit. He wasn't interested in Linza, not a bit. If Cos noticed any of Linza's remarkable female curves at all, it was not obvious because his eyes never lingered on her, even for the briefest of moments, certainly not long enough to show interest or even arousal.

"Was there anything else?" Alia asked. Might as well hear it all.

"There was something about Roman law being a problem, however I think he is working on a solution. One last thing…I got a good look at Cos because I helped him dress this morning. He is a magnificent creature, bulging hard muscle and beautifully constructed. He may think he is too old for you, but I don't."

"Thanks for telling me all this, *Màthair*. It means a lot to me how you look after all of us."

"What are you going to do, Alia?"

Alia was looking off into the distance, her mind pursuing various options and formulating a strategy. She looked right at *Màthair*, catching her full attention, "Would you mind if I arranged for Cos and I to eat our *jentaculum* separately, only this one time?"

"I'll bet I know where!" *Màthair* giggled like a young girl. "At the end of the *peristylum* overlooking the harbor."

"Yes. That spot is private and lovely, and I've never seen him use it before."

"Nor has anyone. I always thought he was saving that for a special day. Let's hurry and get it prepared before he comes down."

The three of them were staring at him as he approached the table. He had a funny feeling that there was something different this morning. There was simply not enough food on the table for breakfast…and where was Alia?

Cos stood, looking back at their faces, wondering at the change and about to demand answers when *Màthair* pointed, and his eyes followed her finger. There, at the far end of the *peristylum*, seated on one of the marble stools near the window to the sea was Alia. From this distance, he could just see her smiling face looking back at him, and the table before her laden with food. She was dressed in white and stood out against the background like a beacon. Without saying a word, he started toward her, understanding that this was a well worked out plot to allow him and Alia to be alone in a romantic spot.

She stood as he neared and moved toward him, arms extended. "I hope you don't mind, Cos," she said. "It just seemed to be the right time."

Cos took her hands in his and looked her over from toe to head. "You look more and more like a marble creation of a myth. I traveled for 2000 years to find you, and here you are."

They sat at the ends of the small oval stone table, not looking at the harbor or the sea spreading out behind it but only each other. Cos put his hands on either side of the table, really feeling it for the first time. He had only occupied this house before, lived in it and worked in it, though at this moment felt for the first time that he actually owned it, was part of it, and part of its history. Someday, when this spot is uncovered after sleeping for two millennia under tons of volcanic ash, he hoped that some man would sit here and, just for a brief instant, imagine how it would feel to be in the year 52 looking across this same table at the woman he loved.

"*Màthair* told me what you discussed," Alia began. "She said that you loved me, and you know that I love you."

"You realized that for months."

"I didn't know that you thought I was too young for you."

"And you are. At first, I was just trying to protect you and restore you to health, yet I couldn't help myself from loving you more each day. The Greeks have a saying that there is only one perfect mate in all the entire world and when you find her you will know that she is the one. For me, it's even better. You and I are caught in a loop, and every two thousand years I will return, and we will meet right in this spot again over and over forever. I will experience this moment with you until the end of time."

"And you should know that I feel no obligation to love you, Cos. I love you out of my own free will, and I will stay with you until death parts us or as long as you will have me."

Alia's hair rustled softly in the morning offshore breeze, and the brilliant glow from the water danced over her face, reflecting the moisture welling up in her eyes. Cos got up, knelt down beside her, pulled her toward him slowly and, with reverence, kissed her for the first time. She encircled his neck with her arms and embraced him tightly, remembering all the moments she wanted to have him this close to be able to show him how she felt.

"Are we one, Cos? Can we begin our life together from this day on?"

Cos sighed and stood, caressing her hair while looking down at her radiant face. "Some would start at this moment…many do, however I want you to have a proper life, to have legitimate Roman children, to feel secure in the coming years, even if I am not around any longer. We have to be married and have it recorded in the required manner. However, there are difficulties."

"What can possibly stop us, Cos?" she asked. In her culture, marriage basically consisted of consent, and the couple who chose to do so started their married life without rules or regulation. Even in that tribal society, it was the custom to have both sets of parents involved or, at least, have their approval. Divorce was rare and so was adultery because adultery was deemed punishable by the tribe. In Alia's view, there was no obstacle to union with Cos, and since she didn't understand the laws of Roman society, there was no need to pay attention to them.

"First things first, my dear Alia," Cos said, kneeling once again beside her. "I would like to ask you an important question." Alia turned to him, a serious look on her face, expecting a question about her virginity.

"Alia, will you marry me?" Cos asked.

"Yes, Cos, I will marry you." She closed her eyes and held her head back, expecting and receiving a tender and prolonged kiss from Cos.

"Now that it is settled, you know my intentions, and I know yours. However, we cannot consummate the marriage until I am able to sort out some legal problems.

"I am here, and you are here, and we are in our home. There are no people above our intentions to tell us what to do," Alia persisted.

"Let me explain," Cos patiently said. "You were never registered as a slave or a freed slave. There was no tax paid on you, and there is no record of where you came from. And…" he paused, "I am considered to be in the senatorial class and am prohibited from marriage to a person of a different rank, especially one who will be accused of being a slave."

"So what are you going to do?" Alia asked, frowning with the thought of another delay.

"I have to approach a *Quaestor sacri palatii* who knows the law and ask him.

"And what if he refuses to help us?"

"Then I need to find a *consul* who will."

"Cos, I have wondered frequently what you paid for me."

"You were given to me because they thought you were going to die," he answered. "Whatever I could have paid wouldn't have been enough because you are worth more to me than any amount of money."

Alia nodded, thinking through the implications. She was never a slave, never sold as a slave. She was a captive only. A huge load was taken off of her mind, and she felt better about herself than she had for months. Now she felt for the first time an equal to Cos, and soon she would join him in marriage, becoming a proper Roman citizen and having proper Roman children. She started smiling broadly, beaming her happiness to the winds and the sun. Life was good and was to become even better.

"Cos, things you have said are confusing to me. Where did you come from?"

"I was born in *Roma*," he answered, looking over the food on the table instead of her while considering how much she could be told and how much of that she could understand.

"Then what did you mean when you mentioned 2000 years?"

"I shouldn't have said that. You won't understand even if I explain it to you."

Alia didn't answer, continuing to stare at him with her intense blue eyes, taking him in as if she had never seen him before. Cos didn't want to have a marriage that hid facts of any kind. He wanted Alia to know everything about him, every detail, if she desired it.

"All right, let me try and see if it is possible to explain this to you. Have you ever heard the word '*futurae*'?"

Alia shook her head that she had not.

"Well, it refers to what has not happened yet. For example, the past is what has happened. You can think of the future as what will happen."

Alia cocked her head and took a drink of wine. "How do you know what will happen?"

"Mostly, you can't know, but let me put it another way. What if you could go backwards…back to the past. If you were able to do that you would already know what was going to happen because you just came from there."

"My people think of only two things, the past and the now. We never speak of the '*futurae,*' as you call it."

"Of course you do. You put away food for the winter and buy cattle so that you can breed more. That's thinking about the future, isn't it? And you are already thinking about our children, aren't you?"

"I'm thinking about right now. I can't think about something that isn't real."

"I'm going to tell you something that I've never told any other person, and you must not repeat it to anyone if you really love me." He waited while his plea sank in. "I was born in the far far future, and I came back to this time to kill a monster."

Alia started to laugh, her eyes sparkled, and her mouth opened wide. She was pleased that he was telling her his mythology of the world, and this opened up the opportunity for her to tell him about her Norse gods as well. She didn't fully understand what he was trying to tell her, but he must have been trying to make her laugh, and it was even more humorous since he was so sincere.

Cos sighed. Well, he tried. He couldn't blame her for not understanding something that still felt impossible, even to him.

"I promised Maccus that we would go to the gladiator school this morning and workout with the young gladiators."

"Does that mean that you will leave me here alone?" she asked.

"You won't be alone. *Màthair* and Linza will be here."

"Why can't I go also?"

Cos thought it over briefly and shook his head. "That's no place for an innocent girl like you. Those are very rough men, and they have no bounds other than captivity."

"I grew up around men who were warriors. That's all they talked about or thought about." She looked a bit sideways at him and lowered her voice a tone. "And I want to see you in action. Anything wrong with that?"

Cos laughed. "You little schemer. Was there any doubt that I will agree to anything you want?" Alia shook her head 'no.'

When Maccus discovered that Cos was bringing Alia, he insisted that Linza be allowed to go also. Cos shrugged. Why not. They could keep each other company in the reviewing stand, and it would be easier to keep two women in view rather than just one.

After some discussion between the women regarding appropriate attire, they left home and started walking the several blocks to the training area. It was slower progress than usual, because they stopped frequently to inspect the latest goods on sale at the shops, and that also meant a small diversion from the shortest route.

Cos and Maccus waited on the busy sidewalk while the women entered a particular shop of interest. After a few moments, Cos began to have a strange sensation that they were being watched. He glanced at Maccus, who was looking intently around, inspecting the faces of passing people, apparently also detecting a threat.

Nothing out of the ordinary could be spotted, nevertheless both became increasingly agitated. It was an old instinct, honed by years of war. Most experienced fighters either develop situational awareness or they quickly perish. Cos had no intention of allowing any threat to take him by surprise.

"We should start moving again," Cos suggested. They had worked out the best tactic years ago, and no discussion was necessary. Cos would take the lead and Maccus would follow far enough behind to avoid a surprise attack from the front while being an obstacle for anything coming from the rear. Cos went inside and signaled Alia and Linza to follow. His stern face caught them by surprise, and they obeyed swiftly. This time, Cos walked in front of both women, a distance of several paces. The women felt the tension, without understanding the reason.

When the arena was in sight, Cos looked behind, seeing no one following. He joined the women and signaled Maccus to do the same.

"What was wrong, Cos?" Alia asked.

"We were being observed, by whom I don't know, but there is no risk of danger here. We will escort you to the viewers platform, and you can watch from there. Don't come down without my approval," he ordered, looking at each of them to be sure they got the message.

The two women were very well dressed but neither wore the *stola,* a piece of clothing designed to cover the more simple tunic underneath, embellishing the wearer with more decoration and substance and which established and announced that the wearer was married. This single piece of cloth was enough to encourage most adventuresome males to keep a respectful attitude and distance since the official punishment for any sport with a married Roman woman was severe and prompt. In a small city like Herculaneum, the consort of *Paulo Fabio Persico Cosimus* was a person to especially avoid because no official would question anything a celebrated *legatus* would do in retribution for an offense against his female partner, no matter what it was.

The platform was elevated from the training area by several sets of stairs and offered a commanding view of the activities below. There were several benches available, and they chose one closest to the railing, smiling broadly and waving each time either of their men came into view.

There was seemingly random motion from the men below who appeared inclined to walk back and forth without purpose. Some were only clothed below their waist while others wore several different types of armor, all were tanned and muscular, their sinews and muscles rippling as they moved. Warm up consisted of calisthenics and stretching, followed by a period of fierce pounding with flashing swords on vertical timbers. A lull followed, but soon the men gathered in groups, forming a loose ring around two particular combatants who circled slowly, keeping a wary eye on their competitor. There were shouts and yells of encouragement, and it was obvious that action was soon to begin.

Alia suddenly realized that one of the men in the center was Cos. He was wearing a chain mail tunic and metal helmet, yet she could still see the broad muscular shoulders and arms of the man she had grown to love. He was almost casual about it, holding his glinting sword low while moving slowly, not even paying attention to his opponent. His fellow combatant was agitated, moving back and forth as if in fear. After a suitable period, Cos held his sword in the air and bowed slightly to the man in front of him, a signal of respect to the man about to be slain. Alia held her breath, she had no idea that this was not play, but serious, conducted with real and very sharp weapons.

Cos turned fully to face the man opposing him. The gladiator was covered in armor and had both sword and shield as well as a full-face metal helmet. The other men were yelling, wanting to see a clash resulting in a body lying in the dirt. Alia couldn't stand to watch, yet could not turn her head. She covered her face with her fingers, peeping through enough to see dimly what she dreaded to see.

In a blindingly fast charge, the gladiator rushed toward Cos, swinging his sword in an arc designed to strike Cos in the neck. In perfectly timed motion, Cos sidestepped the charge, and as the man went by, Cos' sword impacted his body armor with a resounding 'crack.' Instantly, the gladiator went down, thrashing and flailing, while holding his side. The other men held their fists in the air and shouted their approval, chanting "Cosimus, Cosimus." Cos helped his former opponent to his feet, embracing him with affection and back slapping, friends again.

The next pair to step forward included the short, thick Maccus, opposed by a much taller and heavier opponent. Maccus wore no armor and, instead of a sword, wielded a large metal tipped club. His counterpart was clad in glinting armor from head to toe, large colorful fronds sprouted from his helmet. This gladiator was not intimidated by Maccus and circled his prey slowly, swinging his sword from side to side, not losing eye contact for an instant. It seemed to be an obvious mismatch, and Alia wondered why Cos would let his friend enter into a contest he seemed destined to lose.

"Do you know one of those gladiators?" a voice asked. Alia looked up to see a clean-shaven face, a handsome one at that. He was smiling and waiting for a reply.

"I am with Cosimus, and she is with Maccus," Alia answered. There was a sudden outbreak of yelling below, and Alia glanced toward the noise to see Maccus standing beside the armored man, who was already lying immobile on the ground. She looked back at the stranger, noticing he was cloaked in a white toga, a broad band of purple woven vertically into the right side.

"I see. Which one is Cosimus?" he asked, looking over the railing with her.

"The one looking this way," she answered, pointing at Cos who was watching the events in the reviewing stand. He had his hands on his hips and didn't look happy about her new company.

"Yes, I see him. A remarkable fighter. Is he an experienced gladiator? I would assume so from watching that last bout."

"Not really. He is a *legatus*," she answered.

"I understand now. A *legatus!*… he murmured, his hand on his chin. "That would be *Paulo Fabio Persico Cosimus* standing there and threatening me with his eyes just now?"

"He is, and if I were you, I would take it seriously," Alia answered.

"And you, my beautiful young woman, what are you called?" His voice was melodious, not threatening, and he continued to smile at her in an affectionate way.

Alia hesitated to give this stranger any information. She could tell that he was unafraid of the consequences of approaching and conversing with her. How could he be so bold? She decided to ignore his question.

"And you, my dear blonde and interesting woman. Are you with our famous *Persico Cosimus* also?"

The question surprised Linza who was not expecting any interrogation. She was not fully competent with her Latin and still spoke with a pronounced *Germani* accent. She put her hand over her mouth and looked at Alia with big questioning eyes.

"She is with me," Alia answered for her.

"You have an excellent grasp of Latin, my dear. Where in *Germania* were you born?"

Instead of an answer, Alia returned her gaze to the events below and was watching when Cos pulled off his armor and cast it aside. He was bare from the waist up and still wearing the metal embossed leather straps covering his pelvis down to his knees. Cos was breathtakingly muscular, and even from this distance, she could discern several large scars across his chest and back. There were many back slaps and shouts of well-being as he made his way toward the viewing stands.

Cos encountered two heavily armored men guarding the staircase opening. They were carrying the badge of high office, a long axe wrapped with reeds called *fasces*. This meant the man above, seen talking to Alia and Linza, was an elected official of *Roma* with both rank and power.

"You remember me?" one of them asked as Cos approached.

Cos stopped and looked the man over, trying to place his face. Both men were smiling at him and waiting for his reply.

"Should I?" Cos asked.

"*Mario Accius Ponticus*, I was with the 11th at *Colonia Ulpia Traiana*. We crossed the Rhine together on a raid."

"Oh yes, I recall your bravery. You were much discussed," Cos said, putting his arm on the man's shoulder.

"And this is *Aulus Mamilius Hirpinius*," he said, gesturing toward the other *lictor*. "He came after your *Legion XX* departed for *Britannia*."

Cos smiled at the other man and nodded his approval. "Who are you with?" Cos asked, motioning with his head toward the stairs.

"Oh, he is a *consul* and lives nearby. We were directed to leave the other *lictors* there," Ponticus said. Cos recalled that the position of *consul* entitled twelve *lictors* who both symbolized his power and provided for his safety inside or outside of *Roma*, and that most l*ictors* were experienced and tough former *centurions*.

"And his name?" Cos inquired.

They could hear heavy footsteps coming up the stairs, and the stranger stood up and turned toward the sound. He was an attractive man, authoritative in a calm, deliberative way, and showed no fear of what was coming toward him up the wooden staircase. Alia looked back and forth between the stranger and the opening of the staircase. She didn't wish that any violence occur but would be glad to be rid of the persistent and arrogant man who had intruded on their outing.

The first part of Cos to show seemed to be his eyes, narrowed and hard eyes. As the rest of him moved up into the light, they could see sweat and dust still clinging to his chest and shoulders. Without a tunic, Cos looked larger than normal, bigger, more fierce by far, his scarred skin a roadmap of his former life as a warrior serving *Roma* on its frontier.

"A fine performance down there, *Legatus*," *Consul* Piso said, smiling and offering a polite wave. Cos had stopped five feet away and looked first at his women, then at Piso. He could see the strain on Alia's face. She had been in an uncomfortable situation, an unfamiliar one. This was one of the first times she had any contact with strangers without him right beside her.

"We have not met, *Consul*, though I understand we don't live far apart," Cos replied.

"I heard you had retired to Herculaneum. My wife and I don't come here as often as we would like…my duties in *Roma*, you understand."

"Yes. I am, at last, free of duties and combat. My fellow and I come here frequently to help train the young inexperienced gladiators and keep our own skills sharp, however I am through picking up a sword and glad to be finished with it."

"I discovered you have two very lovely women who accompany you. They wouldn't talk to me without you being here. I hope you are not offended," Piso commented.

"I would be with anyone but you. Your reputation is exceptional, and I have heard much about you to respect."

"Thank you, *Legatus*. Hearing that from you is a great honor. By the way, you should call me by my first name…Gaius, if you will. And I have heard much about you. You are still missed by your *legion*, I understand. They clamor for your return."

Cos laughed. "I miss them also. A fine group of men, worthy of the respect of *Roma* and of me."

"May I ask…" Piso started. "Are these women your slaves or servants?" He glanced over toward Linza and Alia who were intently watching and listening.

"They are not slaves, never were. They were rescued by me and Maccus several months ago and are guests in my villa."

"Captured on the other side of the Rhine, I gather," Piso surmised.

"Yes."

"And have you made either or both your concubine?"

"No, they are both treated as members of my family. They are highly regarded by me and are free to live according to their own wishes. Except Alia, who has won my love," Cos answered. He was watching Alia's face as he spoke and could see the tears starting down her cheeks.

"I know what it is like to love a woman. Someday you should meet my wife," Piso said, nodding toward Alia as he spoke. He paused, thinking for a moment, then said, "I would like to invite you and…Alia," he remembered, "to my home. It's not far, though I will send a carriage for you. A little *convivium* in your honor. There will be other guests as well. Will you accept?"

"We will, and thank you, Gaius. And my friends and family call me Cos. Please do so also."

On the walk home, Cos and Alia walked together, ahead of Maccus and Linza. They frequently glanced backwards, noting the difference from before Linza had seen Maccus in action. There was new respect from Linza, and for the first time, the couple chatted, oblivious of anything around them.

Alia laughed, smiling at Cos, her eyes twinkling with mischief and delight. "I think coming with you was good for both of us," she offered. "And I did get to see you in action. I was so afraid of you getting injured, I hid my eyes."

"There was no danger to me. None of them would dare to harm me, even if they could," Cos replied. "You were at more risk than I was, as I could plainly see," he teased.

Alia frowned, "I thought you might harm him, yet you seemed to be friends. Just who is that man?"

"He is *Gaius Calpurnius Piso*. One of the wealthiest men in *Roma*, possibly in the entire world. His family on both sides were wealthy and powerful. On his mother's side, he is related to Julius Caesar. Their home, just outside of Herculaneum, was also home to Julius Caesar, one of the most famous men in history, even in future history. Piso is a Roman senator and, at the moment, also serves as *consul*, a position he will regain later in his lifetime. His authority is only exceeded by the Emperor Claudius."

Alia thought about what Cos said and again she recalled his remarks about coming from the future. "Cos, do you know what is going to happen before it happens?"

Cos was silent for a moment, considering how to explain his life in terms that could be understood. There was nothing he could say which would provide a rational explanation to a simple woman who was raised in a primitive tribe, no matter how intelligent she was. She would only understand, as had Antonius, when she was shown the future in person, something that could never again happen.

"On some things, I do know what will happen and when it will happen. Those are mostly major things, though on occasion, I do know details. For instance, our new friend Piso will die by suicide in about 12 years because he will plot to murder Nero, the next emperor, and get caught."

He could hear her catch her breath. "You know this? You really know?" she asked, her hand reflexly over her mouth.

"It will happen, I assure you."

"Should you not warn him?"

"I said it will happen. That means that it cannot be changed, and no, I will not warn him."

"And me, Cos, and you. What will happen to us?"

"You and I will live in love's embrace for the rest of our lives." He leaned down and kissed the top of her forehead.

"For sure this will happen?" she asked, her eyes big with wonder.

"Honestly, I don't know the answer. What I said was what I hope will happen."

Alia fell silent, walking beside him, occasionally touching his hand but looking straight ahead, not even glancing at him.

"I don't expect you to believe me, Alia. It's too much for anyone to understand. We shouldn't know the future anyway. You can't live your life properly if you already know how it turns out in the end."

His little explanation went unnoticed or perhaps not believed. She was there in body only, walking beside him as if in a dream, detached for a moment from all that she had wished for.

Cos looked ahead, down the long straight street. Looming above the city was the blue outline of a monstrous cone, hovering in wait, the tension inside of it building by the day. Vesuvius was there, its mission unfulfilled. The most famous of all volcanos slept peacefully for a moment of geologic time, giving the skyline an interesting appeal, a mountain in peaceful repose instead of an ominous threat.

He put his arm out, briefly blocking her forward motion. She looked up in question as to why they had stopped, her face calm, waiting on his reasons.

"Look there," he pointed. "Above the street. What do you see?"

Alia looked down his finger and shaded her eyes with her hand. She looked up confused as to what he expected her to see. It was the same sight that she had grown accustomed to seeing.

"See that mountain, the pointed one east of where we are?"

Alia nodded yes, unsure of why Cos had asked.

"That is called Vesuvius, and it will be very famous forever. The reason it will be known by almost every civilized man or woman is because it will suddenly erupt twenty-six years from now and cover this city and Pompeii, with hot rocks and ash, killing everyone who can't get away in time. Suddenly one day, all you see now will be buried under a mountain of rock and only be seen again one thousand eight hundred years later. I have seen this city after it was uncovered. I walked these same streets two thousand years from now."

"Since you know this, will we be be here when it happens and die also?"Alia asked.

"No, if we are still alive then, we will move north along the coast before anything happens. We will have plenty of warning because there will be a big earth shaking in ten years which will cause many buildings to fall. I plan for us to leave before that also."

"I believe you, Cos, because I know you would never lie to me, still it still does not seem possible that what you say is true. Everything I thought I knew and understood has fallen apart. Now, for the first time, I am aware that things and lives are temporary, at least my life is. You must be some sort of God who can live over and over again while I can only live once."

"No, Alia, I am just a man like all the others here. I live and will die just like them. I was hired to do a job as a translator and got sent back to this time not really understanding that it was a very wrong thing to do. I put my best effort into being a good soldier for *Roma*, though when I found you collapsed on the floor of that cage, my life changed for the better. I want to be here as long as I can be with you. To me, it's obvious that you and I were meant to be together all along, and you were the real reason I came back through time and now have the honor of holding your hand and looking into your eyes."

Carole Raddato from FRANKFURT, Germany (https://commons.wikimedia.org/wiki/
File:Fresco_depicting_a_seated_woman,_from_the_Villa_Arianna_at_Stabiae,_Naples_National_Ar
chaeological_Museum_(17393152265).jpg), color by AF, https://creativecommons.org/licenses/by-
sa/2.0/legalcode

Chapter 16

Villa of the Papyri

The man of affluence is not in fact more happy than the possessor of a bare competency, unless, in addition to his wealth, the end of his life be fortunate. We often see misery dwelling in the midst of splendor, whilst real happiness is found in humbler stations.

Herodotus (500 BC)

The worst part a man can suffer is to have insight into much and power over nothing.

Herodotus (500 BC)

Cos was seated in the *tablinum,* the folding wooden doors separating his office from the *atrium,* giving a sensation of privacy. He had a small portable table in front of his chair and had been hard at work all morning tending to the financial needs of his two businesses, the vineyards and wine manufacturing and the small bread industry he had purchased.

A soft voice called out to him. "Cos, are you ready to see us yet?" Alia asked.

"Come in, all of you," he said loud enough for the others to hear, then watched as the four came sheepishly into his inner sanctum. They lined up with Maccus and his mother on the left, Alia and Linza on the right. Each looked back and forth between themselves wondering why Cos had demanded their presence.

"It's time to become more educated," Cos started, watching Maccus begin to fidget with the prospect of disciplined learning. "I have employed a Greek teacher to come in the afternoons three times a week to teach each of you the use of an abacus… for starters. The reason is that I need help managing my business, and since I intend on giving each business to whomever deserves that honor, that person will have to learn to manage numbers, how to write and record, but most of all, there has to be records to show the tax man."

"Cos, do you mean me also?" Linza asked, using a low soft voice.

"Of course, I mean you also. I know this is new to you, however I have watched all of you, and I know you are smart and capable. All you need is to understand what to do."

Màthair spoke up, "I don't want to do this, Cos."

"Of course, you don't have to, *Màthair,* though I believe you will enjoy it. Won't you give it a try? I need you to set an example for the others."

After *Màthair* gave a grudging nod of acceptance, Cos moved to another topic. "There is an invitation lying on my desk. It invites Alia and me to the home of *Consul* Piso. It states that a carriage will arrive for us in mid-afternoon two days from now. I wanted to tell all of you this news, so there there are no surprises and no jealousy." He looked right at Linza to make his point. Alia started to smile, but her face colored quickly to a bright red, and from the way her eyes were rolling around, she had plenty of questions for him.

"Another thing is mentioned," he said, tapping on the rolled invitation. "Piso is sending his personal *ornatrice* and her staff to prepare Alia for her visit. I will be sure to pay her for the additional time it takes to also groom Linza with the latest hairstyle." There were gasps from both women as they folded in laughter and delight.

"May I ask a question, Cos?" Alia inquired.

"And I'm guessing that you wonder what will you wear?" Cos interrupted. She nodded that was at least partially the question.

"Our wealthy new friend has foreseen that need also. He is sending the correct clothing along with the hairdresser. One other thing you both should know. These women are probably slaves and not free women. Female slaves cannot be freed before the age of thirty. So to avoid any resentment, you should keep your present status to yourselves."

After a moment of silence, the little group started filing out and back to whatever tasks had been interrupted. Cos heard a couple of deep sighs as they disappeared around the corner. He was determined to give his wine making company to Maccus and Linza as a wedding present…if and when they were able to manage it themselves. Cos sighed also. It was a very large task to educate people who were used to dependency on others. A noise brought his attention to the door opening where he saw Alia's smiling face peering around the corner at him.

"Come on in, Alia. I was expecting that you had more questions." She turned the corner and came toward him across the decorated floor, barefoot as usual. What a dream she was. Naturally graceful and feminine, each turn of her head was memorable. He couldn't get enough of watching her move.

"I need to ask you something, Cos," she said, pouring her big eyes on his, bending his will to hers without even knowing that she had that power.

"Anything," Cos responded softly.

"This invitation which included me…it's important to you?"

"Piso is a powerful man. I, we, can't refuse, and I believe we will enjoy the experience."

"This is new to me. I won't know how to act or what to do."

"And neither will I, but together we will manage."

"Won't you be ashamed to escort a poor ignorant woman from a small tribe?"

"You have the mind, the body, and the spirit of a goddess. I will never be ashamed to be with you. You will be the most priceless, the most exquisite creature to ever visit with Piso and his wealth."

"Thank you, Cos. I am afraid of being laughed at and ridiculed, and I am afraid of making you look foolish for supporting me as you do."

"Piso is going to a lot of trouble for us, and you have nothing at all to worry about. You will look and act just as you should. Be yourself and be not afraid of anything because I will be by your side."

It was a short carriage ride of only *duo mille passus*, or two miles, though Cos spent most of the time looking at his companion, who had been transformed by an intricate hairdo, tasteful but decorative silk clothing, and priceless jewelry. Alia was a different human, metamorphosed into something timeless, someone too precious to even touch lest the dream be stopped, returning him to reality. The exposure of her long sensual neck drew his eyes to where it started from her scented body tracing its curves upwards to her face in profile. When her eyes turned on him, an electric charge coursed through his body. At first, he had resented Piso's attentions to Alia's attire and her hair, though afterwards, he had to admit what was obvious. She was perfect, with any trace of her barbarian roots now just a distant memory.

Alia could mix with any group without uttering a word because the change in her appearance also had changed her confidence and her poise.

"Alia, you are beautiful."

She smiled, patting his cheek and touching his lips with her finger. "No more of that right now, Cos. I have to concentrate to be what you want me to be. What should I call you in front of all those people?"

"What will you call me when we are married and alone?"

"Cos," she answered, smiling at the thought.

"And that is what you shall call me in public."

"By the way, you are rather handsome in your armor. It looks intimidating but also uncomfortable." She smiled at him and stroked his sparkling breast plate that Maccus had spent most of the previous day polishing.

"I haven't worn this for months, and I hope this might be the last time I put it on," Cos agreed. He looked down at his splendid armor, crafted explicitly for his rank as *legatus*, commander of the famous *Legio vigesima Valeria Victrix*, more than five thousand hardened and experienced men. A time of great responsibility for him which he took on reluctantly and gladly relinquished when his posting was finished.

"Cos," Alia said, looking at his eyes to gain his wandering attention. "What am I to say to Piso's wife?"

"Here is a bit of history about her that you should know. First, her name is Livia Orestilla, and she is from a famous and wealthy family also. She married Gaius Piso, however on her wedding day, she was forced to marry the corrupt Emperor Caligula, who divorced her the next day and forbid her to see Gaius ever again. They, of course, were in love and got back together as the Emperor knew they would. He banished them to a distant island in a fit of revenge. After Caligula was murdered, the next Emperor, Claudius, brought them back together. As you might assume, Claudius and Piso are very close. Though to answer your question, Livia is considered to have been an empress as well as an important person in her own right. I believe that after her ordeal, you will find her to be a kind and gentle person whom you can address by her first name. You will know what to do when you meet her."

The two-wheeled carriage rocked along over the paving stones, and the small city of Herculaneum passed by the small windows. Cos remembered very well the trips he had made here when he was young, and the wish he had that he could see the city before the volcano buried it. And here it is, drifting by, building after building. It looked so normal, not something that was in the past but real and now. He was here and part of it, not an all knowing person from the future looking down at savages from the past. These people were really the same as those he had known in his youth, had the same habits, the same manner of speech, the same wants. And he was proud to be here among them, one of them and no different in any way. At first he had looked on this era as something in a dream, not real, not permanent, its future known to him as a god might know it. Life had changed him, and he realized that it would be more or less the same no matter where in time he visited.

Cos had a sensation and turned as if by reflex, finding the penetrating blue eyes of the incredible creature sitting beside him. He looked back, trying to read her thoughts. Was she frightened, uncomfortable in some way, dreading their coming adventure? "I love you, Cos," she said instead. The happy moisture forming along her lower lids.

"I love you also."

The carriage stopped, and before them lay the entrance to the grandest of all Roman homes, which would be called "The Villa of the Papyri" in the distant future because of the wealth of discovered rolls of manuscripts, an entire library of previously unknown works. At the time Cos left the twenty-first century, there was still no mechanism which allowed the burnt scrolls to be read. The home was never fully excavated. In fact, only a small portion of it had ever been seen since the year 79 AD. This was a most famous villa in its time and even more so since it was re-discovered. Cos exited from the carriage and held his hand for Alia as she dismounted. Standing in front of this villa with this glamorous woman beside him was a thrill he had never expected.

A pair of uniformed men appeared, their bronze and steel armor polished to a mirror finish. "Greetings lady and *Legatus*," one said, extending his arm to indicate that they should precede him and enter the villa. Once past the entry gate, they entered the huge open *peristylum* with its center pool flanked by rows of columns on both sides. At the end was the residence itself, facing the garden with two floors visible. Cos took a breath. This was even more magnificent than he had imagined. Along the path were countless cast bronze statues of people, animals and legends.

"Cos!" Alia said breathlessly, "This is… ." She didn't finish because there was always more to see and experience as they walked.

Cos slowed near the *impluvium,* noticing the many sculpted heads on pedestals. He had often heard of the treasures found here, indicating not only the wealth of the owners but also their culture and appreciation of art and history.

In a short row, he found the busts of Democritus, Silenus, Pythagoras and Epicurus, all in perfect condition and certainly no copies. These were the real thing. He looked about, wondering where the missing image of Alexander was. In the future, it was never found, and its absence gave many reason to ponder why.

"This is amazing, Alia, amazing," he murmured to her. Both were in disbelief of the opulence and size of the villa.

"I thought no place could be better than ours," Alia said, whispering in his ear, "I was wrong."

They were directed into a second entrance in the center of the main building at the end of the walkway. Again, the floors and walls spoke loudly that enough money and taste could create marvels. Cos looked around, realizing that in not too many years this place and all who inhabit it will be covered by a mountain of hot rock and ash, destroying it while also preserving it for the future so that men in latter days can marvel once again at the sophistication of the Romans.

One more turn and they were waved into a large room, decorated by lavish wall paintings, and there in the center was Pizo, smiling sincerely at them.

"Welcome, Cos and Alia," he said. Three other men in *togas* came forward and nodded their approval of *Paulo Fabio Persico Cosimus, Legatus* and his notable companion. Cos glanced at Alia briefly to gauge how she would handle this new experience. Her silk *tunic* was the most elaborate he had ever seen and rippled seductively as she moved, exposing her graceful curves under thin and supple layers of silk. Her *palla* was itself exceptional, and there was enough fabric to wrap around her and cascade over her shoulder creating an image very similar to those statues of various female gods they had just passed. Well done, Piso, Cos thought to himself. The attire chosen was perfect in that a viewer could not see that she was not wearing the garment she would have preferred…the *stola,* which would have indicated marriage.

Alia looked back at Cos and smiled. Yes, she was happy and proud to be with him, and for the first time, she felt like she belonged. She took his hand and gave it a quick squeeze, then turned her attention back to their host.

"I want to introduce you to my other guests, *Legatus*, however I fear their attention is directed at the spectacular jewel with the profoundly blue eyes standing beside you," Piso said, engendering a chuckle from the other men who obviously agreed with him. "The last time we met, I was taken by a fear that the bronzed warrior who mounted the platform was about to part my head from my body because I dared talk to the love of his life." More laughter. "We all heard about the reputation you earned during many years of combat, yet I never understood until I saw you standing there in person with your muscles bulging and your eyes projecting hostility. Now, I hope we can be proper friends." Again the smiles and laugher from the other men.

"I can't help the way I look, Gaius, but I never meant to give you the impression that I would harm you in any way. You are one of the most respected men in *Roma*."

"Thank you, Cos," Piso said sincerely. "These men are sources you should know, and they may prove useful to you in the future. I should mention that they traveled all the way from *Roma* to be here today."

Cos appraised the group more carefully. Piso was well groomed and handsome in features, although two of the others were more typical of politicians in any era. They wore the robes of power easily, yet there was a hint of falsity about them, the smiles coming a bit too readily. *Roma's* system of elections was lubricated by money, especially during the Imperial period.

Piso slapped one on the back as he came forward. "I want you to know my friend, *Quintus Fabius Ambustus*, who is currently serving as *Praetor*, a *magistratus curulis*." Cos nodded his approval and gave the required smile, taking the man more seriously. He was certainly one of the most powerful men serving and could influence or order changes as he saw fit.

"I've heard much about you, Cosimus," Quintus remarked. "It's said that you have more personal fighting experience than any previous *legatus*. We will expect great things from you."

"You have heard then, that I have retired and live in this small city by choice, have you not?" Cos asked.

"A true fighting man is never retired, as you say, is he?" was the answer. A creeping suspicion came over Cos that this was not just a friendly meeting. There was a plan and an expected outcome. Whatever they wanted from him was something they had to coax him into.

Piso interrupted, "And this next official is none other than *Lucius Tettius Julianus,* however don't let his youth make you think less of him because he is enamored with you and your reputation. He is currently a *tribunus militum,* but we expect him to become a *legatus* soon."

Lucius stepped forward and beamed a smile, "When you return to duty, I will request to serve under you."

"Sorry, Lucius, to disappoint, but I am retired because I grew tired of killing my fellow man," Cos responded. Lucius' face fell a bit, and he looked at the others in some disbelief.

"And the last is someone I suspect you have heard about. He is a close friend of our Emperor and has his ear. *Asconius Quintus Pedianus,*" Piso proudly announced. Indeed, Cos had heard about *Asconius* though not in this lifetime, only in the other. *Asconius* was a noted Roman historian who had lived to be an old man. To see him in his prime was indeed an honor.

"I am most pleased to meet you, *Asconius,*" Cos said earnestly, while wondering why, why indeed, these men had traveled so far just to have a meeting with a retired *legatus*.

There was a noise causing the group to turn just in time to see Piso's elegant wife, Livia Orestilla, sweeping through the opening. She was thin, lavishly decorated with jewelry, and Cos noted her elaborately braided hairstyle which was very similar to the one on Alia. He could feel Alia take a step backwards as if in fear of this wealthy and famous woman coming toward her.

"And I understand that you are called Alia. What a pretty name, and it suits your beautiful face," she said. Cos was impressed. A scattering of choice words and Alia was completely in her grasp. He noted the flushing of Alia's face, though she remained steady and didn't look away.

"I never dreamed you would be so gloriously radiant," Alia said, smiling broadly in relief that she would be accepted so easily.

"At my age, it's all an illusion, my dear Alia. Perhaps, when I was as young as you, I had the gift of looking like some sort of delectable fruit as you certainly do. I want to welcome you to our home, and I want to steal you away from these men who only will talk of empire and business anyway. Come see our home." She softly guided Alia out without a glance backward from either of them.

"Alia was right about Livia," Cos said. "She is a remarkable beauty. I can see why it hurt so much to lose her, even for a moment."

Piso's face turned dark, recalling a horrible time that he would have preferred never to discuss again. "Yes, eventually I got her back, and here we are. By the way, I owe that to Claudius, a fine man. In fact, all of us standing here owe our positions to Claudius. Even you, Cosimus. He personally appointed you to be *legatus,* and it was the first time an elevation from rank was made in the history of *Roma*. Do you realize that all positions of *legatus* are earned by progression of elected office? You skipped all that. It was Claudius who decided that, against a lot of complaints from others who thought they deserved your position more than you did. Of course, he was right because you have proved yourself over and over."

"It was a small emergency, Gaius, because *Aulus Plautius* was moved from *legatus* of the *XX Valeria Victrix* to be in charge of all three legions invading Britannia from Gaul. There was a vacancy which needed to be filled rapidly. I was at hand."

Quintus spoke up, joining the discussion. "At the time, I was one of those in line for *legatus*. We tried to find your family history, with no success. You are not of the senatorial class, that is for sure." Quintus had taken a slightly confrontational tone and was evidently waiting for an explanation.

"I was legally adopted by *Aulus Plautius,* the current Governor of Britannia, and, for sure, I am now of senatorial class. I have already been *legatus*, so any discussion of that is water under the bridge," Cos explained.

"No need for ruffled feathers, my friends. We are here to welcome Cos to this town, not discuss ancient politics," Piso stated firmly. The discussion was ended on that topic. "There is one subject more that we need to discuss before the women return," Piso said, looking at each guest in turn. This was to be a command from *Consul* Piso, rather than a request from a friend.

"You have all seen Alia, the rather sumptuous woman at Cosimo's right hand. She and he intend to marry, and they need our help to make it legal." He stopped to hear complaints or objections. There were none, and the group remained attentive. "Tonight, she is to be adopted by me and Livia, and we will host the ceremony right here in our home. I will have the pleasure of giving the bride to Cosimus. You three are here to sign the necessary documents to make that legal. Are there any objections?"

"Gaius, I don't know what to say," Cos stuttered. There were few moments in his life which had come to him so quickly and so unexpectedly.

"No thanks necessary, Cosimus," Piso said softly, laying his hand on Cos' shoulder. "I understand that you purchased a fine home and have started some businesses, and there is no need for money in your life, but a wife is more important than wealth, and I should know that more than anyone. You have earned the privilege of a softer life than you once had. It is my want to see that the second half of your life is better than the first."

Chapter 17

A House Becomes a Home

Happy the man, and happy he alone, he who can call today his own: he who, secure within, can say, tomorrow do thy worst, for I have lived today. Be fair or foul or rain or shine, the joys I have possessed, in spite of fate, are mine. Not Heaven itself upon the past has power, but what has been, has been, and I have had my hour.

Horace (65 BC to 8 BC)

To have a great man for an intimate friend seems pleasant to those who have never tried it; those who have, fear it.

[Dulcis inexpertis cultura potentis amici; Expertus metuit.]

Horace (65 BC to 8 BC)

*T*he evening was approaching, the rim of the sun still showing over the Bay of Napoli as the carriage turned onto the last street, their street, their home nearly in view. It had been almost constant body contact between them since the ceremony, given in one of the palatial rooms of the villa of Piso. Since then, Cos could hardly remember words being spoken to him which did not come out of the mouth of Alia.

She was more than radiant at the wedding ceremony, seeming to be floating effortlessly across the tile toward him. Livia had dressed her in gleaming white, her face and hands the only parts of her body visible, yet what a moment when he first saw that face, isolated by white, the pink glow of her cheeks enhanced by the intensity of her blue eyes which never left his. Only a higher being could look like she did that moment, and all at once he began to believe the stories of a goddess leaving her perch above to mingle with mere men.

"Wasn't it nice of them to let us stay the night?" Alia said, speaking for the first time since leaving the villa. Indeed, what a night. The room selected for them by the owners had a commanding view of the sea on one side, the other of the inner garden, the second *peristylum*. This room was lavished with gold on the walls in spots where the paintings suggested there should be glitter. Even the ceiling, the recessed panels above their heads, were hand painted with scenes of nature. Absolutely the finest room Cos had ever seen with his own eyes.

"Yes, they have given us each other and removed any obstacle to our happiness. I have never known such generosity nor people who were so gracious and refined."

Alia held up her left hand, letting her ring of marriage shine in the receding light. It was identical, except for size, to the one Cos now wore, both gifts from Piso and Livia during the wedding. Alia still wore the matching gold earrings, necklace and bracelets given to her to keep as a wedding present, and her silk *tunic* was at last covered by a *stola*, a fabulous one, given to her by Livia as a personal gift after the wedding.

"Cos, I am so happy now. It's like life is a dream, only I fear I will awaken to find something else instead. I would have been afraid to sleep last night, but I had you beside me, and I know nothing ever can harm me again."

"Not if I can help it."

Alia pulled his face toward her, and her look became serious. "Just how many children should we have?"

"How many do you want to have?"

"All that I can. Is that all right with you?"

"Yes and no. I am selfish, and I have a problem with your perfect body being burdened by a child inside you. My child."

"I would guess that has already happened. Better enjoy me while you can."

Cos sighed deeply and with satisfaction. This new life was to be better than anything he could have imagined. He now had everything a man could hope to have in life, nothing at all was lacking. Leaning forward, he found her waiting lips.

The carriage stopped moving, and Cos looked around. They were home.

After only two days, life was very different for everyone. The dynamics had changed, tilting toward Alia who was now in a different category and had quickly assumed more responsibility as the wife of the *dominus*, not just another servant. They were all still friends, of course, though Alia had grown in stature in everyone's eyes, including her own. The impact was felt most by Linza, who grudgingly relinquished any competition for the attention and affection of Cos. Initially, the realization that Alia had won the competition and was in possession of Cos forever caused endless tears and sorrowful faces, although at last, she realized her dream was over forever, understanding that her future belonged to Maccus, who grew in importance in her eyes.

Her new status didn't prevent Alia from being part of any domestic chores. One morning, she appeared in the culina ready for work, dressed in a simple rough tunic and barefoot. *Màthair* turned toward her surprised, her mouth open in wonder. "You are up early, Alia," she said.

"Ready to help," Alia noted, smiling at her. "Nothing has changed *Màthair*. There is work to be done, and I am here to do my share."

"And your hair, my dear. What happened to it?"

"I took it down. Cos likes it long anyway." As she turned, her glossy hair flowed behind her, catching the morning sun and casting a warm glow into the small room.

"And are you happy now and want for nothing?" *Màthair* asked.

"Only a healthy child," she grinned, giving away her secret.

"My, that is wonderful news, and it's also what I've been waiting for."

"Do you think Linza will produce a child soon?" Alia asked. After all, she and Maccus had been making so much noise that Cos requested that they take one of the rooms near the *atrium* so the rest of the house could sleep.

"Seems likely. She has been gaining weight lately, however I've heard nothing."

At breakfast, Cos was more relaxed than ever, joking with the rest and still flirting with his new wife. He was sliding into a comfortable life, one he had certainly earned. There was love, enough money, health, and he was surrounded by friends, really family, however dissimilar their origins.

"Cos?" *Màthair* called, waiting for his eyes to return to hers. When he was looking at her, she continued, "Alia told me that Vesuvius will arise and destroy everything. Is that true?"

Cos lost his smile and looked around. The truth had to be told. After all, it was their future also. "Yes, it's true. I told her that, and it will happen."

"How did you come to understand that will happen?" she asked.

Cos hesitated again, unwilling to tell the truth, because he wouldn't expect anyone other than Alia to keep his huge secret to themselves.

"Have you, or anyone at this table ever known me to not tell the truth?"

There were shakes of heads all around the table.

"It will happen one month after Titus becomes emperor. Many will die. If you are still living here, you must flee before it happens, otherwise you will die with the rest."

"Can you really see the future, Cos?" Maccus asked. "I have wondered that for a long time."

"I don't know what will happen to anyone at this table, even myself. So, no, I can't tell the future, yet I do know some things."

"Titus?" Maccus repeated the name. "Is he the same one as the child of *Legate* Vespasian?"

"Indeed the same." Cos answered.

"Him?…that fat little spoiled kid will become emperor?" Maccus continued, laughing at the idea.

"Are you doubting me?" Cos asked, wishing that he had not given that particular answer.

"Well, it does seem improbable."

It was before noon when the messenger came. From his chair in the *tablinum*, Cos could see the silhouette of a man in armor standing in the doorway and handing Maccus a scroll. His attention perked up, wondering why an official document found its way to his little corner of the world and what it could mean.

"Message for you, *Dominus*," Maccus said, handing him the scroll and lingering until it was read, in case there was any important news affecting him as well. Maccus craned his neck, but it was of no use anyway because his Latin reading skills were still marginal.

"It states that our friend Piso is paying a visit here this afternoon. Go and get the women because they need to get ready for him," Cos commented. He had been thinking that the generosity of Piso could have a cost, a payment due, and this might indeed be the day it happens. He put aside the scroll as the three women came in.

"We are about to have an important visitor, and you have only two hours to ready yourselves," he announced. They looked at each other in horror. Only two hours and so much to be done. They left in a hurry without another word, and in the distance, Cos could hear their high-pitched excited voices.

"For several days after the wedding, I thought of nothing other than Alia, although in the past week, I have begun to think more clearly. The entire process was well worked out to the last detail. Someone had put in a great deal of planning to have it happen so smoothly. There must have been a reason, and I fear we are about to find out what I owe in return."

"Could it be so bad?" Maccus wondered. "They could offer you another *legion* to command. What else is there?"

"There is a lot. Romans are always conspiring about something. One thing you must know is that, in our present system, there are those who always want more power at the expense of those who currently have power. You are on one side or the other. No one is neutral. At one time, before the Caesars, there was a republic, and in the republic, power was given to those who got the most votes. Today, power is a prize to be seized."

"They wouldn't ask you to kill someone, would they?" Maccus asked.

"The previous Emperor, Caligula, was killed by the *Praetorian* Guard. That will happen again many times in the future. However, not this time because the Guard put Claudius in power. Someone else conspires against Claudius."

"Do you know what will happen, Dominus?"

"If I did, I couldn't change it. History is history."

"I'm confused," Maccus admitted.

"Stay that way, it's often better to not know some things."

In exactly two hours, Piso arrived, surprisingly, on foot, accompanied by six heavily armed men who waited outside at Piso's direction. Cos met him at the door and escorted him inside. He could see Piso looking over the villa, appraising every feature, as though he was about to make an offer to purchase.

"Nice home you have, Cos, one of the better ones in Herculaneum."

"Except yours, Gaius. No home could ever match that one."

Piso laughed, "No, my friend, that is indeed not a home. It acts as a residence for scholars and poets who roam its corridors when we are not there. Also, it's not my handiwork that built it. I only inherited it by marriage, so don't think less of me for possessing it during my lifetime."

They sat in the *tablinum*, across from each other. Cos could see that Piso was working up to whatever request he was about to make.

"Cos, there is something I need to present to you, and you should not fear that there is anything objectionable about it. Look on it as an opportunity." He cleared his throat and looked around while thinking.

"Is your marriage a happy one, Cos?" he asked.

"Very. Thanks so much for everything you have done for me and Alia."

"You both are very lucky to have each other. It was our pleasure to help it happen, and I will recall that happy day for the rest of my life." With that formality out of the way, he directed his attention to the matter at hand. "You are unique, Cosimus, in so many ways. After achieving high office by hard work, you want nothing in return, no power or money. You are the most pure Roman I have met in my entire life…no desire of further position and satisfied with what you have at present. I envy the simplicity of your life. However, there are things you can do for Roma and for Claudius in particular. You will not have to fight in wars this time, and you will become celebrated as well as rich. I am here to offer you a posting to a most coveted position…*Prefect*, in command of the *Praetorian* Guard."

Cos didn't even blink. He expected something like that. "Why me, Gaius?" he asked.

"Because you are uncorrupted and, we believe, incorruptible. Claudius feels that he can trust you completely because you want nothing. As I discovered, you didn't even allow your *legion* to take slaves nor steal the conquered enemy's women or possessions."

"I have a strong sense of what is right and wrong," Cos admitted. "In taking your offer, I would be in the thick of corruption and greed as well as endless plots against somebody."

"Exactly. That is why Claudius asked for you."

"Forgive me, Gaius, but I was in charge of fighting men, not a bunch of pampered sons of senators and retired legionnaires. I would want men who could take direction and fight as needed. I don't believe the *Praetorian* Guard could actually defend *Roma*."

"No, they could not nor are they much of a threat to Roma as they are. They are mostly policemen and, therefore, are decoration, not for fighting an invading enemy. A strong man such as you could forge them into more than they are now, and Claudius could be sure that they would not turn on him with you in charge."

"I am very happy here with my wife. You may not know this, but I have not been in Roma since I was very young. As a member of a fighting *legion*, I was never allowed to return. It would all be new to me, and I don't know anyone there. Forcing Alia to leave her home for a new adventure would be very difficult."

"First of all, I have a very large home just outside of Roma, and you and Alia are welcome to live there with us for as long as you want. I will be glad to take care of this villa while you are away and see to the needs of your current family. You see, everything will be taken care of."

"You have been hard at work figuring all this out. My appreciation to you, Gaius. And given all you have done for me, I find it hard to refuse you. Still, I have some things to tell you that you do not know."

Piso leaned back in his chair to hear this new information, surprised by the resistance Cos was showing to the lucrative appointment, more certain than ever that Cos was the right man for the job.

"I want to emphasize that I have no connection to anyone in *Roma*, no direct knowledge of plots, and I am not a conspirator in any way. I believe the threat to Claudius will not come from the *Praetorians* this time, it will arise close to him…from a member of his own family. I don't want to accuse anyone in particular, however it is logical to fear those who want to inherit the most powerful position in the world. Do you understand what I am suggesting?"

"I do, but speaking of this aloud will get you into scalding water."

"Here is my reason for being hesitant to take this position… my being there won't change anything."

Piso was quiet for a moment, not looking away from his face while turning over in his mind all the possibilities.

"You are telling me that Claudius will be assassinated by a member of his family, and there is nothing we can do to stop it? How can you know this?"

"Perhaps I don't know, perhaps it was just a memory of a dream. You recall the fable about the Parcae, the Three Fates? They decide a person's destiny and the time of death, and nothing changes their decision."

"Cos, there was something said about you that I once overheard. They suspected that you can tell the future because you seem to know things before they happen."

"Sure, it's called *intuito* or intuition, and most generals acquire that ability over time."

"Since we are friends, Cos, can you tell me my fate?" Piso asked.

"Even if I knew, it wouldn't change anything, and a person should not know their own destiny."

"Then you do know," Piso stated, his eyes fixed on Cos, trying to pull information from him, even a small fragment of the future. After a long pause, he said, "I'm afraid that your fate is to travel *Roma* and meet with Claudius or his close advisors," Piso said evenly. "Even if you don't want the post, you are summoned, and it would be very unwise to not obey. Perhaps you can tell this story to Claudius and see if he agrees that it would be better not to know the manner of his own death."

Cos realized that he had made a mistake, a big one, letting Piso believe that he knew the future. He was trapped and always had been. It wasn't Piso making the decisions, it was higher up, much higher up. He had been selected before the wedding, long before. This was an offer which could not be refused.

"When am I expected? Cos asked.

"As soon as my little ship sails and arrives. Your meeting will be in two days. Tonight, ready yourself for departure at sunrise. I am going with you, though I won't be there for your interview, and you may stay at my home while there. The question is…will you go?" Piso asked with furrowed brow, knowing the answer could not be no.

Erin Silversmith, the copyright holder of this work, hereby publishes it under the following license: Permission is granted to copy, distribute and/or modify this document under the terms of the GNU Free Documentation License

Chapter 18

A Trip to Roma

The dawn was only a glimmer of light as Cos prepared to leave. Alia was there beside him and tried to be in physical contact as much as she could. Every time Cos looked at her, he could see a sorrowful and fearful face. He had tried to explain the best he could how impossible it was not to obey a request directly from the Emperor, especially the one who had trusted him enough to lead a *legion*. It was a debt he had to pay. However, he had formulated a path of resistance allowing an escape back to his home and his wife…hopefully. He knew exactly what was to happen in the future, and he didn't want any part in it. Claudius had only two years of life left, and he was destined to be poisoned by his fourth wife, Agrippina the Younger, as her name will be recorded by history. Cos recalled stories about her, written contemporaneously by Roman historians. She was married twice before her marriage to Claudius and suspected of poisoning her second husband. In addition, she had many affairs and was involved in another troubling conspiracy to murder her own brother, Caligula, for which she was exiled for a time. Cos knew that by now, Agrippina was not about to tolerate anyone who could stand against her determination to make her son by another marriage, the young boy going by the name of Nero, the Emperor of *Roma*.

What Cos most wanted at this stage of his life was to live comfortably in the arms of Alia and forget the troubles of *Roma*. He stopped packing and turned toward her, taking her in his arms and smothering her with kisses. "I wish that you could go also," he whispered into her ear.

"And why can't I?" she asked, also whispering, her lips touching his ear, her warm breath creating a delightful sensation.

"I don't know for sure, though Piso said something about a 'small ship.' Anyway, *Roma* is a big place, and you would just be left at another one of Piso's homes. So the long journey over the sea would be for nothing. You are safer here."

"I will be here for you when you return. Promise that nothing will happen to you…promise me," Alia pleaded.

"I have no reason to think that I will be in danger. I'll be back, but I don't know how many days it will take."

Maccus and Linza appeared, both looking rumpled and sleepy. Cos motioned for Macccus to come to him. "I want to remind you that you are in charge of this home and the safety of everyone in it. You understand, don't you?"

"I do, *Dominus*. They will be safe with me, and I will stay here the entire time you are gone. Nevertheless, I would rather be with you."

"I have signed the papers. As of yesterday, you own the vineyards and the wine store. You have to oversee them and keep up with your business. If I am gone a long time, you will be able to make enough money to keep up this home and support the women until I return. I am depending on you."

"Thank you, *Dominus*. I won't let you down."

Cos patted Maccus on the shoulder and looked into his eyes. It would be a different trip, one taken without the dependable man he had so grown accustomed to having beside him. Unfortunately, there was no choice.

Cos stood at the door ready to leave, taking one last look at his family. They looked so small and helpless without him, and he wanted to stay with them more than anything he had ever desired previously. He bent over for one last kiss from Alia, her tears also wetting his face. Then he was gone.

Cos took long strides while carrying a heavy bundle containing his resplendent armor, necessary and required for an appearance before the Emperor. He was wearing a simple long sleeved tunic over long pants. There was no reason to wear something which would pull him to the bottom should the boat flounder. He well understood that a sea voyage, even hugging the coast of *Italia*, had its risks and that boat travel had a minimal margin of safety. Ahead, rocking at the wharf was a small ship bristling with activity, its crew scurrying about, getting ready to sail with the tide.

"*Salve*, Cosimus," a voice called from the pier. It was Piso, waving for Cos to come his way. Drawing nearer, Cos was surprised to see Piso dressed as a simple deck hand in coarse ragged clothing.

"I would have never guessed, Piso." Cos said dryly, looking him over from head to toe.

"Neither would any pirate who stops this vessel. It's wiser to be anonymous at times. You, on the other hand, would pass for a gladiator; in fact, I think you are one," he laughed aloud at his own humor.

"Yes, and I would accept that description with honor. Gladiators, at least, are simple, honest people who live and die by the sword. There is no treachery, scheming, or pretension among them, unlike most of the political class. You, my new friend, are a notable exception, and I don't mean to offend you in any way."

"What you say is, unfortunately, true, and I take no offense. I try to do my part to spread knowledge and enlightenment, and I take no part in duplicity. You are heading into a sticky situation, Cos. Be most careful with your choice of words while there."

Cos studied Piso's face while he turned over in his mind what he could say. He knew what was going to happen to Claudius and also what fate would befall Piso. Nothing he could say would change anything because he was from a time when all those events had long since happened. It was history, immutable, unchangeable, written in stone history. Even his own fate was history, and thankfully, he didn't know what it was. He was living moment by moment as a person should live anyway, regardless of fate. The present counts for more than the future. Live for the future and you lose the present. Alia flickered into his vision as he stared into the distance. She was in his arms again, his hands pressing into her soft flesh, the memory of her aroma wafting into his conscious mind. He had to refocus on the present, the ship, the meeting in *Roma*. Alia would be there when he returned, and he would never leave her side again.

The ship was new, the wood still harboring a tint of red and exuding the odor of fresh cut timber. Even the ropes and rigging were bright and strong. As Cos looked around, he suddenly realized that this boat was lateen rigged, not square rigged as most Roman boats of the period were thought to have been. This rig allowed the sail to be carried more amidship, increasing the ability to move forward into a headwind. Impressive. The crew numbered eight and obviously knew their tasks because the little ship moved briskly northward, heeled over by a strong offshore breeze. In the distance, and sliding ever southward, was the peak of Vesuvius, standing guard over its captive cities nesting along the western slopes.

"We will shortly pass the harbor at *Misenum*, then the ship will head out into the sea," Piso informed him, speaking loudly above the roar of the wind. He pointed to the land's end where they could see the tops of several masts.

"There is Vesuvius, looking down at all of us mortal men," Cos observed, shielding his eyes with one hand.

"A great place to grow grapes, the best in *Italia*," Piso commented.

"Until it explodes a few years from now."

"What do you mean?" Piso asked, looking directly at him instead of the view.

"It's just the two of us here, so I don't mind telling you a few things of importance. You may not believe me, but I need to tell someone," Cos said close to Piso's ear. You see that mountain as nothing more than a lovely piece of rock, covered by delicious grapes, however I see it as a sleeping monster which will awaken and blow rock and hot ash into the sky, and as it falls to earth, it will cover Pompeii and our little city of Herculaneum, smothering the cities and all who remain in them. They will sleep under rock for one thousand seven hundred years and, even then, will never be fully uncovered."

Piso looked at him with interest, not understanding why Cos would say such nonsense to him. Was he jesting or did he believe it, and if he did, where did he hear such a thing? "Cos, this is your idea of humor? How can you say this will happen?"

"Not to worry, my friend, you will not be here when it happens, and I plan to leave well before that time, if I'm still alive, that is."

"I have heard the rumors, Cosimus," Piso said. "There are those who speak your name with a bit of fear. You know the future, they whisper. Tell me…is it so?"

"In truth, Gaius, I do know many things which will happen. Unfortunately, knowing something does not give me the power to change anything. And there is the fact that on most things, I don't know anything at all about what will happen. Take the famous Alexander of Macedonia. You know about his life, what happened and when, and how he died. Nevertheless, you know nothing about the men who served with him. If you were to somehow be able to go back and stand with Alexander, you could help him occasionally yet still be ignorant of most things."

"You are telling me that you are from the future?" Piso asked, his voice rising.

"And how could that be possible?" Cos replied, smiling disarmingly at him.

"It's not possible…is it?"

"Of course not. Vesuvius will still blow twenty-seven years from now. You have my word that it will happen."

After that exchange, Piso changed a bit. He was polite and remained friendly, no longer fully understanding their relationship. Just who was this man called Cosimus, journeying the sea with him, he wondered to himself. How could any man know the future with so much certainty? Perhaps the Roman gods were indeed real, and one of them chose to speak to Cos, giving him insight as to the fate of man.

The evening light was dimming when the port of *Ostia* came into view. Overall, it had been a good trip, though not smooth, nor was there any particular excitement or danger. Just as Cos was wondering what the next step in this process was, he heard Piso calling his name.

"Cos, as soon as we dock, gather your things because I expect a carriage will be there for us," he said, resuming his previous demeanor.

"Say, Gaius, I hope you are not offended by anything I have said," Cos asked.

"Confused, not angry. You are an interesting man, Cosimus. I thought I understood you, however I no longer know what to think."

"Think this, Gaius. I consider you a friend, and I have great respect for you. You are the only one I would trust completely which is why I opened up to you. Consider this gift of mine to see the future as my reward for a hard life of slaying the enemies of *Roma* and nothing sinister."

"I can do that, and having a friend like you is more valuable than all the money in the world. Thank you for being patient with me." They embraced briefly as a line was tossed to dock workers waiting for the ship to come into range.

The trip from Piso's villa on the north of Roma was only three *mille,* but progress was slow because of the congestion of other travelers and commercial wagons as well as frequent mounted legionnaires. Traveling in a carriage over cobblestone pavers while dressed in metal armor was not the most pleasant way to travel. Cos would have preferred to ride on horseback, though Piso wouldn't think of it. They had to stage a grand arrival for such an auspicious meeting. Each time the carriage swayed, Cos' leg slammed into the side of the seat, and he gritted his teeth, trying to remain calm. Piso didn't know exactly who Cos was to meet when he arrived at the Emperor's palace on Palatine Hill, only whoever it was reported directly to Claudius.

Seeing *Roma* in its prime was a shattering experience. Most of the city was covered in *insula*, not grand temples or magnificent public works. The apartment buildings, rows of them, streets of them, all looked the same. Shops were on the street level, the living quarters above. And the streets were narrow and somehow foreboding. At nighttime, there would be no lights of any kind to assist anyone trying to walk very far. The population was obviously massive, and the city overcrowded. By the time they approached the area of the Forum, surrounded by shining white buildings supported by soaring columns, Cos had experienced enough of the grand city and was more than anxious to return to his simple home.

The small two-wheeled carriage transporting Cos bore imperial markings, its driver in armor typical of the *Numerus Batavorum,* the German bodyguards who guarded the Emperor, instead of the *Praetorians.* Cos had heard of them but never previously encountered one.

"What tribe do you come from?" Cos asked the driver who, up to this point, had been silent.

"*Frisii,*"was the answer. This was a tribe of northern *Germania*, who lived near Alia's tribe.

"I see. And how long have you been in *Roma*?"

"Three years," was the clipped response. Cos heard enough to recognize the same accented Latin that Alia spoke, though hers was rapidly diminishing.

"And do you desire to return home?" Cos asked.

"This is my home." So these men had no more thoughts of motherland, Cos realized. They were now Roman and intended to remain in *Roma*.

The carriage wound up the Palatine hill headed to the only structure there completely off limits to the Roman population, the home of the Emperor, the *Domus Augusti,* named for its builder and original occupant, Caesar Augustus. It was said that the home was built over the original palace of Romulus, the first King of

Roma, nearly five hundred years BC. It was a building in nearly total collapse by the twenty-first century, with only a small fragment of decorated walls and ceilings remaining. Cos had seen it in his youth, never dreaming that some day he would see it in its majesty.

The carriage abruptly stopped, and the driver turned to look at Cos, giving him a mental message that the trip was over. He dismounted and straightened his armor and sword. Waiting at the entrance were twelve *Praetorians,* six on each side, all watching him closely. They carried shields as well as long spears. Given their age, Cos guessed that all had been *centurions* at some point in their previous duties.

Instead of a tight row, and in presentation attitude, they were loosely standing on either side of the entrance. Two were conversing while eyeing Cos as he made his way toward them. When he neared the closed entrance, he stopped and looked back and forth at the guard.

"Who is in charge here?" he barked sharply. From the lack of response, he assumed that no higher officer was present.

"You are a sloppy bunch," he exploded. "I'm ashamed to call you fellow legionnaires. Get into position and stay there," he yelled. After a shocked look, they fell into order, facing forward rigidly, not daring to look directly at this unfamiliar superior officer who had come out of nowhere.

"Unless you would enjoy running the perimeter of *Roma* in your armor, I suggest that you look alert and disciplined when I come out of this door," he said menacingly. It was obviously true that this *legate* meant what he threatened.

Cos resumed walking toward the entry door which was snapped open by guards on either side, allowing Cos to get his first glimpse of the home of Claudius, and his predatory, scheming fourth wife, Agrippina the younger.

Chapter 19

Agrippa

---

*An honorable death is better than a
dishonorable life.
[Honesta mors turpi vita potior.]*

Tacitus (56 AD to 111 AD)

Cos was shown into an opulent room by a young *tribune*. Turning the corner, he observed that the room was rectangular, containing a center table flanked by two chairs, one on each end. There was a curtained opening along one of the longer walls, closed at present. A dominant red had been chosen as the principle hue, the walls painted in many shades of subtle color depicting a temple rising into the heavens. The effect was to expand the volume of the room manyfold. Cos looked up and studied the arched ceiling which was broken into rectangles each containing a masterpiece of some epic conquest back in history.

"I see you haven't changed much," the voice behind him said. Cos turned and briefly studied the face of the man coming toward him before realizing that he knew this man very well indeed.

"Agrippa!" he exclaimed and moved forward to embrace this visitor from the past. "It's been many years since I've seen you," he said. "And you look very comfortable in a toga instead of a breast shield over mail."

"I've kept up with you and your exploits, Cos. Most impressive for a man who just walked out of the desert that night. You achieved a rank of *legatus* before I did, and I had served longer than you if I recall correctly."

"The right man at the right time. I was lucky. What are you doing in the *Domus Augusti*, or can I ask that?"

"I'm interviewing you, Cos. I am serving currently as *Praefectus Urbanus*. In other words, I am in charge of *Roma* at the moment. Since I knew you long ago, I was chosen as someone who could ask difficult questions without getting killed."

"No danger of that, my friend. I am most happy to see you again."

"Then, seat yourself, and let me quiz you a bit," Agrippa requested. Cos sat down in the closest chair and pulled it up to the table. He noticed that before Agrippa sat, his eyes flicked for an instant toward the curtain. It was but a brief look, and Cos could not discern if Agrippa was giving notice that someone was behind the curtain listening to the conversation or was it nothing more than an accidental glance. The more Cos thought it over, the more convinced he was that their conversation was not private.

"You gave honor to *Roma* in your service as *legatus* of the XX. Your men thought well of you and, in fact, still do. You have achieved unique distinction in that fewer of your men were lost in combat than any other *legion* serving in *Britannia*. You are known to be fair to your troops and fair to the conquered. A notable achievement." He paused and looked up from his notes as if studying Cos closely.

"It is my understanding that you seek no higher office and consider yourself retired from duty and civic life," Agrippa summarized. His eyes flicked again at the curtain, his face showing no change. Cos was certain that Agrippa was sending a message to him to be very careful in his responses.

"Yes, my goal was to enjoy myself and my new wife for as long as life lasts for me. I tried to be a good soldier, however I am not endowed with the gifts needed for a political life."

"You are being considered for appointment to a lofty position and one, I might add, that brings a considerable salary, far more than a *legatus* makes, at least an honest one such as you. There are no politics in this appointment, and it will mean being in charge of the men who guard *Roma* itself. A great responsibility."

"And, just what is the post you refer to?" Cos asked, already knowing the answer.

"*Praefectus Praetorio*. You would command the *Praetorian* Guard. There are currently fifteen *cohorts* of men, not including additional equestrian units, stationed nearby, larger than the *Legion XX* you commanded."

"Why me? Why was I chosen over, for instance, you?" Cos asked.

"As for me, I am destined for a different path, possibly *consul* next year. All I have to do is win the election," Agrippa laughed softly at the humor of not being elected. It was obviously a sure thing. "As for the choice of you, Cosimus," he continued, "you are thought to be incorruptible, fierce and honest. All desirable traits for leading a force as sensitive as the *Praetorian* Guard."

"I recall Emperor Claudius was saved by the *Praetorians*, and I also recall that they murdered Caligula. It's a bad trend to move from protection to choosing the next emperor themselves. I fear that we have not seen the last of that exercise of power."

"And since you want nothing, and fear nothing, you are an excellent choice. You come highly recommended." With that said, Agrippa again indicated the curtain with his eyes. Claudius must be behind the curtain, listening to the interview himself, Cos reasoned.

"I am honored by the offer, Agrippa, and I owe much to Emperor Claudius for allowing me the opportunity to lead one of his legions. He is a great ruler, the best since Augustus, and I would love to serve him again. Still, I have a request to make before I give my answer, and I think it is a request which will add to the safety of *Roma* and all who reside in it, especially the Emperor himself."

Agrippa put down the paper he was holding and leaned back in his chair. Cos could tell by the expression on his face that he was not happy about Cos giving conditions. In fact, it could be a dangerous request for both of them since Agrippa had undoubtedly endorsed the appointment of a man he had known so long and so well.

"And?" he inquired.

"I reprimanded a group of *Praetorians* when I arrived. They were sloppy and undisciplined. Given that the Guard has life pretty easy and are paid higher than the other *legionaries*, we should demand more of them. I know that many are experienced soldiers and have retired from the fighting units, but I don't believe they could repel an enemy fighting force. It seems to me that rotation of real fighting units into *Roma* would be an insurance against softness as well as duplicity."

Agrippa sighed and nodded, indicating that he heard though disagreed. He cleared his throat, choosing the right words before responding. "Cosimus, you have to understand that the *Praetorians* are themselves feared by the citizens of *Roma*. The *legions* are kept out of *Italia* because they represent an even more serious threat. A *legion* answers to one man only, their *legatus*. Julius Caesar was the first to break the law concerning crossing the Rubicon with his *legions*, and he was slain, partially because of that act. No one wants a hardened, fighting *legion* in *Roma*. We need a police force here, not an army."

"If I am in charge, there will be no danger. They will do exactly what I say. They will obey every command down to the last man. I swear to you that I mean what I say."

"I know you do. What happens if we start this new precedent, and you retire or if something else happens to you? How do we control your army then?"

"Simple. Just choose another honest *prefect*."

"And you understand, don't you, that you are the single, only, *legate* ever chosen from the ranks. All the others were active politically. There are no candidates other than you who are not consumed by politics and other alliances. Many would aspire to being emperor themselves, and others can be bought with money or reward of positions. It's by request that you are sitting here today. Accept this offer with no conditions." Agrippa put his palms down against the polished table and stared at Cos. There would be no conditions met, and it was out of Agrippa's control.

"I understand your position, Agrippa. Yes, I will accept this appointment as long as I can train and discipline this force as I feel appropriate, and that I will be able to reject or retire those men who are not fit or obedient."

"We would expect nothing less from you," Agrippa said, rising to his feet. "You will forgive me, but you should remain here while I report my findings and recommendations." With that, and a nod of respect toward Cos, Agrippa moved rapidly out and down the long hall.

Cos listened as Agrippa's footsteps faded into the distance. He looked around, staring at the closed curtain for a moment, tempted to part it and look into the adjoining room. Not a good option, he told himself. He started to drum his fingers on the polished wood table, lost in consideration about how his answers sounded. It was his plan to be rejected because someone, probably Claudius himself, would and should fear giving him that much power. After all, being completely in charge of over five thousand trained and equipped men would constitute the most powerful force in *Roma*. That is the very way empires have been taken over throughout time. Generals have to be loyal. His expectation was to be rejected because he sought to construct a force which could not easily be controlled or bought off by bribes.

Cos was suddenly alerted by a noise, and he instinctively turned toward the curtain, just as a slender hand parted it long enough for a female figure to emerge as if the curtain was giving birth to a new life. It was a woman, spectacularly attired in silks and jewelry, one with hard eyes and a chiseled face. One glance and he knew who it was. Agrippina the Younger was looking at him with amusement, comprehending that she was completely unexpected. Cos rose to his feet, not knowing what to say to her.

"You looked surprised to see me, *Legate*," she said. "I know about you. I know everything about you, and you will never be promoted to the position you seek."

"I didn't seek anything, Empress," Cos protested.

"There are others more suited than you. I have made my choice, and you will never get this position."

Cos didn't want to protest because her choice was fine by him as long as he was allowed to go home and get away from this hotbed of dishonesty.

Agrippina started walking toward the hall then half-turned back toward him, pausing before she spoke. "I understand that you know the future," she stated, not permitting a denial. "If that is true and you answer my questions, I may change my mind."

Before she voiced her questions, Cos' mind raced ahead with what he knew about her. She was going to murder poor Claudius with poison in two years and install her teenaged son, Nero, on the throne. What she didn't know was that Nero would grow quickly tired of her meddling and have her killed also, just seven years from this moment. Such was the way with absolute power, and it would happen again and again throughout Roman history until the Empire collapsed under its own weight. Cos remained silent, not wanting to answer anything she inquired about.

"Do you know my fate?" she asked bluntly.

"And if I did, would you really want to know the truth?" Cos responded.

"Of course," she said shrilly, giving him a menacing look of her power mixed with loathing of anyone beneath her station.

"If a person has only moments of life remaining, would it be better to let them live those moments peacefully in ignorance or spend that short time in dread of what is inevitable?" Cos asked.

"Answer my question, do you know my fate?"

"If you can answer mine, I will answer yours. Why do you want to know?"

"I want to know if all my plans will work. Is that too much to ask?" she huffed.

"Yes, your plans will work," Cos stated. "Does that change your mind?"

"No," she said, her back turned toward him as she walked away, trailing the ends of thin silk garments which softly fluttered as she disappeared around the corner.

Cos could feel beads of sweat collecting on his forehead. It was like an encounter with a cobra snake, a meeting you always felt fortunate to survive. He sat down heavily, wondering if he had handled it as well as he might. If he could change the future, the first thing he should have done was to sever her treacherous head from her body. Still, he was convinced that events recorded by history were unchangeable and unpreventable. Perhaps the legends from ancient Greek and Roman culture suggesting that gods determined what would happen were correct all along.

He heard footsteps coming his way and tensed, waiting for his next surprise. Agrippa rounded the corner and smiled at him, nodding for him to remain seated. He put his papers on the table and sat also, clearing his thoughts so that he could be perfectly clear. He no longer glanced at the curtain, so Cos assumed that Agrippina had been the only party in there.

"The Emperor is unchanged. He wants you to have this appointment." There was a long pause, and Agrippa's eyes never left his. There was more to his story.

"Unfortunately, his ear is also taken by others. Not mine, because I also favor you, and I know that you are the most trustworthy person in my entire life's experience. This will take some time to sort out. We will get in touch soon. That's all I can tell you at this time." He stopped talking, continuing to appraise Cos with narrowed eyes.

"Thank you, Agrippa, for your faith in me. I will do my duty as required, though I am also happy to return to my wife and to a smaller life of children and happiness instead of this eternal struggle to get ahead." He rose to his feet, as did Agrippa.

"If we don't cross paths again, my friend, I wish you well. Have a long and happy life," Agrippa said. They embraced, possibly for the last time, because neither felt that Cos would be selected for this controversial and important position. A politician would be selected, one that bent his views to match his sponsor, and Cos had a feeling he knew who the sponsor was.

Chapter 20

Empty Hands, Heavy Heart

Nothing is ours except time.

Seneca the Younger (4 BC to 65 AD)

*O*nce onboard, Cos paused to look past the wharf toward long rows of columned buildings crafted of stone and placed in a neat orderly line along a wide stone paved street, a wonderful civilization, full of feats of engineering and stunning architectural designs. However, the Roman government, so intelligently created, so full of checks and balances, and time-tested over a span of nearly five hundred years, was, now and for the remaining period of its existence, simply a dictatorship and nepotistic autocracy, pretending to have popular representation. There would be a few enlightened emperors in the four centuries to come, yet also several who used their power over their fellow men to satisfy some inner demon.

"Sorry you had to leave without discovering your future," Piso said softly. He was standing at Cos' shoulder and had come up from the hold unnoticed. Piso was a handsome, well-groomed man, who was also very educated in many things. He had chosen to become a true friend to Cos, for whatever reason, and they found much in common during their lengthy discussions.

"I always knew that I would never be chosen for that position," Cos said, without taking his eyes off of the receding view of *Ostia*, wondering if he would ever pass this way again.

"I hear that Claudius, himself, asked that you take this position," Piso recalled.

"I heard that also. However, his wife told me to my face that I would never be chosen, to use her words. Agrippina chose Sextus Burris long before I came to *Roma*."

"She is a hard woman. I wonder why in the world that Claudius would make such a choice," Piso mused.

"Politics, not female attractiveness. He will pay for that decision," Cos recalled. This time he turned to face Piso, watching his reaction.

"How do you mean that, Cos?"

"Agrippina wants her son, Nero, to take his place. Do you think she will wait on nature or take matters into her own hands?"

"You wouldn't ask that if you didn't know the answer," Piso observed. "So what is to happen?"

"Two more years, then we will all bow to the new Emperor Nero. You, in particular, won't like it."

"Are you serious, that spoiled brat?" Piso asked.

"Yes."

"Is there anything we can do about it?"

Cos put his hand on Piso's shoulder and leaned closer. "I already told you that I can't change history nor can I save you from yourself. You are a great Roman in every way, yet your love of *Roma* will someday be fatal."

"I have a very large collection of manuscripts, Cos, regarding the philosophy of life and how to live. One quote I recall, though, is actually very recent and from Seneca, whom I have met. He is about our age though wise beyond his years. '*Life without the courage to die is slavery.*' " he told me once. So my view is that I should always do the right thing, even if doing it brings my own death."

"And here is a quote from him that I remember, '*The greatest man is he who chooses right with the most invincible resolution.*' "

"Thank you, Cos, for that," Piso said, his eyes gleaming with moisture.

They stood together as the small ship got underway, slipping back south, down the coast, headed for home and, most of all, returning to their wives. Piso turned at last and headed back below decks, only Cos remained, still thinking about his past and *Roma's* future, while watching history slide by.

He was here, mind and body, part of the sea of humanity who lived their lives as they always had and always will. People in the future were no different than those he knew in the present. They all have the same virtues and the same flaws, the same wants, the same needs. It didn't matter in the least which century you lived. Life was more or less the same in a personal way. The woman you embraced and held softly in the night would feel the same in two thousand years, and you would love her just the same and yearn for her in the same way. Cos sighed. He wished the boat could move faster and faster, bringing the trip to a close all that much sooner. Alia waited for him, and he could almost taste her lips and feel her hot breath on his cheek.

In the shadow of Vesuvius once more, the little ship came around with the wind and stood upright, the offshore breeze popping the sail full in a forceful way, nearly lifting the boat as the sound of water being parted by the prow increased. The docks were in sight now, and Cos could just make out a small party ready to assist in landing, standing in small groups, all looking toward him.

"Did you manage to purchase a gift for your bride?" Piso asked, smiling broadly.

Cos reached inside his tunic and brought out his little surprise tightly clutched in his hand which opened revealing a small gold ring, the stone setting elaborately carved. Piso carefully picked it up and held it up in the fading light, turning it over and over. "Indeed a prize. That is a *Janus* captured in stone and very well done. A good choice," he said handing it back.

"It's sort of me I thought when I saw it. You know the legend… one face looks to the past, the other to the future. I expect Alia will laugh when she sees it and will enjoy the humor every time she looks at her hand."

The ship bumped against the dock, and the crew started rapidly putting the boat's gear away for the night, amid shouting and calling back and forth from the dock and the deck.

"Time to go home," Piso said. "Need any assistance with your gear?"

"It's only a *mille* or so. I will enjoy the walk, but thanks. And thank you for your hospitality this entire week. Someday I will return the favor," Cos said. Mentally, he wanted to extend his hand for a shake however, once again, reminded himself that Romans infrequently shook hands. A friendly pat on the shoulder was the expected gesture. Instead, they briefly embraced, and afterward, Cos walked away into the rapidly dimming evening light.

He came through his *vestibulum* into the *atrium* and dropped his gear on the tile floor, expecting the noise would bring Alia to him at a run. In expectation, he had already formed a big smile, and his arms were ready to pick her up and twirl her around, their faces in contact, their hearts interwoven, their joy mutual.

There was a soft noise, and he noticed a group of three coming toward him, taking their time. It was *Màthair* and Linza, followed by Maccus. He expected to see Alia at any moment. Something was wrong. He could tell by the body language of the three, not only were they not excited to see him, they acted as if they dreaded seeing him.

"Where is Alia?" he asked, intuitively knowing that her absence indicated that some horrible thing could have happened to her. Cos could feel his pulse increasing rapidly. "Where is Alia?" he demanded.

"We don't know," Maccus spoke first. The two women crouched in fear.

Cos could feel a rage building in him, one that could easily get out of control.

"Come on and tell me everything, and tell me quickly," he yelled.

"She went outside into the street to get bread two days ago. We haven't seen her since. None of us have any idea of where she may have gone. No one knows anything, and not a single person was a witness," Maccus said.

"Where have you looked?"

"I have personally searched every street. The *magistrate* was informed, and he sent out men to look also. There is no sign of her anywhere."

"You let her out by herself?" Cos roared.

"Try to calm down, Cos," *Màthair* said and moved toward him. "She was so excited to wear her *stola* and wanted to proudly go out and show off and get the morning bread for me. It was only to the stall by the doorway. She wasn't to go more than a few *passus* from the door. It was a short time before we realized she was missing, and we all went looking for her."

"This is a very small city. Somebody had to see her," Cos said.

"That is what we thought, however nobody seems to have seen anything."

"What about the shopkeeper? Surely he would have seen her taken."

"He never saw her," Linza added.

"Maccus," Cos asked. "How many men did the *magistrate* send to look?"

"A few at first, then he summoned an entire *cohort* of *Praetorians,* and I think they are still looking."

"And have you stopped looking, Maccus?" he asked.

"I thought it was my place to stay here and guard the women and our home, as you asked."

Cos started pacing back and forth. Who could have done this and why, he wondered. Was there a plan or was it a random act? Was it because Alia belonged to him or was it because she was an attractive woman? There were no answers, only speculation. He realized he couldn't rest in this house while she was missing. There would be no resting until she was found, no matter how long it took.

"Maccus, you will stay here, but I must find Alia, and I won't return without her. You understand, don't you?"

"I'm sorry, *Dominus*, very sorry. I have let you down."

"This is not your fault, Maccus. I am angry though not at you."

"What will you do, *Dominus*? We have searched every spot of the entire city. She is simply not here any longer.

"I can't think straight right now. I just have to go out and walk and clear my head." Cos found the pile he brought back and started sorting it out. He took the metal mail armor, along with his trusted *gladius,* and headed toward the door.

"Don't go tonight, Cos. Please sleep before you leave," *Màthair* pleaded.

Cos didn't answer or look back as he disappeared into the darkness, his sword unsheathed and in his hand.

Cos walked briskly north, unsure of what to do or how to begin. He racked his brain searching for some meaning to the abduction of Alia. Not once did he consider that she could have left voluntarily. It was not possible…someone took her by force and did so using a plan. They had to be waiting for her to emerge, patiently waiting while he was away from home. Then he recalled that day they went out to the gladiator school. Someone was watching, he recalled feeling the eyes on him. Whoever had taken Alia was planning it for months because when the opportunity arose, they were ready. Alia had no family or relative who could have acted so far from home, and why now, anyway?

Behind him, Cos heard the clatter of horses coming his way, down the narrow paved street. Carts, the supply kind, used these streets at night, traveling very slowly. This one was making time. He turned, grasping the hilt of his sword tightly and braced his feet. The killing stance. He hoped it was an assault directed at him because they were about to die in the effort.

"Cos!" the familiar voice called out. It was Piso with three armored men. As the carriage stopped, Piso leapt out and took Cos by his arm. "I just heard. A tragedy for you, and I know just how you feel right now. You won't accomplish anything by walking the streets alone. Come with me, and we can talk and develop a plan. Just so you know, I have already sent to *Roma* for three cohorts of men, and they should arrive in two days. We will find her, I promise you. If we need to, we will pull your *Legion XX* out of Britannia and have them search also. As soon as the light comes up, I will send messages north to stop any parties who are traveling with women. She can't get out of *Italia*."

"Any ideas about who could have done this?" Cos asked, his nostrils still dilated, his breath still rapid.

"No. I know what you are thinking, and the order couldn't have come from *Roma*. There just wasn't time. I am told she was taken two days ago, and that was about the time of your meeting with

Agrippa. It has to be a local crime, and if she is still alive, we will find her, and we won't stop until we have the answer."

"Are you prepared to order a search of every villa, every apartment, and every storage room in Herculaneum?" Cos asked.

"That will start when the cohorts get here. Two days, three at maximum. We will turn over every stone in this city," Piso assured him.

"I'll accept your word for it, Gaius. Right now, I'm going to the gladiator school and look around. I can always tell if someone is lying to me, and this time I won't be gentle."

"Why? Do you suspect someone at the school?"

"I have humiliated several of them at times. It's possible. I need to explore this before your troops are roaming around creating a distraction."

The training facility was dark, black dark, and Cos had to feel his way over to the lodge where the men would be sleeping. Finally, he recognized the door by feeling its oversized lock. He hammered on the door with the hilt of his sword, the echo produced rang loudly inside. First were some voices, then scuffling of feet. At last the door was flung open, and Cos could make out at least three large men in the opening. "Why do you awaken us in the night?" a deep voice called out. Before he could answer, a light appeared, and the lamp was passed forward. The speaker held it high, looking Cosimus over from toe to head. "I recall you, Cosimus," he said. "What is it?"

"Move aside and hold the light for me," Cos said pushing the man away from the door. Once inside, the light behind him was held overhead, and the room made dimly visible. A row of cots lay before him with the occupants sitting up and looking his way.

"Hear me, men. Most of you know me. I am *Paulo Fabio Persico Cosimus,* and I have been here many times helping you train, and I have donated money so that you would all have the proper food. Now I need something in return. My wife was taken two days ago, and I am searching for her. If anyone here knows anything, let him come forward and collect a reward. I warn you though, if someone does know about this and does not come forward now, when I discover his name, he will die in front of the rest."

The murmuring rose collectively to a loud roar, only to die down again in silence. No one came forward. "No one here knows anything to help, Cosimus. We are sorry," the deep voice said from behind.

Cos just stood there, sword in hand, glaring ahead at the men, deciding on what to do. "The offer still stands. If anyone helps me find Alia, I will reward him with his freedom. Talk it over," Cos said and spun around toward the door. He felt a hand on his shoulder which turned him toward the man.

"I swear to you that we had no hand in this deed. None of us. You have our utmost respect, and if there is anything any of us can do, all you have to do is to ask."

"I know, Gratus, I know. These men have my high regard, and I trust many of them more than most citizens of the city. However, I am enraged and grieved, and my anger knows no bounds. Sorry to have awakened you. One last question. Have you seen any strangers around lately who seemed to be waiting for something, instead of working?"

Gratus paused in thought. "We usually pay no attention to spectators, yet…there were three young men in the reviewing stand a few days ago. They were strong and healthy, and I wondered briefly about them. Other than that, I know nothing."

Cos patted Gratus on his shoulder and found his way out. Once back in the city, he walked slowly, thinking deeply about what the next step could be. Two days of head start was a problem. They could have been mounted, and if they traveled north, they could

have made it nearly to *Roma* by now. Word of this abduction
would spread widely. People talk. Somebody someplace knew, and
eventually he would discover the truth. His main worry was that
some harm had come to her, and worst of all, she had already
passed into history.

Photo by Tom Oates (https://commons.wikimedia.org/wiki/File:Atropos.jpg), Atropos", color by AF,
https://creativecommons.org/licenses/by-sa/3.0/legalcode

Chapter 21

The Search

Juvenal (? to 130 AD)

Juvenal (? to 130 AD)

---

*A*n orange sun was settling into the sea, casting ever longer and warmer shadows as the moving air was starting to rest, allowing calls of gulls floating over the water to resonate against the stone walls of the outdoor patio. It would have been a nice afternoon spent on this splendid balcony overlooking the peaceful *Sinus Cumanus,* as the Bay of Naples was then named.

Cos stretched sore muscles and sagged again, tired to the core of his being, his mind still searching, even though his body was not moving. All the energy he had expended produced not a single clue. Alia was gone as if she had never existed.

"Could I have the servant bring you some food, Cos?" Piso asked.

"Too tired to eat, thanks though."

"I assume you found nothing up there today or you would be less listless," Piso observed.

"Nothing. No sign of the slave trader, no tracks, no wagons. I don't think he has been there for months."

"Similar to the reports I got regarding our search today. The entire city has been disrupted and under lockdown, and still there is not even a hint of Alia. There is even the rumor circulating that she never existed, and complaints about us and the troops are popping up everywhere. I didn't want to break this news to you… I called off the search today. The *cohorts* will return to *Roma* in the morning. There is nothing left to accomplish."

"I understand. After a month, I am defeated as well. Whoever did this got away with it, and I still don't know the reason she was taken," Cos said, looking out at the last rays of the sun being extinguished at the edge of the sea. "What about the ships and boats arriving and departing? Did you look into that?"

"Thoroughly. All departing during that period were headed to Pompeii, and all were well-known cargo boats. I don't believe she left by the sea route," Piso replied.

"What else is there?" Cos asked. "Where can I look?" His tone was nearly pleading, the fight long gone as acceptance grew larger, slowly replacing his anger.

"I will speak to the Senate and bring this matter up in two days when I'm there. You never know what that will do to stir up the old hornets' nest of rivalries. If there is even the slightest positive personal advantage, someone will take me aside and whisper a rumor. It's our last hope."

"I'm going home tonight. There is one last thing I need to do there before I leave," Cos said.

"Where are you going? Surely you can't go without a plan and by yourself," Piso asked.

"I was thinking about going north toward *Colonia* along the *Rhenus*. If she was ever taken to that area, they would have to pass through one of those forts since there are no other roads. That was my base for years, and I know it well," Cos answered.

"By yourself!" Piso exclaimed. "That will take a month of hard travel to reach, not to mention the many dangers encountered by a solo traveller."

"I never told you this because I didn't know how to explain it so that you could understand. This may be the last time we ever see each other, and I'll say to you what is in my heart and mind."

"There came a point in my life that I clearly saw all living things around me as already dead, long dead, myself included. To my mind, we were all just inconsequential dust and, in a short time, would be forgotten, leaving behind only a few pitiful relics of our lives for others to dig up and wonder about. I was in a state of not caring any longer, just living day to day as if in a dream. Possessions, power or wealth no longer concerned me, and I felt that my entire life had meant nothing, accomplished nothing."

"Then, by accident, I found Alia on the floor of a slave wagon, starving and near death. At first, she engendered only pity within me, and I tried to save her mostly to make up for all the deaths and hardship I had brought to my fellow men. Then, slowly, as she recovered, she opened up a new world for me, and I lived only to look into her loving eyes and feel her next to me. I am still in love with her, wherever she is, and if she is dead, I want to be with her in the afterlife as well. So the dangers of this trip mean nothing to me. My fate will be what is already written, and if I lose her, I lose my reason to live anyway, and I readily accept that."

"It is a sad day in my life to lose your company, Cos. You must promise me to remain here for a while longer so that I can use my influence as *consul* to discover who did this and why. I beg you to go home, rest, regain your strength, and give me a chance. Please,

Cos, just go home and stay there until you hear from me," Piso said with passion.

For a moment, Cos gave no indication that he even heard Piso's plea. He continued to stare into the twilight, not moving and silently breathing. Slowly, he rose to his feet facing Piso, "I've had few real friends in life, a handful only, of whom I could always count on, and you are among them." He moved to a manly embrace with Piso with gentle back patting and a slow release. "I found my first true friend in life in the darkness of Judea only to lose contact with him a few months later. He is still in my thoughts, just as you will always be."

"Who was this man, and what happened to him," Piso asked.

"His name is Antonius, and I don't know what happened after we parted."

"May I help discover his location for you?"

"No. He is gone and won't be seen again for two thousand years, long after we have returned to nothingness."

"How can this be possible, Cos? What are you saying?"

"I am saying that Antonius and I traded places. He is in my world, and I am in his."

"You are telling me that you are not from this time. If true, that would explain how you often seem to know what is going to happen."

Cos stood there in the dark and didn't answer. How could he explain what actually happened, and what difference did it make anyway? It would not benefit Piso to know the truth, and he wouldn't accept it, no matter how sincere Cos was.

"Say, there was a story which circulated some years ago that I heard in my youth. It was about a well-known *centurion* who disappeared in Judea. There were several witnesses who reported that he, accompanied by others, walked into a hole in the ground and were swallowed up. I believe he was also called Antonius. Was this the same man you refer to?"

"It does no good to discuss the past, my friend. Nothing can bring back time which has passed by us. I need to go home, as you suggested, and tomorrow think about what I can do and how I can manage to live with my loss."

"We must, and will, engage in this conversation at a later time," Piso said solemnly. He watched as Cos gathered his few things and dejectedly left the patio, headed for the staircase which led to the wharf area. Piso had done all he could do to help find Alia. He had become convinced that this was no ordinary capture of an attractive woman but a much larger, well-rehearsed and financed plan, directed at Cos, not Alia. If that were true, then she is still alive and being held captive as a motivation of some sort to force Cos to choose an option that he would otherwise not want to do. He had spent enough time with Cos, and he knew the history of the man, to understand that whoever formulated this plan would meet a sudden and violent end should Cos ever discover what it was all about. It all depended on finding Alia before she met the end of her usefulness. Piso shuddered. The most obvious conspirator was just now sitting down to dinner on Capitoline Hill in *Roma*. And he, or she, was at the top of the pyramid of power and well guarded. This was a theory he dared not discuss with Cos until he was sure.

Cos realized that he was awakening, not dreaming, yet his brain still resided in that fog separating sleep from being fully alert. He reached behind him, expecting to find some part of Alia to caress, then pull her in closer contact, feeling the warmth and softness of her body. His hand hit the empty mattress, instantly restoring him to reality and the knowledge that she wasn't there, and if he didn't soon find her, she would never again lie beside him. He sat up and looked at his room, the first time he had slept here since he returned from *Roma*. His mood had been ceaselessly switching from desolation and loss to anger, energy and determination. Over the past thirty days, he had been with men of the *Praetorian* Guard as they searched, by force, the entire city and the surrounding villas. In participating, he had not exactly made friends with his fellow citizens, and there were many who were insulted as well as vindictive about being accused of snatching a woman who most of them had not even heard of. All for nothing. Alia was, for certain, not in Herculaneum nor the surrounding hills. Even the slavers had not been seen nor are present at the moment.

Cos threw the covers aside and stood up. Today…today he must start gathering things for a long, arduous trip to the northeast frontier of Gaul, to the long line of Roman forts keeping the tribes of *Germania* at bay. It was a wild card, an exceedingly small chance of discovering what happened to Alia, simply the only one remaining. Piso said he would persistently pursue any leads in *Roma* and also call on his friends and allies to help in the search, and Cos knew he would keep his word. He couldn't leave for Gaul yet, he must wait, no matter how hard inaction was.

The aroma of cooking drifted up to catch his nose. Yes, time to eat.

They had waited to eat until he came down. The three were seated at the table, all watching him as he came forward, trying to gauge his mood. Their faces were sour, the happiness gone. The absence of Alia had affected them all, and with Cos gone most of the time, they were no longer living in a home, it was simply a house.

"It smells good," Cos said, trying to brighten the mood.

"We hoped you would eat with us," Linza said, her voice a bit high. She was starting to show, her breasts more ample, her lips redder and her entire sense of purpose now fixated on childbirth instead of finding a mate. Cos looked at her a bit longingly, her blossom of youth and beauty making him even more lonely for the small woman who had managed to fulfill all his wants and needs for a period much too short.

"Pregnancy agrees with you, Linza. You are more beautiful than ever," he said.

"And how are you, *Dominus*?" Maccus asked. "Did you sleep?"

"Some…enough. Even my dreams are troubled. If only for today, I am home."

"Is it over?" *Màthair* asked gently.

"No, *Màthair*. It is not over." He could hear her sigh and look away.

"What are your plans, *Dominus*?" Maccus asked.

"I have in mind a trip, though not for a few days. There are things here I need to do first. *Consul* Piso will leave for Roma soon, and he asked that I give him a chance to look there before I do anything else."

They all were studying his face, trying to understand what it meant for him to leave again and what would happen to them as well. *Màthair* broke the silence by passing the food along and pouring Cos a glass full of their wine, the same wine now owned by Maccus and Linza. He took his glass and held it up toward them, an acknowledgement of who were the proper owners, then drank deeply. He could see the gratification in their faces. Their future was secure, their income assured, their happiness evident. It was wonderful for him to see, and he forced himself to concentrate on these few remaining family members and to not think of his own misery, at least for the moment.

"I have to ask you to run a couple of errands for me today, Maccus. Would that be a bother?" Cos asked.

"Not at all, Cos. Whatever you need, you know that."

There was a nice offshore breeze which came through the end of the *peristylum* and fluttered the drapes, softly swinging them from side to side as if the house was breathing, alive, and whispering to him that it felt good to have the master home again. Cos paused his writing and looked into the distance. The grief hit him all at once, his loss nearly unbearable, and for the first time in his adult life, his tears showed no limits. He didn't wipe them away because there was no end to them, no way to turn the spigot off. Cos had reached the lowest point of his life, his soul residing in a deep well with no way to climb back into the light. It was the first time that he regretted returning to the past. The monster waiting for him was not the one he had slain, but the one which had him in his grasp now, the one he could not see or fight against. It was the other side of intense love, the flip side, where there is unhappiness enough to equal the happiness on the bright side. Cos needed to talk to someone who could understand, really understand, and offer advice as to what to do, instruct him how to go on with life. Only one person could satisfy that need, and he lived in the distant future. Antonius was his brother, his mentor, and would always rise to any challenge. He needed Antonius now more than ever…if only he could speak to him, even for a moment.

His gaze came into focus. There was a stone at his feet that became important, a stone like all the other pavers in his *tablinum*. For some reason, he couldn't look away. This stone was significant in some vague way, and his mind started working again, his imagination soaring into the future of how this very stone could provide a mechanism of communication as an image of it being dug up hit him with clarity.

"Maccus!" he called.

Chapter 22

A Familiar Voice Touches the Heart

Of all the things which wisdom provides to make us entirely happy, much the greatest is the possession of friendship.

Epicurus (341 BC to 270 BC)

A strict belief in fate is the worst of slavery, imposing upon our necks an everlasting lord and tyrant, whom we are to stand in awe of night and day.

Epicurus (341 BC to 270 BC)

Setteville, Italia

Tony took a deep breath and glanced at Mary. It was time to disclose the whole truth to their son and, this amazingly preceptive young woman, Rachel.

"You are right, Rachel, I am the *centurion* who disappeared in Judea two thousand years ago. So now you know the truth. Yet knowledge of this fact is a very dangerous thing to possess. If you breathe a word of it, and it gets back to the wrong people, your life, as you know it, is over. They will come for you. So this conversation stays in this room. You must agree to this condition."

"It's earthshaking history! How can something so significant be hidden when it should be celebrated? I am actually talking to someone from the past. It's like I'm dreaming and will wake up, and it will only be a fleeing thought in the night," Rachel gushed.

"Listen closely, and I'll explain it to you," Mary interrupted. "We were sent back in time to change history…on purpose. It didn't work and, instead, nearly caused the biggest conflagration ever. Others, if they knew how, would scheme to go back and change something for their benefit, and the result might alter our world in unpredictable ways. That can't be allowed, so the authorities have tried to erase the project from existence, remove all possibility that it could ever happen again. They have left us alone thus far, so I'm not sure our names are even known to them. We have discussed this at length and are convinced that the project director, Dr. Susan Harmes, destroyed all of her records before she retired, in an attempt to spare us the spotlight. She was the only one who knew how it was done. Please don't do anything which will provoke them to silence us, and you as well."

Rachel stared at her, trying to comprehend the significance, slowly realizing what a big thing she had stumbled into. "I see or, at least, I think I see," she said, nodding her head slowly. "No, you can count on me to be mum about this." Rachel looked up at Cos, who was standing beside her chair. "And you too, Cos." She put her index finger across her lips.

"The Cosimus you found in the records is the same Cos that I traveled across the threshold into the past with. This fellow," she said as she patted her husband's arm, "came back through the portal to be with me. Often, I've wondered if he regretted doing that."

"So you exchanged one for the other?" Cos questioned.

"Not intentionally. Cosimo went back alone to save our civilization…and he did. We witnessed when he went through because we were in Rome watching a small monitor as he gave a little last wave and stepped into the past for good as the opening winked out. Afterward, I cried for three days, and I think Tony shed a few tears himself. We have to accept the fact that the world will never know our story nor any mention of Cos, though a greater hero has never been born."

"And you named me after him," Cos observed.

"When we first met, he went by the name of Cosimo. While in the first century, he wanted to be called Cosimus, a more Latinized version and more appropriate. Mostly, I still think of him as just Cos. You are very much like him in some ways," Mary recalled.

"He was our best friend, and it was to honor you with the name of a very great man," Tony said.

"About the letter we found," Cos asked. "Can you read it to us now?"

Tony sat up, opened his top desk drawer, and took out the copper scroll very carefully, reverently uncoiling it and spreading it flat with his hands, then looked at Mary. "This will be hard to hear, Mary. It's sad, tragic, and much too short. When I read it the first time, Cosimo came back to me so strongly that I nearly thought he was in the room with me. In my mind, he never changes from the young valiant man whom we knew, though when he wrote this letter, I believe he was about the age I am now."

"I want all of you seated and listening, and imagine, if you will, Cos, as he sat down to write the letter he always wanted to write, only was forced to write it at the wrong time…a moment of great stress and trial. As he says himself…by the time this letter is read, he will have become only dust in the wind, but I'll speak for myself when I add that, in our memory, he still lives and will live forever."

In the eleventh year of the Reign of Claudius, first day of the Ides of March

To my dear friend, Antonius Severius Maximus.

I know that someday, somehow, you will read this letter. I am composing it in the tablinum of my home in Herculaneum, and it will be buried under my feet and marked with your name. In twenty-seven years, this spot will be covered by ash and rock for centuries to come and will only be fully uncovered in the twenty-first century. My hope is that some inquisitive person will notice the inscription and extricate this message hidden under the stone. By the time you read this, I, and everything around me, will have disappeared and been long forgotten, swept away by the river of time.

Over the years, I have thought about you and Mary many times, and I always hoped that you were happy and successful together.

It's funny how things turn out, isn't it? You and I switching places…it's a story only a few people ever knew, yet one that everybody should know. And I'll tell you the reason and one that you have already discovered; people are the same. They have the same wants, needs and excesses. Often, they even look the same. I can't count how many times I've seen a person here that I thought I recognized from your time. It even feels the same being here as there. After awhile, I didn't even notice or remember the way things are different, and now, after so many years, I can truly say that I don't miss anything from your time, except you and Mary.

After you saw me enter into the past, you must have always wondered what happened. I served in the Roman Army for twenty years, and I progressed in rank all the way up to legatus, in command of the famous Legion XX in Britannia.

At some time during the struggle for control of Britannia, it became clear to me that I was only fighting ghosts, not men, and I already knew what was to happen. I became discouraged and demoralized, eventually becoming reluctant to engage the enemy, who, after all, were justly fighting for their way of life. After my appointment expired, I gratefully retired and sought a quiet life in this small city. So, by some measure, I achieved success, wealth and respect, and I should be happy and grateful that I am still alive and in good health. However, that is not the case.

For a time, I lost the will to live, lost the joy of being alive. My world changed abruptly when I rescued a little German girl being sold as a slave. She was near death when I took responsibility for her, except she recovered and became the most important person in my life. Alia was the reason I awakened each morning, and every time I beheld her beautiful face, it was like a blessing from God. I fell in love and married her, and I love her more deeply than I can describe in writing, though I know you and Mary have that same feeling toward each other and can understand how I feel. For once in my life, I finally achieved complete happiness, and I looked forward to each day that Alia was near me.

About a month ago, I was in Roma being considered to lead the Praetorian Guard. Somebody took Alia while I was away. I, and hundreds of Roman troops, have searched in vain for her since I returned and discovered that she was missing. There is no person here who knows where she is or why she was taken.

I was not selected to command the Guard because the wife of Claudius, Agrippina, has other plans, so I am free of that responsibility, and I plan to spend the remainder of my life searching for Alia. After I give my possessions away, I will travel north along the Rhine and the border of Germany, my last chance of finding Alia. She was originally from one of the northern tribes, and it is possible that she is being returned to her homeland.

Our home in Herculaneum is the only location that I could use to send this little message, although I will never return here again. My need for your counsel consumes

me, and I wish you were here beside me
because, of the many fearsome things I have
faced, this is the worst of all.

I realize that window between our worlds
can never open again so I bid you farewell and
want you and Mary to know how much I loved
you both.

Cosimo.

Tony quickly wiped a tear from his cheek and looked at the others for comment. Rachel and Cos were looking at each other, but Mary was holding her face in her hands and weeping, sobbing, as Cos came back to her also.

"Oh, why does everything have to happen to him?" she sputtered through her hands. "Tony, what do you think happened? Did he ever find Alia?" Mary asked.

"We'll never know that," he answered, his voice husky and low. "You two are archeology students," he spoke toward Cos and Rachel, "can't you go dig something up and discover the answer for us?"

They both looked back at him, wondering if he was serious or just speaking for Mary's benefit. "Just where should we look, Papà?" Cos questioned. "If my namesake couldn't discover where Alia was taken with the entire Roman army searching, how could anybody from this time find anything?"

"I know a bit about Roman history, as do the three of you," Mary spoke up as she blotted her face with a handkerchief. "We all know little pieces of this era because there were several really excellent contemporary Roman historians whose work has been studied for generations. I suggest we talk over what we know and what we may need to discover."

"Why?" Cos blurted. "After all, whatever happened doesn't matter any longer. It was over so long ago that…well, do we really care if he got Alia back?"

"I care," Tony said.

"And I do also," Mary agreed. "Cos was real to us though, apparently, just a statue for you two. I guess it doesn't really matter to anyone other than us, still, wouldn't you like to know the outcome of this compelling story cut short without an ending? However, to me and Tony… ." Mary couldn't finish because the tears started back and she turned away, lost in grief.

Rachel stood up, her hands on her hips and surveyed the room. "I agree with Mary. We will think about this letter the rest of our lives. I, for one, would love to hear what happened, and if there was a happy ending, it would be most satisfying to know."

"And, what if there was even more tragedy? Would you also wish to know that?" Cos asked.

Tony didn't move from his spot, and his head still hung low, but he was listening, still deciding on what to do. In his mind, he kept seeing the aperture, the opening through time. It was so easy. He had just bent down a bit and stepped through. Like walking through a door, except it was, instead, a jump of two thousand years. Finally, he starting talking while the others watched and listened. After all, this was his era, and surely he knew more than anyone what could have happened.

"I was a simple *centurion* and never based in *Roma*," he said. "Nevertheless, what happened in the center of power concerned us all, and there was always much talk and speculation about what went on there. The level of intrigue, manipulation, and even murder was amazing, even to us, the soldiers of *Roma* at the edges of the Empire where we struggled day to day with death and injury." He cleared his throat as the images of ancient *Roma* civilization came back to him, the people and places he knew were as clearly seen as if they had just been encountered yesterday. "We know little from this letter, only let's examine what he said one step at a time. Cos said he had been called to *Roma* for consideration of appointment to a very powerful position, that being the head of the *Praetorian* Guard. We know from history that he didn't get the job. Why? Cosimus was well qualified, honest, loyal and had no political aspirations. He was happily married…retired, after waking up to the brutality of his life. I feel sure that Cosimus didn't want this position. Claudius, the Emperor himself, must have been interested in Cosimus and would have had to be involved. And we know that *Sextus Afranius Burrus* had just been chosen as *Prefect* in the year 51, only a year prior to this event. There must have been an awakening by Claudius that his wife, Agrippina the Younger, was actively engaged in power moves designed to insure her plans for her son, Nero. He may have chosen Cos to undercut his devious wife."

"Agrippina? Didn't she kill Claudius?" Rachel recalled.

"Yes, I recall that episode now," Cos blurted, now interested. "She was the one all right. Except she was murdered by her own son not long after he gained power."

"More like seven years. And during some of that time she was excluded from proximity to Nero, who didn't trust her any longer. He tried three times to kill her, some the efforts are humorous, if true," Mary clarified.

"Nevertheless," Tony said. "We have narrowed the list down, haven't we? I mean, we are pretty sure that the Emperor Claudius didn't do it. On the other hand, there is the infamous Agrippina who surely had a motive to keep Cos away from power. He couldn't be controlled and, therefore, was dangerous. And don't forget Burris who was about to lose a lucrative and powerful position as *Prefect*. He would not have wanted anyone to take his place."

"Hey!" Cos said excitedly. "We have a conspiracy, and the list is narrow. Do you think Cos, the other Cos, would have also figured this out?"

Mary shook her head. "Cos had no power after he retired. He would have had no men under him to take direction or follow orders. Burris and Agrippina were at the center of power and had only to raise a little finger and things would get done. And there could be no reprisal possible against them, either one of them. I don't even think an inquiry could be done because this was no democracy. Only Claudius could have rooted out the offender, however at the time, Agrippina still had his ear. At least, we think so."

Rachel frowned, trying to understand the political complexity while not fully informed about this particular Roman period before the infamous teenaged Nero took power. "I don't understand," she said, looking around. "Why would this Burris or Agrippina take Alia? How did that change anything? Wouldn't Cos find out and tell Claudius what happened?"

"Since either Burris or Agrippina had access to a virtual army at their disposal, it would be a small thing to snatch a little gal from a small town. I think it was done as insurance to force Cosimus to not accept the position of *prefect*. If he wanted Alia returned, then he had to do what they wanted," Tony said.

"He didn't get the position and didn't even want it. Why didn't they return his wife?" Rachel asked.

"It would be simpler to not return her, since no one apparently knew for sure who had done it. The task was over. There was no need to return her because, then, they would have been exposed. Better to dispose of her quietly and be done with it," Tony suggested.

Cos spoke up, "They played dirty back then."

"Yes, they did but no different than now. Nothing has really changed in human behavior," Mary observed.

"I still don't get it," Rachel said more loudly than she intended. "They searched the entire area. Where did they take her?"

"And that is the question, isn't it?" Tony agreed. "Let's do our diligent research and see if we can give a more educated guess. After all, we have time. The matter has been over for two thousand years. What's a few more days?" He gently patted Mary's back and gave her a smile. She weakly smiled back, at last coming to grips with the idea that, as her son had said, it really didn't matter any longer.

Chapter 23

An Unexpected Answer

The only certainty is that nothing is certain.

Pliny the Elder (23 AD to 79 AD)

"There is no person so severely punished, as those who subject themselves to the whip of their own remorse."

Seneca the Elder (54 BC to 39 AD)

The setting sun cast its horizontal orange rays into the west window of the dining room, painting a heavenly glow and warmth on everything it touched and producing an even more glorious soft reflected light on the faces of Tony and Mary. She looked up from her meal, smiling, her eyes sparkling with the departing energy of the sun.

"A smile," Tony noted aloud. "Something I have not seen for too long." He raised his wine glass to her in a silent toast, and she returned the favor. Her solemn mood had not been unexpected after the appearance of a nearly forgotten ghost, one that Tony also loved only not in the way Mary loved him. Over the years, Tony tried hard to never resurrect the memory of Cosimus in his wife because he feared how her love for him resurfaced so strongly. No matter how long ago it was since they lost Cosimus, Mary's love for him had not diminished. At some moment, Mary had chosen Antonius over Cosimus, and she had given him her love and a child, yet there always remained a lingering longing for what she had also lost.

"Hear any news from Cos or Rachel?" Mary asked. From the prolonged look Tony had given her, she was certain that he was reading her thoughts regarding Cosimo and her worry over something which had occurred in the first century.

"Rachel is back in New York and has returned to class. I don't expect to hear from her directly whatever she finds. Most likely, she has forgotten all about it and moved on."

"I'm not sure about that. She was more excited about the letter and what it meant than our son. He is the one who has moved on."

"Perhaps you are correct, Mary. Better that way, I think." He pondered over it as he finished eating. There was a subject he wanted to discuss but was hesitant about bringing it up. On his own, he had tried, without much success, to discover what had occurred at Fermilab after they left Chicago. In a careful way, though. No good can come of awakening that dragon.

"Tony," Mary said softly, "do you remember Susan Harmes?"

Tony's head jerked up. Talk about mental telepathy. That is exactly who he was thinking about. Dr. Harmes had been the director and physicist in charge of the Fermilab project which had produced the opening in time, and she was the one who painstakingly discovered how to position the opening both in time and location.

"I remember her very well. What brought her name up?"

"Oh, I was thinking of her and tried to look her up recently," Mary replied.

"And what did you find?"

"She passed away about ten years ago. You know, don't you, that she retired from Fermilab after the episode with Cosimus?"

"No, I was sort of hoping she was still around. That's sad," Tony said.

"And why would you want to see her?" Mary asked.

"Look, Mary," Tony said, starting to wave his hands like the Italiano he was or had become. "You and I are thinking the same. We both know it, so let's talk and not play any more games. I wanted to ask her if it was still possible to create an opening. You know that's what I was doing. Are you in this game with me or not?"

"I heard your warning to Rachel. Best to let sleeping dogs lie, isn't that what you meant?"

"It is indeed. Yet there is no harm in a bit of speculation, is there?" Tony asked.

"As long as the American authorities don't find out. We have to be very, very careful. I've thought about this for years. We don't actually know if we have been under surveillance all this time. If that is the case, they are very good because I've never spotted them nor seen any sign."

Tony was silent after that exchange and studied the encroaching twilight through the window. "So it's over," he muttered mostly to himself. The last faint hope of resurrecting a window was really just a thing of the past. When Susan died, so did all the technical talent needed to even think of such a thing.

"Would you want to go through the opening again?" Mary asked, looking at him in a penetrating way.

"Not if a monster was waiting there for us. No. Simply to see Cos again, to help him…I owe him that. We changed places, and my life has been very good, and I owe most of that to him."

"I've wondered how he would look at our age. I suppose he would be much the same."

"No, he wouldn't. I've thought about that as well. After twenty years of being in the Roman Army, he would be brimming with muscle and be as hard as stone. You would be shocked."

"Really?" Mary said, nodding as she thought about it. "You are pretty muscular yourself," she noted, "more than you, you think?"

"I have pretty boy muscles. They look great on film but…Cos would have the real thing. There is a big difference," Tony admitted.

"And you?" Tony asked. "Would you go through?"

"I'm not considering it, and I don't think the possibility will ever occur anyway."

"I wonder why we are even talking about this," Tony said with finality. He pushed back from the table and placed his napkin on the plate.

"She had a son," Mary said. "Did you know that?"

"No. So what?"

"No ordinary son, that one. Susan Harmes was never married but adopted a child from the Chicago ghetto and taught him at home. He was a brilliant child and went to MIT with a full scholarship."

"What was his major, if I have to ask?"

"Nuclear Physics, what else?" Mary replied.

This conversation was starting to show Tony that Mary had been seriously researching the same subject that had been keeping him awake at night. It was the image of poor Cos that had ignited all this energy in both of them about time travel.

"Have you wondered just what this young man knows about his adopted mother's work?" Tony asked.

"I have. The only way to find out would be to ask him in person. You would expect if we could ponder this, the American agencies would also. This man I'm sure is being watched and monitored very carefully."

"Then, my dear, what do you suggest as the next step?" Tony asked.

"First, we have to face the fact that opening a portal may be impossible. Things have moved on, and there are people watching. It's risky, to say the least. And we don't even know if Cos would really want us back in his life. I'm sure that he was a capable man and would know far more than even you about that era. And I have to wonder if you would chance everything we have earned in life to risk such an adventure." Mary put down her paper and gave him a level look, waiting for his reply.

"Well stated, my lovely. My answer is that we don't have enough information about any of it to make a plan. We don't know what happened, and even if we did, could we make a difference? And we don't know the first thing about this young man of Susan's. Would he know what to do, and would he do it? I don't have the answers. We need to just stop talking about it and wait."

"Wait on what, exactly?" Mary asked.

"Well, there is no hurry about this, is there? I believe that if there are any facts, then they will come to us in due time. We have to wait."

New York University, Kimmel Center Student Technology

Rachel glanced around as she entered the computer lab. There had to be a chair that wasn't beside some aggressive male student on the make. She sighed. *Whatever*, she said to herself and chose the nearest free computer work station. She hung her coat on the back of the chair and put her notebook on the desk and sat down. There was a paper due, and she had only the outline done. Another sigh. All she could think about lately was Cosimo back in Italy and his most interesting family. It had been very difficult to not discuss what had happened to her as well as the most exciting news she had ever heard. She had been warned by all of them, and thinking about it, they were right. Best to stay out of the reach of the law. Her family had always emphasized that point as well. Another sigh. She just had to get back to work if she wanted to graduate on time.

She started to notice the male student beside her on the left. He had densely curly hair which had been trimmed to look more like a wig than real. His face was slender, youthful, and pimpled, and his clothing worn and sloppy. She also noticed that he occasionally was staring at her.

"Say, isn't your name Rachel?" he finally asked. Rachel, looking directly at him, just didn't answer.

"OK, so you don't want to talk to me, and I get that. Only I am headed to Naples next month, and I heard you just got back from there."

"So?" Rachel said.

"I don't know the first thing about Italy or Naples, don't even speak the language. There's got to be some advice you have for me."

"I was at Herculaneum most of the time. Where will you be?" Rachel reluctantly answered.

"They tell me that I will mostly be at the Naples museum. I'm more of a computer guy than a digger."

"I don't get it. Why are you going?"

"They are doing some sort of research on charcoal scrolls they have. I will be helping to write the code needed to run the analysis of their new x-ray machine's digital files."

Rachel paused, lost in thought for a moment. She knew he was talking about the famous scrolls found in the so-called Villa of the Papyri, next door to Herculaneum. This was a place of interest to her since she had been spending way too much time trying to find any scrap of information regarding the Cosimus who had written the letter to Tony. A famous general like Cosimus would have had to visit that villa at one time or another. She had wondered if any clue to his wife's disappearance could have been uncovered there during the nearly two centuries of excavation.

"I've been there once. Interesting place. Say, what is your name?" Rachel asked.

"Bobby Steinmeyer," he answered. "And what is your last name, Rachel?"

"Lucchese."

Bobby raised his eyebrows but had no comment.

"Don't worry about your English, Bobby. They all seem to speak it in some fashion. You'll get by."

"Did you discover anything new while you were there?"

"No historically important things. I didn't actually do any digging." She thought about the thunderous explosion of discovery that a team had been sent back in time and returned intact. Even bringing an ancient into the present with them. My God, she thought, can I live with this knowledge locked up in me without telling a soul? Forever?

Rachel jotted a note on a slip of paper and offered it toward Bobby. "Bobby, take this with you, and if you run across either of these two names during your research, send me an email about it."

Bobby took the paper and studied it for a moment, then looked up at her. "What's important about the names Cosimus or Alia?" he asked.

"We know that Alia was a woman who was kidnapped, and Cosimus was her husband. Back before the volcano erupted," Rachel explained.

Bobby nodded and carefully folded the paper and inserted it into his wallet.

Musei Capitolini, Rome

Cos squinted at the computer screen and tilted his head from side to side trying to discern the Latin text on the photocopy of the original manuscript.

"Nuts," he said aloud, gathering disapproving looks from other researchers as he broke their concentration. The question was did he have enough information, and was there anything else that could be learned? He had been studying every text, in the original Latin, in hopes of getting a true picture of the infamous woman, Agrippina the younger, as she was called by later historians. It was a confusing picture given that there were disagreements and probable exaggerations by the original Roman historians. All were subject to literary pressures in different ways. The ones writing about Agrippina before her death were careful to avoid saying things which might arouse the beast. After her death, and Nero's clear control of the Empire, historians were more likely to heap scorn on Agrippina. Where is the truth, he wondered. One thing was for certain, she was no innocent, no virtuous woman. Agrippina was in it for herself and her offspring and would do what it took to make it happen. He recalled the words written by his namesake from the past, "Agrippina has other plans." It was clear that some of the legends were true. As for the poisoning death of Claudius…well, that might or might not be true. He could have died of natural causes just at an opportune time for his fourth wife. She got what she wanted and also the historical blame.

What was most interesting was her involvement in a plot to murder her brother, Caligula, who was a most despised emperor. The plot failed, and Caligula banned Agrippina to the island of Ponza in the Tyrrhenian Sea off the coast of modern Naples. She remained there until her uncle and future husband, Claudius, ended the ban and restored her to Rome. While on Ponza, Agrippina and her sister lived in the *Palazzo Giulia*, built especially for them. The adjacent smaller island of Ventotene had been used earlier by the first Emperor Augustus to imprison his wayward daughter.

Cos sat up, rubbing his chin. There was a history of sequestering people on those two islands, and Agrippina herself had lived on one of them for three or four years. It would have occurred to Agrippina to silently remove Alia to one of them. That would explain why Alia could not be located around Herculaneum. What if she had been taken by boat to one of these two islands?

Searching the Internet about those two islands produced little of value. There were only scant ruins there now. Who would have done the bidding of the wife of Claudius, Cos asked himself? The *Praetorians*, of course, only Cos recalled another military unit acting as Imperial guards. The *Cohors Germanorum*, as they were called. These were German born personal bodyguards who protected the emperor on a more immediate level. "German," Cos repeated to himself. That was also the origin of the missing wife, Alia. She was also German. Cos began to realize that a team of these Germans who could speak to Alia in her language would have no difficulty getting her away from her home, by trickery if not by force. If they transported her as captive to one of the Pontine islands, she could have been held there as long as Agrippina had need of her. "Then what?" Cos asked himself. Would the *Cohors Germanorum* murder Alia if requested? Of course they would. A military unit obeys orders whatever they may be. It was the answer to the riddle. He just had to prove it.

Image by Alexander Francis
adapted from the cover of the novel, *Revenge of Jesus*

Chapter 24

Deception

Seneca the Elder (54 BC to 39 AD)

Rose paused and listened to be sure he wasn't using the phone, engaged in private conversation, though she had never known him to do that, then pushed the door open with her shoulder, her right hand occupied with a steaming cup of black coffee, the left with a fresh mango. As she entered, there was no surprise that Dr. Harmes was at his computer terminal as usual, staring at a screen full of mathematical symbols. Rose shook her head slightly, always wanting to give the young man advice about too much sedentary activity being bad for long-term health. But she didn't and never would venture that far into his private life.

"Can you take a break and drink this coffee before it gets cold?" Rose asked. Dr. Harmes turned to look directly at her, only his eyes and mind were still occupied by whatever math problem was circulating in there. Rose often felt transparent, as if she wasn't actually standing there.

All of a sudden, Dr. Harmes' face cleared in some vague way, and the light returned to his eyes. "Sure, Rose, and thank you. I need a bit of a break. Won't you sit and join me for a moment?" he asked pleasantly and smiled up at her.

Rose's heart fluttered for a brief moment, except her brain reminded her that there were twenty years difference between them, and besides, Dr. Harmes was only displaying his gift of personal warmth that made him so unusual in the lofty realm of genuine geniuses.

"Thanks, Dr. Harmes, only I need to print the week's lecture supplements for you. May I bring you anything else?"

"I insist, Rose," he said and pointed to a chair. Rose sat down somewhat awkwardly and stiff, her back held rigidly off of the chair while Dr. Harmes looked her over as if seeing her for the first time. He took a sip of coffee and cleared his throat. "You recall our conversation about snoopers?" he asked.

"You are referring to those suits who keep asking questions about you?"

"Those and others. Seen anything of them lately?" he asked after another sip.

"Are they police or spies?" she asked instead of answering.

"Spies will bribe. Did they try to do that?"

"Not yet. What should I do if they offer?"

"Take the bribe. You can use the money, I'm sure, and neither of us have done anything legally or morally wrong. Next time they show up, invite them to look at my computer monitor. Perhaps they can help me solve this problem." He chuckled lowly and tapped his finger on the screen, pausing mentally for a split second as a possible solution popped into his head.

"I'll do just that. Only you should know something else, though, before you invite them in. We don't know who they are working for. What if it's the Russians and not the FBI?"

"Of course, I was joking. You know that. By the way, all my papers are published in the journals. All they have to do is buy a copy and then they would know everything that I know. No need for spying."

"Anything else?" Rose asked, impatient to leave since the conversation was not, after all, personal in any way. She looked Barron Rasmon Harmes, PhD over again as she waited for his reply. He was trim, fit, and handsome, and the way he moved implied a muscularity that was unexpected in a full professor of Physics at MIT. Quite the package, this one. She wondered if Barron had a woman stashed someplace to make him happy in his off times. If he did, he kept it to himself.

After Rose left, Barron turned back to the computer screen, but his train of thought had been disrupted, and the equation remained in place for now, unsolved. He thought about the persistent surveillance, present most of his entire life. On occasion, he suspected that his personal living quarters had been examined in detail, except the agency conducting the search was professional in the extreme. Only a brain like his could have detected how they had left traces, however small and insignificant. They would never find what they were looking for. That treasure was hidden away in a place they would never look, and even if they found it, it would be meaningless to anyone other than a brilliant physicist like his mother or himself. Barron knew exactly what they wanted. It was to keep knowledge of time travel out of the hands of mankind, forever. And they were relentless and would never stop until the missing files were located and destroyed. The logical person to own the files and the only person who would be able to act on the knowledge was Barron Harmes, adopted son of the brilliant Susan Harmes. What they didn't know is that Dr. Barron Harmes had read, digested and memorized all of the technical information he needed if he wished to start the project again. There was no need for a printed or digital file, even though one still existed. Barron's file was in his head where they could never get at it.

When Susan Harmes had performed her miracle of time travel, Barron was only ten years of age, too young to fully grasp what was taking place in his mother's life. Later, out of the ear and eye of listeners, she told him the amazing story. Barron understood fully what was involved and why the government didn't want the information distributed in any way and, for sure, didn't want another venture into the past. He agreed…too dangerous, and the authorities didn't know the full story of how the recent past, a horrible nightmare of a past, had been prevented and changed by the brave actions of his mother. She should have won about fourteen Nobel Prizes and worldwide adulation, yet she didn't and died unknown and unloved except by her adopted son. The memories of her persecution and isolation made Barron angry at the world at times. Her contribution to science would not be lost, he would make sure of it.

Chapter 25

First Contact

Tacitus(56 AD to 117 AD)

There is an old saying which, from its truth, has become proverbial, that friendships should be immortal, enmities mortal.

Livy (59 BC to 17 AD)

*B*arron pulled over and looked again at his roadmap, then flung it to the floor of the car. He hated paper maps, and his little rental car had no mapping system and no place to hold his smartphone. He tried to be calm, but the Italian traffic was fast and relentless, nearly like the bumper cars that his mother had let him drive at the state fair. In addition, he had a near sleepless night, worrying if he had managed to lose any team following him. By now, they would have concluded that Dr. Barron Harmes was intentionally avoiding surveillance which would only increase the intensity of the search for him and their determination to find him. It may have even triggered an alert passed on to the European agencies. Or perhaps not, he reasoned. The Americans would never like to see him interrogated by any foreign intelligence agency. Given the size of the secrets he may have, it would be better to avoid any inquisitive foreign agencies and the questions they might pose.

He had flown to Paris in full view with no disguise and no pretense. Just a vacation trip abroad to see the sights and to have fun. Once there, Barron rented a small sports car, one that could, if needed, be hard to pursue. He had exited the Parisian hotel through the freight entrance and gone to a nearby clothing retail shop, changing there and discarding everything he was wearing. In fact, the only items he retained were his watch and wallet. After that, he drove out of Paris, paying for gas using cash, heading for the Italian Alps and, after that, Rome. As far as he could tell, he left no trail to follow…yet. For now, until after his impromptu meeting, he needed to stay under the radar. His intent was to re-emerge in Paris and go on as if nothing had ever happened. He would be suspected, for sure, except what could they do about it? If he ever got questioned, he would claim a liaison with a nameless woman, one whose identity absolutely could not be disclosed.

At last, the driveway he had been expecting came into view, and he turned onto the gravel and stopped at the large closed gate. Barron put down his window and looked at the stone pillar, assuming that someone inside could see him.

After a time, the stone crackled, "q*ual'è lo scopo della tua visita?*"

At first Barron could not be sure that he was talking to a person or a computer system. He decided to treat the entity as a person. "I wish to see Anthony Solomon or Mary Solomon. I am the son of an old friend in Chicago."

There was a lengthy silence before the column responded. "*Dichiara il tuo nome*," it asked. Though Barron could not speak Italian, he was fairly proficient in French, enough to correctly guess what the speaker had asked. It wanted his name.

"Barron, son of Susan," he replied.

The gate clicked and started opening majestically, exposing a long paved driveway with immaculate grounds and orchards. Barron drove slowly, taking in the scene. As the house came into view, he braked to take in a full view of this magnificent yellow stone home set in a working orchard, backed by a rear view of blue, distant hills. A grand home in any society, it spoke of wealth and position. He stopped in front of the house and tentatively got out, briefly stretching before ascending the front steps.

Before Barron made it to the door, it opened and standing in the entry was a very lovely woman, dressed in soft white loose clothing, with dark exquisitely braided hair.

"I only heard about you recently," Mary said. "You were a surprise to us."

"Yes," Barron laughed, "I surprise a lot of people. You are Mary. I recognize you from photos I've seen."

Mary stuck out her hand, and Barron accepted it, looking into her eyes as they softly shook hands. "Please come in," she offered, standing aside. "What shall I call you?"

"Just Barron will do," he answered. Barron looked around when inside and softly whistled to himself. "More than nice. Nearly museum quality," he remarked.

"I agree it's a bit too much, but we are collectors. We can't seem to help ourselves."

Barron stopped in the middle of the hall and turned toward her, a serious look on his face. "You should know that there… ." He stopped when Mary nodded and put her finger across her lips. Silently, she took his arm in hers, and they strolled through the large house, out the patio door and into the open air. Without saying another word, she led him away from the house toward a neat row of olive trees.

"This is a better place to talk, wouldn't you agree?" she asked, turning to face him.

"So you know?"

"I suspect. I'm not positive, only I've had feelings about it for years. Except I'm sure about you. They will be watching you," Mary said.

"And they are. I believe that I escaped their net for the moment, but they will pick up my trail soon."

"They will know you came here. It might have been expected," Mary warned. The idea hit Barron in the face like a slap. Of course, they would, he thought. There was no escape.

"Did you come to visit or was there another reason?" Mary asked.

"I always wanted to talk with you and Antonius. I've seen his photos all over the place, and I know the story, still I had to see both of you first hand at least once. My mother had such high opinions of you both, and the one that returned, Cosimo…she thought he was a true hero. She would tear up every time she thought about him and always wondered what happened."

"There is news about that you will be interested in," Mary said. "My husband got a message from him…from two thousand years ago! He fought the monster and won and then went on to have a glorious career in the Roman army. He retired to Herculaneum and married," Mary paused, looking into the distance as if she didn't want to continue.

"There is something bad, I can tell," Barron said, hoping she would continue.

"Yes, very bad. It has to do with the constant power struggle at the top of the Roman command structure. His young wife was kidnapped while he was away. He never found her and became despondent. After that, we know nothing… ." Mary again couldn't stop the tears, which flowed freely down her face.

Barron remembered his mother saying that Mary seemed to be in love with both men, and she wasn't sure which she would marry until Cosimo decided to return to the past. He was unsure of how to respond, how to help, so he just stood there waiting until Mary regained control.

"Sorry," she said, and once again tried to look normal, except her eyes remained red, and she continued to sniff. "I admit that we, Tony and I, keep thinking of how we could help him, yet we know that whatever happened is long ago and should be forgotten. We, the living, have to concentrate on us and what happens tomorrow, not what occurred ages ago. If you knew Cosimo, you would understand. He should be right here with us instead of long dead. It hurts to think of him, at a moment of true happiness, thrown back into despair."

Barron summoned the nerve to ask the question he had come so far to ask. "Mary, would you go back again if you had the chance?" Mary was stunned and looked at Barron as if trying to be sure that he had actually said what she heard.

"Is it possible?" she asked.

"I know how it was done. There may even be improvements that I can implement. After all, computers are faster and more capable than they were twenty years ago. Of course we would be at extreme risk attempting such a thing. I'm not sure that they would stop at arrest for this particular offense. It's possible that we could just disappear, if you understand what I'm suggesting."

"Only why on earth would you chance such a thing?" Mary asked.

"My mother's research should have made her world famous but, instead, made her isolated and alone. She was ostracized by lies invented to destroy her reputation and insure that, even if she told her story, it would be laughed at. I have always had resentment about it, and on top of that, they watch me, who has done nothing but further the cause of science. Her research is all in my head where they can't destroy it. They could, and perhaps would, kill me, only they are not sure that a hard copy isn't somewhere where it might someday resurface. That's what is keeping me from harm. Once, an old friend told me that if you are being accused of something, you might as well do it. I would enjoy the excitement of creating another portal, but there is a more compelling reason. This field of study will crop up again, by accident if not by design. We might as well learn all we can about it before those with evil intent get the opportunity before us. After hearing about your message from the past, we have reason to think about this subject again."

Mary looked surprised, even startled. She never really considered the remotest possibility of the portal ever opening again. She clearly recalled what chaos the monster had accomplished in a few months after he came through from the past. No one should want to risk the chance of that happening again.

"The first time, and only time, I went into the portal, I was naive, and I was protected by two big men who would never let anything happen to me. Now that I'm older and a bit wiser, I would not do it again, not even for Cosimo. Only, my Tony will feel otherwise. He would return in a heartbeat because, after all, that was his origin, and it holds no fear for him, and he has always harbored guilt after we watched Cosimo go through alone. By the way, Susan went in just behind him. To me it was even braver, if that is possible. An incredible woman, your mother." She paused before continuing. Barron had to know the full story. "Did you know and understand exactly what occurred back then?"

"I was too young to comprehend it all when it happened, except before Susan died, she told me everything she knew about it. From what I gathered, she felt responsible for the demon who came through and nearly destroyed the world, and she resolved it should never happen again, at least by her hand. Except you said that Cosimo had fought and prevailed. Wouldn't that mean that he had killed the creature once and for all?"

"We believed that the monster was the Antichrist, the mythic devil of the ancient world. I saw him myself, and I still shudder at the thought. Could he be killed? We didn't think so at the time, but if he is still waiting for the opportunity to return to this century, you will have to be both quick and prepared to avoid another disaster."

"Well, I am not at the point of making such an enormous decision. I'm not absolutely sure my calculations are correct, and I have to have the right environment for testing. I wanted to see you before I started working on it since you and Tony are the only ones left who have been through an opening and returned. For your information, and in the strictest confidence, I'm scheduled to transfer my research to Fermilab next month." Barron stopped talking, his train of thought lost in anticipation of just how to disguise his experiments so that the authorities could not guess his intent. He came back to life an instant later and focused on her face, "None, other than us, will understand what it might lead to." After he finished speaking, he and Mary remained looking at each other as if they had always been friends, instead of just meeting.

Barron smiled and touched Mary on the cheek. "My, you are still a lovely woman, Mary. I hope you aren't offended by my noticing."

"No woman would be offended, Barron, especially coming from a man with as much dignity and poise as you possess." She smiled back. "I am concerned, though, that every minute you stay here, you endanger all of us."

"Yes, I should leave." Barron agreed. "Please tell Antonius that I'm sorry I missed him. We will stay in touch, won't we?"

Cupids playing with a lyre. Roman fresco from Herculaneum (perhaps the Basilica)This work is in the public domain

Chapter 26

Research

Galen (130 AD to 200 AD)

Fermilab, Batavia Illinois

*B*arron sensed the shadow moving toward him, silently approaching and closely observing. He stopped typing and twisted in his chair, looking upward to the expected. "Ah, another visit from administration," he said mockingly. "What, pray tell, is it this time?" He stonily looked at Jim Fowler and waited for a response.

"Don't get huffy, Dr. Harmes. It's my responsibility to cut spending and waste. That's how people like you get hired, with money that didn't get used unnecessarily," Fowler spat out. He produced a large piece of graph paper from somewhere and unfolded it. Barron rolled his eyes.

"You are spending my time, aren't you? And isn't my time valuable also?" Barron quipped.

"Look here," Fowler said, and pointed at two peaks in the graph, both circled in red wax pencil. "These are energy spikes. They are not supposed to be there. It's your software that is creating them, so you have to explain it since the rest of us are too dumb to figure this out all by ourselves."

"You understand that my software was given to all the senior scientists who unanimously approved the code prior to implementation? And you understand that my research is proceeding according to design and has produced signifiant findings which have garnered praise?"

"We all understand what a brilliant mind you have, Dr. Harmes, and what an incredible scientist your mother was. Yet there is something odd here, would you not agree?"

"A couple of random energy spikes could come from anything, even equipment or monitor malfunction. I don't find it troubling in the least," Barron replied.

"Well, I, for one, do," Fowler said, not letting the subject go. "I will tell you that more unexplained occurrences could result in your project being shut down until the issue is resolved or explained."

"And I will tell you that I have received several requests to join the research team in Geneva and should my project get shut down for a few energy spikes…well, I know CERN would be delighted to see me."

With a last exasperated look in Barron's direction, Fowler turned his back and disappeared around the corner. Barron silently sighed. A rather expected encounter and it might not be the last of them, he thought to himself. Of course, his program was responsible for the spikes, and there were more of them than Fowler's silly graph showed. Most of the extra energy use was fitted between the sheets, so to speak, except now and then more energy was required. The openings, the portals, had been nearly microscopic at first, requiring minimal energy, just enough to be sure they were indeed present. Larger openings require more energy, and a lengthy opening would send an army of administration types running his way. It was a dilemma, for sure. Now that he had proved to himself that his theory worked and that he could control, precisely control, both the time and position of a pin-sized portal, he needed to move on to a practical opening. Impossible for now, he knew, because he was being closely monitored by staff such as Fowler but also by unseen interested parties who listened and looked over everything he touched. They were the people to fear.

Barron smiled to himself as he turned back to his computer terminal. The software idea of his was brilliant. He had created a copy for submission that, after it was compiled, was exactly the same length in bytes as the one running, the very one that was compiled with very different source code and the very same one that he was using to create portals into the past. It was working nicely indeed. Barron only hoped that someone, someday, would appreciate the genius needed to not only create a time portal yet, at the same time, hide it from everyone, even those who suspected what he was doing.

New York City, V Lictoree Cafe

Rachel Lucchese occupied her usual seat at the usual tiny table in the usual coffee shop. It was a routine for her and a time to relax a bit from the grind of graduate school. Harder than she thought and took way much too much of her free time. Mornings like this one were a small treasure where she could indulge in a cup of fine coffee prepared in the Italian way, which she had grown to love so much. Every time she put the cup to her lips, she saw the bushy head of Cosimo on the other side of the table, just long enough to make her yearn for his company. How about that? A brief summer romance of three short months, and she couldn't get him out of her system. It was, regrettably and most likely, love. So this is what it felt like to be in love. All her free time, and many of her dreams, were spent recollecting the very few moments in his arms. He was the one, she knew it, and she hoped that he knew it. Someday. Someday they would get together again, and this time it would be different. She would make the world stand still for Cosimo Solomon and never again would they part.

A small chime from her laptop indicated a message, and since the sound was audible, it was from her small circle of approved senders. She opened the device rather expecting another, all too short, message from Cosimo. Her eyes widened as she saw who the sender was: Bobby Steinmeyer. Wasn't he the bookish kid who had approached her in the computer lab several months ago? Sure, that was the one. She had given him her email address with instructions… .

Rachel read the message and read it two more times. Indeed this was news, and news that she could relay to Cosimo and his parents. What a break. Then the message's contents sunk in. It wasn't a good message but a uniquely bad one. Bobby and his computer skills had helped read a manuscript written on papyrus two thousand years ago and after incineration in the outflow of the most famous volcano in human history. It was like the past had once again come alive.

Dear Rachel. It's been awhile, however I did remember what you asked me to do if I ever discovered either of the two names you gave me. Turns out better than that. Both names were mentioned on the same line, and immediately, it popped into my head that I had seen or heard those names previously. You got what you wanted, Rachel. There was at least a sentence mentioning the names of Cosimus and Alia. When we get the rest of the scroll read by my software, I'll be able to tell you more. But this is what we have found so far.

First, the scroll's author was, from what they tell me, a rather famous Roman named Lucius Annaeus Seneca. I'm no historian so you have to find out more about him than I can tell you. The sentence containing your names was fragmented, and so far, we have recovered only a part of that section of scroll. He wrote: "Alia, wife of Cosimus, was killed by order of Agrippina on the island of Tyrrhenia."

That's all I have, and I also don't have a clue where Tyrrhenia is. I hope this information is helpful to you.

Bobby

P.S. Now that I've done you a favor, the next time I see you I will expect you to be a bit more friendly.

Rachel looked off into the distance, gathering her thoughts. It was news, however certainly not good news. Alia never made it back to Cosimus like they all hoped she would. Mary, in particular, would be devastated. Except a fact is a fact, and the truth is better than ignorance. She decided to forward the mail as is and send copies to all three members of the Solomon family.

Setteville, Italia

Tony tossed his hat on the table beside the entry door and called for Mary. He had noticed that her car was in the garage so she must be home.

"Mary?" he called.

In the distance he heard a reply, "Upstairs," she answered.

A few bounds up the stairs, and he entered their shared bedroom and found her sitting at the little computer table in the corner. Even from the rear, he could see her body sagging a bit as it often did in her low moments.

"Problems?" he asked.

"Ever heard of *Tyrrhenia*?" she asked, with her back to him.

"Sure. It's the ancient name for what we call Ponza today. I've never been there, but it's just offshore from Naples. What is there about that little island of interest to you?"

"It's where Alia was killed. You must have seen the message from Rachel."

"No, I haven't read my mail yet. Killed? That's really too bad. Not what we wanted to hear. Poor Cos. Fate is sometimes so unfair." Tony sat on the bed and stared at Mary's back. She did not love Cos more than he did, except her emotions were always on the surface, there for everyone to read. His feelings were deep and rarely surfaced. Again, he regretted that Cos went back alone to not only face the monster but, even if he won, be trapped in the past. Yet would he have wanted to change places with Cos and lose all these years beside Mary? Selfishly…no. It was hard to admit, even to himself, only there was no other way for things to turn out good for himself and Mary. If they both had returned with Cos, Mary would have found herself alone in a strange time and in a strange place. Cos was right all along. Only Cos should have returned, and that is what happened.

"Ever hear from that Dr. Harmes again?" Tony asked.

Mary shook her head but didn't otherwise answer.

"Do you need to talk this out, Mary? Is there anything we can do to change what happened so long ago?" Tony asked.

Finally, Mary turned toward him, her eyes red, but there were no longer any tears. "I researched the name *Lucius Annaeus Seneca* and the island of Ponza. You left before any of these names and places came to prominence, so you also may learn some facts of interest."

"No, I'm not up to speed on the history of *Roma* after 27 AD, the year we left the past."

"OK, then. You know that Agrippina the Younger became the wife of Claudius, the Emperor, and that her son, Nero, became emperor after the death of Claudius."

"Sure, we all know that much," Tony replied.

"Did you ever hear that Agrippina had been exiled for three years to the island of Ponza by her brother, Caligula, and eventually brought back by Claudius?"

"No, I missed that fact. Interesting."

"It's more interesting than you think. Julia Livilla was the younger sister of Agrippina and was actually exiled with her during the reign of their brother Caligula, except Julia Livilla was later returned to exile to the island of Ventotene, another nearby island, and was starved to death there by order of Claudius. Even their older brother was exiled there and eventually killed. See a pattern yet? The two islands, Ventotene and Ponza were frequently used to imprison people who were in the way. The message we got today from Rachel confirms it for me. Alia was sent to Ponza to keep Cos out of Rome. She was later murdered there, and we know that by the pen of none other than Seneca, who was a senior adviser to the young Nero. Seneca was in a position to know what had happened."

"All right, we know, or actually think we know, where Alia was taken and that she was murdered rather than set free. So what can we do with that knowledge?" Tony asked.

"Wouldn't you guess that Alia was kept alive there until Claudius was murdered in 54 AD? It was insurance against Cos, who couldn't be controlled by Agrippina. When Cos wrote to you, it was only a month or so after Alia had gone missing. If he had known where she was, he would have found a way to the island and rescued her. Surely Alia was still alive at that time."

"I see where you are going with this. If we had a way, we could just tell Cos where she was, and then history would be changed and he and Alia could spend the rest of their lives together. I get it."

"Not so fast. Think about this for a moment. The wife of the Emperor, Agrippina the Younger, was totally ruthless. After Cos rescued his wife, he would have come for Agrippina out of revenge and anger. She would be certain to have Cos killed and as quickly as possible. Cos has no way out of this. Find his wife and get killed or get killed trying to find his wife. It's a dead end."

"And, my dear imaginative wife, what are you saying we should do?" Tony asked.

"It's obvious, we have to bring both of them back through a portal."

"Are you kidding? Didn't Barron Harmes tell you that he is under constant surveillance? And, as I recall hearing, there is a huge energy expenditure while creating a portal. How could that be done without anyone knowing, especially if they are already suspicious?"

"I don't have an answer for that," Mary replied, "only, together, we may figure it out. Barron was sure that he could recreate another portal, and by this time, I'm sure he has. We need to talk to him, directly, face to face, in a place that no listeners can overhear our conversations. That means we have to travel to America together, and I think we should take our son with us."

"No doubt our son would readily agree, especially if we stop by New York so that he and Rachel can get together again."

Chapter 27

Birds of a Feather

First, have a definite, clear practical ideal; a goal, an objective. Second, have the necessary means to achieve your ends; wisdom, money, materials, and methods. Third, adjust all your means to that end.

Aristotle (384 BC to 322 BC)

Edhams Resturant, Park Avenue, New York

Not all upscale restaurants in New York have separate, enclosed dining areas for wealthy patrons, except this one did, and Cos and his parents were seated at a secluded table for four, waiting impatiently for their invited guest. Rachel was at least thirty minutes late, and they started to wonder if she was coming at all.

"Why don't you call her, son? Find out where she is," Tony suggested again.

"No, I'm sure she is coming. Rachel likes to make a grand appearance, so she will be here eventually," Cos said with confidence. Mary looked between her men, mentally willing them not to start an argument, especially not now.

Tony summoned the waiter, pointing to the nearby empty wine bottle luxuriating in the silver cooling pitcher. To the others, he motioned for them to tip their glasses and, while smiling, demonstrated with his own glass.

The door opened again, and instead of the waiter, Rachel swept in. She was dressed lavishly, decorated with abundant though restrained jewelry, and the effect was one of a movie star or Broadway legend consenting to dine with her adoring public. They all stood to welcome her, with Tony being first to extend his hand.

Instead of accepting a simple handshake, Rachel moved closer to briefly embrace Tony, then quickly turned to give a much longer and more intimate embrace to the man she most wanted to see again.

"Sorry to keep you waiting," she said, looking between them. It's so good to see you all again. I can't count the times I've thought of you." She was looking directly at Cos while speaking, making sure that he knew that she was talking about him.

They could all see the pronounced flush in Cos' face. He was, for the moment, intellectually paralyzed by the presence of this very intelligent, confident, and most beautiful woman who was capturing him with her unblinking eyes. Cos recovered enough to offer Rachel a chair beside his and stood behind her while she seated herself.

"Got your message, Rachel," Mary said, "though the brutality of if was hard to take."

"I'm sure. Not what any of us wanted to hear," Rachel replied. She looked back and forth and wondered just exactly what this meeting was about. Could it be that Cos was accompanied by his parents in anticipation of a proposal? It would be how Italians, in their appreciation of tradition, would want it to happen. And Rachel's parents were also close by, to not only consent but to celebrate the event together with their eventual new in-laws.

"Welcome to New York," Rachel said, raising her wine glass in a toast. "While you are here, is there any place in particular that you want to see or visit?"

"Some other time, Rachel," Tony said. "In fact, we are passing through to Chicago, however we had to stop by and see you again."

Rachel's face fell a bit. It wasn't a proposal after all. She tried not to let her disappointment give her away, though abundant tears were just below the surface.

Cos' eyes hadn't left hers for a moment, and he witnessed her face fall and the luster momentarily leave her eyes. He put his hand on her bare shoulder and pulled her close for a whisper. "You and I have to have a quiet moment together this evening. I am counting on it."

Rachel brightened and turned enough to give him a quick kiss, then looked back across the table. "Can you tell me what is going on?" she asked.

"We have a long story to tell you, and I'm sure you will be interested," Mary said, speaking lowly. "First, you should know that the scientist who made our trips possible had a son who came to see us recently. He is in the same field as his mother and is interested in making another attempt."

"No!" Rachel blurted, her hand rising to cover her open mouth. "You mean you are going again?"

"We think that Cosimus and Alia should be rescued and brought back," Tony affirmed. The news was indeed big, bigger than anything Rachel had ever heard. They were going back in time and bringing two people back with them. It was historic, exciting, explosive.

"It can be done again? Are you sure?" she asked.

"If it could be done the first time, then of course it can. It all depends on our young scientist. We are going to have a meeting with him, face to face, to discuss it," Mary answered.

"The whole thing is a secret, I assume," Rachel calculated. "Can something this newsworthy be kept a secret? Does the government know about it?" So many questions were in her head, all fighting to be answered.

"This is something that must be kept secret for many reasons," Mary explained. "The truth is, the U.S. Government would never permit another opening, and they must never find out about any of this or our lives would be jeopardized. Certainly they would try to remove any evidence, any mechanism, and any scientific theory about time travel…also, any witnesses that it was ever done. We would not involve you, still you figured it out by yourself and would again. You are in this with us, like it or not."

"How can I help, Mary? I don't know the first thing about science," she said.

For the first time, Cos spoke, "We need some way to avoid the surveillance which we believe encircles Dr. Harmes. He is sure they are constantly watching him. Can you ask your family if they know anyone around Chicago who could help us out and keep their mouth shut about it?"

It didn't take long for her tears to form, and nearly instantly they were rolling from Rachel's big eyes down her powdered cheeks. "So you knew all along?" she asked.

"Of course. It doesn't make any difference to me. I love you completely and forever and always will. These several months have been torture to me without you around. A phone call or letter is not enough." Cos had moist eyes himself after speaking. He had intended to pour his heart out to her in private, though her sudden tears had changed everything.

Rachel patted Cos' hand and blotted her tears. "Sure, I think that can be arranged. Can I come along with you?"

"I would love that to happen," Cos replied. He looked at his parents to make sure they had no objections.

However, Tony did have some reservations. "You might be putting yourself in harm's way, Rachel. Better if you stayed here where you are protected and not involved. We don't know if it can be done, but we are ready to go right now, if possible."

"Just so you know," Mary added. "I am not going through this time. You can stay beside me and watch the men go in."

Rachel drew a big breath and turned toward Cos. "You! You are thinking of going without me?" she said accusingly.

Cos raised his hand in protest. "Wait a minute. We don't know if anyone is going. They don't even know if Cosimus wants to come back. The entire thing is just imagination at the moment. However, from the stories I've been told over the last month, I don't think a rational person like you would even want to go. I surely wouldn't want the woman I love and hope to marry to be in harm's way, never for a minute or a second."

"You crazy *Italiano*, is that your way of asking to marry me?"

"It's sincere at least. Will you?"

"On one condition. If you go in there, I go with you. Deal?"

"You crazy *Americano*. Did you just say yes?"

"I did. Where is the ring?"

A Dark Street, Chicago South Side, 11:30 PM

The dark blue maxi van slowed and stopped, its motor still running for a moment, then shut down and waited, its dark windows allowing no possible observation of any occupants. After a long moment, both front doors opened, and two men got out and looked up and down the silent street. Both were bulky, neckless, and dressed in cheap dark suits. They exchanged inaudible words before taking up positions in sheltered doorways on opposite sides of the street. The remaining occupants looked around trying to discern any activity, any landmarks, which would give them a clue as to their exact location though to no avail. They were dependent on their guides, who gave out minimal conversation other than grunts where appropriate. Once commenced, the operation seemed well planned and executed, and it was obvious that their contacts were used to avoiding any risk of detection. In a careless moment, one of them opened his jacket a bit too far exposing a large firearm carried in a low slung shoulder holster.

"What are they doing now?" Cos asked.

"Keeping us safe, I expect," Tony answered. No matter what century, bodyguards acted mostly the same. They needed room for maneuver and surprise. Taking up positions for good crossfire was standard procedure no matter if it were in ancient Rome or the rough streets of Chicago. These were experienced and tough men guarding them, no doubt about it.

They sat in silence for long ticking moments, the anticipation of the coming meeting being enhanced from second to second. In the distance, crossing under one of the few still operating street lights, a person was walking toward them. He was in no hurry and strolled almost casually in their direction. As he got closer, passing into near total darkness, he looked back and forth and briefly behind him once or twice. When he drew opposite the dark doorway sheltering a bodyguard, he paused briefly but didn't look toward the shadow. As if guided by an unseen force, he headed straight for the blue van and, without hesitation, opened the side door.

"Can I come in?" Barron asked.

"Please and welcome," Mary said. On the sound of a familiar voice, Barron dipped low and disappeared inside the van, the door closing softly behind him.

Barron extended his hand in the darkness toward whoever was in there with him. Tony was first to take it and said, "Hi, Doctor Harmes. I'm Tony. Sorry I missed you in Rome, but I'm very glad to meet you at last."

"And glad to meet you, Antonius. You are a legend to me. At least, I can say that I heard your voice, though I can truthfully say that I never saw you in person." They all laughed at this display of humor in an otherwise somber and tense moment.

"Hi, professor," Cos said. "I'm their son, and this person beside me is my fiancé, Rachel. My new fiancé, I should add."

"Well, delighted to meet you both and congratulations," Barron replied. "You all should call me Barron and drop the formality. We are all rowing in a small boat through troubled waters and should be friends first and foremost. Trust is a precious thing, and sharing it between more than one is even more special."

"Thanks for coming, Barron," Mary said. "Sorry to put you through all this security and secrecy, however I'm sure you understand. We had to talk to you in person because none of us trust any electronic communication given who could be watching."

"Oh, be assured that they are watching, very closely watching, and they are probably using every possible method, old and new. Your friends out there seem to have their own methods, albeit a bit rough ones, to avoid the authority's scrutiny. I was literally snatched from a gas station by surprise. At first, I thought they were intelligence agency goons although quickly realized that it was only real goons, and they were not interested in harming me. I wasn't sure about any of it until I gratefully heard Mary's sweet voice just now."

"I can tell you that all of us want to know one thing first and foremost. Is it possible to open another aperture into the past?" Tony asked.

"Indeed it is. I have so far opened twelve of them. They were all nearly invisible to the naked eye, however my algorithms work, and I have confidence that they are repeatable. In addition, I have improved my mother's calculations, and the passage may be placed in time and space with confidence."

"That's wonderful news to us," Tony said. He started to continue but paused, thinking out how it should be stated.

"And you must be ready to try it again or else you wouldn't be here," Barron guessed. "So what has changed? Certainly not the past because it just hangs there in silence, unchanging and unchangeable."

"Are you suggesting that the past cannot be changed?" Tony asked.

"Depends on how you look at it. If you go back in time and do something, anything really, you are already part of the past. It didn't change anything. The past has recorded events that are what they are. No one says exactly why or how, they just are."

"On the other hand… ," Mary objected, "didn't you hear of the carnage brought on because the beast came through the opening? Cosimo went back in time to prevent him from coming in. The future changed, and I know this and so does Tony because we witnessed it."

"Depends how you look at it," Barron repeated. Obviously, he was not about to explain his concept of those events. It could wait for another day. "And just why do you, some of you I'll bet, want to go back in time again?"

"To rescue Cosimus and his wife. Otherwise, they will be killed," Mary said.

"However, I repeat, that history is history. Do you know for sure that they will be killed or, should I say the more factual, were killed?"

"A recent translation from a newly discovered scroll says that Alia was killed on the island of *Tyrrhenia,*" Rachel explained.

"So, I assume that you would go back to a date that you are sure she is still alive and take her into the future with you?" Barron suggested.

"That's about it. We need to rescue her from the island before she is murdered."

"Still, your historian says that she was killed. Then was he lying or wrong?" Barron persisted.

"Maybe he just assumed she was killed. He may have just known the order for her killing was given," Tony interjected.

"That is possible," Barron admitted. "Though, you could 'rescue' her before she was taken to the island."

"No, because she wouldn't leave then. She was happy where she was and so was her husband. They would only leave that life if there were no other choices," Tony explained.

"Yes, well…hmmm…," Barron murmured as he thought it through. "Say, that means that there has to be more than one opening. You need to fetch this Alia from the island and then at some other place, get her husband. And they have to agree to come back. At least four openings. Just open long enough to pass through, close and open again to allow you to come back in. It has to all be done in one night because after this huge power drain is discovered, I am done at Fermilab. They will close me down, possibly arrest me. It's not certain that they haven't already rigged some system to prevent me from using so much power. If that is the case, then the entire scheme is not possible. We will all just end up in prison."

"We don't want to ruin your career, Barron, and none of us want to see you or us in prison. Perhaps we should just write this off as impossible," Rachel suggested.

"For sure on that. I don't think we should take that kind of risk. It's bad enough just thinking about going through the portal," Cos agreed.

"For one thing, you should know that if anyone goes through, it will be me and only me," Tony declared.

Barron came out of his thoughts and put an end to their speculation. "Listen up. I want to open a portal, even it it accomplishes nothing. It's my contempt for the spies, watching me and waiting on me to make a mistake, that makes me want to do this. Nevertheless, first I have to know where, exactly where, you want these openings placed and the exact moment in time. I have to know the precise coordinates so that I can use my program to decide where in the ancient world it would be located. One thing you should understand is that the earth is not in the same location in space that it was at that time. Far from it. The earth is not only orbiting and tilting, but the solar system and our galaxy are also moving. This is not as easy as it sounds." He stopped without finishing as his mind strove to grasp the totality of the proposed task. Suddenly he came back to the present and finished speaking. "Look, I have an idea about the power drain, though I have to experiment a bit first. You people have a task while I'm working on this and that is to get me those coordinates and decide exactly what you need and how long it will take. Give me a month, and we will meet again and talk it over. By then, I should know if it can be done safely and, most importantly, quietly."

Chapter 28

Deception

Tacitus (56 AD to 117 AD)

Fermilab, Batavia, Illinois 8:00 AM

Dr. Barron Harmes got out of his low slung sports car and stood upright, partially to stretch and partly to look around and observe who was looking his way. He locked the door, then opened the trunk and extracted a handsome leather briefcase. He was dressed not in a white lab coat with an open collar shirt underneath but in a fitted wool suit complete with vest. There was an important meeting this morning, and his brain kept searching the parameters of his presentation, recalling each significant point and the arguments both for and against his proposal. Representatives from the AEC would be there, as well as the directors of Fermilab and, most importantly, eminent scientists who would have been invited. Dr. Harmes would be proposing a new field of study, a high energy project, which would require many megawatts of energy, all brought in by the many high tension wires leading into the Fermilab complex. It was to be a costly proposal, indeed, and one that required a financial commitment from the Atomic Energy Commission, representing the U.S. Government nuclear physics research efforts.

Barron stopped by the main office before heading to the conference room. Down the hall, he could already see the security team in place, their scanning unit being set up beside the table holding the admission badges. He was looking for his self-declared nemesis, Dr. James Fowler, himself a published nuclear expert, however now acting as the supervisor in charge of others' pet projects.

"Jim in yet?" he asked the pert secretary. She nodded her head and chin-pointed toward the closed door.

"May I enter?" he asked her. She shrugged. Barron took this as an invitation and opened the door and walked in.

"Well, young man, is there some deception I can help you with, or are you just trying to be nice before your presentation?" There was dripping sarcasm from Fowler who had become convinced that Barron was lying about his project's energy use. The problem for Fowler is that few, other than Barron, actually fully understood the scientific merit of his research, and certainly, it was above the head of Jim Fowler.

"Now, Jim, try to be nice. If I pull this off it means a lot of money for our lab, does it not? You should be in there as my clapping support section instead of tossing snippy cutting remarks. You need to apologize."

"You are smart. I'll give you that. However, there are others than me who are suspicious of you. Someday you will be uncovered."

"Yes, Jim, and that would delight you that a smart cookie like me was finally brought down by a lowlife like you. I give up trying to explain to you how we don't fully understand Particle Physics yet, even fewer totally grasp Quantum Mechanics, and there are bound to be unexplained glitches. Come on, get over it and work with me."

"I don't trust you any more than others before me trusted your mother. We still don't know exactly what she was doing, certainly not what she said. And she was receiving funding from some rather suspicious sources."

"My mother again, is it? The reason her research is beyond your understanding is simply a matter of IQ, same as my research. Frankly, Jim, you are hopeless, and this is the last time I will make an attempt to gain your confidence." With that last final statement, Barron turned on his heel and slammed the door on his way out. He ignored the secretary and passed her in silence yet could feel her eyes on his back as he made for the conference center.

A poster stood beside the open conference door noting the topic for presentation. It read:

Proton Spin Crisis...A Possible Solution
Using high energy muons to create quark spin,
a novel approach
to a vexing question

Presented by Barron Rasmon Harmes, PhD

Barron smiled at the topic, knowing that it would arouse interest and money, especially if an American physicist could be the first to solve a historic problem. He picked up his name tag at the desk and was waved through by security.

Outside the Tevatron, Fermilab, Batavia, Illinois 10 PM

Barron pulled up his coat against the omnipresent winter wind coming off big Lake Michigan, just to the north. He squinted, holding his hand to his eye, shielding the fog of snow just now gathering in quantity. The entry door, the same one his mother used the times he had accompanied her to her basement level lab, was just ahead, the small vapor light over the door sparkling in the snow. Once there, he held his security badge to the sensor and, after a few seconds, heard the bolt go back, releasing the door. He wondered at the delay, which should have been instantaneous given the computer processing speed available. Could it be that his card triggered and relayed information to another party, a supervisory party or even a nefarious government agency or two, he wondered. Barron shrugged. They could look all they wanted, except they could never see what they wanted because it wasn't visible nor was it in the computer code that he had written himself. The time travel aperture was a side effect of his and his mother's research, not a direct effect which could be predicted. To an investigator, even if he discovered the opening, would never be able to associate a direct link to research by the respected Dr. Barron Harmes.

The poorly lit basement stairs were the most dangerous thing in the building, especially with snow covered shoes. He proceeded cautiously, looking around as he descended. No assistants or scientists were present, and the authorities simply could not place conventional cameras and listening devices in this cavernous space because electronic forces emanating from the accelerated beam made that impossible. Barron liked to work at night because he could think things out without distraction. He had the area to himself, that was certain.

Once at tunnel level, he strolled down the massive circular opening until he came to the Switchyard, so called because that is where accelerated particles were separated, sorted and directed at targets not far away. It was eerily quiet just now because the equipment stood silent, waiting on the correct computer signal to proceed. The heavily shielded computer work station he used was sitting on the right side of the tunnel, slowly blinking its readiness. Tonight was the real test, the culmination of months of work, and most importantly, the utilization of a project mainly designed to provide cover for the enormous energy costs of opening a time portal. He had in his pocket the exact coordinates, as provided by Tony and Mary, and their calculations of the time needed for the duration of a portal opening and, importantly, the calendar date down to the exact hour, minute and second. They were ready and waiting to be called and, at the moment, residing in one of the swanky downtown Chicago hotels overlooking Lake Michigan.

He wakened the computer, entered his password and hit the start key. There was a gradual, nearly inaudible whine at first which rapidly built in volume and presence. The machine was ready, waiting only on his final instructions which Barron rapidly typed into the keyboard. He checked his entries three times, making absolutely sure that they were correct, then looked up and around one last time.

Once the process started, the ambient energy released by the subatomic particles streaming through overhead tubes tingled his skin and vibrated his entire body, making his hair feel as though it was standing on end. Barron closely watched the location where the portal was to be created as the whine turned into a scream and then to a howl. Suddenly, there it was, a circular opening nearly two meters in diameter, hovering about ten centimeters from the floor, and as clear and crisp as if it were only an optical illusion. He rushed over to it and peered in. It was just where it was supposed to be, facing a rising hill just past the harbor on the island of Ponza or *Tyrrhenia* as it was called in ancient times. On the hill top, spotlighted by the rising sun, was a Roman villa, the *Palazzo Giulia* of legend. It was spectacular and in perfect condition, its elaborate stone work breathtaking even from this distance. Barron could hear voices, and they were becoming louder as they approached the opening from an unseen direction. He quickly ran to the terminal and hit the 'abort' key and was relieved when the opening snapped closed. He could feel sweat beads forming on his forehead in spite of the cool conditions in the tunnel. Barron remembered the tale of what had happened previously when his mother was standing about where he was at the moment. A monster had come through, an unstoppable presence of evil. Could it happen again and without warning? He didn't know and that was troubling.

Barron usually felt secure about himself in that he was a person recognized in his field yet also physically fit, very fit, attained by vigorous workouts for most of his life. He wasn't used to the sensation of fear, although it was with him now, and he felt his heart leaping about, pumping blood in preparation for some flight or fight for his life. His hands were wet and clammy, his thoughts fuzzy. The reality struck him that he had opened a portal and looked through it to a time in earth's history roughly two thousand years ago. The sensation he felt looking into the portal was not one of delight at the miracle of scientific accomplishment but of terrifying, abject fear encircling him. Barron was faced with the enormity of what he had done. No wonder that the authorities didn't want a portal opened again. It wasn't right, and it was dangerous for many, many reasons. Had he made a mistake? Barron felt more like Dr. Frankenstein who created a creature out of dead parts and watched as it opened its eyes. There was no control, no turning back after the monster became alive, and things once impossible were possible. He tried to calm down, tried to let his body burn off the extra epinephrine so his brain could function like a scientist instead of an adolescent afraid of the dark. Still… there was one more setting he had to check, this one was an exact location in the home of the Cosimus in question. No matter how fearful it was to open another portal in time, he had to make sure that when the moment came, the process would be accurate and safe. He looked at his trembling hands. "Calm down, Barron," he said aloud, though his body wouldn't listen. His instincts were proving smarter than his intellectual processes, demanding that he run away.

Once more, Barron checked the coordinates. He specified that the portal would open in Herculaneum late at night, hopefully avoiding notice, and, he hoped, avoiding any dangerous entities lurking nearby ready to rush through and cause chaos. This time, before hitting the key initiating a high energy cascade coursing through the overhead tubes, he took a deep breath and briefly closed his eyes. Again, he felt his body tingle as if being charged with electrons and the sensation that his hair was standing upright. Barron forced himself to watch for the opening, even though he didn't want to see it there. Yet there it was, hanging like the mirror from some German fairy tale, a hole in space through which lived the past. He had to look in, and he had to do it quickly, then close the opening as soon as possible. Barron took long strides toward the opening and saw exactly what he didn't want to see. A man was on the other side looking back. And this was no ordinary man. The man on the other side was thick with muscle and something else… he exuded danger, radiated it. Barron caught his breath, not able to move for a moment, as if a tiger had just appeared on a trail right in front of him.

"Just who are you?" the man asked. Even his voice was threatening, dark and suddenly Barron realized that his words were spoken using English!

"My name is Barron…who are you?"

"Barron what?"

"Barron Harmes."

"Are you related to Susan Harmes?" the man asked.

"My mother. I was adopted."

"What year is it there?"

"It's 22 years after you left. I assume you are Cosimus."

"I was once called Cosimo where you are. Why did you open a portal?"

"Your friends, Antonius and Mary, wanted it. I'm sorry, Cosimo, however I have to close this portal. They aren't here now, but stay there, and I'll open it again when they arrive."

"Wait," Cosimus said. "Why now? Do you know?"

"It's about Alia. They have an idea." After he spoke, he rushed to the terminal and hit the key.

Herculaneum, June 52 AD

Cos stared at the floor right where the opening had just winked out, lost in thought. Something just happened that he never thought he would see again and suddenly he felt out of place, in the wrong time. It hit him that here, he was only a visitor, never really belonging, a simple actor in a role pretending to be part of this ancient human drama. He felt the tears welling up in his eyes and about to run down his face. The man, Barron, said that his friends knew about Alia. His friends so long ago lost to him were just on the other side of an imaginary wall. Cos looked at his feet where the stone with the inscription to Antonius was still fresh. It was only yesterday that he had inserted it, knowing that it was nearly impossible for the message underneath to survive and be read by the single person in earth's history that should read it. Nevertheless, it worked. The message was received and read, just as he hoped. A gulf of two thousand years and it took only one day for the answer to arrive. And, Antonius and Mary had some plan to recover Alia. His heart soared, the weight lifted from his shoulders, and he smiled. Help had arrived.

Chapter 29

Truth

Tacitus (56 AD to 117 AD)

Outside the Tevatron, Fermilab, Batavia, Illinois 1:15 AM

With Dr. Fowler in the lead, the little group started for the side entry door. The snow was coming down hard, and puffy gusts of wind swirled around their heads. All seven men were hunched over, their heads down, trying to avoid the tearing effect of a rapidly declining temperature against bare skin and eyes. There was a short steel platform just visible against the looming concrete mass. The entry door was there though hidden in the shadow cast by a small vapor light mounted high on the wall.

As they mounted the stairs, Agent Brimm called out to Fowler, "Can you tell me one more time why we are doing this in the middle of the night?"

"I've been monitoring the energy expenditure of Dr. Harmes' research. There are frequent surges of power, nearly all of them are at night when other staff isn't present. There's something going on, and I, for one, think he is up to something illegal, immoral or devious, certainly not within the bounds of his stated research." Fowler started to pull his pass key, but Brimm's big hand stopped him, grasping his wrist.

"And what do you expect to see in there, Dr. Fowler?"

Fowler hesitated, looking at the closed metal door and then back to Brimm's shielded face. "I don't know, although there must be something amiss. We'll see when we get in there."

"Hold it," Brimm insisted, "if we find nothing, nothing at all, then you have alerted Harmes and only accomplished giving him warning that you are watching. What if all the activity you saw is imbedded in computer code? Have you looked at the programming, and if you did, what did that show?"

"Yes, we looked at it in detail. Several times, in fact. We don't think the program will create spikes of that nature," Fowler admitted.

"Frankly, Fowler, this is a stupid misadventure calling for a raid with nothing but suspicion to go on. I've been around a long time looking for spies, finding some, missing some. You know, I've begun to believe that this is just a grudge match between scientists." Agent Brimm let go of Fowler's hand then pushed him away from the door, turning him face to face. "I've decided to go in there alone and check it out. You and my men will wait here until I call for you. Got that?"

It wasn't what Fowler wanted, however Brimm had authority and an overpowering personality. Besides, he had several heavily armed men with him. Fowler stepped back and waved his hand toward the door, an offer of first entry.

"I'll need your pass key. Thanks," Brimm said and took it out of Fowler's hand. Quickly, he held it up to the scanner, and the door bolt popped open.

The warm air rushed out, enveloping the party gathered on the stairs in a frosty mist as the additional humidity turned to ice. With a last contemptuous look at Fowler, Brimm entered and allowed the door to slam behind him. He stood, for a long moment letting his eyes adjust to the dim available light, and listened. He wanted to be sure there were no human voices drifting toward him from the huge tunnel below. All he heard was the threatening hum of the science project working, producing a flow of subatomic particles through the overhead tubes. Brimm shook his head. No matter what they paid him, he would never consent to work around all this energy flowing here and there. There was no way it could be good for a human body to be exposed for very long.

Brimm went carefully down the long metal staircase, holding on to the rail at all times. A fall here would clearly result in severe injury or even death. Once at the bottom, he looked both ways in the tunnel. One side was dark and foreboding, the other held more light and more probability that Dr. Harmes was down there some place. He started walking while looking around. The place was, in some ways, cavelike, filled with millions of dollars worth of gear and equipment. Ahead, he found what he was looking for. A man was seated at a computer terminal, busily typing at the keyboard, unaware that someone was headed his way.

Brimm stood at a distance and watched before calling attention to his presence. All he saw was what he expected to see. Dr. Harmes was hard at work, and there was nothing around him but bare concrete floor, not a single other person present. Brimm cleared his throat and watched Harmes' head snap around toward the sound. The quickness of the move did imply some guilt, some dread of being exposed while doing something he wanted no one to see.

"Hello, Dr. Harmes. My name is Brimm, and I am with the AEC. This is an unannounced visit, and I apologize for startling you."

Barron turned on his seat and stared at the man walking toward him. He saw a middle-aged man with a taut weatherbeaten face. A winter hat hid his hair, although above the ears, the hair was mottled grey, matching the small mustache on his upper lip. Behind the squinting narrow eyes there was obvious intelligence, a prying stealthy intelligence formed by long experience. Barron read the signs. This was a dangerous man, and he had to be very careful with his interactions.

"Just what are you doing here, whoever you are? This area is off limits without supervised guidance. Even you should know that," Barron said.

"You may rest assured that I do know that. Put simply, I am here to see what you are doing," Brimm answered.

"And what have you discovered?"

"Not much so far. We were alerted about the energy spikes produced during your experimentation. I thought I would ask first. What about that?" Brimm asked.

"Know anything about particle physics?" Barron retorted.

"More than you may have guessed. I was around when your mother worked here."

"So you knew my mother. Did you have problems with her research as well?"

"I knew enough to understand that there was more going on than what was stated. There were the same spikes of electrical consumption, yet there was something else. She was being funded by some pretty strange sources."

"And, did you ever find anything that was illegal or unpatriotic about her work?" Barron quizzed.

"It came to an end suddenly, before we could fully understand what was happening. And she retired almost immediately afterwards. I continue to have my suspicions."

Barron stood up and faced Brimm, his hands on his hips. Once standing, Barron found himself a bit larger than Brimm, certainly younger and fitter.

"And you harbor the same suspicions about my research, is that stating it clearly?"

"I'll get right to the point, Professor Harmes," Brimm said forcefully. "I think…I know… what this is all about. It's time travel. And you are working on the same thing. All of us at the agency have been looking for the extensive files your mother kept and then hid from us. You undoubtedly know where they are, and I'm certain that her files are the basis for your current research, if you can call it that."

"What an imagination, Brimm," Barron hissed. "Time travel! Where in the hell did that science fiction come from? It's laughable."

"You won't be laughing if I turn off the power one day. You'll be standing out on the street looking in or, better still, looking out from behind bars like some animal."

"Where's your proof? I hope your people can defend against the biggest lawsuit anyone has ever seen. And I'll bet when this story comes out in the press, you will be considered the biggest fools in history as well. Time travel. Grow up, Brimm. That stuff was in the funny books you read as a child. There is no such thing as time travel."

Brimm grew red in the face. He did know more than he was allowed to speak about. Dr. Barron Harmes was doing exactly what his mother had done. Brimm had had a recent meeting with his supervisor who gave explicit instructions. The public must never discover that time travel was actually possible. The news would erupt and travel around the world in seconds. And immediately, experimentation in a dozen labs would follow in a race to see who could duplicate openings in time. The world would never be the same. Brimm guessed that Harmes would react in anger if provoked, and afterwards, you couldn't be sure what would happen. There were only two possible solutions. Barron Harmes could be dragged off into a dark corner and disposed of or… perhaps he could be tempted by an offer of cooperation. Brimm would propose Barron Harmes silence in return for giving up his methods and files.

"Tell you what, Harmes," Brimm said softly. "If you want to keep working on this, you have to let me in. We both understand how top secret this is. The deal you must agree to is that when whatever you are working on is complete, you will never go back to it again and, in addition, we must destroy all your and your mother's records. This entire process must be erased from history. A smart fellow like you should agree that it's too dangerous to attempt time travel. No one should ever know that it is possible, and certainly no one should ever realize that it was actually done. I want this matter to return to the level of 'funny books' and science fiction."

The bluntness of Brimm's little speech took the fight out of Barron. Brimm wasn't guessing. He knew for certain about the time travel Susan had been a part of. Brimm was the tip of the spear. There were others, an entire agency, who knew enough to guess the rest. There was no secret to protect. He also admitted to himself that Brimm was right. This had to be the end of it forever. The fear he felt during those two brief openings had aged him by years. No, he didn't actually want to continue. At some point, one of the openings will allow another element to invade the present. A horror out of time.

"I don't see why I should trust you, Brimm. If you feel that way, just back off, and let me handle it."

"I can't do that. Things may spiral out of your control. All that on one person's shoulders is too much. You are taking responsibility for all of humanity, for everyone who has ever lived. No matter how smart you are, that's too big a burden. You need me."

"Sure. And you need proof, and once you get it, I'm history," Barron snapped.

Brimm looked around the vicinity, scanning for any small thing which might lead to implications of going beyond the scope of the research protocols. There was nothing at all to use, no tool or clue. It was either all in Barron Harmes head or his computer code and that had already been examined by very smart people. "Look, Harmes, I can choose to shut you down right now, or you can start trusting me. Your choice and I don't have all night."

Barron responded by typing on his keyboard in a short burst and immediately, the roar of particles overhead started diminishing. The machinery had been turned off. Barron looked up and toward Brimm with a smile. He had made his decision, and he had chosen to be defiant.

"I'm done here, Brimm. You can stay as long as you like, however I'm finished. You'll hear about this tomorrow when I report to the board of directors that you caused so much interference that I could not continue. It will be interesting to see what they say."

Brimm rubbed his chin, his hard eyes squinting at Barron Harmes, trying to decide if this was a bluff or a serious challenge to his authority. He knew what the board would say because he had been down this road before. They trusted Dr. Harmes completely. He was widely admired and cultivated, and walking out on an ongoing science project would be heard round the globe for years. Damn. Strike out for Brimm's side.

"Whatever you decide, Dr. Harmes. We can meet soon and give this more discussion if you like."

"No chance of that. I'm quitting, moving to Europe where I'm not likely to be second guessed by a gumshoe. Over there, scientists are admired, not arrested. The lab is yours Brimm, and you can do whatever you like with it." Barron snatched his coat from the rear of his chair and started walking down the corridor using brisk, long strides, not looking back even once.

Brimm had a sudden thought. Barron Harmes still had an active pass key. He called out and ran toward him, catching him just before the long ascent up the iron staircase. "I'll have to have your badge and pass key, you know," he said breathlessly.

"Not unless I am arrested, and if you try to take it from me now, you and your face will be headed to the emergency room." Barron stopped walking and glared back. Brimm hesitated. An arrest without any proof of any kind would be personal suicide in the department, especially of a renowned scientist. And, worse, the newspapers would sniff around and just might discover what it was all about. No arrest at the moment, he quickly decided. Brimm stopped where he was and watched as the younger and fitter Dr. Harmes took the stairs two at a time, heading for the exit.

Chapter 30

The Open Portal

Epicurus (341 BC to 270 BC)

arron slid down in his seat, watching with one eye over the dash as Fowler and Brimm got into their respective cars after their long conversation while standing in the snow and leaning close together. As their tail lights disappeared into the night, he sat upright and reached for his phone, the unregistered, toss away phone given to him by one of the tough guys who had arranged his first and only face to face meeting with Tony and Mary after they arrived in the U.S.

He quickly dialed the number which would connect with another phone of the same type…both untraceable without significant effort by the FBI.

"Hello," Mary answered, her voice giving away her hesitance and lack of trust that whoever was on the other end was friend instead of foe.

"This is Barron. Are all of you together?" he asked.

"We are, at least the ones who intend on going. Count me out, though Tony, Cos and Rachel are ready."

"I thought Tony said that he was the only one."

"It's not up to me. Should I put Tony on?"

"Yes, time is short."

"Hi," Tony said.

"This is the time and the only time we will ever get. Are you ready?" Barron asked.

"Anytime. Should we come now?"

"As soon as possible. I'll meet you in the parking lot. Hurry if you want this done."

They disconnected, and Barron slumped back in his seat, covering his face with his parka hood. There were few other cars in the parking lot, and security made rounds every two hours. Barron reasoned that it would take about a half hour for Tony and the others to arrive by cab. He tried to calm down and think. This might work, then again, he had to consider that Fowler might have rigged an alarm system to alert him if power surges occurred again. They would get one chance and then it was over. As he thought about the timing, it occurred to him that there only needed to be two openings, very close to each other in time. Open the first, shut it down, reset the parameters then open the second. If the parties were there and ready, they could all be out of the building before Brimm was called and returned. Yes, his research at Fermilab was effectively over tonight, still, if he pulled this off, it would be very hard for Brimm to prove that anything was amiss, just more research in the middle of the night. Barron took a deep breath, trying to steady himself against his fears of both opening a window into the past and getting away with such an audacious experiment.

A car's engine and the sound of tires crunching ice woke him, and he carefully looked over the dash, seeing the illuminated marker of a taxi moving toward him. Barron sat upright and rubbed his face, trying to wake up fully before the excitement began. He saw the broad shoulders of Tony emerge, and as he watched, the cab emitted two more people, one of them a woman. He opened his car door and three heads turned toward him.

"Hi," Barron said and started walking rapidly toward them. "Let's go before anyone knows we are here." He headed over the open snow field, hearing footsteps behind him, and bounded up the short staircase, holding his breath as he held his card up to the scanner. The bolt went back, and Barron exhaled a column of frosty smoke. Fowler had not had time to reset the security computer. They were in.

With Barron in the lead, the group hurried down the long tunnel. In the distance was the computer workstation that would make the entire thing possible. Once there, Barron stopped, turned and studied the three before speaking.

"Let me explain how this is going to work. I will open a portal which will remain open just long enough for you to go through, then close it down behind you. You should find yourselves in the home of Cosimus, and I think he will be there to greet you. You will have six days there to do whatever you plan to do, and then, exactly at the same time of day, I will open the portal, and you can come back."

"I thought you would only have this one chance,"Tony asked. "You are going to do this again in less than a week?"

"No," Barron explained. "I have only to reset the system to appear in six days of time in the past; for me, it will only be a few seconds. We will not be operating in parallel time." He studied them for the impact of his words, then added, "One other thing you should consider. Once you go back in time, it is possible that something will go wrong on this end, and you will be there forever or until you die. I have not tested this process, and it is only a guess that it will work. And, there are people watching me and this system. If they discover what I am doing, they could shut off the power before I can get you back."

"So about the island that we presume that Alia is being held?" Tony asked, "You are not going to open a window there?"

"I don't think we should take that chance. It means more energy spikes and more chance of detection plus a big delay while you go find Alia and bring her to the portal. You will have to catch a boat to the island and rescue her yourself. Just be back in six days exactly or practice your Latin skills."

Tony looked at his son and Rachel, and they looked back. "You both want to go, I understand. You heard Barron. It's dangerous in many ways. If I go back alone and something happens that I don't come back, you can say that I returned to the time that was my heritage and know that I was thankful that I had these years with you and Mary. Neither of you would ever be happy back in that time. So my advice is to stay here and be safe."

"It's dangerous for you also, *Papà*. I remember that you said they would consider you to have deserted your post and, therefore, you would be treated as a criminal," Cos reminded him.

"I doubt that anyone there would remember an event from that long ago," Tony said. "Although if such a thing did happen, where would that leave you? Cos, you don't know the first thing about survival in ancient times. And Rachel, you don't even speak a bit of Latin. You might find yourselves captive and in slavery."

No doubt that Tony's warning had a chilling effect on Cos and Rachel, and they looked at each other with new concern. It was a big decision going through a portal, and they didn't have any more time to think it through.

"Dr. Harmes," Cos called out, "I have an idea that we should consider." They all turned to look his way, waiting on him to voice his plan. "What if you open a portal and let Cosimus come in with us then quickly open another on the island where Alia is for him. He would rescue his wife all by himself, and none of us would take any risk."

Rachel raised her hand, "History tells us that Agrippina was ruthless and capable of killing anyone standing in her way. Mary and I have researched her to the extent the historical record allows, and we agree that she would never stop until Cosimus is eliminated. Saving Alia is only one part of his problem."

"And I agree with that. Thanks, Rachel," Tony said. "I was a warrior at one time, and I might be able to assist my brother once again. I owe him that. We have no idea of what awaits us on the other side, and I see no reason either of you need to go in."

"Listen up, folks," Barron interrupted. "We don't have time to spend arguing. The longer we are here, the more likely it is that we will be discovered and then no one goes anywhere. I'm ready to begin right now, so whoever is actually willing to go in, get your gear on."

Cos and Tony began rapidly opening the bundles they had carried with them, and as they laid out the clothing and armor, they began to undress, tossing aside the modern and putting on the ancient.

"I guess that means you are going in also, Cos," Rachel noted. He nodded in agreement as he pulled on a chain mail garment.

"I am going through. You stay here with Barron."

Rachel undid her coat and let it fall to the floor, revealing a proper Roman tunic and palla. She picked up a long stola and flipped it around her shoulder, looking back at the men with defiance. "And I'm going also," she announced.

The ambient humming started. Low at first, rapidly building to a penetrating and threatening vibration, creating an undisguised fear in the faces of Barron's guests. After a series of low frequency clangs in rapid progression, Barron yelled over the noise, "It's up! Look over to the left near the floor!" Indeed it was open, at first hard to see because the dark opening blended into the unlit corridor behind it.

Tony was first to look in, and he smiled, "Good to see you again, brother." He extended his hand, and another one came out from the past to take it. Tony started disappearing into the circle and yelled behind him, "Come, if you are coming," and then disappeared. Rachel and Cos glanced at each other and swallowed hard. This was the actual moment, and when it finally came, the decision to enter was not so easy as they imagined.

"Hurry!" Barron screamed.

Cos took Rachel's hand, and together they started through. When they stood erect on the other side, the opening behind them silently winked out.

Barron stood for a moment before wiping the tension sweat off his upper lip, ignoring the omnipresent hum overhead, the massive particle accelerator patiently waiting on his next move. His fingers rapidly clicked at the keys, calculating and inserting the exact numerical positions for the next opening, which would be scheduled to exist after mere moments of his time but six long days in the past. Just before his finger touched the key to start the power surge, he heard a low voice behind him.

"Turn it off, Harmes. You are done here," Brimm said. Barron twisted to look at the source of the voice, and the first thing he saw was the barrel of a large caliber pistol pointed at his chest.

"You again!" Barron exclaimed. He backed away from the terminal, not striking any keys.

"Me? Sure. What did you expect…a host of admirers celebrating your illegal activity?" You are under arrest, Barron Harmes. By rights, I should shoot you here because a trial might expose exactly what you are up to. One tiny false move on your part will give my finger the excuse it needs. Just try it and see."

"You don't understand, Brimm. If you let me explain you would agree and be part of this instead of creating another tragedy."

"You are creating time travel. I know all I need to know. The public entrusts me with the responsibility to prevent nuts like you from perverting science and endangering the future of the human race. You have to be stopped by whatever method possible. Now put up your hands and move away from that keyboard."

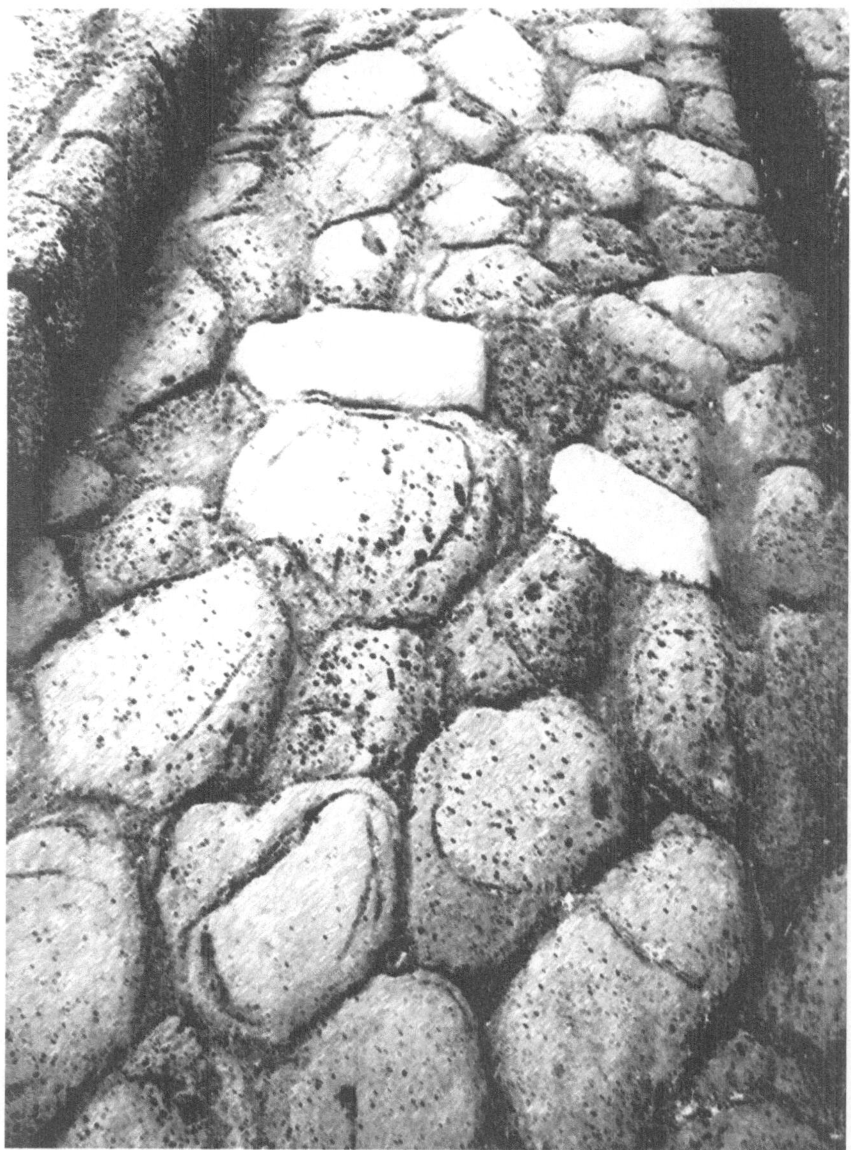

Surface of a roman road in Herculaneum, which was buried by the eruption of mount Vesuvius 79 AD (public domain image)

Chapter 31

No Better Friend

All men have one refuge, a good friend,
with whom you can weep and know that he
does not smile.

Menander(342 BC to 291 BC)

The first thing Rachel saw was the glorious sight of Antonius embracing Cosimus, and then the first thing she noticed was the utter darkness of the room, lit by two small, smoking oil lamps. She looked around trying to make out the room and the objects within. It dawned on her that this was the very site where she and Cos had discovered the bronze inlaid stone which started this entire adventure. Reflexly glancing down at her feet, she saw it. It was there in plain view, the bronze still fresh from the hand of a master craftsman, reflecting the dim ambient light. She nudged Cos and pointed at the floor, and he looked down and smiled.

"And who are these two brave souls?" Cosimus asked, looking for the first time at Cos and Rachel.

"Hi!" Cos spoke up. "I'm named after you, I believe. They call me Cosimo, however you can just call me Cos."

"You are the son of Antonius and Mary?" Cosimus asked.

"Indeed I am, and this is my fiancé, Rachel," he announced proudly, placing his arm over Rachel's shoulder.

"A beautiful woman," Cosimus remarked, looking her over. "I would have expected no less from a man named after me. Except what are any of you doing here?" he asked, glancing at the new faces, each in turn.

"We have come to help you find Alia," Tony answered and placed his hand on his friend's shoulder, "and to perhaps save you from Agrippina."

"And how can you do what I have failed to do?"

"We have studied your letter and researched history. A recent discovery at the Villa of the Papyrii gave us some disturbing news. Alia was killed…murdered on the order of Agrippina."

"Where, when?" Cosimus asked. The news visibly weakened him, and he turned his face away from his friend.

"We don't think it has happened yet. All of us agree on one thing. Alia was taken to the island of Ponza, just off the coast. Agrippina was previously exiled there herself and knows the place very well. I believe that her bodyguard, the *Numerus Batavorum,* carried out her orders. They speak German, the same as your Alia, and most likely lured her away by trickery. There would be no reason to kill her until after Agrippina poisons Claudius and acquires power for her son, the young Nero. We believe Alia is still alive and being held captive as a bargaining device to keep you away from Rome. Once you rescue Alia and the word gets back to Agrippina, she is sure to order your death, since she has no hold over you any longer. While you are alive, you endanger her plans."

"Are you here to help rescue Alia?" Cosimus asked.

"We all are," Tony replied.

"And then what? How can you help me repel the evil that Agrippina represents?"

"We would like…invite, I mean…you and your Alia to return with us…to return to the twenty-first century."

"It's hard to leave my homeland in which I have earned a place, developed friends, and become respected by most people I encounter. I am part of this society and this time period. I belong here now and so does my wife. Leaving means adapting to a new environment, earning a living and being someone of no importance that not a single person knows or even wants to know. Until you came through time, I was already dead to you, just dust that had blended with all the other indistinguishable dust blown willy-nilly through the air. Whatever had happened to me was long ago, far away in time, and best forgotten."

"Tell you what, Cosimus. Let me help you recover Alia, and you can talk to her about it and decide together what you would like to do. Over twenty years ago Mary and I watched you go through the portal alone to face the demon. All the years since, we wondered what had happened and whether you had ever found happiness. Mary and I are grateful to you, as should be the entire world population. You saved humanity that day, and no one but us and Susan Harmes ever knew. I needed to return to repay that debt, and it is the least I could do for my brother."

"If the *Numerus Batavorum* are holding her, they will fight to the death, every last one of them. Are you willing to risk death or injury for a man you knew so long ago?" Cosimus asked.

"I am."

Cosimus studied him and nodded agreement. Antonius was the same *centurion* that he had once known and respected, and he would still be fearless in combat, a man to have at your side when there was a life or death struggle.

"We will talk of this again when the sun comes up. Now allow me to show you to your rooms and let you sleep on it. A decision like we face comes easier after a morning meal," Cosimus suggested. He then turned to Cos and Rachel. "I have not forgotten that you are here also. Whatever we decide tomorrow will not include either of you. You will stay at my villa until it's time for you to leave."

"Thanks," Cos said. "I don't know what I should call you."

"I usually go by the name Cos, just like you do, though when we are together, I think Cosimus will do fine. By the way, I can see traces of your beautiful mother in your face. How is she?"

"She is very happy and successful. She often spoke of you, and I know she holds you in the highest regard. At this moment, she is alone in a hotel room waiting in fear and hoping all of us return safely."

"I thought about your dad and Mary many times in my life, although after a few years, I decided that I should not dwell on things that cannot be changed. The letter I wrote to Antonius was my last goodby before I gave away my possessions and headed to the north frontier in a final desperate search for Alia. I hope your theory about where she is being kept is true, though we will never know until we go there ourselves."

There was a muffled noise causing the four to look up and see shapes moving through the darkness toward them.

"We heard voices, *Dominus*," Maccus said. "Are you in need of assistance?" Behind Maccus was the shining blonde hair of the very pregnant Linza and just emerging into the scant light was the elderly *Màthair,* who was holding a small glowing oil lamp.

"Come in, my family, and meet our newest members," Cosimus said. Before he introduced anyone, he announced, "Cos, you and Rachel should be informed that Romans don't use a handshake. They won't understand it. Hugs are more familiar, and it is what the members of a family would want anyway."

"Cosimus," the young Cos called out, "We have a small problem in that Rachel speaks no Latin and hasn't understood a word of what has been said."

"Yes, that is a problem and no small one," Cosimus acknowledged. He studied Rachel for a moment and then spoke to her using English. "Rachel, you can use English around me, and I will speak back to you in it, however the others speak even Latin with difficulty and, of course, no English is spoken at this time anywhere, including Britannia. Don't leave this home by yourself while you are here."

He turned and put his hand on Maccus' broad shoulder. "This is Maccus. We have been together for years and a more dependable and honest man could not be found. And the beautiful woman behind him is his wife, Linza, and beside her is the mother of all of us, *Màthair*. She will try to take charge of you also, but she is wise and always speaks the truth. *Màthair* will become your mother also, even if you don't want her to."

"Where did these people come from, *Dominus?*" Maccus asked.

"They came from far away to help me find Alia. We will talk about that in the morning. For now, we just have to find everyone a room."

The room chosen for Rachel had no windows, and instead of a door, there was a finely woven drape hanging where a door would be expected. Although the drape covered the opening from top to floor, the morning light poured around and filtered through enough to light up the room. Rachel awakened to bird calls, and a nearby fluttering of wings meant that birds were flying uninvited down corridors from the *atrium* to the *peristyle*. As her consciousness clarified her thoughts, she jerked alert, realizing where and when she had awakened. She partially sat up and studied the room, trying to recall if this room was familiar in any way. The four walls were painted in color, and large rectangular areas recalling nature scenes were interposed by architectural columns and fanciful walls. It was beautiful beyond description. The colors were bright, sharp, and the realism created was striking. There were several pieces of furniture near the bed, and she reached out to feel the contours of an elaborately carved chair. One thing that was lacking in the excavation and restoration of Pompeii and Herculaneum were wooden items. The heat and live embers of the volcano had destroyed nearly all of it. In fact, very few perishable items like furniture had survived anywhere from the ancient Roman civilization. To see and touch any of it was a stunning moment. In the distance, she heard voices speaking clearly, though she could not make out any of it. She felt completely helpless and realized she was dependent on others, something she usually successfully avoided.

A soft male voice called from the other side of the curtain. "Rachel? You up yet?" Cos asked.

"Just about," she answered.

"Breakfast soon. Come down when you are ready, and I'll show you the toilet."

"OK." She pulled the cover back, stood up and stretched, looking around once again. She looked down at her bare feet and saw the tiled floor for the first time. There must have been tens of thousands of small tiles beneath her feet, all skillfully and artistically arranged to provide geometric borders and scenes of fish and fowl. "Amazing!" she said aloud to herself. No restoration does this justice, she thought. Smiling, she pulled on her garments and headed out, anxious to see the rest of the villa.

Once on the balcony, she went to the railing and looked down toward the *impluvium*, and the breathtaking tile work surrounding it. "My God!" she exclaimed out loud.

"Stunning, isn't it?" Cos answered. He was standing at the bottom of the stairwell waiting for her. He smiled broadly and opened his arms, slowly turning in a circle. "This isn't the same place as in our time, is it?"

"No. I had no idea it would actually be this grand," Rachel replied while coming down the stairs. She took his arm and pulled him close, smiling up at him. "Thanks for letting me come."

"I didn't let you. You were determined. I just didn't prevent you. Remember that if we get into trouble," Cos reminded her.

"Did you notice how muscular Cosimus is?"

"He is a hard man, isn't he? I'm not sure even Dad is a match for him." They strolled together, both heads twisting here and there trying to take it all in. Through the *tablinum* they could see the brightly lit *peristyle* and a table full of food with people moving about. They were all there and smiling back. The experience was like coming home after long absence. Rachel chose to sit beside the radiant Linza who eyed her with something between interest and envy. Linza was obviously in her third trimester and was self-conscious of the loss of her natural feminine grace. She blushed deeply as Rachel studied her. Noticing, Rachel patted the back of Linza's hand and reassured her that she was still strikingly beautiful, and even though Linza could understand none of it, she did understand the sentiment.

"Welcome," Cosimus said and smiled at his enlarged family, all looking expectantly toward him. He started to say something and then hesitated, "Cos, I need to speak in Latin, and you will translate for Rachel, please." Cos nodded that he would and leaned toward Rachel's ear and explained.

"Today is an eventful day. Help for me has arrived, and his name is Antonius. I was subordinate to him once, and now he will obey my orders," he said sternly and looked at Antonius for his agreement. "We are going to sea to look for Alia, and we may be gone several days. Maccus will go also and that leaves young Cos to safeguard the women. Cos, I want you to go outside as little as possible because I don't know if any danger is waiting out there for you, and though your father trained you, it's not enough for real combat. Is there any disagreement?" He looked around at all the faces looking back and saw no argument. "One other thing," he said and waited until there was silence, "there are going to be big changes for everyone if we return with Alia or not. Our time of being together as a family is over after today. We can look back on the happy times, the wonderful meals we ate together, and the feeling that each of us was important to the others. Things are happening that are out of our control, and we must adapt and accept what the future brings."

Cosimus put his hand on the shoulder of Maccus and spoke directly to him. "Today, I am giving you ownership of this house and everything in it. You will also own the bakery and the store. You are to be proclaimed a Roman citizen as of today and full legal rights will be Linza's as well. I hope the future brings both of you happiness."

Maccus wiped a tear and sniffed, "*Dominus*, are you leaving us just when you are getting Alia returned to you?"

"I can't fight the wife of the Emperor. When she dies, it will be safe for us again, however until then, we have to disappear."

"Seven years," Antonius offered. "Where can you hide for seven years? You would rather hide than return with us?"

"You recall that you suggested that I discuss it with Alia? I intend to," Cosimus answered. "Either way, we have to leave here where we can be found. Nevertheless, if we can't find or rescue Alia, I fully intend to keep looking, even if it means I will never find her."

Antonius pursed his lips and looked away. He would do the same. "What do we do next?" he asked.

"I intend to ask my friend, Piso, if we can use his ship and his men, and if he agrees, then we might as well leave today."

"Piso?" the young Cos recalled. "Isn't he the owner of the Villa of the Papyri?" he asked.

"We don't call it that in this time. It is his home, that is true, at least one of them. Piso is currently serving as *consul*, a powerful position, however he is close friends with the Emperor Claudius, so I have some misgivings about his loyalty to me. So far, he has treated me and Alia very well, but at this moment, Claudius does what Agrippina wants, and Piso does what Claudius wants. You understand, I hope."

"What will you tell him as the reason for the use of his ship?" Antonius wondered.

"I'm not sure. This morning, you and I will go see him and only then will we understand if there is a problem."

Ángel M. Felicísimo from Mérida, España (https://commons.wikimedia.org/wiki/
File:Retrato_femenino_(26771127162).jpg), color by AF, https://creativecommons.org/licenses/by/
2.0/legalcode

Chapter 32

Out to Sea

Adversity has the effect of eliciting talents which, in prosperous circumstances, would have lain dormant.

Anger is a momentary madness, so control your passion or it will control you.

Horace(65 BC to 8 BC)

*T*hey walked side by side, their shoulders occasionally brushed as their speech became more animated. Both wore a chain mail tunic over their linen one, and both carried daggers in their belts.

"Had you ever visited Herculaneum in either previous life?" Cosimus asked.

"Only once and not in my youth when it still looked like it does today. I was briefly here at the ruins a few months ago, however only to see one of Cos' professors who was rather harsh after he read your buried note to me," Tony answered and then laughed at the memory. "He seemed to think that I faked it for publicity." He laughed again. "A remarkable insight you had when you buried that. In English yet! Well, it was almost discarded and would have been had not Cos and Rachel been the ones who found it."

"I didn't intend that you come rescue me, you understand. I was trying to tell you how much I missed you, and in my desperation, you seemed to be the only one who would have been able to help. And here you are. You brought hope to me, at least, and if we can find Alia where you think she is…it's a debt that I can't repay."

"You already paid that debt. I watched helplessly that night as you did it. Being back here with you at my side is an adventure that I wouldn't have missed for the world," Tony said and slapped his brother on the back.

They rounded a corner near the waterfront and in the near distance could be seen the rising white columns of Piso's villa. Cosimus stopped walking and stared ahead wordlessly. "Something wrong?" Tony asked.

"There are two boats at Piso's wharf. One of them I haven't seen before."

Tony looked again, and there were two small ships bobbing in the water, going up and down slowly in the morning waves, their hawsers taut to the wharf. One was a bit larger and still wore the light tan of new wood. The other craft was older and much darker.

"What does that mean," Tony asked, unable to discern any significance to seeing two small ships together.

"It means communication from *Roma*. Someone new is at the villa," Cosimus answered and then started walking again. As they drew closer to the entrance, four armed men stepped out of the shadows.

"*Stabit*" was called out, and one raised his hand toward them, an order to halt. A well-appointed, armor-clad officer stepped forward and stood in their path.

"What do you want, and who are you?" he demanded.

"I am *Paulo Fabio Persico Cosimus, Legatus,* and you are standing in my way. I don't answer to *Praetorians.* Move aside, and that is an order."

The guard hesitated, fury burning in his eyes. This muscular pair standing in front of him looked formidable and unafraid. With reluctance, he decided on the path of least resistance and moved out of the way, keeping his hand on the hilt of his sword as an obvious threat. He let them pass, however when they came out, it would be another story entirely.

They strolled down the impressive path of gardens, laden with flowers and sculpture, toward the villa house, itself stunning and implicating great wealth. "Wow," Antonius said, "better than I expected, better than most, perhaps better than all of *Roma* itself."

"Not quite, my brother. I've been to his villa just outside of *Roma,* and it is even bigger. Piso is the wealthiest man in the world at this moment though also very educated and polite. You'll see."

They were greeted at the door by a bronzed slave, but one who was obviously well nourished and clothed. He lowered his eyes at the sight of the *legatus* he had become accustomed to seeing. Without words, he waved them in and stood by as they walked the hallway toward the magnificent *tablinum,* and as Cosimus expected, Piso was there at his desk, bent over scattered documents. When he saw his guests approaching, he stood to greet them.

"A surprise and a welcome one. Please enter and be comfortable," he said. He looked long and hard at Antonius, trying to place him in his vast memory of people and places. "And who are you, my new friend?" he asked.

"Allow me to introduce," Cosimus interrupted.

"*Gaius Calpurnius Piso,* meet my oldest and best friend, my brother, my right hand, *Antonius Severius Maximus.* Piso stood there for a moment looking him up and down before speaking.

"Good to know you, Antonius. You have the look of a warrior yourself, I might say, and that leads me to ask of your service to *Roma*," Piso said, a thin smile on his lips. His active mind was jumping around trying to place the name which was, at the moment, just out of reach.

"I served with Cosimus long ago. We fought together once and became close," Antonius answered, aware that his answer sounded vague and hoping to move on to other subjects quickly.

"Yes," Piso murmured, his quick eyes darting back and forth between the men. "Yes…I have heard your name previously. In fact, I recall Cosimus and I discussing you. You are legend in some parts of the Empire. The famous, or should I say notorious, Antonius, the missing *centurion*. Am I correct?"

Antonius glanced at Cosimus and then back at Piso, deciding on how to answer this pointed question. He felt Cosimus' hand on his shoulder, and he turned to face him.

"Piso is very bright and has a capacious memory. He was told my story once, but I scarcely expected him to believe me. Go ahead and be honest with him. He is a man we can trust."

Antonius took a big breath and allowed himself to relax. "Yes, that legend is true. I am the one."

"And Cosimus said once that he and you traded places. I took it to mean that you went to the future from the past, and he stayed here instead of returning. Then, I ask you, how and why are you here?"

"I came from the future to help my brother find his wife. I have ideas of where she may be, and I believe that she is still alive only she won't be for long."

"And if my information is correct, you left this time to keep a woman safe, and you return to save another?" Piso asked.

"True enough," Antonius answered.

"And how is the future, Antonius, and would I like it there or not?"

"The future is much like the past in that people are the same, so it doesn't take long to feel as if you had always been there, same as here. I live well there and, by some measurements, am wealthy. You, though, live better than anyone in the future, and you have not only wealth but power and influence. Be happy that you are here, however be careful."

"I've been warned by my friend, Cosimus, also, so you both know something about my fate, I presume. Simply don't tell me what will happen and don't tell me that I cannot, out of my own free will, change it. If my life is ordained by the gods, then just allow me to live it as they have chosen."

"You are a man for all times, Gaius, and I am honored to have known you," Cosimus said.

"Sounds like our companionship is to be short lived, Cosimus. Whatever do you mean?"

"I am leaving our city. If we find and rescue Alia, then I have to explain things to her and see if she is willing to travel to the future and risk all its unknowns. If she is dead or still missing, then I will stay here and take my vengeance. We are certain that Agrippina would like to see me gone where I can't disrupt her plans. I can't fight the *Praetorians* by myself. I'll have to hide from them."

"And you would be correct on that," Piso agreed. "You saw the black ship on the way in, I presume? That was an exchange of my guards fresh from *Roma*. I believe they have orders concerning you already, and I was not to be told about any of it. You are lucky to have gotten in here this morning."

"And you are suggesting that we might have to fight our way out?"

"It's possible. though even if they let you leave, they will come for you at some point. Don't despair because I am here to help," Piso said. "By the way, you came for some reason this morning. What can I do for you?"

Antonius spoke up. "I believe that Alia is being held captive on the island of *Tyrrhenia* or, as some call it, Ponza because Agrippina was herself held there in exile for a time. We were going to ask you for the use of your private ship."

Piso looked away lost in thought. "You might be on to something. Both of those islands were used for that purpose, and to get there, you need something bigger than a small boat. I should have considered that myself instead of spending all our time searching every room in this city." He rubbed his chin for a moment, then held his hand up to signal that he was about to say something profound.

"Listen closely, both of you," he nearly whispered. "I don't trust my *Praetorian* Guard. Never did. They can protect you or kill you depending on orders from *Roma*. I never needed them anyway, but I'm stuck with them. If I give you the boat right now, they will get word to *Roma* within a day's time, and you can be sure that this new batch is looking for something or someone. I now know who…it's you, Cosimus. You. Now what do we do about it?"

"May I suggest a plan, Gaius?" Cosimus inquired. Piso nodded enthusiastically, anxious to find a solution. "We will stay with you all day. Order your ship to be prepared to return to *Roma* in the morning after the sun comes up and order that the ship's crew stand by. After dark, we will slip down to the ship and silently take her into the harbor. When they finally realize that we are gone, they will probably take off toward *Roma,* trying to catch us."

"One addition I might add, my brother," Antonius suggested. "We disable the other ship before we depart, just to be sure. After all, if we are already outlaws, we might as well act like it."

"Or," Piso laughed, "I could just order the entire bunch to leave and return to *Roma*."

"Would they comply?" Antonius asked.

"It would take force. They have been commanded to be my escort. None would leave without orders from their commander, and he is in *Roma*."

"Then it's settled. We will leave in the middle of the night," Cosimus said.

Piso answered quickly, "That will be more difficult than you expect. The crews of ships are hesitant to sail at night, with few exceptions. They like to have the land in view at all times."

"Then we sail out of the harbor and wait on the sunrise before proceeding to Ponza," Antonius suggested.

"I'll be going with you," Piso said. "You'll need me to command the crew. They won't obey you, only me."

"There could be risks. We face at least ten or more of the *Numerus Batavorum,* and they will all require killing. No easy task for just two men."

"Looking at you two, I have nothing to worry about," Piso chuckled.

"One last thing, Gaius," Cosimus said. "I need another favor. Could you have a messenger take a note to someone for me?"

"Of course," he answered. "To whom?"

"To Gratus."

"You mean, The Gratus? That one?" He looked puzzled nevertheless nodded that he would see that it was done. Piso took the paper and looked at the name on the outside of the folded note. He shrugged and wandered out of the room, looking for a servant.

"What was that about?" Antonius asked.

"A little insurance from someone who owes me a favor or two."

Tyrrhenian Sea, Sunrise

The ship was bobbing in the sea as constant waves passed under her, also creating an unpleasant rocking from side to side. The harbor of Herculaneum was still in view although nearly a *mille* away. This was the area the Romans correctly referred to as the *Crator* because of the cup-like extensions of the mainland, visible on three sides. They were waiting on something to happen at the villa, and one of the crew was first to spot the activity. "The sail is going up," he exclaimed from his higher perch.

"Think they have spotted us?" Cosimus asked.

Piso chuckled, "It's obvious that someone has. We are sitting out here like a wart on the back of a hand. We will start sailing in earnest once they get underway. No worry about them catching us because this is the faster ship," Piso assured them.

Sure enough, the black ship was getting ready to sail, and even from this distance, they could see the sparkle and reflection of the sun from the various polished breastplates aboard, and soon they saw sweep oars hard at work.

"They look pretty determined," Antonius commented, the wrinkles between his brow giving away his concern.

"Yes, they were ordered to stay with me at all times, and if something happens to me when they are not present…well, they won't live long. My guess is that all of them are in that boat, and they will follow us as long as they can," Piso said.

"No, they won't," Cosimus said dryly. "Once they reach the open waters, the strain on the rudder will cause it to shear off. They will be afloat for days before drifting to shore. I should know because I sawed the rudder shaft nearly in half last night."

"How long?" Cosimus asked to anyone on deck who was listening. There was no answer except the splash of the breaking waves against the prow. The craft was making good time with a fine quartering wind and clear skies. He looked around, observing that men were at their stations and looking forward as if to wish the sudden appearance of their destination, the small islands in the vast Mediterranean Sea. Cosimus glanced at Antonius, who stood by the mast, engaged in conversation with the curious and glib Piso, who ravenously digested every morsel of information about the future and, most important, the history which was to occur between now and the distant future. No harm in him knowing, Cosimus thought, as long as he didn't ask about his own future. Piso would eventually have a belly full of Nero and his extravagances and plot to have him murdered. Unfortunately for Piso, an informant would give him away and the point of the spear would be aimed at his chest instead of Nero's. He shrugged, wondering about his own fate and even where would life take him next. There was no need of endless speculation until he found Alia. She was the force driving him, and he would never discard her memory. Finding something so precious as Alia lying on the floor of a slave wagon…he resisted thinking about it because the anger raised up in him like a wave from the sea, destroying his logic forsaken for rage.

"*Legatus*?" a voice called. Cosimus turned to see a senior sailor looking his way.

"Yes?"

"You asked about the time for travel," the man shouted above the white noise of the wind and waves. "We should get there about dark. Good fortune today for sailing," he added.

"Thanks," Cosimus said and raised his hand to the man. Arriving in near darkness would be an asset. There were bound to be watchers posted for arriving ships. The Emperor's private guard, the *Numerus Batavorum,* were well known for fierce loyalty and were not in anyone's control below the Emperor himself. That made Cosimus think again about how Agrippina could have managed to command them to do anything without the knowledge of her husband. Money would do it, and if they acted for profit only, then their willingness to die for it might be a thin thread. He looked up and saw Antonius and Piso calling him over.

"We thought that a strategy should be developed before we make it to Ponza," Antonius said over the wind. "It was obvious that the most senior military man should be the one deciding and that man is Cosimus."

"I've been thinking about it. Seems to me that if we see just one *Germani* anywhere on Ponza, it will be a sign that Alia is still there."

"And there is bound to be more of them than two," Piso observed.

"No more than ten, perhaps fewer," Cosimus guessed.

"We can't let them get together as a group or give them warning what our intentions are," Antonius proposed.

"Then you think that we should start killing immediately before an alarm can be sounded?"

"Yes."

"Wait," Piso interrupted. "There may be an easier way. After all, I am *consul*, even the *Germani* would understand my authority. I can demand to be brought to Alia. If they act suspicious or hostile, then we start killing."

"We?" Cosimus asked.

"You both know when and how I am to die. We haven't discussed it because I don't want to know. Just tell me one thing… am I to die on Ponza…yes or no?"

"No!" They both answered in unison and started laughing. Piso was right, his plan just might work.

The little harbor in Ponza faced to the west, a grateful relief from the wind and waves of the sea, and its waters were smooth and quiet, necessitating a slow approach to the wharfs. It was twilight, and the deep shadows of the island disclosed only glimpses of men moving about on the land. Things were silhouettes, not men or ships. High above on the right was a rise still lit by the setting sun and on it rose a majestic Roman villa of some extravagance, a decidedly comfortable spot for an exiled wife or child of an emperor.

Antonius and Piso squinted and studied the villa as the ship bumped into the wharf amid the calls back and forth from dock workers who sought to secure the ship.

"See anything?" Cosimus asked.

"A bit of movement though too far away in this light to see much. Have you seen anything around the dock?" Antonius asked.

Cosimus pointed with his chin, "There are two watching us, and both have a *Suebian* knot of hair on the right side. No doubt of who they are and where they come from. She is here, or at least, was here. If she has been harmed… . " He couldn't finish, however Antonius and Piso knew exactly what he meant.

"Do you think they see a threat coming?" Piso wondered.

"We are dressed like sailors, not Roman Army. How could they know?" Antonius asked.

"Well, you both look like something other than sailors," Piso observed.

"Too far away. It's going to be a surprise," Cosimus whispered.

The small ship was firmly roped to the padded wharf, and the three of them disembarked, getting their legs under them once again. "Stay here and keep watch," Piso ordered, and started walking directly toward the two *Germani* warriors.

When he got closer, both men stood up alertly watching him, their hands already gripping their swords. Both kept glancing past

Piso, carefully observing the two muscular men standing on the dock who looked back at them.

"I am *Consul* Piso, and I have a message for your prisoner from the wife of Claudius. Take me to her," he commanded.

Piso couldn't be sure that they had understood his Latin, though he was sure that they were far more interested in the two large men moving slowly toward them.

"Did you understand me?" Piso yelled at them.

"We don't take commands from you," one answered in near perfect Latin.

"Do you expect Agrippina to travel here directly and give you orders?" Piso returned at the top of his lungs.

"She would send a scroll," the man stated.

"Not this time. Look, if I wanted to harm you I would have brought a *legion* with me. Take me to Alia right now or face the consequences."

The two men looked at each other for guidance and then at the two large men coming toward them, now only a few *passus* from them and nearly within striking range. It was time to submit, flee, or fight. They were out of time.

"We protect her. How do we know your intentions?" the man answered. He partially withdrew his sword, thought better of it, and let if fall back into its scabbard. Both approaching men were carrying swords held discreetly at their sides, and he could see the hard faces of experience they wore. These kind of men were not easily bested in a one on one fight, something the Romans, in particular, were very good at.

Cosimus and Antonius stopped just behind Piso. Their body language said more than words. Both were killers, and both had long experience in the Roman Army.

"We have not harmed Alia. We protect her," the man said indignantly, looking quickly at the faces looking back at him.

"I am Cosimus. She is my wife. Take us to her without further talk. We will be right behind you so if you try to run or call out, you will both lose your heads."

The threat was real indeed, and both *Germani* put up their hands in submission. "No need for that. Alia is unharmed and waits for your coming. Follow us." And with that last statement, both *Germani* turned and started moving up the steep path toward the villa, now sitting in near absolute darkness with only traces of the structure visible by starlight.

There were armed *Germani* at the entrance, all dressed in loose fitting clothing, armed with spears and especially long swords hanging from their waist. Just as Julius Caesar had reported, the young warriors all wore the *Suebian* knot hair style and all had distinctly red hair. They quickly conferred in their native language with glancing and pointing back at the three Roman men just entering the gate.

One man finally stepped forward and put up his open hand to halt. At this, both Antonius and Cosimus brought his *gladius* up into view and stiffened visibly. "We mean you no harm," he said with accented Latin. "You are welcome here, and you will find your lady unharmed and well cared for," he continued, then slowly put his hand down. It was a tense moment with Cosimus considering the recent advice of his former *centurion*, Antonius, that the killing should start early. The farther they entered into the expansive villa, the greater the chance that at some turn of a hallway, they would be overtaken by several *Numerus Batavorum*, recreating in a small way the massacre at the Teutoburg Forest in nine AD. Those were *Germani* adversaries also, and their treachery was legend among the Roman *legionaries*, a lesson never to be erased by time.

"Get to the rear, *Consul* Piso, and if any action starts, make for the entrance as fast as you can," Antonius ordered. Piso obeyed and fell behind the two large men in front of him. They walked slowly, alert to every shadow and sound. The hallway led to an open *atrium* and its *impluvium,* which had running water at both ends and an inviting stone surround just the right height for sitting and contemplating the abundant fresh water. As typical for villas of this importance, the walls were painted, this one with nautical scenes in restful shades of blue.

"If you wait here, I will bring Alia to you," the one in charge announced. The perimeter walls started silently collecting *Germani* warriors, all armed. Cosimus counted eighteen of them, and he assumed more were outside at the entrance. He glanced at Antonius and saw his jaw tighten and his eyes narrow. Both were mentally calculating which to strike first when fighting started.

"I will go with you," Cosimus announced and strode confidently out of the group to the center the room and looked around defiantly.

"I am called Farvlad," the man announced and nodded at Cosimus, expecting a name in return.

"Paulo Fabio Persico Cosimus, Legatus."

The man's eyebrows went up. "You are just as she described you," he remarked and continued walking toward a darkened corridor.

"I want to ask you a question," Cosimus said, and Farvlad stopped, turning toward him. "Were you ordered to kill Alia?"

"No. We were ordered to capture her, take her here and stay with her."

"If ordered, would you kill her?" It was a direct and tough question, and its asking made Farvlad hesitate.

"We obey commands. Yet…none of us would slay a defenseless *Germani* woman, especially a pregnant one."

"Then if such an order comes to you, what will you do?"

Farvlad stroked his chin. "We have discussed that among us. Do you have knowledge that such an order is coming?"

"Eventually, the command will come. It might take two more years, but it will come," Cosimus predicted.

"Then, to answer you, we will report that Alia was killed. You should take her with you and hide her well to protect us all"

"I will, and thank you for being honest."

"We do this for a fellow *Germani*, not for you, for we all know about you and that you once fought against our fellow countrymen," Farvlad answered. "Will you leave tonight?"

"If possible, else early in the morning."

"She will be more comfortable here than on your small ship," Farvlad suggested.

"Do you trust us, and should I trust you and your men?"

"We all want the same thing for Alia. All of us respect her, and for tonight, there will be no reprisal, no hostility. You are welcome to stay and eat with us for the last time."

"How will you answer any inquiry about Alia after she is no longer here?" Cosimus asked.

"Simple," Farvlad answered confidently. "If they come before we are ordered to slay her, then we will report that she flung herself off the cliff. If the order comes, as you predict, then we will report that she has been slain on the command of the Emperor."

"That should work. I am in your debt, and if there is anything I can do for you... ."

Farvlad cut him off. "We need nothing from you, and you owe us nothing."

At the end of the long corridor was a door, closed although admitting a faint light under and above. Cosimus took a deep breath. This was a moment at the peak of the curve of life where absolute fulfillment was obtained, where worry was abandoned for a brief moment in the arms of a lover, and where a profound change in life would start to occur, the unknown other side of the curve. There was no going back to the idyllic life in their lavish home in Herculaneum, the cool nights of near absolute darkness when their faces were pressed together as their bodies blended into one soul, one heart, and one mind.

Cosimus held up his hand and nodded that Farvlad should retreat and leave him to encounter his love by himself, not wanting to share this intensity with any living thing other than Alia. Farvlad turned without comment and strode away, disappearing in the darkness.

Cosimus knocked softly and listened with his ear nearly touching the wooden door. "Yes?" Alia's voice said. "Are we ready to eat?" she asked. Cosimus pushed the door open slowly, wanting the moment to last. Alia was seated at a small desk, quill and wax tablet at hand, and she slowly, casually, looked up toward the door. For a moment, she didn't react, her brain processing information that seemed impossible, that the sight of her Cos was just an active imagination that could not be real. She blinked, her big eyes looking directly at him as he smiled back at her. Suddenly, she came out of the chair and rushed toward him, burying her face into his chest. Big arms enveloped her and slowly raised her from the floor to face level, and they pressed against each other, tears from both wetting their faces, clouding their eyes. Cosimus adjusted his hold so that no undue pressure would be exerted on her distended abdomen. She held his face between her hands, looking in awe at this man she so loved, the same face which had appeared constantly in her dreams, the face she saw floating over the sea when she looked out of the window in her room.

"I always thought you would come to me someday. There was never a day that I gave up hope," Alia whispered into his ear, then slid her face and lips across his, finding his lips and warm breath.

"And I searched everywhere, nearly giving up hope. I would have never stopped looking. You are my entire world, the only reason I live."

"And you have more than me to love now. There will be three of us…could be four!" She beamed at him and looked down toward her pregnancy, then back to his eyes. "You didn't know before, did you?" she asked.

"I thought it was possible, hoped it was…but *Màthair*, she knew, she always knows." He laughed and gently put her down and with a light touch, stroked her belly, shocked at the size and the change in her. Alia was more beautiful than ever. Her hair was down and full, reflecting the dim light from the single oil lamp, and she was more full of curves, though most notable was the radiance from her lovely face. She seemed more mature in some way, no longer shy. She looked him in the eyes as an equal, a partner as well as a lover and devoted expectant mother. They had been parted for only two months, but the Alia which was standing in front of him, her eyes sparkling with intelligence, was more woman than the one he had lost.

"How have you been treated?" he asked.

"Those men treat me with every respect, every consideration possible. They see that I have the freshest food, the warmest bath, and the best clothing they can find. They seem to me to be my brothers, my blood relatives, who share my beliefs and my values. They tricked me, and before I realized it, I was being carried away on a boat which headed into the sea. I watched as our city grew smaller and smaller, and I called out to you, however you were far away at the time. For a moment, I wanted to leap into the sea and die because without you, life and a child didn't have the same meaning. But those young men quickly grew to care for me, and we have acted as family while on this island. They don't understand why I was taken or how long I am to be captive, however they were ordered to stay and care for me until it was over. And now, with you here, it must be over."

"And it is. I have come to take you with me. We will be together for as long as we live. You will never be captured or harmed again."

"And our family? Are they still there and is nothing changed?"

"Everything has changed except you and I. We are all that matters. The future will be different than we expected, and together, we have our love which will never leave us. Now come with me, I have two friends waiting to see you."

Chapter 33

Tourists

All things change, nothing is extinguished. There is nothing in the whole world which is permanent. Everything flows onward; all things are brought into being with a changing nature; the ages themselves glide by in constant movement.

Ovid(43 BC to 1 BC)

ave you noticed the men standing in the street?" Rachel asked.

"Sure, they meet my eyes every time I look their way. They seem friendly, although I've never seen tougher looking chaps than those. And when they leave, others just like them take their place," Cos answered.

"Do you think we are in any danger?

"They have had plenty of opportunity to harm us if they chose to do so. I think someone has instructed them to look after us, probably Cosimus himself."

"Why do we need protection?" Rachel asked.

"Well, you do recall Cosimus telling you not to leave this house while you are here? There is something going on that

Cosimus is in the middle of. That's why Alia was taken. I only hope my dad and Cosimus are successful in finding her still alive."

"How are you getting along with Maccus?"

"He will respond to any question I ask, and he is especially polite to us…though he seems to be angry about something and avoids me whenever possible," Cos answered. "And how is it going with you and *Màthair* and Linza?"

"Grand. I love those two. *Màthair* is so intuitive about everything and so considerate. Linza is preoccupied with her unborn child and, I think, worried about the delivery process. Even this far along in her pregnancy, she is a very beautiful woman and seems to know it. A real handful for Maccus, whom I would describe as a primitive."

"Rough around the edges, yet from what I hear, a very tough man in a fight. I'm glad they left him here. It makes me feel safer, especially with men in the street watching the house."

"Want to go for a walk around town with me?" Rachel asked, her face upturned and pleading. "I just have to see something while we are here. Think of what we are missing!"

"I have to think about it, nevertheless I can see your point, and I want to see it myself. We should, however, do as we were told and wait here for *Papà* and Cosimus first."

Rachel knew he was right, yet looking out the windows onto the bay just wasn't enough. They were actually here! It was not a dream but reality, and when she went around the house and through the rooms, it struck her how marvelous, how artistic, everything is. Then there was the toilet. She had such a strong aversion to using what they called a toilet that she held off as long as possible. Not only was the odor coming from the opening strong, it held the possibility of something sinister, a dreaded reality of creatures inhabiting the sewer who had access to the house and…her. It was the worse experience so far. The lack of a morning shower was beginning to make her feel soiled, and there were public baths just down the street, though so far, she couldn't use them or even see them.

Rachel looked around the *tablinum* again. It was indeed the most central area of the entire structure, and it was intended to be since it was the office of the *paterfamilias* who was the most important person living here. From the little she saw of Cosimus before he abruptly left, she had already formed an indelible impression of him. What a man, she thought. He was everything a man could possibly be, both inside and outside. She felt a strong magnetic pull toward him, realizing that all of them thought of Cosimus in the same way…well, nearly in the same way. For her, there was a nearly instant sexual attraction that had hit her in the face like a slap. As much as she tried to repress the sensation, it welled up in her, taking over her thoughts at times. Of course, Cosimus was old enough to be her father…still…he was handsome, rugged, commanding and gentle, all at the same time. The nearly perfect package of sexual attraction in spite of the age difference between them.

"You know what I want to do?" Cos asked, breaking her fantasy and bringing her focus back to him.

"No, but I can imagine," she said and flicked her eyes at him. Her natural skills at attraction were undiminished by a little thing like time travel.

Cos was flustered by the pull toward her and lost his train of thought for a moment. "Yes…and it's not that at the moment. I want us to dine on the table on the second floor overlooking the bay. You know, the one we first ate lunch at when you lured me in here."

"Lured? I never lured. You will know when I lure. That was pure archeology, my handsome companion, and you should know the difference by now."

Cos sighed. Rachel could be such a handful at times. "Don't you want to recreate that moment with me?" he asked, wondering as usual, if Rachel was just teasing.

"Of course, I do. It's a wonderful idea. When?"

"I'd say at evening when the sun sets across the bay. We can sit there as long as we want and just look at each other."

"And I'd say we will do that when we finish helping the overworked *Màthair,* who has assumed responsibility for everything since Alia is missing and Linza is limited on what she can do. Then, there is poor Maccus, who has to go out and buy the food, tend to his two businesses, care for Linza, and fix anything which breaks. We have to hold up our end, wouldn't you agree? That means that our pleasures come in last."

Cos sighed and nodded. She was right, as usual. "Where do we start?"

"We clean. You take the upper floors, and I'll do the lower. Dust and sweep…you can do that, can't you? You'll find the broom and cloths near the *culina.*"

Cos sighed again and stood up slowly, resigning himself to labor rather than visually feasting on Rachel.

At that moment, the bushy round head of Maccus appeared looking around the corner. "I was looking for you two. Are you busy at the moment?" he asked and smiled his broad smile showing his flattened and worn incisors.

"No, not at all," Cos answered quickly. "Do you need something or anything we can do for you?"

"I was wondering if you would like to get out and see the city and also help me with a cartload of fresh bread for the bakery next door."

"Yes, we can!" Cos reached for Rachel's hand and pulled her to her feet.

"What did he say?" she wondered.

"He wants us to go outside with him. Isn't that what you wanted anyway?"

"Great. Can you wait until I change my clothes?" Rachel asked.

"You look fine. Better than fine, I'd say. How can you improve perfection?"

"Look, Cos, I have to do what the Romans expect of their women. You will wait right here, and don't move until I come down." She smiled at Maccus on the way past and hurried up stairs.

"Something wrong with her?" Maccus asked, watching her disappear with out warning.

"Doesn't Linza fuss with her clothes when you take her out?" Cos asked.

Maccus understood completely. There was no difference in women wherever they came from.

Rachel walked beside Cos, her arm in his as they walked the narrow sidewalk a few feet behind the broad shoulders of Maccus. As they left, they saw Maccus stop and talk to the men lingering outside the villa. He seemed friendly and even happy about them being there and hugged both of them more than once. Cos got up the nerve to ask Maccus about it once they commenced walking. He said that the men were gladiators from the nearby school on the outskirts of the city, and they had been asked to stand guard while Cosimus was away. Maccus apparently knew all of them and smiled about it when he talked. Cos relayed the message to Rachel who then understood completely. She felt safer already.

"Cos, do you notice how much better everything looks? I mean, the street is level and even, and all the buildings are faced with smooth plaster. It's all so...perfect!"

"You remember that this city was already here for a long time, perhaps two hundred years, even more, before the Romans started making it a resort for themselves. There is a lot of old here. It just looks so much better than when we saw it."

"And you remember the little sidewalk restaurant you pretended to serve me food from? Well, it's just ahead. Want to buy me something to eat?" she asked playfully.

"No money. Sorry."

"Well, ask Maccus. We can pay him back when your father returns," Rachel insisted.

Cos tapped Maccus on the shoulder, "Can I borrow a few coins from you? Rachel would like to try the food at the *thermopolium*." Maccus shrugged and dug into his purse, pulling out several denarii and handing them over. "Do you want any food?" Cos asked him.

Maccus shrugged, then said, 'No."

"This is the very same spot we stopped at," Rachel said in excited English. The shopkeeper looked at her funny and then back at Cos.

"She is from Britannia," he explained, then pointed to one of the large steaming flasks of mostly beans and held up two fingers. The man looked down at the marble top expecting money prior to service. Cos placed one coin on the counter and was rewarded by two steaming bowls of lintels and chickpeas, combined with some sort of meat.

"Want *garum*?" the cook asked.

"What?" Cos responded, not understanding the question.

"He asked if you wanted fish sauce on yours. Say yes," Rachel advised from behind him. Cos twisted and looked at her smiling face. Resourceful gal, he thought.

Maccus stood partially in the street looking up and down while they ate. There were no spoons available so it was eating with fingers only and no place to rinse their hands after eating. They laughed at each others distress, enjoying the experience. And the food was very good.

Cos noticed Maccus looking at him in an odd way. "Something troubling you, Maccus?" Cos asked. Maccus nodded subtly and rolled his eyes down the street. Cos looked up to understand what he meant. There were four armed soldiers moving their way along the sidewalk, still a block away. Each wore a metal breastplate and carried a long spear as well as a sheathed sword. There was something confrontational about them, the way they moved together and the looks of hostility projected at anyone they passed.

"Trouble," Maccus stated. It was obvious, but why, Cos wondered. Maccus signaled that Rachel and Cos should come with him, and he crossed the small street and headed smoothly away, the two time travelers following behind him. They turned left at the first corner, heading away from the soldiers or so they thought. There was a noise behind them and when they looked back, the soldiers had partially closed the distance between them. It seemed that they were the target, and the appearance of armed *Praetorians* was not random.

"What do you think they want?" Cos asked.

"I shouldn't have taken you with me. They will want to find out who you and the girl are and where you are staying. Do you know how to use a sword?" Maccus asked.

"Yes, however I don't have one."

"I do. And there is an extra one under my cloak. If the need arises, I'll toss it to you. If we kill one, we have to kill them all and quickly. Remember that."

Cos felt his mouth go dry and his pulse increase. Never in his life had he had to actually defend himself. All the sword work he had done with his father was just play. He didn't think he was ready for the real thing, and besides, these men wore armor and were experienced.

"What is this all about?" Rachel asked. She was watching and understood that the approaching men were somehow hostile though didn't understand what to do and what Cos and Maccus were about to do.

"I don't know. Just try to remain calm, and if anything starts, duck into any doorway and get away as fast as you can."

"*Subsisto*," one of them called out. It was an order to halt. They did and turned around as the men approached.

"I haven't seen you before," one of them asked Cos. "Where are you staying?" He moved closer and started looking Rachel over. She pulled her *stola* more over her face and looked away.

"We just arrived. I am looking for my father's brother's home," Cos lied.

"Who is that?" the man asked.

"His name is Piso. *Consul* Piso. Ever heard of him?" Cos said and tried to look affronted or angry.

"Yes, we have. We have been assigned to that home. No one told us about any arrivals. I think you lie." With that, the other men started to fan out a bit, their hard eyes fixed on Cos.

"You can escort us there, and we'll ask him in person," Cos retorted.

"He isn't at his home at this time," the man answered.

"When will he return? Where are we to stay in the meantime?" Cos asked.

"You and your lady can stay with me until Piso returns," Maccus interjected.

This bit of information was difficult for the soldier to digest or refute. If this young man was indeed a relative of *Consul* Piso, then harming him would definitely be off limits. Still, he wasn't sure that the young man wasn't just a skillful liar. It was a dilemma not easily traversed without undue risk. He decided to back off for the moment but keep this unknown person under close observation.

Maccus broke out into a big smile and stepped forward, "I own the bakery just down the street, also the wine shop. If you men accompany me there, I'll see that you get your fill of both. It's the least I can do for fellow men of arms. I once served *Roma* also, both against the *Germani* and the tribes in *Britannia*. Twenty years I served."

That broke the ice, and the hostility melted away like the late snows of April. Maccus moved into close contact with them and started telling old war stories accompanied by much back slapping and camaraderie. After a time, he looked up at Cos and indicated with his eyes that they were to slowly move away and return home.

"I've never felt so good about returning home," Rachel said, pulling off her *stola* at last and letting her long, full hair drop behind her back. "Maccus saved us just then, didn't he?"

"Sure did. Good old Maccus. We owe him for this," Cos admitted. His pulse had not yet returned to normal nor had his breathing. And, he didn't want to say it, but on the way in he noticed that their gladiator guards were gone. They were on their own, it seemed. He decided that he would not alert Rachel to that fact just now.

"What were you saying to that man?" she asked.

"He asked me where we were staying. I lied and said we were looking for Piso's home."

"Why there?"

"He is powerful, rich, and a good friend of Cosimus. It was a good bet that they wouldn't want to get him angry when he comes back. Anyway, it worked for the time being."

"Now that I have seen the city, part of it at least, and had my excitement, it's time for you and I to get to work and earn our keep," Rachel informed him.

When Maccus returned two hours later, Cos approached him with questions. It didn't take long to be aware of Maccus' inebriated state. He was blurry in the eyes and moved somewhat clumsily. He held his finger to his lips to request that Cos be quiet.

"Maccus, can you tell me about those four soldiers we encountered, and why they were interested in me?" Cos asked anyway.

"I just spent the afternoon with them and watched as they gulped gallons of my good wine. They are not a bad bunch. They just take orders, however I got it out of them… their secrets. Don't tell anyone." He held his finger across his lips again and smiled.

"Still, you can tell me. I need to know. Come on, Maccus, it's important."

Maccus fixed him with bloodshot eyes which wandered a bit, and he pursed his lips for a moment, obviously thinking and recalling what he had picked up.

"Please, Maccus, try to remember," Cos pleaded.

"They don't have orders yet. They are waiting on orders," Maccus finally recalled.

"There must be something more than that," Cos said loudly.

"Oh, there is," Maccus said and grinned. He gently let himself down until he was sitting on the floor and then looked confused as to where he was.

"I'm waiting, Maccus. You can do this."

"They are going to arrest somebody, somebody big." Maccus used his hands far apart to demonstrate the very large importance of the arrest.

"Who?"

"These men didn't know. They were told it might be a *legatus*. That's pretty big." He smiled again and rubbed his face with his hand.

"There is only one *legatus* in Herculaneum, isn't there?" Cos asked.

Maccus nodded the truth of it, then frowned, the realization finally hitting him. He struggled to regain his feet, and Cos helped him stand.

"So they are going to arrest Cosimus," Cos stated. "When…do you know?"

"When the rest of them get back," Maccus recalled. "They are not *legionaries*, they are only *Praetorian* trash, and they will do anything as long as they get paid for it." The reality finally sank in, and Maccus seemed to toss off the alcohol by the second.

"They will come for my *dominus*. It will be soon." Maccus stood more erect and his face grew darker, the shadows of his rugged face deepening with resolve.

It was well after dark when Piso's ship slid up to his private wharf and bumped gently against the timbers. Two men leapt off, secured the lines and then motioned that the rest could disembark. Cosimus was first off, and he reached out and took Alia's hand and then gently guided her as she stepped onto the solid and nonmoving dock. Piso quickly followed, and they started walking toward his expansive villa, hovering in the nearly nonexistent light.

"Will you stay with me tonight or return to your home?" Piso asked. Cosimus looked at Alia for a response though he felt very sure which she would decide.

"I would rather see our home again, but thank you, *Consul*, for your kindness, your help, and your generous offer," Alia said. She glanced at Cosimus to be sure he agreed.

"That seems to be the right decision," Cosimus responded. "One question for you, my friend," he said, then continued, "I am convinced that Agrippina has sent out an order for my arrest or even death. What can you do on your part?"

"You may be correct. If there has been such an order, it has been kept from me. I am angry that they would use the very guards assigned to protect me to carry out such a foul deed. I can stop it, but unfortunately, I have to travel to *Roma* and talk to Claudius himself. He would never permit such an act. They will, of course, deny it, though that is the only way that I can see to actually stop her plans."

"You may recall that I know Claudius will be poisoned by Agrippina or her agents in less than two years. I don't think Agrippina will stop trying to position herself and young Nero unless someone removes her foul head."

"It's true. She is an aggressive, devious woman, and some of us, including me, tried to talk Claudius out of wedding her. I'm sure she knows these facts and hates me for it. I promise to try, but don't count on me being much help. Though it pains me to admit it, you may be safer somewhere that they can't find you or your lovely wife."

"I've come to the same conclusion, however my final decision will depend on how Alia feels after we've discussed the facts and our options. Thank you, Piso, for your help, advice and support. Without you, I would have never recovered my wife."

"I know exactly how that feels. The evil Caligula took my wife on my wedding day, used her then cast her out. When we tried to reunite, he banned both of us, and we were sent far apart. It took his death and the actions of Claudius for us to find each other again. I am happy for you both, and I would not want anything to happen to either of you." Piso manfully wiped away a tear, and his smiling teeth gleamed in the moonlight. "Now if you would allow me to accompany you home, I would appreciate it."

Cosimus realized that Piso would have to return alone in the dark without protection. It was a fine offer but, given the circumstances, too generous by far. "We would be honored, however you should stay here where your wife is undoubtedly still up and waiting for you. I promise that Antonius and I are capable of protecting Alia."

"I'm sure you are, yet I hope it doesn't come to that," Piso answered.

"How long do you think we have before your *Praetorian's* make it back to shore?" Antonius asked.

"We saw their ship in the distance at least twenty *mille passus* from shore on our return voyage. If they are lucky and don't encounter a storm, I would guess they are still several days from returning on their own. On the other hand, they could get lucky and be found by a *bellicae soloturae Intus* and be towed back earlier than that. When they return, I will send you a message."

Cosimus sighed and looked down at his wife who upturned her lovely face toward him, listening to him and relishing having him back in her life. She was visibly showing her pregnancy though she had a couple of months or more before childbirth. He had to find a safe place for her, one that had access to at least the best, however primitive, medical care. *Roma*, itself, was out of the question as was the neighboring Pompeii. As he pondered where to escape, he came back to the prospect presented to him by Antonius. They could return to the future when the portal opened, if it did that is. There could be some unknown reason that the portal would never appear again and that possibility had to be considered.

"What's next?" Antonius asked.

"I don't know," Cosimus answered.

"I have a question," Alia blurted. She had remained silent up to now, letting the men be in charge of events. She was impressed with Cosimus' friend, Antonius, however she was burning with questions. "I heard about you, Antonius. I heard a lot. Cosimus loves you, and we both feel lucky to have you with us. Except I heard that you had taken Cosimus' place and had returned to the land he had left. How are you here with us? Where did you come from? And when will you leave us?"

Antonius laughed, "I thought you would never ask. You should understand that I would not have worried about dear Cosimus had I known that he had married such a wonderful woman. And I didn't understand how intelligent and perceptive a woman could be until I met you."

"And what are the answers to my questions," she retorted.

"First, my dear Alia, you have a couple of unexpected surprises coming in a few minutes. My son, whom we named Cosimo after your husband, and his companion, Rachel, came with me. You are about to meet them."

"And can I just talk to them as we are talking?"

"With Cos you can, however I'm afraid that Rachel doesn't understand Latin."

"What does she speak?"

"She can only communicate in English, though I'm sure you will find a way to make your feelings known to each other."

Alia smiled, even though it could not be seen by her companions. "And you still have not answered my questions," she persisted.

"We came from the future. I know that is a hard thing to understand, and I barely understand it myself. We are returning in three days. Cosimus will explain that more fully to you in private. Just so you know, these two young people who came with me are about your age and are from the future. They have seen this city after it was dug up from the ash and rock that smothered it, and they have even seen the home that you live in. Together, they discovered the message that Cosimus left for me and that is why we are here. We returned to help rescue you."

"How is it done? I mean, how do you travel?"

"For us, it's simple. A big machine opens a little window, and we walk through it. There is no pain or effort. We just leave one room and enter another."

"So I could go through also, and my baby could go with me?"

"Easily. You just have to be willing to step into the opening," Antonius answered.

"Wait a moment," Cosimus interrupted. "We have not had time to discuss this yet. Alia and I will talk this over in the morning. There is much to decide."

They were all there waiting by the *impluvium,* as if they knew something was about to happen. Cos and Rachel were standing together holding on to each other. Maccus and Linza were doing much the same. Old *Màthair* was standing apart from the others, wearing her tattered clothing and her moth eaten *stola,* feet widely spaced and hands on her hips. Alia was first to appear from the entryway, and as she entered the *atrium,* there were whoops of joy, and the three members of her family rushed to greet her. As they were hugging her and throwing questions, Alia looked long and hard at the two strangers trying to gauge their personalities.

Then Cosimus and Antonius entered and threw their sacks on the tile floor. Cos rushed toward them dragging Rachel behind him. "You did it. You got her back," he exclaimed. "Any trouble?"

"No one was killed, and Alia had been well treated. However, it has been a long journey," Cosimus answered, thinking of Alia, her pregnancy and how tired she must be.

"What happened to the people who stole Alia? Did you give them what they deserved?" *Màthair* asked.

"They were *Germanii*. They had looked out for her and treated her as well as they could. I do not hold them to blame because they were only following orders," Cosimus answered. Then he looked at his brother's son, still holding on to Rachel. "Any problems here while we were away?"

Maccus answered instead. "We were guarded by a few gladiators until the *Praetorians* threatened them and forced them to leave. The four we encountered yesterday said that they were here to arrest an important person soon. I believe that person is you, *Dominus*."

"I know about it. We will talk in the morning about our plans," Cosimus said.

While the others were listening to Cosimus, Alia moved toward Cos and Rachel. This was the first time Rachel had a good look at the now rather famous Alia, and she was forced to take a deep breath. Nowhere had she seen a more beautiful woman as Alia. Rachel was used to the appraising looks men would give her, and she was told many times by many people how attractive she was, yet for the first time in her life, she felt plain and unattractive. The woman walking toward her held her head high and moved with grace, intelligence radiating from her eyes, her long lustrous red tinged hair flowing behind her like a scarf. In spite of her obvious pregnancy, she radiated beauty as if she had just come alive from a Greek statue of a goddess. Her eyes never left Rachel's, and Rachel was unable to look away from this apparition of loveliness coming directly toward her.

"Hi, my name is Alia. I understand that you are Rachel, and you come from the future."

Rachel blinked and looked again at Alia. Had she just heard English from this woman or had she imagined it? "I'm sorry, did you just speak to me using my language?" Rachel stuttered.

"Yes, I speak English. Probably not so good, but I'll get more better," Alia smiled and reached for Rachel's hand. "Welcome to my world. I hope you are not disappointed."

"How…no one here speaks that language. Where did you learn it?" Rachel asked.

"Cos…my Cos…taught me. It is our private language so we talk between us only. Do you get me well?" Alia asked. It wasn't just her physical beauty, Rachel comprehended, it was her entire presence. It was like being introduced to the most sought after, the most glamorous of all movie idols, a woman who knew she was beautiful and was aware of how her beauty humbled most people, even other women.

"To answer your question, I love this place. It is better than anything in our time. I have been very fortunate to see it before it is destroyed," Rachel finally got out.

"Compared to my family farm, this is heaven for me also. Cos makes me very happy and gives me everything. He is the only person I thought of when I was taken from here. I knew that someday he would come for me. Now that I am home we can go on and have our baby and be happy forever." Alia turned her head toward Cos and blew him a kiss. Her profile was a shock to Rachel, the intensity of her perfection, her complexion and her cascading radiant hair was nearly an out-of-body experience to witness. What a marvelous creature for a man to possess, Rachel mused. She glanced at Cos, who was staring at Alia, hardly believing what his eyes were seeing.

Alia turned her attention to Cos, "And you must be the son of Antonius. I understand they named you for my husband. I am glad to meet you," she said and held out her hand. It was taken by Cos, though he held it limply, not fully understanding what to do with it.

"Glad to know you also, Alia. Has anyone told you that you are beautiful?"

Alia laughed at him and retracted her hand. "A few, however you should not ignore Rachel who is also very wonderful and is yours."

Once more, Alia turned her attention to Rachel, asking, "Have you had a baby yet or do you know anything about childbirth?"

"I don't know the first thing about it," Rachel admitted.

Alia nodded to them again, smiled, and moved toward Maccus, Linza and *Màthair*. The way they embraced and kissed each other was a spectacle to watch. Neither Rachel nor Cos had ever experienced the love and affection by others that was on full view in front of them. It was a reunion that was heartfelt and sincere, people who had truly bonded, people who assumed responsibility for each other no matter what came along.

"The hour is late," Cosimus announced. "We all need to retire now, and in the morning, we will discuss what comes next."

"Are you still leaving us, *Dominus*?" Maccus asked. His question hung in the air like a gigantic weight, ready to fall to earth obliterating everything around it. Alia's head snapped around. Her eyes holding Cosimus in an intense and questioning look. Cosimus felt like he was standing on a mount about to decide the fate of a multitude. His decision would affect them all in one way or another.

"Tomorrow, not tonight, we will all discuss that," he answered. He gathered Alia's arm in his and headed toward the stairs. She continued to look up at his face trying to decide for herself what his intentions may be. "We need to discuss this between ourselves first. I intend to hear your thoughts before deciding anything," he whispered to her.

Chapter 34

One Last Glorious Day

Ah, what is more blessed than to put cares away, when the mind lays by its burden, and tired with labor of far travel we have come to our own home and rest on the couch we longed for? This it is which alone is worth all these toils

---

Catullus (? to 54 BC)

QUI NUNC IT PER ITER TENEBRICOSUM ILLUE UNDE NEGANT REDIRE QUEMQUAM

(Who now travels that dark path from whose bourne they say no one returns)

Catullus (? to 54 BC)

---

*D*awn moved across the ceiling, creeping in like a cat who is being watched and casting light into the corners of the otherwise dark room. Cosimus lay there watching its inexorable progress, his thoughts very far away. One part of him was listening for any human noises drifting in on the air, though so far, the other occupants were still enjoying their sleep. Alia shifted and moved closer to him, a sure sign that she was nearing awakening. Having her beside him where he could feel the heat of her body and touch her when she came to his mind was wonderful, even more wonderful since their forced separation made him realize how temporary and fragile those in your life are, no matter their importance to you. Life is not a continuous process but comes in jumps, starts and waves. Riding one of those wonderful waves has to be accompanied by the knowledge that it, one day, one hour, will play out and end.

"Good morning," her soft voice said, then her delicate hand started caressing his chest. Cosimus looked into those deep wonderful eyes and had to fight back the tears. Alia was his again to nourish, protect, amuse, most of all to love. She found his wrist and moved his hand to her protruding belly. "Just concentrate and you can feel the baby moving," she said. He did and closed his eyes, picturing a small fetus moving around in a confined space. Sure enough, there was a delicate flutter which came and went according to some process known only to the unborn infant.

"I feel it," he said and then turned toward her and kissed her forehead softly. "It's wonderful to have you back beside me. I took you for granted, thinking that you would always be here with me. Now I know for sure that I can no longer live without you." Alia used her finger to outline the shape of his lips, then let her arm reach around to his back drawing him closer.

"I feel the same. How did I get through my previous life without you there?" She rolled to her back and looked at the ceiling, the sun's rays streaking it with ever increasing brightness. "I understood last night that you intend on leaving here for good. And I thought we would resume our lives as before, you and I and the others. We were very happy. Why would you want to change that?"

"Actually, when I said that, I had nearly given up hope of finding you close by. I was preparing to travel to your homeland to see if someone took you up there. However there is another problem, a big one. Antonius and his family discovered a document found in the remains of Piso's home which recorded that you were murdered by order of Agrippina, the wife of the Emperor. She is trying to keep me out of *Roma*, even though I had no intention of ever moving there. Recently, she has sent out a command that I be killed by the *Praetorian* Guard. I assume that your murder would have followed mine. There is no stopping her while we can still be found. We have to run away and hide for the next eight years. Then, Agrippina will be murdered by her own son, Nero, whom she is fighting so hard to install as the next emperor. So, my dear, even though I don't want to leave, we have no choice, and the worst news is that we have to leave soon, in no more than two days."

"You mean we have to leave this home and our friends and never return again?" Cos could sense her tears even though he couldn't see them.

"Well, we could return after eight years when it will be safe for us, but remember what I told you about this city, that someday it will be covered by hot ash from Vesuvius. Many will die, and this city and others nearby will disappear for almost two thousand years. At some point, we would have to leave here anyway."

"Where could we go? I am going to have this baby soon, and we can't be walking in the forest when it happens."

"If we make it back to *Britannia*, my *legion* is still there and will gladly protect us. Or there might be some small village not far away to hide in. And you know already that Antonius has offered us a chance to return to the future with him and his family."

"What do you think about that? You know that world, wouldn't you want to return to it?"

"It depends on you and what you want. I am comfortable here now, and I have many friends, more than I would have back in the future world. Still, I could do it. I worry about the effect of that world on you, though. You may know a language which would allow you to converse, but things are very different there. If we decide to leave this time, there will be no returning, and I promise you, when you see this very house, this very room, in the future, it will bring you to tears recalling our time here, and you will always wonder what happened to Linza, her baby, and the others. It's a big decision to make, and we have little time to think it out."

Alia took a big breath and exhaled noisily. "I have to ponder it. Can I let you know my feelings tonight?"

"That will be fine, though by tomorrow, we should be preparing to leave, wherever we are going. I hear someone moving about downstairs, so I think we have to get up."

Cosimus and Alia walked down the stairs slowly, listening to the active conversations coming from somewhere on the first floor. Before they made the turn into the *peristylum*, Cosimus heard his name.

"Not this morning," *Màthair* called loudly from the *culina*. She stuck her head around the corner and pointed to the *triclinium*. "We decided," she said and then grinned. It was the most spectacular room in the villa and almost never used. This occasion, with everybody present, was the special circumstance that called for the best, and all were aware that there may never be another opportunity to use this room or to be together again. Cosimus led Alia around the corner, and there it was, all set up for an extravagant breakfast. The room had three wide padded benches surrounding a table where food was placed for all to access. Already, two were occupied by smiling couples…one held Maccus and Linza, the other Cos and Rachel. They were reclining together as couples and laughing. The bench on the left was reserved for Cosimus and Alia. Cosimus looked around wondering about the two others when he heard chairs being moved in by Antonius, which he placed at the end of the food table.

Rachel studied Cosimus and Alia as they positioned themselves, awkwardly at first, on the padded bench. She blushed as she fixated on Cosimus, his muscularity and his manliness on full display as he tenderly and gently caressed his marvelously attractive wife. For a moment, Rachel wished that she was the one in Cosimus' arms, it was her hair that he buried his nose in, her ear that he whispered into, and her laugh that caused him to smile. Her thoughts were disrupted when Cos snuggled up with her and kissed her cheek and neck. She put her palm against his face and patted him softly. Cos was a handsome fellow also and very much in love with her. Why could she not let those images go? "You need a shave," she said softly, then turned her big eyes on him.

"And you," Cos whispered, "never looked more appealing. That tunic shows you off you know. Any man who sees you would be jealous of me."

Alia stole glances at young Cos and Rachel. She was determined to spend as much time with Rachel as possible this day, pumping her for information about living in the future and what it actually meant to be there. It was a fearful thing to give up all you know and everything familiar. On the other hand, there were Cos and Rachel, both decidedly normal, intelligent, well-informed as well as open and friendly. If that's what the future holds, it can't be so awful to contemplate moving there. Still, the concept of time travel was impossible for her to grasp. No matter how many times it came to her mind, she rejected it as silly, more or less as she regarded the nearly endless legends about Roman gods. All of it was just a story, an entertaining tale, nothing more.

Antonius looked over the room with satisfaction. After living so long in the twenty-first century, it was delightful to return to the first century and compare as no one else could, other than Cosimus, that is. He was comfortable here in this marvelous villa, in this adorable little city on the Bay of Naples. The Romans certainly did know how to live, at least the wealthy ones did. His few moments outside this house did remind him of how, in general, healthy the majority of people were. There were no fat ones and no inactive ones. They all looked happy and whatever they did, they put their best efforts into it. Yes, he missed this era very much, even given the shortcomings of it and the lack of industrial things which made life easier. The largest shortcoming was the state of medical care. There was little of that, and what was available was administered more by tradition than directed by the science of reason and research, as would become the norm in the distant future. He leaned back in his chair and studied the walls. This room was a masterpiece of some unknown painter who had painstakingly applied his decorations on wet plaster, yet had preserved the lifelike quality of a work done on canvas. The scene was continuous around the room on three walls and painted within a demarcating border made to resemble marble. It told a tale of the mythical Titans and their heroic struggles against other gods. The floor was intricate, of lighter color and largely geometric, in this way avoiding conflict with the action taking place on the walls. He shook his head. Most of his life in this era had been spent in the dirt of distant lands. This home was as foreign and extravagant to him as it was to his son or Rachel.

Màthair came in, struggling with a large glass flask of wine, put it down noisily, and pulled up her chair, sitting down beside Antonius at the end of the table. It was the final signal to begin eating since they were all there. "I think you and I are destined to be sweethearts also," Antonius said and put his arm over her thin shoulders and smiled at her. What a dear and what a hard worker she was. Cosimus had introduced her as the mother of them all, and he was completely correct. *Màthair* was often overlooked yet clearly the most indispensable person in the family. She gave him a furtive glance though otherwise ignored his humor.

Cosimus passed the flask of wine around, and when the cups were full, he cleared his throat, and they all ceased talking and turned their attention on him.

"My family," he started, "My wonderful family…at last all together. What a moment to celebrate. How fortunate I am to have the loyalty of my friend Maccus who has protected me and served me for a great part of my life." He raised his cup to Maccus and then took a drink of wine. "And what beauty his lovely wife Linza lends to this room." Linza blushed and looked around to see if anyone was admiring her. Cosimus continued, "I would never forget to bring praise on *Màthair* who is the glue that holds us together." He raised his cup again and smiled her way.

"Consider what a friend I have in Antonius. He taught me to be a soldier, in fact taught me nearly everything, and was willing to travel back in time to help me once again at his and his family's peril. There are no words to express my gratitude for their help in rescuing my dear wife, Alia, who would not be at my side today except for their assistance." Cosimus stopped talking and just looked at Antonius, holding his eyes. Everyone there could see the tears slowly dripping down his face. He used his hand to wipe his face clean while the others respectfully stayed silent. "There are hard choices ahead for me and Alia. This vengeance against us will continue until they succeed or we hide from them. Alia and I have to leave this home and our dear family. Maccus and Linza now own this house and everything in it. They also own my winery and my bakery, and I know they will prosper and be happy. I'm sorry that Alia and I won't be here to help them and witness the birth of their child. This is the only home I have ever known, and the people in this room are the ones closest to me through my entire life. Nothing will ever erase this moment from my memory." After the murmuring started, Cosimus sat down and hugged Alia who was also running with tears.

Antonius stood up and raised his cup in return. "This is to the most noble Roman of them all, the finest man I have ever known. To you, Cosimus. May you and Alia find happiness once more." He put his cup to his lips and drank deeply.

Once again Cosimus spoke with firmness, "For the last time, Maccus, you are to stay here and guard the women. I know you want to protect me, but I assure you that Antonius and his son will do that." Maccus looked dejected and turned away, disappearing down the hallway without another protest.

"Good man, that one," Antonius observed then turned toward Cos. "Son, you are well trained. Trust yourself and follow our lead if anything happens. However, if you do have to use your sword, make every strike count." Cos nodded understanding, though inside, his confidence was low and the stress building.

"It's only a half hour walk to Piso's villa, and I don't expect trouble until we arrive. Once we get to him, he will take control of the *Praetorians*, I'm sure," Cosimus said. All three men were dressed in loose fitting tunics, though also wore overlying chain mail, and all three were armed with a sheathed *gladius,* carried on their right side.

"I feel a bit exposed going into battle without a helmet," Antonius commented.

"Let's hope it doesn't come to that. Everyone ready?" Cosimus asked and started forward, walking at a brisk pace. During the daylight hours in Herculaneum, commercial carts were forbidden in the streets, partially because the sidewalks were narrow and a great deal of pedestrian traffic was, by necessity, spilled onto the paved streets. Cosimus chose to walk down the middle, and this way avoided any surprise attack from the many alcoves and side streets. They neither met, nor saw, any armed men as they made their way toward the waterfront. After turning north, Piso's villa could be seen looming in the distance, its distinctive three storied main structure set well back, surrounded by an expansive garden with pools and statuary along the way.

"This sure looks different than what we saw while working here," Cos remarked.

Cosimus laughed, "All of it lying under twenty meters of compacted ash and rock. Yes, I saw this area at one time in my youth. From what I recall, only a small part of the city had been excavated. What you see now gives you understanding of just how much work yet needs to be done."

"Sure does. It's like digging up a grave and finding bones instead of bodies. This city is far more attractive than I even imagined. And the colors and the occupants… " he trailed off, saddened to think that it would all disappear in one fiery day.

As they drew closer, the villa suddenly erupted with shouts. They caught glimpses of shiny armor moving about inside the front *peristylum*. "We've been spotted," Cosimus dryly observed. There was no surprising an alert Roman guard, and he expected what was about to happen.

Just before reaching the entrance, there was a commanding shout. "*Stabit*!" The three men stopped walking and spread out, alert to whatever was about to come through the gate. A soldier emerged, his hand resting on the pommel of his sheathed sword, and following him were four more. All were wearing battle armor including shield and *pilum*. One stepped forward as the others moved laterally.

"You are called Cosimus, is that right?" he stated brusquely. When there was no returning answer, he smiled and looked quickly to his men, seeing that they were in good position. "I am instructed to arrest you. Put down your swords," he commanded.

"If you know about me, then you must also know my rank as *legatus*. And you should also know that I take no orders from any *Praetorian*. Move away from the entrance, and let us pass."

"You are under arrest. I warn you; if you do not do as I say, then you force my hand," the officer said.

"I am giving you a chance to live, soldier. Your orders did not originate with Claudius but from his wife. Move away from the entrance or you will be the first to die." Cosimus moved slowly to one side, away from the one giving the orders and closer to one of the end men. He was watching the eyes of his adversary, gauging when the order would come and who would attempt to strike first. Then, he saw the man's eyes narrow, and the glance to one side to confirm that his men were ready. It was coming.

In a movement too rapid to understand, Cosimus twisted, grabbing the long spear, the iron tipped *pilum*, from the surprised end guard and at the same time striking the man in the throat with his elbow causing him to loosen his grasp of his spear. In a blur, the spear tip was directed at the exposed throat of the commanding officer, piercing his neck from front to back. Cosimus continued to push the spear forward, driving the flailing man backward until he struck the wall behind him causing the spear to be imbedded in the plaster, suspending him by his gushing neck.

The swords came out quickly, flashing in the morning sun and Cosimus held up his hand, palm out. "You men!" he announced. "You are taking orders from me now. I mean you no harm, and we understand that you are just doing what you were instructed. However, your officer gives no more orders, and you are under no more obligation to follow his previous orders." It was obvious that this tactic took the guards by surprise, and they looked back and forth between themselves trying to decide what their course of action should be. One man uttered a fierce scream and launched himself toward Cosimus with fury, his sword aimed directly at Cosimus neck. He only covered two feet before his progress was halted by a thrust from Antonius who had been expecting this particular guard to attack. His *gladius* was precisely aimed at the unprotected arm pit just above the breast plate, and deeply penetrated the man's chest, a rapidly fatal wound. He dropped to the floor, grimacing in death. The three remaining guards realized that they were now evenly matched in number, however their opponents were experienced fighters and not about to surrender. It was a moment that they had to choose which side to be on, and the decision was a matter of life or death.

"We surrender," one said, and his sword and spear clattered to the stone pavers.

The two remaining men realized that they were hopelessly outnumbered and, somewhat defiantly, dropped their swords and spears.

"Good choice," Antonius remarked, his bloody sword still positioned to resume its fearsome work.

"You men are to remain here and dispose of these two bodies. Be sure and clean the stones of blood after you do so," Cosimus ordered. He was aware that the task was to be a humiliating one, bound to cause outrage, however suppressed. He stood for a moment watching them, making sure that they all would do as he directed or face the consequences. They began by pulling their officer down from his impalement, letting his limp body fall noisily to the earth.

Cos held his tongue and tried not to visibly shake on the outside as he was doing on the inside. It all had happened so quickly. In just a couple of confusing moments, two men lay dead before him. The reality came to him that sword training is no substitute for actual battle. He felt useless, incapable of the decisive action that his father and Cosimus did by instinct, and worse, he felt both of them glance his way to be sure he was still standing and not pulling away.

"Be on your guard because we still have to run the gauntlet before we make it to the villa. There are many opportunities for ambush over the next two hundred *passus,*" Cosimus remarked. He held his sword by the hilt, allowing it to drop beside his leg as he started walking forward, alertly watching as he entered the vast *peristylum.* Antonius motioned for his son to go ahead of him and behind Cosimus. Antonius would take the rear, the most likely position inviting attack. Before they arrived at the villa, the door opened and a steady stream of armed men poured out. Cosimus held up his hand, an order for those behind him to stop. Ahead, the *Praetorian* Guard assumed a line, spreading from the entry door in both directions, shields up and spears ready. Between them passed a smaller figure, clad in a radiantly white toga, a double stripe of rich purple covering his right breast. It was Piso himself, and he rapidly walked toward them, his guards remaining in their defensive posture behind him.

"Greetings," he shouted. "I was just informed as to what was taking place outside the gate. My hope is that no one was injured." As he came closer, Cos got his first look at this rather legendary figure, a man whom history will treat favorably yet also a man willing to die for what he believed was in the best interests of *Roma.* Piso was a handsome man and walked with a bearing suitable for someone of immense wealth and political power.

"Forgive me, *Consul* Piso," Cosimus said while sheathing his *gladius.* "We encountered violence and responded with the same. You have lost two men. The others are cleaning up the entrance."

"Regrettable…and problematic," Piso said, glancing backward at the long line of *Praetorians.* "It will be hard to explain it to them," he said, motioning with his thumb toward the glistening armor behind him. "What brings you here this morning?" he asked.

"I have made the decision to leave Herculaneum as soon as tomorrow. If I can have some assistance from you, I plan to take

Alia with me and travel to *Britannia*, rejoining my *legion* for the next eight years."

"Why eight years?" Piso wondered.

"That's when Agrippina's son, Nero, will grow tired of her meddling and have her killed. Afterwards, we will be free to return." Cosimus could feel the surprised stares from his two companions from the future. He would not be returning with them as they had hoped. Cosimus had become part of the past and willingly had chosen to remain so.

"And how can I help, Cosimus?" Piso asked.

"You can help us find a ship bound for *Britannia* as soon as possible."

Piso rubbed his chin as he considered how to accommodate Cosimus. "I can no longer trust my *Praetorians* to obey me. They are commanded by *Roma* only, and until our Emperor takes charge, they are out of my control. And no ship from here heads to *Brittania*. We will have to find one heading out from *Ostium*, and one that is carrying *legionaries*, not *Praetorians*. It's going to be difficult." He looked with sadness at his friend, wishing that he could protect him and his wife, while realizing that he could not control forces set in motion by Agrippina in her lust for power. "It may not be the best plan. I need to think it through, if you will allow me. Return to your home and remain there. I will come to you tomorrow, and together we will come up with something to keep you safe from harm."

Players of Astragali, from Herculaneum, on marble, by Alexander of Athens. Phoebe tries to pacify Latona and Niobe, while two of the niobides, Hilearia and Agle,continue to play with the astragali, unaware of their impending death. This work is in the public domain

Chapter 35

Fatí Plaga

The hour is ripe, and yonder lies the way.

Virgil (70 BC to 19 BC)

With a last look up and down the long straight street, assuring himself that no one was coming…yet, Cosimus entered his home and allowed himself to sigh, his muscles loosening and his nose taking in the wonderful aroma of fresh baked bread. Across the *atrium*, he caught a glimpse of Alia's eyes and saw her fluid motion appear briefly in the distance. Whatever happened, wherever they found themselves, he could bear no separation from her. He needed Alia, and she needed him. His entire life had lead to union with this small wonderful woman, the years of struggle and risk, the vast distances he had crossed, and even the transportation back in time, all had been for a reason. And as he watched her come toward him, a small smile on her lips, the happiness beaming from her eyes, he knew that this was what his life had been directed toward all along.

"Did Piso offer anything helpful?" she asked as her slender arms enveloped his neck and pulled his face toward hers.

"He's thinking about it. It's not simple as I had hoped it would be. Have you any suggestions?"

Alia's face took on a serious look, her face dropping slightly, partly shielding his view of her radiant eyes. "I've spent the morning with Rachel because I needed to hear all about where she and Cos came from and what it would be like for me to be there."

"And?"

"We have to move from here, you said." She paused as she waited for Cosimus to nod the truth of it. "And we will be in a new place, a new home, and things will be different. We will not have Maccus, Linza and *Màthair* with us ever again. Is that right?" Again she waited until he responded, this time with his eyes. It was true, their lives were to be vastly different. "So, if we go with Antonius and his family, we will have them with us, they will be our family, and no one will harm us there. Is that true?" Her reasoning was clear and to the point. Cosimus pulled her in, forgetting for a moment the protrusion of her pregnant abdomen, again made aware that a baby was present and needed to have its opinion heard as well.

"I see your point. Until you were taken from me, we were both happy here. I know what is on the other side of that opening, however you and I are from this time now. Crossing over again… " Cosimus stopped for a moment, allowing his thoughts to catch up to his emotions. The last time he saw the future, it was under attack. The world he had known was coming apart, and the demon was succeeding in causing the destruction of thousands of years of civilization and ending the lives of millions of its citizens. And that was the reason he had left and returned to the past. It was to save mankind, to preserve the essence of what it meant to be a human and respect your fellow men. And it had worked. The future had been restored to what it should have been.

"So you have made up your mind. You think we should return with Antonius," Cosimus asked in a near whisper.

"Many women die while giving birth, and many children don't live to grow up. Rachel tells me that almost never happens where she came from. She even offered us to live with her family if we need to."

Cosimus gently let her go and looked past her at the home they shared. He had managed to survive many battles and was lucky enough to find Alia. It was hard to give up all his hopes for a comfortable and fulfilled life here among people that he loved, in a place that was so marvelous, and in a city where he was respected and honored. Clearly, little Alia was correct. She and the baby would have a much better chance to live with better medical care and all the things modern civilization can offer. His rational mind agreed that they should return with Antonius, but emotionally, he didn't want to return to the complexity of modern life. He liked it here, enjoyed the people, the sights and the clean air free of automobile smoke and noise. It all depended on Piso and what he could come up with. If there was a reasonable solution offered, then he would insist that they take it. It was only for eight years. Surely they could live comfortably and safely for that short time. And money was no problem. He had plenty of money, and it was no longer being held by money lenders or buried in a temple. Maccus and he had collected all he could acquire and quietly and secretly buried it in a place unlikely to be disturbed in this time or any other. It was his security, and Maccus could be trusted with this knowledge as no other person could.

Cos found Rachel looking out toward the peaceful bay and the several ships under sail, moving slowly across toward unknown destinations. He put his hands on her shoulders and nuzzled her neck. "Is it what you expected?" he asked. She turned around and embraced him, pressing her cheek into his chest and enveloping him with her arms.

"No, it's better than I ever thought. I've not seen very much of it, though so far I would be willing to live here forever. How about you?"

"We encountered trouble over at Piso's place. Dad and Cosimus killed two men so fast you could hardly see it happen. Luckily the others gave up, or I would have been trying to kill one of them also. The city is beautiful, as is the entire region, but death is always just around the corner here."

"It is no different than home, is it? I mean, people get killed by autos all the time, planes crash and people get sick and die of things. Life isn't permanent. It comes to you for a few years and then leaves. Shouldn't we live moment to moment and savor every second of it instead of fretting how we might die?"

"Of course you are right about that. One thing I noticed is that most would expect that these people would be somewhat primitive by our standards. Well, they aren't primitive at all. All I have met are very smart and savvy as well as talented and well trained in what they do. And I hope you get a chance to meet Piso. What a guy. He is very educated and wealthy though also humble in some ways. I can tell he has a lot of respect for Cosimus and Dad. We never made it inside his villa, however the garden is full of spectacular statues and art. What a treat to see it as it was…or is, excuse the mistake."

"Say, do you recall the first day when I took you here, and we had lunch together imagining what it would be like?"

"Sure, you had a surprise box lunch prepared, and we used the little table by the window upstairs."

"Since we are leaving tomorrow, I think you and I should do it again today, and this time we will have a better view."

It didn't take very long for Cos to agree that this would be a memorable experience. "I'll have to ask *Màthair,* but there should be no problem, and it would be delightful."

Cosimus found Antonius in the *culina* talking with *Màthair* and Maccus. They seemed to be in animated conversation and looked surprised when they saw him enter. "Greetings, Cosimus," Antonius said, smiling broadly and offering him a seat at the small table.

"You are leaving tomorrow?" Cosimus asked. "About what time?"

"According to the scientist helping us…precisely at six o'clock in the afternoon. He was most explicit. Did you discuss this with your wife?"

"Yes. She wants us to go with you."

Antonius could not suppress his delight. "Wonderful. Did you agree?"

"No. Not yet. I await suggestions from Piso who is coming here tomorrow. Frankly, I would rather stay here. There is nothing for me in your world. I am older now and have no modern skills in order to provide a living for Alia and our child. Here, I am a wealthy, respected Roman citizen."

"And one who is hunted by the first lady of *Roma* and her numberless *Praetorians*."

"True, though Piso has promised to speak to Claudius on my behalf, and I know that Claudius would never permit such a thing if he knew about it."

"And in two years, Claudius will be gone. Then what?" Antonius asked.

"Then I'm no longer a threat. I think she will forget about me."

"You hope she will."

Cosimus had no returning comment. It was true enough. Agrippina was unpredictable. He rubbed his chin, lost in thought.

"Cos… ." *Màthair* spoke, gaining his attention and his eyes on her. "I have been listening patiently and expecting you at some point to ask what I think. Since you don't seem inclined to ask, I'll tell you anyway." Cosimus smiled at her and waited for her to finish.

"You are planning to leave this city and travel with Alia to some distant place. I know that much, and I think I know why. Still, exactly how do you travel with a woman who is advanced in her pregnancy? Do you expect her to straddle a horse or to be bumped along in a cart? Have you thought this out and given her situation consideration?"

Cosimus could feel the eyes on him. *Màthair* had exposed a weakness in his plan. They would have to travel very slowly and if pursued could not escape. He sighed. The pull of the portal was becoming very strong indeed.

"No, my dear, I had not given that appropriate consideration and thank you for enlightening me. Have you any suggestions for that problem?"

"Can't you use Piso's ship to take you to a bigger ship so Alia can travel in some comfort?" she asked.

"That would be an answer. The problem is that the *Praetorians* who seek to harm us might find out, and we would be at their mercy on board the ship."

"I heard Antonius say that Alia wants you both to leave with them. How, exactly, are they leaving?"

"Its complicated, *Màthair,*" he answered, reluctant to explain time travel to her, knowing that she would laugh at the idea.

"I'm listening," she retorted.

"Tomorrow, we will show you, *Màthair,*" Antonius answered instead. "It's simple, and there is no danger to Alia, I assure you."

Màthair frowned, not liking the lack of trust in her intelligence. She had already seen more in life than any of them and not much would surprise or confuse her.

"One more thing, Cos, and then I'll be quiet," she said and patted his arm. "Young Cos and Rachel have in mind dining tonight upstairs on the end table. I think if you are really leaving tomorrow, you should do the same with Alia and use the downstairs table. It will be your last chance, and I know it is what she would want."

The idea was a good one. A last meal overlooking the bay as the sun set and the evening shadows grew longer. It reminded him of dining there with Alia before they were married, when he was discovering his love for her and her love for him. Yes, a grand idea. He grinned at the ever resourceful *Màthair* and softly patted her arm. He nodded his approval to her.

"And don't worry about me and Maccus and Linza. They are good company, and I enjoy eating with them," Antonius said, then remembering, added, "and *Màthair* also."

Herculaneum lies due west of Vesuvius and as such has an earlier onset of evening. The *Tyrrhenum Mare*, to the east, sparkles and moves in the sun as a somber evening shadow creeps over the city, and as night approaches, the songs of evening birds grow louder and more insistent.

"I thought this would be nice, and it is," Rachel beamed across the table. It was too early for a lit candle or oil lamp, and most of the light was being reflected from the water, moving across her face in subtle little waves, accenting her natural beauty.

"You make me feel good to just look across the table at you, and I feel even better knowing that you will someday be my wife, and we can recall this adventure together," Cos said. They were sitting at the same table that they used once in the far future, yet the effect was nearly the same. Even the table and stools wrought in marble were in the same condition as they had seen previously. Cos rubbed his palm over the smooth surface just as he had done before and looked over the bay, still moving under the direct light of the setting sun. "This place is marvelous. No wonder Cosimus doesn't want to leave."

"I felt helpless once we arrived, and I wanted to talk to someone, anyone. Then along came Alia and her English. It almost knocked me down when she spoke to me. Now that she and I have become good friends, I feel like I fit in, that this is my home also. I'm not sure I want to leave either," Rachel said, her teeth gleaming in the reflected sunlight. Cos wasn't sure if she was serious or not. With Rachel, you could never be sure.

Cos could easily understand her feelings. "You know, I wish we could stay longer, much longer. Even a year. There is so much I would like to see now that we are here. Rome is just north of us, and it is sitting there in its prime, and we will never get to see it."

"Be thankful that we were able to come at all. Though seriously, do you worry about returning? I mean, what if Barron Harmes can't open the portal again or if something happened to him or even if he changed his mind about getting us back? We could be here forever."

Cos frowned. He never really considered that the process could somehow fail. Could they survive here for the rest of their lives? What would actually happen if Cosimus is arrested or even murdered? Where would they go?

"A sobering thought, Rachel. Let's try to enjoy this meal, our company, and our good fortune, just for the moment. The future will take care of us somehow."

Alia felt that sitting across from Cosimus was just too far away, and after fretting about for a moment or two, she suddenly smiled and came around the table and softly held onto his shoulder, looking down at him with her longing eyes. "Can I sit on your lap instead?" she murmured. Cosimus picked her up carefully and sat her across his lap. She responded by leaning into his other arm and letting her head rest so that her face was turned up to him. Her playful fingers stroked his cheek, and her eyes glistened with tears.

"Something the matter, my dearest Alia?

"I'm happy being with you. I'll be happy any place as long as you are close by. Only… ." She paused, the tears flowing down the sides of her face onto her neck.

"Only you don't want to leave this lovely place and all your new friends," Cosimus suggested.

"No," she admitted. He waited, but there was no further explanation from her and none needed.

Cosimus didn't try to convince her about anything because he had nearly made up his mind to stay if at all possible. He too felt saddened about leaving, about going anywhere. After all those years of struggle, those deaths all around him, finally he had earned the right to have a life of his own. Now, because of one woman's greed, it all had to be discarded. All except the small wonderful woman in his arms. He would trade it all for her. She was everything that he wanted in life, the only thing he could not part with.

"It's lovely here, the gentle evening breeze coming off the water and the purple shadows just now reaching the shore's edge. We should have dined together at this table more often. And you are correct, it's so much better holding you than looking across the table and wishing I was holding you."

Alia chuckled and wiped some tears away with her hands. "I'm sorry to be sorrowful just now when I should be so happy. I have your child, and I have you. That's all I want. Anywhere you are I want to be there also."

Cosimus leaned toward her, and they kissed a long and passionate kiss. "Now sit up, and I will feed you your supper," he teased. She sat erect and brushed back her long hair, tucking it behind one of her ears, then turned and smiled at him, opening her mouth like a bird while she giggled.

Chapter 36

Longum Vitae

Josephus (37 AD to 100 AD)

From somewhere distant there came a sound, and Cos opened his eyes. The room was still mostly dark yet glowing as the morning approached and ambient light increased by the minute. He looked at the wall nearest his bed, straining to see the art work, still nearly fresh from the artist's brush. If only he could bring this entire house back through the portal with everyone inside as well. What a loss, what a tragedy that the earth will choose to swallow everything in sight, and there was nothing anyone could do about it. He stretched and his first awake thoughts were about Rachel, who slept in the adjoining room. Parting from her and watching as she entered her room last night was nearly the low point of his entire life. It was the last look she gave him over her shoulder. She had paused for a moment in that position allowing for the greatest impact possible. And she had been successful because most of the night wasn't spent in sleep. It was passed in wakeful yearning for her body to be beside his, her arms to be intertwined with his and her lips to be pressed against his. He pulled the cover off and stood up trying to shake off her image, trying to concentrate on today, their last day in the first century.

Cos looked around at the floor for his clothing, still partially lost in thought.

"Are you up?" the soft voice said from the other side of the curtained doorway.

"Not dressed yet, though sort of up," he answered. The curtain parted, and Rachel slipped into the room. She was clothed only with her underwear, and her long hair swung behind her. Without hesitation she came to him and pressed against his chest and belly.

"I was miserable without you last night. Didn't sleep. How did you do?" she asked.

"Much the same. My mind was active with all kind of thoughts, mostly about you."

"Looks like we need an early wedding, doesn't it?"

"Seeing those two couples in love and together clinched it for me. I'm more than ready."

"Me, too."

They kissed, and Cos put his arms around her back, drawing her to him with force. "We better quit this before it goes too far. They don't like this sort of thing in the first century. And neither does my Dad, who is not far away."

Rachel made a pout with her lips and cast her eyes down. "What are the plans for today?" she asked.

"Well, I think Cosimus is waiting for *Consul* Piso. Our portal is supposed to open at six, so we have some time yet."

"Can't we just go for a walk?" Rachel asked.

"I don't think we should. After they killed those two soldiers, there may be consequences or revenge from the other men. It's all up to Piso now. Anyway, we were warned by Barron that there would only be this one last opening. If we got detained…well, we don't want to chance that."

The pile in the *atrium* wasn't very large considering the bags and the two wooden trunks contained everything that Cosimus and Alia would be taking with them, their entire possessions, the sum total of a lifetime. Each time Antonius passed by, he stared at it. Such a small amount of items to start a new life. If only Cosimus would reconsider, he thought. Once back in the future, he would make sure that Cosimus earned a good income and had a fine place to live. Antonius again sighed deeply and passed by, shaking his head.

They all assembled in the *peristylum*, and it was by mutual consent, not by request. The three former colleagues in war, Antonius, Cosimus, and Maccus, stood together, laughing and exchanging tales, as the three young women, Rachel, Alia and Linza, grouped together displaying all the traits of young women who share interests and hopes. That left Cos and *Màthair,* who eyed each other trying to think about common interests other than departure which steadily crept forward in time and in their minds. Cosimus and Alia's destination was as yet undetermined, but the portal opening was not to be avoided. It was a once in forever moment and would never repeat.

"And, young Cos, how do you like it here?" *Màthair* asked.

"Wonderful. Much better than I thought. And, by the way, the food you prepare each meal is something I will remember with fondness."

"Now can you tell me why you are leaving since you like it here so much?" she asked.

Cos pursed his lips and squinted, trying to think of a way to explain it to her. "My father came to help find Alia. I came with him, and Rachel came with me. We have to return home at some point, and today is the day."

"I understand. Just a visit then. And how do you get home and by what manner do you travel?" she asked

Cos thought for a moment. *Màthair* would be there when the portal opened. She would watch them leave. There was no reason to keep it a secret any longer. "*Màthair*, we didn't travel by distance, we traveled by time. I was born a very long time after you died. We came through an opening and will return that way. After we pass, the opening will vanish forever."

Màthair stopped what she was doing and looked directly at Cos, evidently thinking about what he had just said.

"How does this opening happen?" she asked.

"I don't understand it. It is created by a vast machine."

"You seem to me to be an honest young man, though I will believe my own eyes when I see it." She paused in mid thought, turning her head slowly from side to side. Cos watched her, unsure of what she was thinking.

"There is the sound of marching feet outside on the street," she announced, causing Cos to stand and look around. Listening carefully and tuning out the ongoing conversations in the room, he could hear it also.

"You'd better go look," *Màthair* advised, and pointed to the *posticum*, the rear entrance, which led to a small path between the adjacent villa and then to the street.

Cos headed for the door, hesitating for a moment before grabbing a *gladius* from the pile of Cosimus' belongings. Out of his peripheral vision, he noticed Antonius was following his moments with his eyes. Once through the door, he found the alley, just wide enough to pass if he turned sideways a bit. At the entrance ahead, he saw several men pass in a column, marching together in formation. He peered around the corner just in time to see *Consul* Piso enter through the front entrance. The armor clad guards relaxed and broke formation, looking up and down the street in a casual manner.

Cos decided to observe the men rather than returning, at least for the moment. After a few minutes, he could see one of them pointing down the street, and there seemed to be general agreement as to a course of action. Evidently, one man was elected to remain, posted at the door, while the others went down the street. Cos recalled the food stall about a block away and presumed that the others had gone for food. One man was left, and he occasionally stood in the doorway looking in, a well-worn crossbow slung across his shoulder. He looked furtively back and forth as if expecting something or to see who might be watching. Just out of sight of the doorway, he bent over while standing on his crossbow arms and with both hands pulled the bowstring back, locking it in place, then placed a short heavy bolt in the tract. For some reason, he had armed his weapon out of the view of anyone, or so he may have thought. The man glanced around once more, then peered around the corner of the doorway, observing someone inside as the group gathered around Piso.

Cos swallowed hard. This guard was an assassin, bent on killing someone inside. He had conspired to remain as the other guards withdrew, leaving him free to launch his arrow when the right opportunity presented itself. Cos didn't have time to alert anyone inside. He was the only one who could act. Sweat broke out on his upper lip, and his hands grew moist. What should he do? If he attacked the man and was in error, there was no saving him from retribution. He would face Roman criminal justice which was swift and severe. Not only that, the other men, nine of them, would rush back down the street to protect one of their own. Still, he couldn't let this man kill if he could help it. Mentally debating his position, he drew his *gladius* from its sheath and took another look around the corner.

Piso observed the bundles and trunks in the middle of the *atrium*. "So you are ready to leave?" he asked, stating the obvious.

"Not in spirit but in fact," Cosimus answered. He spoke with his arm around his wife, Alia, and Piso could see her moist eyes looking back at him, hoping for an answer to her distress. "Have you a plan which would change our minds?" he asked Piso.

"Yes and no, I'm afraid. You should know that I spent yesterday and this morning sorting out the men assigned to me and rooting out the ones who might be tempted to carry out an order to harm you right under my nose. I found ten whom I didn't trust, and they left on foot for *Roma* earlier today. May they enjoy the long walk. The remaining men have been with me for months, and I trust them to obey my orders and my orders only. So to answer your question, I would offer for you to move into my villa while I travel to *Roma* to see Claudius. I believe you would be safe there in my absence and well protected. By the time I return, I assure you that Claudius will have ordered your protection, and you will be able to resume your life."

A shout from the street made Cosimus reflexly look that way, and in the doorway was a guard in firing stance, holding a crossbow which seemed to be aimed at Piso. Cosimus flung himself at Piso, knocking him to one side thereby putting his own body in the path of the missile. As he fell to the floor, he felt a stabbing pain from his left flank and realized that the arrow had passed into the side of his abdomen. The room became chaotic with Antonius and Maccus sprinting for the doorway, and the women crying out in anguish and fright. Cosimus rolled to a sitting position, the arrow still imbedded in his flesh, the tip penetrating through his back.

The crossbowman was standing fully in the doorway, his feet apart and his weapon raised to the firing position. Without thinking further, Cos burst out of the alley and rushed toward the man, yelling as loud as he could to distract him from firing. A twitch of his head showed that the man was aware that Cos was coming at him from the side, nevertheless he continued to fixate on his target. Cos' *gladius* was directed at the man's neck, the only exposed and vulnerable area not covered by armor. A split second before the sword thrust made it to its target, the weapon fired, sending the heavy short arrow hurtling into the room. The blade made contact before Cos did, and the two men went down in a pile, Cos on top. There was yelling from inside and the sound of running feet. Cos pushed himself away from the body under him, and as he sat up, he was aware that blood covered everything including his own chest and hands. Someone with strong arms picked him up from behind, and as he was spun around, he saw the women's faces, hands over their mouths, their eyes wide with alarm.

"Are you injured, son?" Antonius asked, gently putting Cos back on his feet. Cos glanced down at the lifeless body of the crossbowman and the expanding pool of blood beneath his body. Antonius clasped Cos to his chest, "You acted bravely, Cos. I am proud of you."

"Cosimus, you saved my life," Piso announced. "We just cannot let you die."

"I'm injured, Piso, not dead, at least not yet," he answered. "For your information, I believe I was the target and the action by Cos caused the assassin to miss. You were simply in the path of the arrow."

"You pushed me out of the way! It happened too fast for me to understand it at the time," Piso remarked. "I would be the one dead right now if you hadn't acted."

Cos and Antonius appeared by Cosimus' side, and they knelt beside him inspecting his wound. There was minimal blood loss, however the arrow had penetrated through the left side of his abdomen and was still imbedded there.

"How does it look?" Cosimus asked. Just then, Alia reached his side and threw her arms around his neck, her face pressed into his.

"Well, if this was modern times, I think you would survive. Here, it looks like a wound which will cause your death in a couple of days or less. Can you reconsider going back with us now?"

"I am now convinced. Yes, we will go with you. Now help me get this arrow out."

There was a furious clamor coming from the street and two armed men entered, swords drawn. Piso turned toward them and shouted. "Back! Back all of you and get in formation. There is no need for you to be in this house." They lowered their swords and retreated, glancing angrily around at the occupants. Piso followed them out and all could hear his shouts and orders being given in rapid succession from the street.

"Oh, Cosimus," Alia cried. "They got you anyway. Are you in pain?" She couldn't control her abundant tears, and she sobbed her words out, unable to restrain her grief. Cos gently pushed her away and rose to his feet.

"Someone cut the tip from this arrow," he ordered. Maccus came forward, knife in hand, and started working on severing the arrow. When he was done, he looked at Cosimus' face for a moment, then quickly withdrew the arrow. Cosimus briefly folded over in pain but resumed standing, his chin defiantly protruded.

Màthair pushed her way forward and put her pail noisily down. She had brought a fresh flask of wine and a bolt of woven cloth for use as a bandage. "Give me some room here," she ordered. She quickly doused the wound with wine and tightly bandaged it, wrapping the long cloth around his belly. "I've seen worse," she announced and patted Cosimus on his butt.

"When are we leaving?" Cosimus asked to whoever was listening.

"One hour," Rachel answered. Cosimus glanced at her and realized that she was smiling though full of tears also. Cos had his arm over her and was looking directly at Cosimus.

"Sorry I wasn't quick enough," he said.

"He missed because of you. He didn't kill me or Piso. That's good enough. Good work," Cosimus answered. He gave Cos a half salute and a thankful nod of appreciation.

Alia came softly to his side and leaned against him, looking up to his face.

"Ready to see the future?" he asked her. She wiped another tear and nodded yes.

Piso returned, shaking his head. "I should have the entire lot of them executed. How are you doing, Cosimus?" he asked.

"I'll need some surgery, but I'll live. That is if the portal opens when it is supposed to."

"You saved my life, and don't disagree. I was there you know. I owe you much, and if you leave, I shall never be able to repay you."

"I am alive, and I have Alia beside me, thanks to you. We are even, Gaius. However I want to tell you something important and you should listen to my words. After Claudius dies, you should stay away from *Roma* and its politics. Go enjoy your money, and don't get involved again, no matter what happens."

"And you know the future and you know the past. In fact, all four of you do, and you all think you know what is going to happen to me. On the other hand, it seems to me that I can do whatever I want, and it will be recorded that way. Does what will happen have to already be written or can I change it of my own free will?"

Alia spoke up as she walked toward Piso, gesturing with her hands. "It is the *Norns* who decide at your birth. *Urðr, Verðandi* and *Skuld* appear when your eyes first open, and they decide what your life will be and when and how you will die. You cannot change your fate."

Piso nodded. He understood the concept of the three fates, the *Moirai*. It was much the same in Greek or Roman culture, just the names were different. "So my fate is already written. I had my doubts about the concept of fate, however I now concede that it's true. You people do know my fate. It has already been written and cannot be changed. So no matter what I do, it will turn out the same. So much for your advice, Cosimus."

"And you will realize that what Cosimus has been telling you, what I have been telling you, is also true. We come from the future, and we will return shortly. You will have been dead for two thousand years when the opening closes behind us, though you will be alive in our memory for the rest of our allotted time. Piso, you are one of *Roma's* finest. You make me proud of my heritage," Antonius said.

"You are all leaving us?" Maccus wondered. "Can you make this journey, *Dominus*?" he asked.

"In a few moments, an opening will appear, and we are going to pass through it and then it will close. This is goodbye, Maccus. You have been a good friend all of my life, and I will miss you every time the sun comes up in the east or sets in the west. I wish you a fine long life and much happiness. One last gift from me, Maccus. It was given to me the day I took command of the *Legion XX*. Now it's yours." He took the big ring off his finger and passed it to a surprised Maccus, who turned the heavy gold ring over and over admiring the insignia designating *Valeria Victrix*, the wild boar. It was the first time Cosimus ever saw tears from Maccus.

Cosimus looked pale and unsteady on his feet, nevertheless he motioned to Linza and *Màthair* to come by his side. When they arrived he placed an arm over each of them and looked affectionately at them in turn. "And you two wonderful women have taught me the meaning of family. How can I awaken in the morning without the aroma of your cooking and the friendship I see in your eyes. Take care of each other and of Maccus."

"Five minutes," Rachel announced, consulting her wrist. She looked up and saw Linza staring at her. She removed her watch and, without words, held it out for her. It was a gift of an item previously admired by Linza, who accepted it with a big smile.

Source: Britannica.com
The Trellis House (left), Herculaneum, Italy.
Werner Forman Archive

Chapter 37

Portal…A Glimpse of Another World

Fermilab, Batavia Illinois

*B*arron Harmes stood there, his hands partially in the air and glared at Agent Brimm. He studied the pistol in Brimm's hand then his eyes went back to Brimm's face. "So, if you want the system shut down, I can't comply with my hands in the air. Do you want it shut down or should it continue to run and draw that expensive energy you seem to be so concerned over?"

Brimm looked back, his face seething with anger, thinking about what should be done. There was no evidence of any wrongdoing, other than in his head. If he managed to shoot a well-respected physicist in his own lab, there better be a clear factual record of necessity, or he might as well turn the pistol on himself. Most detectives require provocation even if they are facing a desperate and dangerous criminal. There was nothing here other than Brimm's certain knowledge that the so-called science experiment was no more than a cover for time travel.

"I'll shut it down myself. I don't trust you to do it," Brimm finally said and moved toward the computer console, keeping his gun aimed at Harmes.

"You'd better know exactly what you are doing because there is a lot of energy flowing above our heads and the keyboard tells it where to go," Harmes said sarcastically.

Ignoring the warning, Brimm looked at the terminal screen, then back at Harmes. It was a complex, cluttered page of data, charts, and options along both the top and bottom rows. This would take time to digest, and he couldn't act alone while holding Harmes at bay and studying the choices to turn the energy off.

Barron sensed his dilemma and smiled. "What's the matter, Agent Brimm? Can't figure it out?"

No, he couldn't figure it out, not by himself and not easily anyway. Brimm could see the satisfaction on Barron Harmes face, causing his anger to grow and his face to flush.

"OK, Doctor Harmes. Come over here and shut it down, though one false move will be your last. I'll be watching every key you touch."

Barron strode confidently toward the terminal, glaring at Brimm. There was no way that Brimm had any idea of the process and certainly not a glimmer of understanding of the physics involved. He waved his hand to shoo Agent Brimm away from the keyboard and watched him sullenly move out of the way. "Let me explain the process, Brimm, since you aren't bright enough to understand it all by yourself. First, I'm going to hit a key which will purge the system, and then all we have to do is leave it alone, and it will slowly wind down. Otherwise, it will damage the target modules and cost a lot to repair. Understand?"

Brimm's hard eyes narrowed, suspecting a ploy. He was ready to act, but clearly Harmes was in charge as soon as he got his fingers on that keyboard. What was the correct way to handle this? It was impossible to know because his opponent was not some street thug with a dull brain. This man standing there grinning at him was smarter than nearly anyone in the world. He had to rely on the threat from his weapon alone because he would be unable to outthink Barron Harmes.

The strike of one key, that's all it took, and things began to happen. Barron had always been in awe of the energy released with that one key stroke, the command to begin to open an aperture in time. At first nothing seemed to happen, although as Barron stepped away from the terminal, the ambient noise started to build. There was more going through their bodies than increased noise. It was energy, raw energy, waves of it, making their skin tingle, their orientation to gravity and position be tested, and the process getting more intense by the half-second. No one who had ever been present just before the portal opened was not frightened by the sensation. Most, including Barron himself, concluded that there was intense radiation coursing through their bodies, a not only unpleasant sensation, but one you were convinced was damaging. Then, as suddenly, it stopped.

"What the hell was that?" Brimm shouted. "What did you just do?" he demanded. He was standing several paces from Harmes, facing him and leveling his pistol at his chest. Something had just happened, and it was frightening. Barron Harmes was smiling at him, gloating that he had the upper hand, that he had somehow pulled off what he wanted, in spite of the threats and the handgun. Brimm didn't know what to do, the energy level about him was diminished, yet still intense, and the man in his sights was happy about it.

Without warning or noise, a hand came from behind him, gripping his throat like a steel vice. Another hand hit his gun arm, sending the pistol clattering to the concrete and spinning away. Brimm felt himself being dragged by his neck backward, his heels sliding across the floor. The room took on a different hue, a darker one, and just as abruptly, he was released and fell to the floor. For a moment, he lost his orientation and rolled to his belly to push his way off the floor and recover his bearing. The floor wasn't concrete, it was finely finished and polished marble, cut into small perfect pieces, a geometric pattern spreading out in all directions. He looked forward and saw the feet standing before him, all clad in sandals, then up at the faces, several of them, all staring at him in an unfriendly way.

"Get up," was the order from a deep commanding voice. Two pairs of arms effortlessly lifted him into the air as if he were attached to a crane and then let him go. He was not in the lab at all. This was an unfamiliar room that he had never seen before.

Antonius hugged Piso and patted his back. "Your assistance was indispensable, *Consul*. Thank you for all the help." Then he turned to Maccus and did the same. "You were warned about Vesuvius, I think. If you are still around twenty-five years from now, get out before it happens and tell your wife and children so that they won't be trapped either." Maccus nodded that he understood and smiled back at him. Antonius kissed *Màthair* on the cheek and pulled her close to him. "You are special. I'm going to miss you."

"And I just got to know you. You seem like another tough guy with a soft inside to me. I'll miss you all. At least I still have one baby to take care of," *Màthair* said, wiping away a tear that no one had ever seen before this moment.

Cos and Antonius steadied Cosimus by the shoulders, one on either side, and moved through the opening, carefully avoiding the shimmering sides. They were followed by Alia and Rachel who both glanced behind them with tearful eyes, looking backward at their extended family with fondness and parting from them with reluctance knowing that in a moment or two, they no longer would exist.

Piso moved forward like a cat and leaned into the portal opening with his head, looking around. "It doesn't look that different," he remarked. "Now, I've seen everything and my head, at least, has been to the future and back again. Good fortune to you all and may your life be full." He waved and withdrew, remaining in front of the portal and looking at his friends standing in a group, on the other side of time.

"Wait!" Brimm shouted. "Are you going to leave me in here?"

"Yes, we are, Brimm," Barron shouted back, his hand hovering above the keyboard. "You've investigated time travel from this side, and now you can do the same from the other side. Good luck to you." The last image Brimm saw was of Barron's hand coming down toward the keys, and then it was gone. The opening to the future was no more and never would open again. He looked around at his new circumstances in horror.

"And just who might you be?" Piso asked the newcomer. He nearly felt sorry for the fellow who stood in one spot, casting around with wondering eyes and shaking visibly. Piso had seen the dark blue object in the man's hand before Antonius skillfully knocked it away. Piso presumed that it was some sort of weapon but didn't understand how something so small could be worth holding. Nevertheless, this man had been dragged unwillingly back from the future, and Antonius never looked back at him or gave a reason for his actions, so Piso presumed that no one really cared what happened to him.

"I don't understand what you said to me," Brimm finally responded.

Piso nodded understanding. This one was from a later time and didn't communicate in Latin or probably any understandable language. He had little practical use. "Guards!" Piso shouted, and two appeared in seconds, weapons drawn. "Take this man out of here," was the order. They picked Brimm off his feet and quickly disappeared back into the street.

"What will happen to him?" Maccus wondered.

Piso shrugged. He really didn't concern himself with that issue. Instead he found a chair in the *tablinum*, probably the one that Cosimus used, and sat down heavily, indicating with a gesture for Maccus to do the same.

"What an amazing experience. We saw something just now that I still don't understand. There was a hole that appeared as if by magic and disappeared the same way. It was open…they just walked through it, and just like that it was gone and four people with it. They said it was the future we saw in there. What do you think, Maccus?"

"Cosimus or his friend, Antonius, were not given to lies. They said it was the future and so I believe them, yet I don't understand it either. I miss them all already."

"And so do I, my friend," Piso said with his face contorted in sadness. "Can you tell me how Antonius knew that Cosimus needed him, why he came back through time?"

"Sure. Cosimus sent a message and so they came. It only took one day."

"Exactly how do you send a message to the future?" Piso asked.

"Cosimus wrote a message on a piece of thin copper and put it under a stone in the floor. He said that since this place will be buried for a long time, no one will find it until the time they came from."

"Amazing! And it worked," Piso marveled.

"I thought it was silly at the time we did it, though I was wrong. They came right away. It sure did work."

"And, can I ask, where exactly did you hide the message?" Piso asked.

"That I can't say. Cosimus made me promise never to disturb it or tell anyone about it."

"And for good reason. Forgive me for asking." Piso's mind started turning over possibilities. Where would he hide such a thing. Where could it be found by accident and yet stay safe for… they said for twenty centuries. Piso blew a puff of breath out. So long! He continued to ponder this subject and wonder how he could also leave a message for the man who had saved his life. Piso thought of what he could say to express his feelings of admiration for Cosimus and his regrets that he and his marvelously beautiful wife had been subject to the whims of a corrupt woman. Clearly, there must be some way to tell Cosimus in what regard he was held by so many people. Cosimus was one of the great men of history, now gone as if dead. Piso held his head low, his mood somber, and reflected on the times that he had spent with Cosimus. So few, really. He had missed a great opportunity to become closer with a special human being, one that had the rare stamp of being exceptional.

Piso shifted in the chair, many things running through his thoughts. He stretched his leg out and settled in. There was something that caught his eye on the floor. An object was glinting in the sun, whose evening rays were slanting in from the opening in the roof over the *atrium*. Then he looked more closely. A message had been engraved in a stone paver right at his feet. *"Quoniam Antonius"* it announced with the bronze inlay. Piso chuckled. Of course. It was right here and was in the perfect spot. He read it again and rolled his eyes about trying to understand the logic of these two particular words. It was seemingly in praise of Cosimus' old friend and mentor, Antonius, however the first word was confusing. Then he saw it for what it was. An intentionally misleading message, one that did not imply that something was beneath the stone. Piso laughed out loud this time.

"Something the matter, *Consul*?" Maccus asked.

"Not a thing. I just realized once more how intelligent your master actually was. Say, Maccus, I just figured out that this stone at my feet was where the message was placed. I need a favor from you, if you are willing."

"Sure, anything I can ever do for you is yours for the asking."

"I want to place a message there myself but not one asking for help. I want the message to say all the things that I should have said to Cosimus today. The things he should hear from a man long ago dead and forgotten by the time he reads it. Will you help me?"

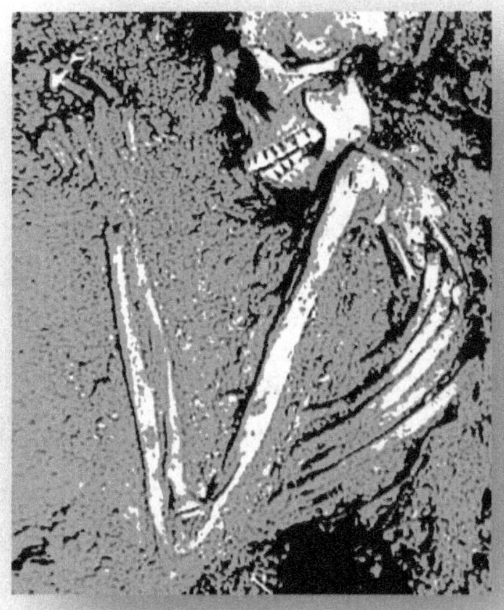

Epilogue

Milan-Bicocca, Italia 0600 AM

*R*achel drew open the drapes and stood for a moment in the morning light, looking over the green landscaped park spreading out beneath their window, the twinkling rainbow sparkle of dew still fresh on the leaves. She sighed and turned away from the view and began the process of fixing breakfast. Cos would come out of the bathroom soon, fresh from his shave, and kiss her politely on her cheek, then hurriedly eat breakfast while consulting his watch, never wanting to be late. She sighed again. Life was grand, and she had everything a woman could want…at least on paper. Nevertheless, the excitement of life, the thrills, the newness, was slowly slipping away and being smothered by the ordinary, the routine, the safety and security, that most people fought so hard to achieve. Once you achieved success, you had to keep it to have it, she thought to herself, more as an explanation of her dilemma than a solution. Just as she put the last plate on the table, Cos came out and kissed her cheek.

"Morning, my dear. Did you sleep well?" he asked perfunctorily and pulled out a chair, reflexly glancing at his watch. Rachel didn't answer him, wondering if he would even notice her silence. He didn't.

"So what is ahead for you today?" she wondered, pushing his morning paper aside so she could see his face.

"I have three patients in a row this morning. One of them came in last night and got worked up for surgery by my staff. My resident tells me that this one might be a long case. There goes my schedule," he commented, before concentrating on the paper again. Rachel sighed, audibly hoping to get his attention turned on her and not the paper.

"Something amiss?" he asked, this time giving her his full attention and putting away the paper. He looked steadily at her, studying her face, concerned that there may be a medical issue that he had overlooked.

"I'm amiss," Rachel answered. "I'm getting old, and life for me is boring. Now that our son has started living in the dormitory, there is nothing for me to do. You rush off to work and come back late every day. Me? I go to the gym, I shop, I clean. At times I read, but it can't go on like this much longer. Suddenly some morning, we both will wake up and be ancient, and life will have passed us by."

Cos got up and came around the breakfast table and knelt beside her. "Some things I can't help. The life of a general surgeon is not a good match for an intelligent, restless wife who gave up her youth so that he could go to school nearly forever. Now that we have arrived…more, that I have arrived," he corrected, "we find that when we were young and full of adventure and passion it was what we wanted all along and not what we were working toward. I understand, I think, how you must feel." Cos pulled her face toward him and gave her a long kiss. Her lifeless expression didn't change though she accepted his kiss. It dawned on Cos that just a display of affection wouldn't change anything for his lovely and devoted wife. Perhaps they both needed a change.

"You know, I've been thinking of taking an extended leave of absence from the university. I can't just quit, though seeing your distress just now makes me determined to change our direction. Our son won't miss us if we take off for places unknown for awhile. There, it's settled. When I come home tonight, I'll tell you when it will happen." This time, Rachel's kiss was different, more like when they were first married, and Cos had to force himself to part from her. He glanced at his watch. "Oops, got to run," he said, "the first case starts in thirty minutes."

Cos stood quickly and located his jacket and bag. Rachel watched as he robotically and quickly moved around the apartment preparing to leave for the day.

"And where would we be going, if I might ask?" she called to him. "I hope not another surgical sabbatical in some distant city where I will be stuck in a hotel room."

"We'll discuss it later," Cos said, waved her goodby and blew her a kiss before shutting the apartment door behind him.

Rachel sighed again, this time to herself, and picked up her cup of coffee and opened the paper Cos had been so anxious to read. She flipped through the first few pages which were full of the usual political and financial news. Her wandering eye caught a small item tucked away on a corner which had an interesting headline.

"Heartbreaking Discovery at Herculaneum," it read. Rachel continued to peruse the column with more than a little interest. This was an article that Cos might have found, that is, if she had not distracted him. They both were always interested in any new finding from the Roman period. As she continued to read, the story grew ever more interesting, and her pupils dilated while her eyelids raised. There was indeed an interesting story here, and she needed more details than was reported.

Rachel picked up her phone and dialed a familiar number, the one belonging to her dear mother-in-law, Mary. In a few seconds, her sweet voice came through to the tiny speaker by her ear.

"Hi, Mary, it's Rachel. Hope I'm not interrupting something."

"Why no, Rachel. I always have time for you. Anything wrong?" she asked. Rachel felt a bit humbled because she had to admit that her calls had become more and more infrequent.

"I was wondering if you saw the news from Herculaneum that I just read."

"Well, for sure. In fact, Tony and Cos are on their way over there this morning. I'll call you with what they find as soon as they return," Mary promised.

"I was thinking that I owe you a visit. Would it be a lot of trouble if I headed down there, like today perhaps?"

"Will Cos be with you?" Mary asked.

"No, at least not today. I'll try to get him to come down later. He is a very busy man these days."

"Well, there is always room for either or both of you. Please come."

"How are the boys, and how is Alia and the kids?"

"The boys are no longer boys, although they still act that way. And they are a bit slower these days, however, I don't let them know that. Alia and her children are just fine. You can see them all when you arrive, if you like."

"I'm coming. Don't know how or when, but I'm on the way."

Setteville, Italia

Rachel was seated in the large armchair by the fire, engaged in conversation with Mary, when the front door chimed its opening. "Well, at last." Mary said and got up to greet them. Rachel stood also, feeling some mild apprehension about her surprise visit and the effect she would have on the family without Cos beside her. The first one through the door was Alia, causing Rachel to recall the first time she had ever seen that face which seemed to always have a radiant presence. They locked eyes, just as the first time, and Alia formed a slight smile and came directly toward her, having much the same effect as the first time they met two thousand years ago. Alia was intensely beautiful. There was no other description which would fit. It was not only her physical beauty, the confident and graceful way she moved, but most of her presence was created by penetrating intelligence broadcast from her eyes.

"Hi, Rachel," she said and enveloped Rachel with a warm embrace. Instead of letting go, she continued to hold Rachel by the shoulders at arm length while studying her face.

"This is a most pleasant surprise, my dear. We don't see enough of either of you."

"I am here on an impulse, I'm afraid. Poor Cos will be so surprised to find my note tonight when he gets home. He just might show up here in a couple of days."

"And you came at the right time. My husband and Tony were over at the dig all day, and what they found out will be of interest to you."

Rachel looked up to see Tony and Cos come in, both showing big smiles when they caught sight of her. As they came forward she noticed that both men were still fit and healthy, however their age was starting to show more than she expected. She hugged each of them in turn and was rewarded by big kisses on her cheeks, simultaneously delivered.

"Rachel!" Tony blurted. "You'll never guess where we were today."

"It was pretty sad. I'm glad you didn't see what we saw," Cos added.

"I'm all ears. What's this all about?" Rachel asked.

"No, you don't," Mary commanded. "The table is set and all talk will be after we sit down and start eating." They all laughed and followed Mary into the expansive dining room.

It was the looks back and forth between Tony and Cos that signaled that they shared a most interesting tidbit of news. Rachel could wait no longer. "OK, we are eating now. Just what did you find over there?" she asked.

"We were tipped off that a recent excavation had uncovered a pair of bodies never before seen. There was a report that one of the bodies was most likely a ranking Roman officer. A *legatus*, they said. It certainly piqued our interest so we wanted to see for ourselves," Tony reported.

"Let me finish this, if it's all right with you, since I'm the one involved," Cos interrupted. "You see, Rachel, they determined that the body was an officer because of the particular ring he had on when he died. A unique one. I had to see this for myself so Tony and I went over there today to see it in person."

"Don't drag this out, Cos," Tony complained. "Just tell her."

"I already read about that part," Rachel commented, "it was in today's paper."

"Yes, except the ring was cast with an image of a wild boar on the face and marked with 'XX' on both sides," Tony explained.

Rachel's mind started processing this information and then it came to her. "That was your *legion*, wasn't it?" she asked Cos. He nodded slightly, his eyes cast downward. Then the information impacted her with force as she remembered clearly what had happened just before they left the past. "That was your ring! You gave it to Maccus just before we left," she recalled.

"I did. And you remember that I warned him again about leaving in time before the eruption occurred."

"Sure you did, I remember the conversation." Rachel said. "Wonder why he was still there?"

"And there is more," Tony ventured, casting a quick glance at Cos. "There was a body with the one wearing the ring. It has been identified as a female, a younger one. They were embracing at the last moments of life. The image of those two together like that would make anyone cry. We feel sure that the female was Linza."

"Oh, my," Rachel said and put her hand to her mouth in surprise. Out of the corner of her eye, she saw Alia wiping away a tear. Yes, Rachel thought, as she analyzed the facts. Most likely the reason they had been caught in the volcano's trap was because they loved their life in Herculaneum and put off leaving until it was too late. "I'm sorry to hear that. You and Alia knew Linza better than I did because I couldn't converse with her, though I found her to be a genuinely sweet person."

Alia straightened up, her face brightening. "You never knew this, but Linza and I competed once for the affection of Cosimus. She could offer sex appeal, and she had plenty of it. All I had to offer was a bunch of head lice. Nevertheless, I won." Her comments drew laughter all around, and she had managed to dispel the depressing mood. Rachel reached under the table and squeezed her hand.

"You all remember Piso, I'm sure," Cos stated, remembering another person from the distant past. "I've been thinking him since we saw those skeletons today. I wonder if Maccus told him about the message we buried. Maccus wasn't nearly as mentally quick as Piso, and it wouldn't have been all that difficult to get that secret out of him."

"And what would he have done with that information?" Tony asked. "After all, the message was undisturbed and delivered just as you expected it would be."

"I have a hunch, that's all. A feeling. Piso and I became very close over the short time I knew him. He had a great deal of respect for me, and as you may recall, he was convinced that I took the arrow for him."

"And how would he express that, dear?" Alia inquired. She, too, recalled Piso fondly. Given her status as a slave at one time, she was treated very well indeed by Piso, who actually adopted her, at least legally.

"We know he was the one who had my image cast in bronze because it was found at his villa during an earlier excavation. I suspect he would want to send me a note also since he would have been aware that I actually got the first one."

"But where would that be found?" Tony asked, not being able to envision any other place a message could be left.

"In the same place as the first one. He could be sure that it would be secure there since the first message made it to me."

"There was only one message in the flask. I saw it with my own eyes." Tony protested.

"No, it wasn't placed there. I know that because you would have found both of them at the same time," Cos explained. "If he did place a message, he would put it beneath the first."

A light dawned on Tony's face. Of course. There may not actually be a second message, though if there ever was one, it is still there under the same marked paver and still unread or delivered.

"There is only one way to find out," Alia suggested. "You boys have to go there and dig it up and see for yourself," she continued, smiling broadly at them.

Mary was silent until now, listening to the excited speculation from two old men who still thought young. "Listen carefully, both of you. Before you go digging, remember that Italy considers that site to be protected. That means if you try this yourself and get caught, you will spend a great many of your precious remaining years behind bars. Think this over please."

Tony looked affectionately at Mary, her judgement was often so much better than his own because both he and his brother, Cos, were given to rash action and quick thinking. Thank God that somebody other than them controlled the throttle.

"Mary is right," Cos admitted. I guess we should let this idea die. The risk is too great, and I know that we would never get the authorities to dig there again. Even if they did, no one would believe that the message was meant for me."

"I propose a toast, long overdue," Rachel said and stood up. "This is to all the dear friends around this table and to the ones we left behind. In my memory, you and they will always be alive, and the adventure will always continue." She raised her glass with her outstretched arm and waited until the others did also, then took a long drink of wine with her eyes closed, seeing the faces of those so long ago parted standing in that little group, their eyes reflecting the wonder of a small glimpse of the future.

Finis

Glossary

Apertum	Area free from obstacles, open/exposed space
Atrium	The entry to a home, may be of large size, more like a court or hall, or just a few square feet
Balbus Thermae	Thermal baths, called suburban baths donated by Balbus to the people of Herculaneum
Bellicae Soloturae Intus	Roman warship
Caesarea Maritima	Ancient Roman city in the Sharon Plain on the coast of the Mediterranean
Caro	Italian, meaning 'dear'
Caupona	Tavern or pub
Centralis Thermae	Private thermal bath in Herculaneum
Centurion	Commander of 100 Roman men
Colonia Ulpia Traiana	Capitol of the Roman province Germania inferior
Consul	A consul held the highest elected political office of the Roman Republic but later became mere symbolic representatives of Rome's republican heritage
Convivium	A Roman dinner party was called a convivium. Convivium is Latin for 'living together' This means that the Romans viewed the meal as a not only an occasion to eat, but also an occasion to socialize
Denarii	A roman coin of silver worth ten asses (small coins)

Dominus	Dominus is the Latin word for master or owner
Domus	The domus was the type of house occupied by the upper classes and some wealthy freedmen during the Republican and Imperial eras
Ercolano	Ercolano (Italian: [erkoˈlaːno]) is a town and commune in the Metropolitan City of Naples, Campania of Southern Italy
Est	Latin for 'it is'
Fasces	Roman symbol of power and authority, a bundle of wooden rods and an axe bound together by leather thongs. Fasces represented that a man held imperium, or executive authority
Futurae	Latin for 'future'
Gaius Calpurnius Piso	Piso was extremely well liked throughout Rome. He inherited from his father (never identified) connection with many distinguished families and from his mother great wealth. Piso came from the ancient and noble house of Calpurnii, and he distributed his great wealth among many beneficiaries of all Roman social classes. Among a wide range of interests, Piso sang on the tragic stage, wrote poetry, played an expert game of draughts, and owned a villa at Baiae
Garum	Fermented fish sauce used as a condiment in the cuisines of ancient Greece and Rome
Genua	Early name for Genoa, a city in Italy

Germania	Ancient region of central Europe corresponding largely with present-day Germany but extending west into the Low Countries and what is now northeast France. The portions of Germania west of the Rhine and south of the Danube were conquered and colonized by the Roman Empire, while most of the land to the east and north of those rivers remained largely in the hands of Germanic tribes
Gingiber	Latin word for ginger
Gladius	Latin word for sword, used to represent the primary sword of Roman soldiers
Graeci	Latin for Greece
Herculaneum	Ancient city of 5000 in Campania, buried in 79 AD and abandoned
Impluvium	The sunken part of the atrium in a Greek or Roman domus designed to store and carry away rainwater coming through the compluvium (a square opening in the roof)
Intuito	Latin for intuition
Jentaculum	First meal, as in breakfast
Latrinea	A simple toilet with a pour flush system
Legatus Legionis	Roman general commanding a legion of 5000 soldiers. First in command
Lucius Annaeus Seneca	Roman historian (4 BC to 65 AD). later, advisor to Nero until his forced suicide
Magistrate	An elected Roman official

Magistratus Curulis	A supreme power held by consuls and emperors
Massacre at the Teutoburg Forest	The Varian Disaster took place in the Teutoburg Forest in 9 AD, when an alliance of Germanic tribes ambushed and destroyed three Roman legions and their auxiliaries, led by Publius Quinctilius Varus
Misenum	Misenum was first established as a naval base during the civil wars in 27 BC. It was then developed into the largest Roman port for the Classis Misenensis, the most important fleet
Moirai	In ancient Greek religion and mythology, the Moirai, often known in English as the Fates, were the white-robed incarnations of destiny
Mulsum	Sweet Roman drink, a mixture of wine and honey
Musei Capitolini	The Capitoline Museums is a single museum containing a group of art and archaeological museums in Piazza del Campidoglio, on top of the Capitoline Hill in Rome, Italy
Neapolis	Ancient Naples
Numerus Batavorum	The numerus Batavorum also called the cohors Germanorum, was a personal, imperial guards unit for the Roman emperors of the Julio-Claudian dynasty (30 BC – AD 68) composed of Germanic soldiers
Ornatrice	Hairdresser, usually a female slave

Ostium	Main Roman port at the mouth of the Tiber
Palla	Traditional ancient Roman mantle worn by women, fastened by brooches
Paterfamilias	Head of a Roman family. The paterfamilias was the oldest living male in a Roman familia
Peristylum	Continuous porch formed by a row of columns surrounding the perimeter of building or a courtyard
Pilum	A javelin commonly used by the Roman army in ancient times. It was generally about 6 ft 7 inches long
Ponza	Largest island of the Pontine Islands, located 33 km south of Cape Circeo in the Tyrrhenian Sea.
Praefectus Urbanus	Prefect of the city of Rome
Praetor	Title granted by the government of Ancient Rome to men acting in one of two official capacities: the commander of an army or an elected magistratus
Praetorian	Elite unit of the Imperial Roman army whose members served as personal bodyguards and intelligence for the Roman emperors
Quaestor sacri palatii	Quaestor of the Sacred Palace was the senior legal authority responsible for drafting laws.
Quoniam	because, since, seeing that
Rhenus	Latin name of the Rhine

Sextus Afranius Burrus	Prefect of the Praetorian Guard and was, together with Seneca the Younger, an advisor to the Roman Emperor Nero, making him a very powerful man in the early years of Nero's reign
Sinus Cumanus	Bay of Naples
Stabit	stand, stay, remain
Stola	Long, loose tunic or robe, with or without sleeves, worn by women of ancient Rome
Subsisto	stop, stand, stay, halt
Supervisore	Italian for Supervisor
Tablinum	An anteroom in a house of ancient Rome, opening out of the atrium opposite the main entry and often containing the family statues and archives
Thermopolium	Cook-shop, literally "a place where (something) hot is sold", was a commercial establishment where it was possible to purchase ready-to-eat food
Transennae	latticework
Tribunus Militum	A military tribune who was an officer of the Roman army ranked below legate and above centurion
Tyrrhenia	Land areas around the Tyrrhenian Sea
Urðr, Verðandi and Skul	The Norns: Urðr (past), Verðandi (present) and Skuld (future); female beings who rule the destiny of gods and men
Vestibulum	Main entrance hall of the Roman domus

Villa of the Papyrii	Villa dei Pisoni was an ancient Roman villa in Herculaneum. The Villa was considered to be one of the most luxurious houses in all of Herculaneum and in the Roman world
XX Valeria Victrix	Twentieth Victorious Valeria Legion was a legion of the Imperial Roman army

9 781942 420279